# The Cane-Cutter's Song

# *the* Cane-Cutter's Song

Raphaël Confiant

*Translated from the French by* Dr Vidya Vencatesan

(in collaboration with Christine Raguet)

SPEAKING TIGER

SPEAKING TIGER BOOKS LLP
4381/4, Ansari Road, Daryaganj
New Delhi 110002

First published in France as *La panse du chacal* by
Editions Mercure de France, 2004
This edition first published in India in English by
Speaking Tiger Books 2021



PAP
TAGORE

The Work is published with the support of the
Publication Assistance Programmes of the Institut français

ISBN: 978-93-5447-076-9
eISBN: 978-93-5447-077-6

10 9 8 7 6 5 4 3 2 1

Typeset in Scala by SÜRYA, New Delhi
Printed at Chaman Enterprises, New Delhi

To Gerry L'Etang, my brother and friend.

To those who left; tens of thousands of Indians who emigrated to the archipelago of the Antilles in the middle of the nineteenth century.

'Here everything dies, burnt by the sun, and the ponds have dried up. The people from the countryside, hunted by hunger, abandon their small homes. It is better to emigrate to the Antilles or the Mascarene Islands with wife and children, with the guarantee of an official contract, rather than to die of starvation down the road and to have for a tomb the belly of a jackal.'

—Maurice Maindron, *Dans l'Inde du Sud,* (le Coromandel), 1907.

My most heartfelt thanks go to Jean-Samuel Sahaï, Gerry L'Étang, Gilbert Francis Ponnaman, Camille Moutoussamy, Philippe Pratx, great experts in Creole Indianness as well as to Pierre Pinalie, for proofreading this text.

# Contents

# Translator's Introduction

*In the sugarcane fields, oh!*
*In those sugarcane fields...*

*They labour till their limbs*
*Weaken and are ready to fall.*
*Ceaseless smouldering has shrunk*
*The hearts of those Hindu women.*
*Isn't there a way to reduce their sorrow?*
*Isn't there a potion to lessen their pain?*
*Like bullocks at an oil-press,*
*They toil in those cane fields. (In the sugarcane fields...)**

Raphaël Confiant is one of Martinique's most prolific litterateurs who writes in both French and Creole. A militant proponent of Creole culture**, this master storyteller delves into his island's history to spin one of the most riveting of human sagas, peopled with truculent characters.

This island of Martinique which he celebrates is an overseas *département* of the Republic of France and is part of the arc of volcanic islands, called the lesser Antilles, nestled in the Carribean Sea between the two Americas. Originally populated by Arawak and Carib peoples, it was charted in 1493 by Christopher Columbus and became a French colony in 1635, when Pierre Belain d'Esnambuc founded the first French

---

*Subramania Bharati, *Selected Poems*, trans. Usha Rajagopalan, The Everyman Library, Hachette India, 2012, p. 139.

**Jean Bernabé, Patrick Chamoiseau, *Raphaël Confiant, Eloge de la Créolité*, Paris Gallimard, 1989.

colony at Saint-Pierre. Sugarcane was first planted here in the seventeenth century and slaves were shipped from Africa to work on the plantations. When slavery was finally abolished in 1848, Indian and Chinese workers were brought in from the French and British colonies as indentured labour. They were paid weekly wages, provided housing and medical facilities and given a free passage to India at the end of their five-year contract. The descendants of those African slaves—who were now French citizens—looked down upon the Coolies—the Indian indentured labourers, who braved the inhumane conditions and remained resolutely attached to their language and culture. Guilt consumed them for having crossed the kaala paani as they pined to return to India.

*La panse du chacal* (literally translated as the Belly of the Jackal) first published in 2004, tells the story of the Dorassamy family and its migration to Martinique. The intrigue is embedded in three locations: drought- and famine-stricken India, steeped in caste and reeling under colonial oppression; the *White Adder*, the British ship with its British captain and crew, transporting the indentured labourers, where race and caste intermingle to everyone's dismay; and, finally, Martinique, where the new Creole identity emerges out of the miasma of exploitation, interracial hatred and the angst of exile.

The story follows Adhiyaman, a former spinning mill owner Ambu Dorassamy's son, who flees for his life and from Madurai after seeing a pack of jackals devour his parents. On reaching Pondicherry he marries below his caste and boards the ship to America, which after weathering terrible storms and surviving a smallpox epidemic reaches the coast of Martinique. The climate and luxuriant vegetation reminds him of home. He, along with his wife and two sons, toils in the fields from dawn to dusk for a pittance. On this island the Coolies are pariahs, the lowest of the low, who can be refused repatriation on false charges, whose women can be raped and whose children have no right to education. Meanwhile the intermingling of races in this strange land shocks them as they desperately try to preserve and hold onto their Tamil identity.

But one day, Indian emigration is outlawed. The fifty-fifth ship is the last one to bring Indians to Martinique. All ties with Mother India are snapped.

Today, more than 150 years later, the descendants of Coolies speak Creole, master the *danmyé,* the dance fight of the Blacks, revel in the Carnival and dance the biguine, mazurka, and bolero with gay abandon to the beat of the *bèlè* drum rather than the *tappu-tambour.* They are now Indian Creoles who may attend mass at church, a Hindu ceremony in a temple and also visit the African obeahman. They are not caged in a single monolithic identity, they are an exquisite mosaic of colours, races, cultures and languages.

Raphaël Confiant chooses to tell the story of the early Tamil emigrants in a potpurri of French, Creole and Tamil as an ode to his multilingual Martinique. He says, he grew up hearing Latin and Greek in church, Creole at home and in the street, French at school and a smattering of Arabic and Tamil on the streets. Creole remains his muse and he has even written a dictionary of Martinican Creole, patiently gleaning words from written texts, oral traditions but also the common parlance.* Confiant's writing is a heady mixture of French and Creole, peppered with any other language that the story calls for. There is no culture without language, and without the sonorous Creole tongue—so vivid, flavourful, rich in colour and texture—Martinique will lose its soul. History and literature work together in the author's world to nurture the memory of all these communities who came to weave their own special thread into the fabric of this rainbow island.

In *La panse du chacal,* Creole is used in conversations, Tamil is introduced largely through proverbs. British sailors speak pidgin English with the Coolies. Verses from the Upanishads, Manusmriti and Bhagavad Gita are quoted in French translation, albeit transcribed in the Roman script.

*http://www.potomitan.info/dictionnaire/

There is never a dull moment in Confiant's narrative. His language is a merry medley of classical French from the *métropole*—a turn of phrase typical of Martinique—a rare word or expression from medieval French, and neologisms whose meanings the reader must figure out from the context. Even his minor characters remain etched in the reader's memory—be it Eugénie de Maucourt, Z'Oiseau, or Coucoune Diable. The main protagonist however is sugarcane, this weed that breaks the back of the former slave and the Coolie alike, unjustly favours the White master, transforms into golden brown sugar and heady rum or *tafia*, and rules this island and all those who live on it.

Confiant's early childhood memories are centred around his grandfather's plantation—a few hectares of sugarcane and a small rum distillery. In the nineteenth century, Martinique's countryside was full of large sugarcane plantations like Courbaril, Gradis, Eyma and Fonds d'Or. Each plantation was the private property of the *Béké* who lived with his family and servants in the sprawling villa called the *Grand'Case* or Big House. The plantation was run by the White overseer, and a foreman and a steward, who were usually of mixed race. The Coolies and Black labourers assembled in the courtyard in front of the *Grand'Case* where the foreman assigned tasks for the day before they trudged up to their workposts.

The Indian reader will be intrigued by the tales from Indian mythology told differently. Some of the spellings like Kannavédi, Ouméavali, Malimouté may be baffling. Consequently, I have opted for familiar spellings in the translation after consulting specialists and whenever I have not been able to trace the word, have retained the spelling provided by the author, like in the case of 'Penpirenday' or 'Irattavati'. In any diasporic culture, myths, customs and beliefs get refracted as they traverse the kaala paani and are revisted, reimagined, repurposed to suit the new context.

Over time, Tamil has ceased to be the language of communication and has become the sacred language reserved for religious ceremonies.* Prayers and devotional songs are orally transmitted from generation to generation and many words have become phonetically creolized like Maldévilin for Maduraiviran.

As a mark of respect for the multilingual narrative imagined by Confiant, this translation has also chosen to toggle between English, French, Creole and Tamil. For instance Creole expressions like *devant-jour, femme-dehors, taxi-pays, nègre-griffe*, have been retained and are followed by a translation the first time they appear in a chapter. Thereafter only the Creole word is used. Or consider *Vèpèlè* which is the Tamil word for *azadirachta indica* that has been translated as neem and *l'eau safranée* as turmeric. A glossary has also been provided towards the very end for ready reference.

Like the original, this translation pays homage to all those brave women and men who crossed the kaala paani, driven by hunger, despair and oppression, to toil relentlessly under the scorching sun in sugar plantations of Martinique. The Creole culture that Confiant seeks to nurture and disseminate has been enriched by Tamoulitude.** The colourful 'madras' fabric, *kolbu* also known as colombo, the mélange of spices, the temples that still buzz with devotees...all tell a touching story.

As a child, I grew up listening to my mother sing the Tamil poet Subramania Bharati's *Karumbu tottattile* (In the Sugarcane Plantations) wherein the poet asks the wind to carry back the sorrowful outpourings of the women toiling in the cane fields in an island lost in the oceans, so far from home, exploited, abandoned to their fate. When I first read *La panse*

---

*Appasamy Murugaiyan, *Chants tamouls aux Antilles: un patrimoine entre écrit et oral*, L'Etang Gerry (ed) Archipélies no 3–4, *De la créolisation culturelle*, 2012, p. 215–234.

**Appasamy Murugaiyan, *Chants tamouls en diaspora francophone : corpus appropriation, transmission et reconstitution*, Nicholas Dejenne et Claudine Leblanc (eds), *Diasporas: Etudes des singularités indiennes, l'Inde de leurs textes: Littérature d'Asie du sud en diaspora*, DESI La Revue, Presse Universitaire de Bordeaux, No 4, May 2019, p. 33–53.

*du chacal,* I knew that the wind, wet with their tears, had finally reached our shores.

A visit to Guadeloupe where I met and interacted with Tamil Creoles impacted me profoundly. When I first read this Tamil tale told in French, I knew I had to ferry it to the Anglophone world in my role as translator-passeur. Prof Christine Raguet, poet Jerry Pinto, Christine Cornet from the Institut français en Inde and Ravi Singh from Speaking Tiger made this translation possible.

As Walter Benjamin says in 'The Task of the Translator', '...all translation is only a somewhat provisional way of coming to terms with the foreignness of languages'.* So I have kept the rough edges, preserved the whiff of otherness and allowed the echoes of the original to resonate throughout this translation.

How successful this attempt was is a decision I must leave to the reader.

Vidya Vencatesan
University of Mumbai,
Mumbai, India
March 2021

*Walter Benjamin, 'The Task of the Translator' [1923], in *Selected Writings, Vol. 1 (1913–1926)*, ed. Marcus Bullock and Michael W. Jennings, Cambridge, Massachusetts, The Belknap Press of Harvard University Press, 1996, (pp. 253–263), p. 257.

# 1

## Song of the Lost Light

*Exuding a bittersweet odour, the tamarind trees strew the earth with fruits that nobody gathers any more. The distress of the tutelary mango trees whose shade is deserted. The soles of our feet are tired of moving forward, of scraping the loose overheated stones on the side roads, the ones we take to escape the Englishman whose language of hoarse sounds makes us shudder even in our sleep. And the gods turn a deaf ear to us as if we had committed some unpardonable sin. O Mariamman, why don't you guide our steps? And you, Shiva, god of a thousand arms, why do you no longer embrace us? Our scorned offerings are left to mangy dogs and vultures. The wind sweeps away the hibiscus garlands patiently woven in your honour, disperses the coconut palms, blows out the flame of the oil lamps, dries our throats and burns the back of our eyes.*

'Hey, Coolie, dog-eater!'

Vinesh had been about to sharpen his machete on a scarred and pitted makeshift grindstone, placed at the entrance of workshops like a statue with auspicious powers, when the insult made him jump.

He had thought he was still alone at this early hour. He had woken early, before *devant-jour*, daybreak, to avoid the droves of noisy Negroes who showed up in carts from all the quarters of Macouba and Basse-Pointe. Already half drunk, they would be trading bawdy remarks about the women from Gradis Plantation, who had the reputation of being less virtuous than women elsewhere, especially the Indian ones. Although he had come here as a baby, Vinesh believed he remembered the first hour, the first day, the first night, the first week, and even the first month he spent in this country. Later, his memory was only that of never-ending and tedious suffering, the repetition of the same gestures—grab the cane in the middle, sever it at the base, then cut it into three segments of equal length. All this in the muggy heat, in the company of red ants and sometimes those fearsome and treacherous snakes, the lanceheads, lurking in the hay. Alongside, in the line drawn by the foreman, dozens of arms kept moving forward, cutting, slicing, hoeing, and stopping only for a brief moment to drink a little water from a calabash. Indians locked into inviolable silence on the steepest plots; Negroes in the plains singing to the beat of their drums to put their heart and soul into the job.

He did not dare turn around. On his back he felt the breath of the man who had doubtlessly come to challenge him; he could hear his heavy step, he could sense the hatred that infused him, the villainous pleasure that this man already felt at the idea of beating up someone weaker than himself. Vinesh had been surprised by the brutish strength of this race that he was told had been slaves until just a short while ago. Tall and muscular, the Negroes were a mystery to him not because of their colour, often being less dark than him—he who was a Dravidian—but very much so because of their strange hair. Picky-picky* hair like a heap of peppercorns, which he had not so far dared to touch, even when some bold boys came by his hut on Sunday afternoons to sell him traditional cakes and sweets. He was also greatly struck by their pride that bordered on haughtiness even though they were so poor that most of them went barefoot and were dressed in tattered rags. They always looked at you with a glimmer of irony, only bowing to the one whom they called Papa Béké, the white owner of the plantation, ambling across the plantation riding La Dorée, a mare with an impressive chest. The mare—La Dorée—could

*Picky-picky hair—Jamaican English word for frizzy black African hair

be seen grazing in the late afternoons, alone, free to move about in a savannah of Guinea grass specially laid out for her without anyone ever thinking of stealing her. She received the same respect as her master and the Negroes wished her good morning or good evening as if she were a human being. They usually showed absolute contempt towards all other animals especially the dogs with whom they had an old bone to pick due to a very old dispute, the reason for which escaped the Indians.

*'Ou pa tann man palé ba'w, Kouli? Zowey-ou sal oben ki sa?'* (Didn't you hear what I said, Coolie? Your ears dirty or what?), said the voice again, the tone less aggressive now but tinged with mockery.

Vinesh, who was nervously tapping his thigh with the flat side of his machete, moved his head slightly to the side, still not turning around. He did not feel up to fighting that morning because he was just recovering from the flu which had nailed a number of workers to their mattresses. Chest flu was the diagnosis of the doctor who had come from town at the request of Houblin de Maucourt, otherwise known as Papa Béké. He was a sexagenarian with a gaunt face, whose blue eyes terrorised the plantation workers. 'Chest flu *hein*!' A disease unknown to Indians, doubtlessly a manifestation of the diablerie that the jealous Negroes got up to on full moon nights in the dense woods in order to wipe out those who—as they said—had landed in Martinique in order to help the Whiteman slyly restore slavery. They scorned these Indian Coolies in public, attacked them without reason on festival days, and raped their women, all while claiming after the dastardly deed was done that they were bitches in heat whose pussy hair was as sharp as a barber's blade.

*'Sa ou lé?'* (What do you want?) Vinesh finally asked, hesitantly.

The man did not reply. He must have positioned himself to attack, fists raised, and was waiting only for one thing: that the Indian turn around so that he could fly into him. It was without doubt Hermann, the braggart from the Hauteurs Bourdon quarter, the most famous *danmyé* fighter, an exponent of the dancing combat that the quarrelsome Negroes would engage in after payday on Saturday afternoon, which they allowed the Indians to watch only from afar. On a memorable Holy Saturday as the Christian feast of Easter drew near, Vinesh had seen Hermann smash an opponent's spinal cord, while a raging crowd applauded. Under the light of the burning torches, the rictus of Hermann's thick lips terrified Vinesh. He could read some secret prayer oozing through the blood trickling down Hermann's chin. The opponent, a simple chap 'long as the Mississippi', as the Negro expression went, had succeeded in dealing him a kick at the beginning of the combat, and proud of his success, had jumped about in circles mocking Hermann. He was accompanied by his supporters from his faraway municipality who were applauding, shouting while remaining on guard as they were encircled by the people of the area. At first, it seemed like a game to Vinesh because the two men took a perverse pleasure in avoiding and whirling around each other, throwing punches in the air for ever so long, when suddenly the tough Negro from Basse-Pointe slammed into his opponent, picked him up as if he were a bundle of sugarcane and sent him flying outside the fighting circle. A terrible joy seized the workers of Courbaril Plantation where Hermann officiated as the assistant foreman. Yells, congratulations, bursts of sardonic laughter, smutty ribbing, you name it. Vinesh slipped away before any of them could think of attacking him just for fun, a favourite pastime of the Negroes when Indians were around. He heard that the loser had been taken home only to die two or three days later, without it affecting Hermann or his supporters in the least. Such savagery had left Vinesh flabbergasted and he had refused for a long time after to watch, even from very far, these fights which enthralled the cane-cutters and the mule-drivers. Did they not discuss it endlessly in Man Ninise's rum shack? She encouraged them while pretending to take up cudgels for the losers, something that had the knack of enraging foreman Sosthène—a Chabin man, white of skin and redhaired—

who bragged that he was one of the numerous *fils-dehors*, illegitimate sons, of the M. de Maucourt's father. Vinesh felt an irrepressible fear every time he ran into Sosthène who held the envied post of plantation foreman. He found them disturbing, these mixed-race people, part White and part Negro, more disturbing than the Mulattoes—the other products of the shameless fornication between land owners and black workers. 'The Mulatto is vicious,' they said, 'he looks down upon you. The Chabin is ferocious, he glares at you with his light eyes and gets angry for nothing.' Not a day passed, in fact, without foreman Sosthène looking to pick a fight with somebody and, if he had not found a way to exercise his talent as a public nuisance, he went about everywhere grumbling.

'I need to fight, dammit. Who would like to fight me? Come on! Don't be scared, mate. No faggots here, right?'

Vinesh felt a surprisingly soft hand settle on his shoulder, a hand so soft that he almost passed out. His fear evaporated when he faced the person who had called out to him so early in the morning. It was a woman! One heck of woman! She stood tall above him, with a bandana in bright red Madras cotton, a fabric from the Indies that the local people had adopted. She was standing with her legs apart, as provocative as can be, hands on her hips, barely holding back the giggle which offended the Indian man. She must not be from here, not from Courbaril, or Eyma or Gradis in any case, because her imposing stature could not have passed unnoticed. She stared at him shamelessly as Creole women, creatures without modesty who seemed to be unaware that man was their master, do. He still heard his father recollect the very first time he had seen a Negress and the stupefaction that had gripped him. At the disembarkation at Fort-de-France, on the wharfs where a row of coalwomen were waiting to come aboard to dump the contents of the enormous baskets balanced on their heads, their arms dangling. One of them had had a bone to pick with a docker and had not hesitated to stand up to him, responding sharply by raising her right hand as if she were about to slap him. Since then, Vinesh's father, Adhiyaman, had endeavoured to teach him these two verses of the fifth book of the Laws of Manu:

*A little girl, a young woman, a woman of advanced age, should never do anything of her own will, even in her house.*

*During her childhood a woman must depend on her father; during her youth she depends on her husband; once her husband is dead, she depends on her sons; if she has no sons, she depends on her husband's close relatives or, in the absence of the latter, she depends on the relatives of her father; if she doesn't have paternal relatives, she depends on the king; a woman should never govern herself as she pleases.**

It was not surprising then that Vinesh found it difficult to consider Negresses real women and had avoided associating with them, even though every morning the foreman assigned him an *attacheuse*, a woman who walks behind the cane cutter gathering the cut cane and tying it up in bundles—a sullen creature who endeavoured to follow the rhythm of his cutting—not offering a word of encouragement or even a knowing wink during the twelve hours they worked together. And the one who stood now before him, while a lazy sun was beginning to poke out of the top of the hills, was even more impressive than all the others his mother, Devi, had not stopped warning him about!

'Negress equals She-Devil,' she muttered every time the higgler went by their house. She used to remind him of the gloomy fate of Sinamallé who had had the misfortune of

---

**The Laws of Manu*, translated by Wendy Doniger and Brian K. Smith, Penguin, 1991, chapter 5, p.115: London

147) A girl, a young woman, or even an old woman should not do anything independently, even in ( her own) house.

148) In childhood a woman should be under her father's control, in youth under her husband's and when her husband is dead, under her son's, she should not have independence.

3) Her father guides her in childhood, her husband guards her in youth, and her sons guard her in old age. A woman is not fit for independence (chapter 9, p. 197).

getting involved with a *Câpresse* from town. Never had one seen a character with a more commanding bearing than Sinamallé; even some men used to stop to gape at him, speechless. Nobody ever knew how he got friendly and then fell in love with the pretentious and flighty seamstress—Hortense. She was well known throughout the north of Martinique for having ripped apart the most stable of couples, some Mulattoes and some Whites of humble origin. Malicious gossips confirmed that she made her lovers pay a heavy price for the use of her charms. Hortense had not known the shackles of slavery, neither had her mother nor her grandmother. At least that was the legend she carefully cultivated, making sure her innumerable lovers carried it to the four corners of Macouba, because having reached a certain age now she was not granting her favours as liberally as she had in her youth.

The liaison between Sinamallé and Hortense should never have happened because the handsome Indian man was a *poussari*, an intercessor between the gods and the poor humans. He knew the prayers to summon Nagourmira, the one who had saved the first ship of immigrants making its way to the Antilles half a century ago, when a storm without a name threatened to shatter it against the rocky coast of the Cape of Good Hope. This epic had been recounted ever since, enriched each time with new details which glorified this Muslim deity even more and Nagourmira had ended up being integrated into the Hindu pantheon. Sinamallé also spoke directly to Mariamman, to Bomi, to Paklayen, asking them for only one grace: not to die here. They had become Coolies on this island where famine had cast them. This was the only boon they sought: not to be buried in this land with its hellish reign of Christian religion and Negro sorcery. To hold on till the date of their repatriation to beloved India. To hold on for five years in the mugginess of the sugarcane fields, at ridiculously low salaries, under the threat of unknown diseases and gun shots fired without any warning by the policemen on horseback.

One year, when January was drawing to a close and the harvest was beginning, the Negroes decided to lay down their machetes. '*Manman, ô, manman, la grève nous a barré la route*' (Mother oh mother, the strike has blocked the road!), they screamed, roaming the countryside day and night in clusters, demanding that the Coolies join them, most often in vain. It was 1899, and Vinesh had just turned thirteen. The date had remained etched in his mind because for the second time the government had refused his family repatriation on the grounds that his father, Adhiyaman, had not finished paying his debts. At that time, he had been too young to gauge the distress that had gripped his father, turning him into a withdrawn creature, stingy with his words and smiles.

'Debts, *hein*! What debts were they talking about?' His father managed to mutter. Every morning his mother sent Vinesh to the plantation shop to buy the same provisions: a quarter gallon of oil, half a pound of dried cod, a pot of rice and a clove of garlic. Man Ninise rolled her eyes at his toes, mudstained in the rainy season and dusty in dry weather and made him wash them with half a calabash of water that he had to draw from a rainwater barrel.

She wrote down the purchases in a mysterious notebook attached to the counter by a string. On Saturday afternoons, after wages, Vinesh went back there to settle his family bill in the company of a multitude of *Négrillons*, Negro and Indian pickneys, who exchanged taps of the head and punches on the ribs. All seemed to be going well until at the end of the fifth year, when repatriation time came, the shop owner let M. Houblin de Maucourt know that the families—Souprayen, Andragon, et Dorassamy—had not paid their dues. The Béké informed Vinesh's father that he owed him several thousand francs and decreed that he must continue to stay on the plantation for quite some time in order to repay him.

**First Name**

When my mother saw her hips grow wide and her stomach become round, she found herself in a buoyant mood. It was this very temperament that had made her one of the most ravishing young women back home in the city of Madurai. It is said that one day, when she had come to the temple of Tiruparrankunram to pray, a man of high caste who was no longer young, was stunned by what he believed to be a sudden apparition of the Goddess Parvati. Interrupting his meditation, he stopped to question her but my mother only smiled at him. She knew that this kind of man had only contempt for the employees of the spinning mill and would be happy to honour her bed for a few weeks before disappearing. On several occasions the Brahmin struck again, but to no avail, and was reduced to threatening her. My mother had not breathed a word about this to her parents and, wearing the same smile as always, had decided to change temples. She became a devotee of Minakshisundareshvara.

My father too seemed to find a semblance of serenity with my mother's pregnancy, even though he was worried for this child who was about to be born in a foreign country. Would he really belong to our race? Would he understand the meaning of our devotion to Kali, to Mariamman or to Kannavédi? Especially because from the shape of Devi's stomach, the matrons of Courbaril predicted that it was a girl. It was much more difficult to protect girls from the eyes of Negroes and Whites. Indian women were thought to be of easy virtue by the Negroes, although in reality, these women only gave in to their brutal courting out of terror. As for the White men, were they not the masters of the land and the mill? To refuse them was tantamount to not getting a job anywhere and ending up like these Indians on the road to perdition, who haunted the ill-famed quarters of towns and the city centre, when they were not being dragged to court and deported to the prison in Toulon.

My mother's pregnancy went without a hitch. This was miraculous because so many typhoid fevers, malaria, smallpox, inexplicable diarrhoea and other terrifying diseases ravaged the country. She gave birth to a little girl who she decided to name Arulmani. The very next day onwards, the overseer de Sainte-Foix came to regularly warn her that she must go to the town hall of Macouba to announce the birth. Such was the law and there was no getting away from it. Since this sensitive task required a certain mastery over French, my mother got my younger brother Ganadin to accompany her. At the registry office they were received coldly. The Negroes from town detested the Indian race as much as their own peers in the plantations did, even though we were not stealing their bread.

The person in charge of registration did not even raise her eyes, nor did she deign to cast a glance at Arulmani whom my mother had wrapped up in a beautiful swathe of orange Madras cotton.

'What's her name?' she asked.

'A...Arulmani.'

'*Ki sa? Aroul ki sa? Kouman ou pa sav nou pa ka asepté prénon kouli isiya!*'

(What! Arul what? Don't you know we don't accept these Coolie first names?)

My mother could not speak. She clasped her baby against her chest and pushed Ganadin in front of her, under the mocking gaze of the other employees of the town hall.

'He speaks French this one?' started the Negress again. 'Since when do the Coolies speak our language, *hein*?'

My brother negotiated in vain. The registry office was no pigsty! Only Christian first names had a rightful place there. The woman suggested the ridiculous name of Paulette. Then she imposed it on them and through the journey back, Ganadin told me, my mother did not stop mumbling:

'We will never call you like that! Arulmani you are, Arulmani you will be forever.'

Alas! This forever only lasted seventeen days. An untreatable lung disease took our little lotus flower and my mother became inconsolable. She cursed herself for letting this senseless first name be written in the birth register.

*

And now, this robust creature who was standing in front of Vinesh, who he had mistakenly thought had challenged him to a *danmyé* fight, was none other than that famous Hortense, the stuff of legends. Vinesh had thought she would be more feminine, more enchanting. He thought she would be like a she-devil from the Créole folk tales, caked in make-up, taking a perverse pleasure in throwing from a cliff those whom she had successfully enticed. Hortense was obviously returning from the fields. She was still dressed in a greyish gaule gathered at the waist with Madras cotton, in the style of an *amarreuse*. Taking off her bakoua hat, she gazed at him mischievously.

'We are late this morning, *Z'Indien*?' she tossed at him.

Vinesh jumped. Raising his eyes to the sky, he realised that it must be past eight o'clock at least. The sun was already piercing the foliage of the mango trees in the courtyard of the *Grand'Case*, Big House, where the master's cooks bustled about. They jabbered in hushed tones as they plucked the poultry and peeled the horse plantains. They had noticed neither Hortense's presence nor his.

'I finished before everyone else,' continued the woman. 'I have to go to Basse-Pointe for some work. The foreman Sosthène was asking about you. Where were you, my poor fellow?'

'I didn't see the sun rise.'

'Partied too hard last evening or what? You Coolies must avoid rum. Ha-ha-ha! You don't have the head for it. Unless you spent the night in a dame's arms...'

Vinesh had neither drunk too much sugarcane alcohol nor had he been gallivanting. He remembered his nocturnal journey with blinding clarity. Usually his dreams faded away with the first blaze of day break, but this particular morning, quite inexplicably, he seemed to feel against his skin the softness of the Kaveri water, the little sister of the sacred Ganga, smell the scent of incense that burnt at the feet of funerary deities mixed with the scent of *vèpèlè*, neem, whose petals were the colour of the sky. He still heard the litany of prayers offered to the dying. The near and dear ones left them on the banks of the greatest waterway of the Tamil country so that they were assured of a good reincarnation. And all these pilgrims came in hundreds from the most remote regions of the interior. They submerged themselves up to the neck, still and radiant, indifferent to the dead branches, to the putrid excrement, and sometimes the rotting bodies of animals that the current swept along. All of India, Mother India, welcomed him into her arms, clasped him against her and it was such ecstasy that each night he wished it would never end. His mother, a tiny bit of a tease, quipped at him:

'Vinesh slept well as usual! You can tell from his face. Why don't you give me a bit of your sleep? I always wake up three or four times each night for no reason. As for Adhiyaman, I don't think he sleeps a wink.'

'I will do that only when I return to Madurai,' muttered her husband, blowing on his morning coffee.

'Madurai! Madurai! You only have that word on your lips. Have you forgotten that you have to cross two oceans before you get there, *hein*? It has been a long time since I stopped believing that India is still waiting for us. They have forgotten us there, Adhiyaman. Well and truly forgotten.'

'Shut up, woman! You are going to stuff dreadful ideas into the boys' heads. Hey Ganadin, get up, time for school!'

Vinesh's younger brother always had difficulty waking up; he did not like notebooks and textbooks. Being taciturn, he refused to explain why he came home so often with grazed arms and black eyes. However, he was the only one in the Dorassamy family who could speak a little French and who could decipher it, which made him the one in charge of verifying the credit note book, which they could check at Man Ninise's shop. That ageless, deliberately nasty Mulatress did not hesitate to con the Indians by writing down merchandise that they had never bought or by exaggerating the amount of their weekly bill. This caused constant bickering between Man Ninise and the Coolies. Ganadin's knowledge of French spared his family such exploitation. Nevertheless the young lad did not get any credit for it and he laughed at his brother when Vinesh declared that Théophile, the European school teacher, had offered to give him free lessons. As for Adhiyaman, he had shrugged his shoulders, because he was certain that his elder son would remain chained to the plantation just like himself. He would end up a zealous servant of sugarcane, the accursed weed that made the riches of the White men, beginning with M. de Maucourt, the owner of Courbaril. Devi, sceptical, had only said:

'Watch out for yourself, Vinesh! You know Théophile is a socialist. If the master discovers that you are hobnobbing too much with him, you know what you risk? He will ask the manager to sack you, and that chap, he doesn't like Indians. He gets along better with the Negroes. You know that.'

'He gets along better with the Negresses, *oui*!' Sniggered the young man.

'Naturally! They are women without modesty.'

And here, lo and behold, for the first time in his life, Vinesh was confronted by one of them. Till then he had hardly had the chance to exchange a few words with the sister of Gaston, his best friend. Gaston was one of the few Negroes who did not look to pick a quarrel with Indians, perhaps because, being lame, he was the whipping boy of the good-for-nothings of the quarter. Their friendship had been built by pure chance and was undemonstrative. Three times the foreman Sosthène had placed them side by side in the fields, where Gaston had had trouble keeping pace because of his debility. Vinesh had lent him a hand in order to spare him reprimands and pay cuts. Patte Crochue, as he was cruelly nicknamed, had not thanked him, but one day had quite simply saved his life. Vinesh was getting ready to grab a stalk of cane when he saw the flash of a machete. The head of a lancehead rolled on the ground while the body of the reptile continued to squirm around his arm for endless minutes. The young Indian remained tongue tied, incapable of getting back to work, till the foreman Sosthène, who was doing his rounds bullied him:

'What is happening to you, mate? I was told Coolies don't fear serpents. So get back to work, understood?'

Hortense moistened her face with the water from the small pond into which freezing spring water flowed, transported by a piece of bamboo plonked directly on the embankment. Then she disrobed and began to wash herself, without bothering about Vinesh. Realising that he had lost a day's work because of waking up late, he looked in vain for a plausible excuse to offer the foreman. He was, however, not too worried because it was common knowledge that Sosthène had a weakness for his mother Devi. For a long time, this had spared the two boys—when they were younger—from the fate of the little *Négrillons* who were thrown into small groups to collect the bits of cane forgotten by the *attacheuses*. Ganadin had even escaped this completely because he was among the rare children who went regularly to primary school in Macouba. M. de Maucourt was not in favour of Indians going to school because he claimed that their parents were not French. What's more, a number of them still demanded that they be repatriated to India, beginning with Adhiyaman Dorassamy, Ganadin's father. Apparently, the foreman Sosthène had succeeded in convincing M. de Maucourt to allow Vinesh's younger brother to go to study ABCD, as they said jokingly.

Hortense was a miracle of nature and she knew it. Her skin which was perfectly black, iridescent with droplets, caught the attention of the young Indian man who was following each movement as if hypnotised. The swaying of her generous hips stirred him so much that he felt his tongue go dry. She energetically rubbed the delightfully frizzy triangle of hair that adorned her crotch. Every time she leaned forward, the firm globes of her breasts dangled alluringly. Vinesh was rooted to the spot. He felt as ridiculous as a puppet in a carnival and prayed that no one would come near the pond. Out there, under the mango trees, the cooks had finished their preparations. They could be heard squabbling in the *Grand'Case*. Vinesh and Hortense were all alone—an unusual pair—that morning in the dry season when the heat was beginning to overwhelm the world.

'Dry me, *Z'Indien*!'

And the Negress held out a piece of coarse canvas cloth that she kept folded in her knapsack. Vinesh did as he was told, almost unwillingly, turning away from this temptress, more shapely than the women of his race. Especially her well rounded, even protruding, rump which he patted shyly, impressed by his own indecent insolence.

'Ha-ha-ha! You folks, the Indians, you have flat bums!'

Hortense guffawed, grabbing his wrist. 'But the Good Lord, he gave you beautiful hair. The Good Lord is just. To the Whites, he offered blue eyes. Only the Chinese, the poor things, got nothing at all. Ha-ha-ha!'

'I like their perfectly round faces...'

He stammered, remembering the brief passage of the two indisciplined workers, Li Feng and Chang Sen, through Courbaril Plantation. They were so pugnacious that the overseer de Sainte-Foix had had to get rid of them at the end of two months.

'I was joking, young man. All the races have something good, if not, the Good Lord would not be the Good Lord. Well, He still has His preferences! As for me, he never liked me. I had to give up my work as a seamstress because my clients were no longer paying me. What's more, now many prefer to buy from wily Syrian peddlers. What else could I do but return to the cane fields, *hein*?'

She took the canvas towel out of his hands with a brusqueness that once again intimidated him, and dragged him to the stables. At this hour of the day, all the mules were in the fields, where they carted bundles of cane along the colonial road. From there, the carts picked up the load to take it to the final destination, to this world forbidden to the Indians: the three distilleries of Macouba and the Basse-Pointe mill. There, where the two principal riches of the country, rum and sugar, were manufactured; riches that only the Whites and a handful of Mulattoes benefitted from.

'Good morning, Madame!' said Hortense to La Dorée, the mare of the boss of Courbaril Plantation, no hint of laughter in her voice.

The animal reared up a bit, looked at them with big glaucous eyes, before going back to chomping the bundle of fresh Guinea grass that the groom brought her every morning. Hortense lay down on the floor on a heap of blankets and well-worn saddles, and spread her thighs wide.

'Do it quickly!' She whispered. 'Someone could come at any moment, *oui*...'

# 2

## Sugarcane, Age-Old Pain, O Tenderness!

*With extremely gentle gestures, these hands—whose tanned palms are no different from the back of the hand—grab stalks, furrowed with dryness. This is because sugarcane secretes tenderness and bitterness. It slashes, scratches, scrapes, skins their dreams, leaving indelible scars—to decipher them is a Story-History; but sugarcane also knows how to weave the wind into its silvery-white hair, to make hearts pound wildly. From its core, the love song of sugar steadily rises; with its four secret notes, the fields on the hill slopes make the vibrant morning air heavenly. Tranquil determination can be read on these faces carved in black basalt who ask neither favour nor fees from destiny. This is why each gesture is shaped with such perfect precision. They know the art of bending the machete blade to the point of distortion while the grinding stone rattles like on Good Friday. They neither smile nor frown nor remain indifferent. To be on the job, to launch an attack on the tightly packed battalions of cane and then to move to the next destination. Expanses of cane, which appear monotonous and immobile only to the outsider, greet the eye. To gaze upon the scene, you need to put the machete behind your shoulders and hold it by the two edges. Because sugarcane is alive, each cane is alive, each plant cries out the suffering of the Negro and the Indian while paradoxically exalting the future. That future is brown sugar that slips between the fingers quick, quickened as if it were the prisoner of some hourglass. It is the colourless elixir whose wild heat welters in the distillation columns.*

*Have you already considered the* amarreuses, *these women kitted out in* hardes-cabane, *rags wrapped around the arms and legs to protect them, wearing Madras cotton and bakoua hats, who, with incomparable gravitas, tie the bundles of cane with such skilful knots? They never stop because time is racing, arms rise high to the sky as they strike. Muscles are drawn taut, jaws grow tense, eyes crinkle from sweat and excessive light—fuck the scorching sun! And the sugarcane falls to the ground, dry, dense. Negroes and Indians fight it, neither looking ahead nor behind. Cutting cane is the big fight. A fight unto death, unto life! Sometimes the* amarreuse *freezes into a statue, hat and machete lowered, nocturnal goddess in the flamboyance of the day, her cheekbones outlining saucy eyes. These eyes transfix the foreman and his zealous viciousness, the overseer and his boastful ways, the Béké on horseback, galloping at will on the stone tracks raising whirlwinds of red dust. These eyes say simply: 'I'm here!' It is their way of claiming solitude. The* amarreuse *has forever been rooted in the most profound of solitudes. When a song escapes her thick sensual lips—a love song in French, a bawdy song in Creole—she sings for no one. These vocal exercises warm up her heartstrings, those fine invisible membranes that link our body to life. Once the sugarcane plots are cut, they look like Negresses' heads coiffed with surprisingly regular braids. These alternatively brown and black stripes melt at dizzying speed into the fringes of the overhanging sky, and playfully blur the horizon. At this moment, the Negro's gaze becomes almost compassionate, the Indian's becomes sugary, but to tell the real truth, both are only disarming. They shout mutely: 'The earth is stronger than us,* oui! *Tomorrow, in ten days or a bunch of months, everything will grow back exactly as before and the cane fields will sketch out the curve of the hills in a crew cut, almost military style. You will see,* oui!'

# 3

## The Procession of Elephants

*They move forward as if in their dreams, their slow pace bringing the world to order. Ever since they left the Mullai Forest, they have not stopped showing us the Way, from village to village, drawing a halo of dust around themselves and we have abandoned everything at once. We turned our backs upon the infamy of our existence, upon the acres of ungrateful earth that the English invaders had condescended to grant us. We are Shudras, born of the feet of the Purusha, the Primordial Man, and thus condemned to serve those who have come forth from his most noble parts. Amongst us we number the dregs of the earth, the untouchables called 'Chandalas', dog eaters so impure that it is forbidden for other castes to touch them. We walk with the elephants, humbly, attentive to their smallest desires and our hopes have no limits.*

The man was moving forward, staggering along, a veil intermittently blocking his view, overwhelmed by the heat and dust that rose from the dirt track. For months now, one could not tell the tracks from the ricefields through which they meandered. The world had become a greyish smear that spread out endlessly, a desiccated smear, the earth cracked and strewn with countless skeletons. Silence reigned supreme, hardly disturbed by the scraping of Adhiyaman's swollen feet. Yet his heart was light. He was clutching against his chest about a pound of rice, grains that he had patiently harvested in the rat holes that lined the Vaigai River which had become a thin trickle. His father had given him this idea. A man full of wisdom, whom people used to consult, travelling from all the neighbouring villages before the English captured the country. 'The rats are smarter than we are,' he said to Adhiyaman, 'they sense the times of drought drawing close and stock up what they need to get them through till the monsoon. Don't forget that it is for this reason that the venerable Ganesh chose the shrew for his vehicle!'

This suggestion astonished Adhiyaman for his father had always been obsessive about cleanliness. Owner of a spinning mill in the city of Madurai, Ambu Dorassamy had built a vast residence, surrounded by an orchard which passers-by admired. Mango, tamarind, sapota, papaya, and banana trees grew here naturally. Rare trees from the northern parts of the country were lovingly cultivated here too. A small number bore fruits that ripened but most others sprouted only buds which never reached maturity. Well-placed families would visit the premises and go into raptures over the apple, peach and prune trees which tried to grow between the other trees that were used to hot weather. Ambu—which meant 'love'—was both an unusual man and a loving father. His generosity did not stop with his family but extended to those who came to seek his help, whatever their caste. At the time of the celebrations of Diwali, the festival of lights, he would hang a multitude of coloured lanterns on the branches of his fruit trees. This drew a rowdy lot of people from the suburbs of the city who knew that they would be rewarded with bunches of litchis, pink mangoes and bananas so plump that one fruit could fill your stomach for the day. Adhiyaman and his sister Chellamani were appointed to distribute the fruit, while their mother made tea on the footpath, serving the low caste people herself. From the first light of dawn to late into the night they all came: the *Yadaval* who were shepherds and milkmen and impertinently claimed that Krishna was born of their bosoms; the *Coumoutty*, the merchants who wear the red spot in the middle of the forehead; the *Nattaman*, the most impure of them all, because they engaged in tanning; the *Panchalatar*, this gaggle of carpenters, ironsmiths, boilermakers who strutted about impudently wearing the sacred thread of the 'twice-born'. In the eyes of the superior castes, all this was fine feathers trying to make fine birds; they were still the pariahs, the dregs of humanity, cow eaters, manual scavengers, corpse transporters, walking garbage themselves who never bathe as you can see from the layers of grime that cover their skin. In those days the prodigality of the Dorassamy family was limitless.

As soon as a post fell vacant in the spinning mill, a crowd would gather at dawn in front of the house, waiting to be received by Ambu who took a decision only after deep thought. Most often he gave preference to widows or men with a reputation for piety, because he worshipped Parvati, the gentle Parvati, daughter of Menadevi and Parvataraja, King of the Mountains. In the heart of the orchard, between the centenarian tamarind trees, he had built a *koïlou,* a shrine in her honour. Every morning, even in the thick of the monsoon, he meticulously swept the temple and lit lamps at the feet of the Goddess's statue before going to the mill in a rickshaw. A thousand times, he had told Adhiyaman and Chellamani the magnificent story of this young girl who fell in love with Shiva. Dismissing all her suitors, she had succeeded in convincing her parents to marry her to the God, whose thousand and eight names she chanted daily. They agreed without great enthusiasm. Everyone knew that Shiva led the life of an implacable ascetic. He could stay for several months without drinking or eating, plunged in intense meditation, with no other shelter but a cave on a mountain. Sometimes, he transformed himself into a mendicant and roamed the world, a begging bowl in hand, accepting humiliations, insults, blows, and the bites of stray dogs. At still other times one saw him in the posture of a yogi, his legs folded under his body, his eyes sealed shut and his hands joined together, oblivious to the surrounding din and bustle. Therefore nobody was astonished that Shiva rejected the offer of marriage from Parvataraja. Not that Parvati wasn't beautiful; the light of day dimmed by comparison; nor did she lack intelligence but Shiva did not want to give in to illusory pleasures which would spoil the purity of his meditation.

'So the gentle and tender Parvati,' Ambu said, now caught up in the passion of his storytelling, 'decided that she too would withdraw from the world. She chose the darkest of forests where she spent several years to the great despair of her mother Menadevi. All of creation was greatly moved. They started worshipping her and she became the very symbol of devotion. Shiva could not remain indifferent any more. Disguised as a Brahmin, he went looking for the young girl. He questioned her about the depths of her feelings, without revealing his identity. Shiva came back, overwhelmed and immediately asked for Parvati's hand. Their wedding was an event which has had no equal.'

The purpose of this story, always narrated at the time of the evening meal, was not only to educate the Dorassamy family. It was aimed mainly at Chellamani, who since she frequented the English school, had hung a portrait of Queen Victoria in her room and had become besotted with a young professor of literature with blond hair. Her attitude had changed. She used to be so cheerful and adored teasing her father. Stylish, she used to love trying out the latest saris that Ambu brought back from the mill. Now she appeared dreamy, even distant. At twilight, she walked in the orchard where she recited aloud the verses of English poets, notably a certain Coleridge, to the great displeasure of her parents who did not speak a single word of the language of the invader. Ambu had incidentally refused to enrol Adhiyaman in the English school in spite of the pressing entreaties from local representatives of British authority. His son would take over the spinning mill from him and for that he had no need to rub shoulders with the world of Christians, who incidentally wore neither tunics nor saris. Ambu asked himself if he had not committed a grave error by entrusting his only daughter to the school masters who were trying skilfully to turn away students from Hinduism. After all, had he not caught Chellamani one day making a strange gesture which he learnt later on to be the Sign of the Cross?

'Every young girl must follow the example of Parvati,' he said sententiously without looking at Chellamani before ordering his two children to recite some verses from the Laws of Manu, a text that he maintained was a thousand times more ancient and wiser than the Christian Bible and the Mohammedan Koran.

The two major catastrophes that were going to befall Ambu Dorassamy were doubtlessly written in the book of Fate. Even though he was not guilty of any offence against the Gods and even though he continued to pray to Parvati every day—he had even extended her *koïlou*—his business began to decline suddenly. The traders who he entrusted with the job of selling his products objected to the prices, found flaws in the saris, and did not pay on time. This was over and above the orders that they cancelled at the last minute, just before delivery. In fact recently, the English had flooded the country with clothes that mimicked the traditional designs but they were stitched, which was a serious infringement of religious taboos. They were one-third the cost of those manufactured in the country. Sixty rupees a sari! Fifty for a *kaïli*, hardly thirty for a *choli*, the kind of blouse that tenderly reveals the belly button. And so on. What's more, they had created such a thin fabric, so soft to touch, called 'muslin', that high caste women went crazy about it. Soon, the entire population only swore by the word 'Lancashire' which referred to a region in England from where this devilish merchandise came. Ambu had to let go of his apprentices, stopped offering food and water to the most senior women weavers and was compelled, with a heavy heart, to forbid them from helping themselves freely to the orchard. Times were becoming very difficult. Already five spinning mills had gone bankrupt in the province of Madurai. The evil was spreading in all directions: to the west, it was Teni which was buckling under the assault of this unfair competition; in the south, Tuticorin and Virudanagar; in the east, Sivagaruna and Ramanathapuram. It was even being said that in the faraway capital of Madras, hordes of unemployed people haunted the streets. Sikh battalions kept them in check.

In short, the entire Tamil country was on the path to perdition. Everywhere, the black goddess Kali was invoked, the only one who could overcome the terrible demon Raktabija. Every drop of blood which escaped from his body during his battles with the Gods, gave birth to an exact replica of himself. In other words this demon was invincible! However Kali knew how to find a way out. She surrounded Raktabija with her red tongue thus preventing his blood from reaching the ground. Then she impaled him with her trident, sparing the world millennia of suffering. What was the difference between this evil creature and the English, who were ripping India apart?

Not only did they ruin mills, they also grabbed the best lands to auction them. The rich owners of large spinning mills, traitors swollen with conceit, were the first beneficiaries while millions of poor wretches converged on the cities. In fact, the British resident was worse than Raktabija!

The offerings to Kali multiplied in vain, she did not attack the invader. It was as if she feared the clangour of the bells that rose from the Protestant temples, troubling the meditation of the *sadhus*, the holy men who dedicated their lives to the study of sacred texts in complete deprivation. Ambu Dorassamy's mill ended up closing like the hundreds of others across the country, even though he did try to convert it into a mill for Pondicherry Guinea. It was a shimmering blue fabric that the people of a faraway French colony in Africa, Mauritania, went crazy over. The lack of sufficient quantities of indigo in the Madurai province defeated Ambu Dorassamy's attempt at resistance. Fortunately he had acquired, years ago, some acres of land in the countryside and sought refuge there with his people when times got tough in the city of Madurai. In the beginning, all seemed to go well even if Dorassamy's adaptation to the life of a farmer was not the easiest. The cows gave plenty of milk and the first harvest of their modest ricefield allowed them to stave off hunger that was ravaging the world around them. The desperadoes haunted the countryside, thin enough to strike fear, often aggressive and even the dogs had difficulty chasing them away. Ambu was compelled to tamp down his proverbial generosity and this broke his heart. Especially because his daughter, Chellamani, could not accustom herself to such rough a life, so far away from her dreams as a young girl. She could not be asked to do much more than wash the dishes and take care of some hens which cackled in an enclosure too vast for them. Even the thought of working in the fields under the hot sun filled her with horror; and this irritated her father. He reprimanded her for having become a stupid and arrogant English woman using very harsh words, unusual from his mouth. She did not react. One fine morning, a car stopped in front of their shanty and a white man with a proud look emerged from it. Without saying a word or greeting Ambu and his wife, he held out a hand to Chellamani and took her away with him. The young woman did not hesitate for a single second. She did not say goodbye to her family.

'It is perhaps better this way,' said her mother looking at the car jolting down the road to meet the horizon.

After her departure, the situation got worse. Suddenly the rivers ran dry and the springs petered out. Eyes turned to the sky for months on end, desperately awaiting the monsoon. Ambu lost three cows and the majority of his goats. The ricefield became a mass of dried mud.

*'Uralil agappatadu ulakkai thappa* (If you fall into the mortar, you will not escape the pestle),' murmured his wife, a fatalist. Hunger tormented them but worse, a great shame darkened their soul. Here they were almost reduced to the level of pariahs, obedient servants, they who had for three generations now prospered in the manufacture of textiles! 'Whatever happens,' Ambu repeated without conviction, 'we will remain Vaishya forever because it is Brahma who once decreed it.' Around them, the world seemed to have fallen prey to a terrible devastation, as if the demon Ravana had woken up from death and had defied the divine Rama again. They saw women, who had lost their minds, wandering down the road, clutching dead babies in their arms, begging. They saw old men, abandoned and haggard, scrawny men who spoke

languages incomprehensible to them. All of India seemed to be on the move, migrating without thought or hope.

'We only have rats left,' said Ambu one day as his family looked on dumbfounded. 'Rest assured, we are not going to eat these creatures of God,' he said. 'But know that they are foresight itself! They don't live from day to day like us, I have taken care to observe them.'

With infinite patience, rats would gather grains of rice, one by one, storing them in their holes in anticipation of the monsoon floods, when it became dangerous for them to venture outside. They would help themselves to rice from the silos of rich landowners. These unusual granaries had to be flushed out, that is all! Adhiyaman had not expected his father to designate him as the rice gatherer. Was he not the eldest son, the apple of his eye; the one who would replace him in case of his sudden death? But two days later, Adhiyaman set off towards the mountains armed with a knapsack and a pointed stick. On the way, he marvelled at the genius of these little animals he had paid no attention to till now: they moved into the crevices in rocks, shielded from the wind and rain, in places inaccessible to jackals. Their endurance was worthy of admiration too, because they had to cover several leagues between ricefields situated in the plains and the holes in the mountains, their secure shelter. Adhiyaman dreaded digging this soil, an arduous task, because here the entire region was laterite. So much effort for a few miserable grains of rice! In reality, the rats, which were still there, demonstrated great intelligence by hiding their loot in a sort of tiny pocket, adjacent to the rat hole which was relatively easily accessible. The young man understood that this allowed them to flee from cobras that were common in these mountains. With the little strength he had left, he started extracting the rice grains with the help of the tip of his stick before stuffing them into his knapsack. In the beginning, this task seemed so pointless that he almost called it quits but, thinking of the emaciated faces and the sunken eyes of his parents, he forced himself to go on. At the end of a day, he realised that he had gathered enough to make a meal, albeit a frugal one. This would be a change from the boiled leaves that they ate to try and stave off hunger. And controlling his disgust, he killed three foolhardy rats and added them to his store of food. The afternoon was fading into a sinister twilight, the overcast sky traversed by the slow flight of vultures. Adhiyaman returned to his hamlet, light-hearted for once. A song, the mantra *Om Namah Shivaya* which had moved him during the last *Maha Shivaratri*, this annual celebration for Shiva vanquishing the forces of evil during the night, suddenly rose to his lips and helped him walk all the way back home. As soon as he noticed the thatched roof of the family hut, he called out:

'Amma! Appa! Where are you? I have brought back...'

A strange sound, a sort of continuous scraping, made him jump. Nobody answered him. Worried, he brandished his stick, a derisory weapon against thieves who had probably come to rob his parents of their last belongings: silver teapots, some jewellery and two carpets embroidered in the Rajasthani style, vestiges of former glory. For months, the provinces of Madurai and Dindigul had become the preferred site of action for gangs of murderers who had renounced the precepts of Hinduism. Drinking, raping, pillaging, blaspheming, they did not hesitate to slash with a machete all those who dared to oppose them, while the British watched in complete indifference. Many of them were not from the Tamil country but from very far up north, that is the Karnatak or the Andhra country. Adhiyaman bypassed the hut, on tiptoes, his stick ready to attack like a bayonet. The scraping did not stop. A sort of 'Crrrrsssh! Crrrrsssh!' which made his limbs quake. Suddenly he recognised his mother's voice. In a death rattle, she said: '*Appavukku udhavi thevaippadukiradu!*' (Your father needs help!)

The spectacle that lay before the young boy's eyes left him transfixed: a pack of wild dogs, jackals, were in the process of devouring his mother and father voraciously and had not even caught scent of him. His mother was still struggling, eyes open in spite of the trickles of blood which covered her face. His father had lost consciousness and his entrails spilled from his torn stomach. The animals were eating his father alive, enjoying this gruesome meal. Adhiyaman charged at the assailants, screaming but, against all expectations, the animals confronted him, bared their teeth ready to protect their prey. One of the jackals jumped on him and lacerated his arms. Terrorised, the young boy took to his heels. The sound of a tibia cracking—the one that belonged to his poor father—pursued him for endless minutes. He ran straight on at a frantic pace, though night was falling, not knowing where his steps took him. When he was exhausted, he slowed down but kept moving, stopping only to quench his thirst wherever he could find a puddle of muddy water that was once a pond. He wandered through the countryside, through forests and rivers, indifferent to humans who imagined that he had lost his mind. Many days passed. The fear that had seized him at the sight of the jackal invasion did not diminish. He knew, from the accent of a woman who held out a piece of grilled meat to him that he had reached Namakkal. Here the poverty seemed less ferocious than in his native place, Madurai. In fact, most of the villages were empty of men and there were less mouths to feed.

'You too are going to Pondicherry?' asked a sympathetic woman.

It seemed like a century had passed since someone spoke to him humanely. He agreed to follow her home and spent a wonderful evening, surrounded by her sisters and her mother, without realising that these people were untouchables. It only struck him when he saw the cow carcass in the backyard. From what remained of the body of the animal, he guessed that it must have been very scrawny. The bones from her shoulders poked out of her skin. Adhiyaman felt nauseous. The woman had served him beef! Curse upon his head! The Gods would soon seek revenge no doubt. Hanuman, his favourite, would henceforth turn his back on him. He was lost, finished. Torn between anger and gratitude towards his hosts, he froze into silence which got them laughing.

'Whatever your thoughts may be,' said the woman, 'know this: the times are changing! Confronted with the English who are non-believers, what is the use of distinguishing between Brahmins and untouchables? Between Kshatriyas and Shudras? Come on, speak! Looking at you, I suppose you are a Vaishya?'

'I am a Vaishya!' Adhiyaman snarled.

'Ha-ha-ha! Today nobody understands this language, young man. I was a servant in a Brahmin family for a long time in Pondicherry and I can assure you that they are people like you and me, with their faults, their pettiness, and their nastiness too.'

It was too much for Adhiyaman who got up on his frail feet and without thanking those who had welcomed him with so much generosity, started off again on his frantic race. It took him thirty-five days to cross the desolate province of Perambalur and reach the city of Pondicherry. Quite unwittingly, he began to follow a herd of elephants led by a male elephant with a gleaming white coat. The herd advanced inexorably, never pausing, moving with determination. As they passed, people gave way with respect, some saying that the herd was heading to the city of Madras where it would trample the English invaders. Bouquets of lilacs and bougainvillea were thrown at them, people sprinkled *mandja*, turmeric, and water on them. Taking Adhiyaman to be a holy man, they joined their hands at eye level and solicited his grace. He paid them no attention, haunted as he was by the memory of his parents that the jackals had devoured. He still heard the cracking of his father's legs under their demonic teeth. He smelt the acrid odour of blood which flowed from his mother's chest and above all he saw, again and again, the satisfied belly of the animal which had served itself first and which was resting at the foot of a guava tree. That was the animal which had jumped on him.

As Pondicherry drew near, the elephants lay down by a river bank and did not get up again. They slept like this for several days. Through this time, Adhiyaman could not summon up the courage to approach them. Then one morning, the white elephant trumpeted for the last time and died. Adhiyaman understood that the others had reincarnated quite some time ago. He reached the gates of the city whose air was laden with sea-spray. Discovering the sea for the first time in his life, he felt a limitless admiration for Vishnu, the Protector of the Universe.

This vast blue sheet, spotted with foam which flew about carried by the whimsical wind, soothed him and gave him a sense of well-being. He gathered confidence again. Adhiyaman mingled with the crowd in the noisy roads jammed with rickshaws, horse carriages which inched past cows rummaging in rubbish heaps. The noise taught him that here too, although they were not as poor as those in the inland provinces, people were disheartened by the goddess they had invoked each day, turning to her in their distress. That year, the monsoon had delayed pouring its regenerative benison on the ricefields and certain priests talked enigmatically about an ancient prophecy to be found inscribed in the holy books for millennia. It was said that thousands of Indians would have to leave the country chosen by Brahma to go beyond the seas as atonement for the sacrileges committed by their ancestors. It was not enough that the White men from Europe had appropriated the best land or that they had reduced the maharajahs and sultans to birds in a cage. There was more to pay and the price was so high that Adhiyaman Dorassamy could not believe it. Incidentally he had never seen so many foreigners with his own eyes. For a long time he had believed that White men were the fruit of the feverish imagination of the people from the north who held the inhabitants of Madurai and Virudanagar in low esteem. Or, one of those legends that was narrated during the festival of Holi when spring came and when each one sprayed coloured powder on one's neighbours and danced with gay abandon. He only understood that all this was true, really truly true, the day that a brougham, a kind of car without a roof, mounted on high wheels nearly ran over him.

'Coolie bastard!' muttered the White driver who almost lost his colonial hat as he hit the brake.

## Devil Hunt

He lead the procession, scarlet like a *Bondamanjak* red chilly, in sandals and an immaculate cassock, a heavy wooden cross around his neck, followed by three priests who had recently landed in Martinique. From time to time, he made a stop, talked to those in the procession, arms raised high, his stentorian voice defeating the murmur of the trade winds. Soon, the Negroes knelt down to launch into a vibrant prayer and made the sign of the cross. Father Xavier, the vicar of Macouba, had had enough of waiting for permission from Frédéric Houblin de Maucourt, the master of the Courbaril Plantation. He had sent him many messages through his very pious wife to warn him against the pagan ceremonies organised by his Hindu workers but there had been no response. The *Grands Blancs*, wealthy White plantation owners, protected their immigrants, who they found more malleable than the Negroes, 'more docile and more compliant,' raged Anthénor, the trade unionist with socialist leanings. Although they were Christian so to say, they used to baulk at work, went absent for no reason, and struck work with their perpetual demands for better wages. If they were not satisfied, some of them did not hesitate to set fire to the cane fields just before the harvest. The time of slavery was over, they repeated every time a foreman or an overseer made a point. As for the Hindus, they had come to this country specifically to work and almost never contested orders (except those who were victims of a devastating insanity and were soon sent off to the prisons of Cayenne or Toulon). Letting them practice their cult, no matter how barbaric, it appeared, was the least that they could be granted.

'My brothers,' exclaimed Father Xavier in front of his fanatical flock. 'Today is a big day. We are going to re-establish the reign of Our Lord in the land of Macouba. Thanks to the help of our brothers in Jesus, the Belgian Redemptorists, we are going to hunt the devils, these statues with four arms, grimacing, hideous and in whose honour these pagans make animal sacrifices. A new era of evangelisation begins and you are its first and most valorous crusaders!'

The crowd was swaying, yelling frenetic halleluiahs. They brandished machetes, pikes, cudgels and vials of holy water. As it went by each hut, it swelled with one or two Christian zealots. Soon, the miserable shacks where the Indians were cooped up were surrounded and they were ordered to come out. Terrified, the women and children begged in their incomprehensible tongue, the men protested in a semblance of Creole, but they were quickly outnumbered and outshouted. Father Xavier and the Redemptorists were the first to enter the houses and brought out oil lamps, portraits of divinities in gaudy colours, books and even statuettes. The Negroes rushed in after them and soon the mud courtyard of the hamlet was transformed into a heap of these objects. Two men, including Vinesh's father, tried to flee through a savannah of Guinea grass but were captured by the mob. Beaten black and blue, they abandoned the portraits of Kannavédi, the elephant-headed God, of Maldévilin, the knight with a sabre, to the prosecution of the Negroes. A bonfire burned all night long. The vicar of Macouba had a three-metre high bamboo cross planted in the middle of the courtyard and preached to the Indians, who were quaking:

'You are in a Christian country! We don't worship either idols or demons but the Holy Trinity. God sent us His son on earth to save us from our sins and Our Lord died for it. Out of goodness for us! Because His love is immense! You are all going to recite the "Our Father" after me.'

Their fetishes burnt to ashes, the Indians stammered the words of prayer without knowing what they meant. Once the crusaders of Christ the King as they called themselves had left and night fell, they cried bittersweet tears over the cruel fate that had brought them to Martinique where the Indian was worse than the dregs of humanity.

*Mestri!* Adhiyaman Dorassamy had heard this word a hundred times since he arrived in the city of Pondicherry. He had ended up recognising these fair-skinned Indians, dressed in English style shorts, ankle socks and black leather boots—

insensitive like the non-believers to the impurity of the material. They lead groups of about twenty poor wretches, mostly Shudras or untouchables, to the port. Here they are cooped up for days, even weeks before being taken on board huge ships flying the British flag or more infrequently the French one. (For Pondicherry belonged to the French!) Adhiyaman discovered, not without surprise, that diverse European nations had taken the initiative to dismember India, to bring her to her knees, in the wake of much older and reputedly less rapacious Portuguese colonialists. In fact, the latter had contracted matrimonial alliances with local royal families while the new arrivals disdained them. These nations seemed to have an unquenchable thirst for labour in a faraway country that they named 'America'. They described it as the antechamber of Mount Meru, the residence of the Gods. However, Pondicherry was a beehive buzzing with activity, a trading post which gathered most of the riches of India for export: rice from Tanjore, opium and saltpetre from Bengal, spices from Malabar, arak from the island of Ceylon, gold and silver from Calcutta and even teakwood from the faraway and mysterious Burma. But this was not enough to hire the tens of thousands of people who had been rushing here since famine was ravaging the land chosen amongst all others by Brahma, the Almighty being.

'All that you need to do in the Americas is to put the sugar out in the sun,' announced the *mestri* who he had ended up approaching. 'It is not tiring work. Incidentally you will be given housing; you will be fed and paid. What's more, at the end of five years you will be brought home at the cost of the French East India Company.' The offices of this recruitment agency were spread out all over the city but its head office was in the port. It was there that the serious decisions were taken. Adhiyaman had prowled around the area, each time reprimanded by the guards, armed with guns. He had seen men and women in tears rolling on the floor for not having been selected. Too ill, too weak, too old, too this, too that. They heard the irrevocable sentences lash them like whips. Those who were rejected were then mercilessly pushed back to the port quarter but not before an officer applied an indelible ink mark on their forearms to avoid their coming back. Incidentally the *mestris* did not present their candidates as soon as they arrived in the city. Paid per head, the *mestris* first got them treated by a doctor, gave them plenty of food which was not edible because it was prepared with cheap European produce. When they reckoned that their clients were in better health, they forced them to bathe in the sea several times a day in order to wipe out all traces of skin diseases, or wounds, both of which might have been caused by the arduous journey from the interior of the Tamil country to the coast. Very quickly, Adhiyaman found his compatriots from the province of Madurai, particularly an entire family that had worked in his father's spinning mill. These Shudras who were in Pondicherry for months welcomed him like a prodigal son and accommodated him in the shack that the father had rented in a quarter close to the port. Everyone remembered the goodness of his own father Ambu, who they constantly cited as an example. Out of reticence, nobody asked him what happened to Ambu or his wife who was so gentle, she who made tea for the workers during religious festivals and distributed gifts to their children. Adhiyaman did not dare confess the horrible truth. He could not get used to the idea that his parents had ended up devoured by jackals like common Shudras. He felt bad that he had not fought off the famished beasts and had not lit the funeral pyre which would have procured a good reincarnation for his parents. Had Yama, the sovereign of the kingdom of the dead, taken care of their souls?

'We leave for the Americas, young man,' announced the father after a *mestri* had visited them twice. 'Alas there is no hope for us here.'

'Where is the country?' asked Adhiyaman, worried.

The man pointed vaguely to the east. This question troubled him, too. Only his daughter, Devi, seemed enthusiastic at the idea of such a journey. She must have been about fourteen or fifteen years old but looked younger because she was so puny.

At first, Adhiyaman did not notice how ravishing she was. In his eyes, she had become a kind of younger sister who served his meals, and washed his only dhoti once a week. A kind of reincarnation of Chellamani, his beloved sister who had fled with her English school teacher.

'Where is it?' the young man asked again, for he had retrieved the haughty tone of a Vaishya.

'I was told, you have to cross two oceans...,' Devi's father replied. 'The sailors call it the Sea of Fire and the Sea of Darkness.'

'Rubbish,' his wife intervened with unusual authority for a Tamil woman.

'The *mestri* showed us the Americas on a map, remember, Anandam! A simple sound separates the Coromandel Coast from these enchanted islands which comes up to four or five hours by ship, the *mestri* said. Incidentally, America has exactly the same climate as Madras and...'

'Shut up, woman! If you imagine that there you can behave like a White woman you are wrong. You will always have to obey me no matter which country we go to.'

Adhiyaman, who had trembled at hearing phrases like the 'Sea of Fire' and 'Sea of Darkness' was far from convinced. Neither corresponded to the resplendent azure expanse that he had gazed upon with keen pleasure from the docks. The taste of salt-water fish had delighted his palate from the very first. But he had noticed that those who ventured into the open sea and returned in the evening with nets full to the brim were most often *Toulken* or Muslims. They did not seem to pay great attention to Hindu customs because they served those who came first, be they Brahmins or untouchables. The only things that interested them were the fistful of rupees that they asked for a pound of fish; the purity or the impurity of the hand that paid did not matter. Adhiyaman smiled every time he saw them kneel down together on their dirty mats, touching their forehead to the earth, turning towards Mecca.

'I don't know what awaits us there. They say that sugar is so abundant that the favourite game of children is to shoot each other with sugar pellets. They say that it is the paradise described in the *Mahabharata*. Is it true?'

'I don't know,' Anandam Vellayoudon told him on the eve of their departure. 'If you marry my daughter, you can accompany us. I will make a deal with the *mestri*...'

The young man was taken aback. The idea of marrying a Shudra, even if she were as pretty as Devi, had never crossed his mind. Already he knew that crossing the kaala paani, the black waters, was to invoke a curse upon his head. To die and be buried abroad was the equivalent of renouncing fusion with the Absolute. His soul would wander from body to body, each reincarnation more painful than the preceding one.

'If not, Devi cannot travel,' said Anandam's wife, her voice quivering. 'They only hire married women...'

'But, I assure you that married women are exempted from signing a contract,' added the man. 'They have no obligation to work once they arrive in America. Devi will serve you in your house. She is a loving girl.'

Adhiyaman mulled over it till midnight, then, coming close to the pallet on which Anandam slept lightly, gave him his consent. The latter woke up the entire family, sent for a priest to whom he handed over his meagre savings. The holy man deciphered the horoscope of the newlyweds and predicted happiness for them. Then the neighbours enjoyed millet pancakes and flasks of arak that Anandam had been saving for a long time. After having tied the *tali* around her neck, a cord that symbolised marriage, Adhiyaman lay down alongside Devi till the morning without daring to touch her. She huddled up to him and her warm breath enchanted him so much that he could not sleep. He thought of his parents who, without doubt, would have protested against this unnatural union, no matter how full of goodness they were. Who would have said that he, Adiyaman Dorassamy, son of one of the richest manufacturers of Madurai would have thus defied the ancestral taboos?

'You were three!' the *mestri* was annoyed when he came to look for the Vellayoudon family. 'Now, you inform me that your last daughter has a husband. How am I going to explain this to the Company gentlemen, *hein*?'

'Devi will not leave without him,' said Anandam stubbornly. 'Nor will we!'

With bad grace, the recruiter accepted the hundred rupees that the mother of the young girl exhumed from the pleats of her sari. The last asset of the Vellayoudon family! If the Company refused to allow their son-in-law to embark, they would be pilloried. They would end up amongst the garbage collectors of Pondicherry, this city which had become a stranger to the rules that had governed Indian life for several centuries. This city where everyone rubbed shoulders, everyone mingled: Brahmins and European sailors, Kshatriyas and untouchable prostitutes, recruiters who had come from faraway Bengal and Indo-Portuguese half-breeds. Seized with holy terror, Anandam said in his heart of hearts, 'This is a foretaste of the Americas.' He constantly felt the little bag of Indian soil which he had hidden in the folds of his *kaïli* as if it were a talisman. At the time of lining up in front of the officers of the Company, his resolution wavered but he clenched his teeth, wiped the tear that came to his eye with the back of his sleeve and clumsily signed the indentureship contract that was presented to him, a contract that the *mestri* translated in a loud voice, in a monotonous ritual, for each emigrant. Miraculously, there was no difficulty for Adhiyaman. Perhaps the *mestri* had shared the hundred rupees with the officer in charge of last minute checks, he thought. Around them swarmed an impressive crowd of people who had come from the deep south of the country, especially men. Among them were the natives of the southernmost province of the Tamil country—Kanyakumari—noticeable because of the striking blackness of their complexion. They pushed, cursed in their raucous dialect or reeled off a litany of prayers to Kannavédi or to Mariamman, doubtlessly their favourite Gods. The others, those from Tuticorin, from Teni, from Virudanagar, from Madurai, Adhiyaman's land, were listless. With empty eyes, stiff movements, and bundles under skinny arms, they were boarding the *pattamars*. These large dhows without a keel could sail through the three lines of breakers which blocked access to the main beach of Pondicherry. The ordeal over, the boats huddled together along the sides of the ship which swayed as a result of the strong swell of the sea.

When everyone was on board, the English sailors assembled them on the aft deck, the largest, so that the emigrants could be directed to the locations planned for them in advance. Contrary to what the young man had imagined, their family ties and their native provinces were not taken into account. Three groups of unequal importance were constituted.

An interpreter indicated that the men would travel in the holds. Then young children and women had a shelter made of tarpaulin reserved on the foredeck. And finally the few Muslims, recognisable in their white *gandouras*, would be on the aft deck. Adhiyaman found himself torn both from his wife and his in-laws. Although he was more than twenty years old nothing quite distinguished him from the carefree adolescents who were already playing at pulling each other's hair and happily accepting sweets from the European sailors. The captain, a ruddy Englishman who wore a curled moustache, made a speech that the interpreter abridged in these words:

'Have no fear, dear friends! The voyage will be long, perhaps three months, perhaps more, it will depend on the mood of the sea, but know that I'm on my seventh crossing and that my ship has never been damaged. I am your captain, Captain Alwyn, at the service of her Majesty since 1847. You must trust me and my team. We promise to get you to your destination, safe and sound. If you have the slightest problem, contact me personally or Quartermaster Henderson. We are at your service!'

While the English were reciting Christian prayers, Anandam took this opportunity to come up to his son-in-law and stealthily slipped a small sachet containing a few ounces of soil from India to him.

'I will not last till the end of the journey, Adhiyaman, I know it, I am too old,' he whispered. 'Keep this carefully and open it if one day you find yourself in distress. Promise me that you will look after Devi as I would have. That child is frail...'

The ship horn tore the evening silence, night was coming in huge strides. Adhiyaman only had time to nod in agreement. His throat was dry, drier than the ricefields of Madurai that used to be luminous, drier than the India he was leaving, perhaps forever, without even being able to gaze upon its contours for one last time.

# 4

# Sugarcane, Age-Old Pain, O Tenderness!

*The Mill is never far away. Its turrets are visible at every turn; its long thin arms grab the cane from the stomach of the cart and the tractor for weighing. Inside it is a dark cathedral without stained glass windows or golden basins. Light falls from indentations in the corrugated iron roof, forming haloes on the rods and the huge serrated wheels—haloes of gold with a pinch of curcuma, turmeric. We walk silently between the crushing mills which make a deafening noise, past cooking stoves which blow like bull-frogs, chimneys that snigger as if they have cigars in their mouths. To screw, to unscrew with gigantic tools, all in a jiffy.* Tak! Braps! Blo! *You do not tarry. To saunter, to daydream is to endanger your body. So many fingers have been crushed, so many arms severed, so many faces slashed or even burned from vapour inhaled too closely. Between the machine frames and the meandering pipes, men are no more than improbable shadows who seem to submit to the obscure will of some jealous or distrustful God. The sugarcane juice flows like the Ganges, carting along a monstrous stream of lava. The surface looks like elephant hide,* oui! *The circular patterns on this surface openly declare whether the cane was planted well, the fields cleared properly before the fury of the rains, whether the beginning of the dry weather rushed the growth of the sugarcane so that its juice could spurt forth from the entrails of the earth and shoot sky high. Water drizzles on the wagons on wheels to clean the miasma accumulated over half a year: the almost invisible aphids, the crazy ants, the crumbs of soil, the dribble of the common lancehead...*

*And finally, when the sugar appears in the palms of black hands, every single time it is a miracle, it is dumbfounding. This is no magic; this is simply unbelievable. It is here, brown gold-tinged with russet, raw, indestructible. Here is the fruit of so much accumulated sweat. Muscles tense as if it weighed so much that even the biggest scale in the universe could not weigh it. That is because it is venerable, this new sugar, fresh like the bright blood of an endless passion. Only the man whose sole mission is to measure its richness dares to taste it. This new sugar is tender upon his tongue. It unleashes a joy which distorts and distends the face of the knowledgeable Negro.*

*The Plantation, known here as The Habitation, is the Siamese twin of the mill. When the work for the day is done and night falls, the Black Shack Alley shakes itself up, making sure it keeps its insolent dignity. Three people are needed to remove boots that long hours of toil have soldered to the feet; this, one might swear, is a danmyé fight. Then the cane-cutter sits on the stone step of his home, bare-chested, his chin in one hand, the other on his knee, a thousand folds lining his forehead as he stares into the shadows of the cool evening. Or placing a plastic basin on an old crate of Lorraine Beer, he lathers his khaki rags as if performing some ancient ritual. These rags are hung out of doors and windows to dry on quick-stick staffs; they are the colour and fabric of The Habitation, the uniform at once of great poverty and supreme grandeur. More often than not, the savagery of the sugarcane leaves, sharper than the pen-knives or razors wielded by braggarts, has to be patched. This is the story the story-teller announces to the suddenly petrified audience: 'I am here to sew your life together again, dammit.' The younger lot degrade themselves at the little shop where a firm hand had written in chalk, 'No credit!' or more harshly, 'Credit is dead', forgetting the word 'fuck' which usually would follow such a decree. It is just that on Saturday, at the beginning of the afternoon, each one is dressed in clean, starched and neatly ironed clothes.*

*They form a line, one behind the other, like well-behaved school kids, each waiting for his name to be called out from the window. Immaculate envelopes, bulging with the fruit of Negro and Indian sweat, appear. Their names in solemn black calligraphy are beautiful:* Bellonie Marc-André, Venceslas Alain, Vinesh Dorassamy, Baradin Frédéric, Singa Vellayoudon, Téramène Hyppolite, Ladouceur Sidonise. *You expect nothing from these absurdly sealed envelopes, no divine surprise in any case but you still pretend to grab yours eagerly and rush to open it in secret.*

# 5

## Plantation Courbaril

*This country to which our poverty has dragged us is but a huge sugarcane field. It rises, towering, right up to the foothills of the mountains, cutting down trees of old ancestry and tree ferns, day after day. Its flower, always a single one, unfurls its pearly splendour as winter draws near, infusing an odd tenderness into the hearts of men who toil away in the fields as long as the dry season makes itself at home. Then they sing to forget and the yowling of their bel-air drums helps knit our dreams and makes our pile of sorrows collapse.*

Everyone felt the master was anxious. They could see it in the nervous gesture that he repeated umpteen times a day without reason: he kept striking his boot with a stick as if it were his mare's flanks. His mount, whom the Negroes had nicknamed La Dorée for her eyes were golden like fire, had a stately bearing. In the *Grand'Case*, Big House, the cooks who usually jabbered away, were quiet, on the alert, expecting a sharp and almost brutal order at any moment. 'Doriane, bring me some rum right away! Octavia, check that the child is not playing too close to the pond! Cécile this! Hermancia that!' You had to obey on the spot, otherwise M. Houblin de Maucourt got into a devastating rage. Even his wife Eugénie and their only progeny, whom everyone affectionately called P'tite Mamzelle, had deserted the drawing room and its mahogany furniture where every afternoon the mother used to teach the daughter the rudiments of the piano. The *Négrillons,* little Negro pickneys, would assemble at the windows to observe the scene, squabbling with each other to get the best spot from which they could see everything and not be chased away. Today, they preferred to go roaming in the fields. When the master was in a rage you had better not cross his path or you would be crushed. Firmine, an alluring Mulatress with curly hair—his mistress—was testing her power over him. She used to boast about how she kept him on a tight leash and would flaunt the different pieces of gold jewellery he bestowed on her for the New Year. Returning from Macouba with her arms loaded with provisions, she indulged in her favourite provocation, her way of hurting the pride of the mistress of the house, yet again. Planting herself in the middle of the courtyard, her fists on her hips, she said to the Béké:

'*Frédérik, ki sa ou ka atann pou vini koké mwen? Ou nè lé man ouvè dé fant katjé-mwen ba an vié Neg soubawou oben ki sa? Ha-ha-ha!*' (Frédéric, what are you waiting for to fuck me? Would you like me to spread my legs out for a boorish Negro, Ha-ha-ha!)

Nobody was offended by such vulgarity. Firmine was a *femme matador,* a coquettish domineering woman, as they say, whom Houblin de Maucourt had wrested from a brothel in the city of Saint-Pierre at a very high price. Out there, she had turned the heads of dozens of White men, each richer than the next, and had ruined some of them. Households had been destroyed because of her. Poets had committed suicide by flinging themselves from Morne Abel because she had not obliged them. She was no great beauty, but but so much sensuality emanated from her that you would quiver as she walked by. Da Gervaise, De Maucourt's nanny, an ageless Negress who had raised three generations of Whites and who, as a result, could stand up to them and even bullied the master when he came back home drunk, would tease Firmine as she entered the *Grand'Case*:

'*S'ou wè man té an nonm, haaa Firmine, man té ké za koupé'w venn-twa fwa!*'

(Aah, Firmine, if I were a man, I would have already fucked you twenty-three times!)

On the infamous day of the master's rage, Nanny Da Gervaise's wrinkled face was sullen. She knew him inside out. She was the one who had breastfed him when he was a baby, swaddled him, washed and clothed him; she had helped him take his first steps. She had led him proudly to church on the day of his First Communion and had even been consulted by the family when they were choosing a wife for him. Yet, Nanny Da Gervaise did not understand why he was in such a foul mood. This sudden mood swing left her perplexed, and she loathed doubt. She did not smile at the provocation of the *femme matador* and did not ask her, as she usually did, what little gift she had brought her from town. For Firmine never forgot Nanny Da Gervaise. They were allies. Firmine brought her hair clips, ormolu necklaces, chewing tobacco or biscuit boxes from Brittany with magnificent miniatures in which the old woman stored her needlework material. In exchange, Nanny informed Firmine about Houblin de Maucourt's new conquests, for he was one of those who devoured nubile Negresses by the dozen. She advised Firmine on how to move those pretty, carefree, chatty maidens called *capistrelles*, out of the way so that none of them would ever nurture the crazy hope of becoming the first mistress of the Béké. A luscious creature of about thirty, Firmine did not have to fear her rivals too much yet, but she had to keep an eye out for them. For this she even had the approval of Mme de Maucourt who treated her like a distant cousin and encouraged her to come to the *Grand'Case* more often where she always welcomed the hussy most warmly. Firmine lived in the middle of Macouba Town, several kilometres from Courbaril Plantation. It was a real pleasure to see the *Blanche-pays*, White woman from France—already a victim of advancing years though still in good shape and having retained the hard look—have a friendly chat with the woman who was no more than the strumpet who took her husband to bed several times a week; the wife resting on her rocking-chair and the mistress leaning on the balustrade of the verandah. The world was all admiration; especially the Negro cane-cutters who went as far as to say:

'*Hon*! If only my Negress was as understanding as Mme de Maucourt, I would drown in happiness, *oui*!'

That infamous day, in the course of which the master did not calm down, something happened that would be talked about for months during the endless discussions at wakes. Houblin de Maucourt delivered Firmine a resounding slap; when she staggered, a second slap, this one so hard that the sound of his fingers on the young woman's cheek could be heard in the seven rooms of the house. From the rooms on the upper floor, the chamber maids—a flock of young women grown arrogant because they interacted with Whites daily—rushed to the windows. At the sight of Firmine who had fallen to her knees, her sublime Madonna face on fire, they let out 'Ohs' and 'Aahs' suffused with false compassion. Not one of them felt sorry for the Mulatress for they were all deeply jealous of her. On the ground floor, Nanny Da Gervaise came out on the verandah with the heavy step of an octogenarian and began to chide M. de Maucourt, whom she regarded as her son:

'*Frédérik, ou vini dekdek an mitan tet oben ki sa ? Sé vié Kouli-a ki mété an zenzen an tet-ou, neg-mwen?*' (Frédéric, have you gone mad? Has that bloody Coolie bewitched you or what?)

Embarrassed, the master helped the young woman—who was whining like a spoilt child—to get up and patted her head. But there was such indifference in the gesture that the lackeys immediately guessed what the old governess of the De Maucourts, who moved with difficulty and could only see with one eye, had seen before anyone else. She had guessed that M. Frédéric had just repudiated his mistress of fifteen years in favour of this enticing Indian beauty, this Nalima, who had arrived only recently at the Courbaril Plantation. That he had constructed a little house for her, not far from the flower garden, was no surprise; each of his *femmes-dehors*, mistresses, had always received similar rewards. These were not cheap trinkets, *deux francs-quatre sous*, that the Negroes used to buy from Syrian peddlers, but solid stuff! Long lasting. Something you could show off. And that is how, Berthe, the Chabine from Moulin L'Etang could boast that M. Frédéric, the father of her first son, had bought him a *taxi-pays*, local taxi, which he plied on the road from Macouba to Trinité. Emérancienne, once the most alluring washerwoman in the region, was granted a piece of land on the edge of the Coulisses Ravine, where she had been able to build a decent house. Why go on? It would be futile to draw up a list of M. Houblin de Maucourt's mistresses. Even at the age of sixty, he continued to indulge in sexual pleasures. Myrtha, Francelise, Didière, Floriane and company could each boast that she had been taken care of. Incidentally, many of them had borne a child for the *Grand Blanc*, wealthy White man and, in the multitude of kids that they hauled to church on Sunday, the child with the fairest skin was the best dressed and also the best fed. If this chosen one, as an adult, married fairer than him, and his children did the same thing for sixteen generations, then the final descendants could perhaps hope to integrate into the class of Whites. Adhiyaman often mocked this rule, clearly stricter than the one decreed by Manu whose verse from the tenth book he liked to quote:

*If the daughter of a Shudra and a Brahmin, united with a Brahmin to give birth to a girl who similarly united with a Brahmin and so on, the low class will rise to the most distinguished of class by the seventh generation.**

In fact, the great tragedy in the life of Firmine, the dethroned first mistress, was that she was sterile! O yes, her entrails had always refused to be impregnated by the master's seed. The sweet-tongued gossips claimed that this was because in her adolescence, before de Maucourt noticed her, she had undergone too many abortions using a concoction of green pineapple.

'That is what awaits females who are too hot,' they whispered when she was seen stopping to caress a new-born or to hold him close while covering him with kisses.

---

**Manusmriti*, edited and translated by Shri A.J. Prabhu, Pune, Vidarbh Marathwada Book Company, 2003, Book 10 verse 64.

The more charitable claimed that a jealous person had sealed her womb with the help of *quimbois*, Obeah. Some even suspected that Gerard-Congo, the bearer of malevolent powers that he had brought from his native Africa, was the perpetrator. The Mulatress woman had in fact turned up her nose in public at his person and had rejected his advances with such exaggerated indignation that it had become a Carnival biguine. Its bawdy refrains were sung every February, mangling the poor man's honour. Thus Firmine was one of the very rare mistresses of Houblin de Maucourt who had not given him a descendant and that is why, that day, his anger knew no bounds. If he had pretended to regret his resounding slaps, it was only out of fear for Nanny Da Gervaise who had always treated him like a kid in shorts even though he was as White as a magnolia flower and she was as Black as mortal sin. Mme de Maucourt, who was playing a Fauré piano piece in the drawing room, in turn, felt obliged to take up the cudgels for Firmine, for which she was sharply rebuked and sent right back to her principal activity. Eugénie Houblin de Maucourt was after all a pianist renowned all over the north of the country, and was often solicited to showcase her talent at receptions organised by the Whites, some at Macouba, some elsewhere. A piano was proudly displayed in every planter's residence, next to sideboards in solid mahogany, chaises longues and English arm chairs. These pianos lay unused 'for lack of fighters' as Théophile, the school teacher from the metropolis, would say mockingly. What was most extraordinary was that Eugénie had learnt to play because it was impossible to find a music teacher so far away from Fort-de-France. Incidentally, this idle activity would have heaped great disdain upon whoever dared to engage in it in a place where only sugarcane and rum reigned supreme. Real work meant planting sugarcane, weeding, cutting the cane in early January, transporting it to the sugar mills and the distilleries, making them work double quick because they had the nasty habit of breaking down when least expected. And when that was done, they had to transfer sacks of sugar and barrels of rum to the barges which stayed off the coast of Basse-Pointe because of the monstrous breakers that hammered its beach. Such were the occupations of serious people, be they White, Mulatto, Chabin, Negro Creoles, Coramantee Negroes, Indians or Chinese. So they said condescendingly:

'Fuck Mme Eugénie, what she plays is no music! You fall asleep when she taps the piano. Your feet don't even itch to dance, *non*!'

It is true that as soon as drums started beating on the plantation, the thin sound of the piano did not even make its way through the *Grand'Case*. Confined only to the drawing room, she created a near-sepulchral atmosphere which frightened the servants. Mme de Maucourt thus acted as the high priestess of a mysterious cult which she practiced alone, her husband much preferred to unwind at a bash improvised by the Negroes. But all this gave Eugénie some authority over her husband and, armed with the support of Nanny Da Gervaise, she took the liberty to reprimand her man whenever she judged it necessary. M. de Maucourt would remain unperturbed, kowtowed or let out an enigmatic '*hon*!' before seeking refuge in his office, amidst the books of accounts and ship models locked up in bottles which he collected, a passion incomprehensible to his lackeys. That is why, when he rebuffed Eugénie that day, the infamous day when he gave a double slap to his mistress Firmine in broad daylight, it was obvious to everyone that something had changed in the Courbaril Plantation. The Indian woman had 'possessed his mind!' nothing less! This foreigner, this Coolie always wrapped in her gaudy saris—red, yellow, saffron or shimmering green like the forewings of common tiger beetles—deployed her diabolical charms to take M. Frédéric under her control. This annoyed the Negresses who were quite elegant themselves. Unbelievable! Extraordinary! A Coolie, *oui*!

In fact, though Houblin de Maucourt was well and truly besotted with Nalima, to the extent that he asked for a portion of his own lunch, the one he shared with his wife and P'tite Mamzelle to be served to her at noon, his ire was motivated by quite another concern. He had just learnt, from reading *Les Antilles*, the White Creoles' newspaper, that strikes were planned by the trade union of the agricultural labourers when the harvest was still far from finished. The owner of Courbaril Plantation shared the indignation of the author of the article in question.

*Good Lord, strikes in such a small country? Is it not ridiculous, and worrying too? Why? Why on earth? To do as the others do, out there, beyond the Atlantic, to walk in the disoriented footsteps of the other strikers of France? In order to join forces with their pernicious progress, to affirm as ridiculously as they do, these human rights, citizens' rights, workers' rights, rights of the proletariat?*

Another article announced, most importantly, that the General Council of Martinique was about to vote to stop Indian immigration. As things were, de Maucourt hated this tie-wearing gang of Mulattoes who ruled there. They were the school teachers, lawyers, doctors and other scientists who were proud of having studied in the city of Bordeaux and who pretended to be familiar with the French language. Now there was one more reason to curse Victor Schœlcher who was the sole cause of all the misfortunes that plagued the colonies. What was worse, he was not even a French citizen. According to the White Creoles, when France had ceded these territories to Germany after the Franco-Prussian War of 1870, Alsace and Lorraine had lost all claim to being French. Had this frenetic Alsatian not devoted himself, heart and soul, to the abolition of slavery which he decried as a repugnant institution? Let's not forget that if the Whites had pulled out the Negroes from their native Africa, it was for their greater good! Without that, would they not have continued to live like savages and to engage in fratricidal wars in the wilds which were infested with animals as savage as themselves? And that traitor Schœlcher had not stopped there. He had then incited if not helped these arrogant Mulattoes to oust the White Creoles from almost all the elected posts. Mayors, departmental councillors, members of Parliment, senators were all Mulattoes now! They had succeeded in their schemes by conning the Negroes shamelessly so that they aligned themselves with these half-breeds. This had been convincingly demonstrated in Gaston Souquet-Basiège's book *Le Préjugé de race aux Antilles françaises* (Preconceived Notions of Race in the French Antilles), who was Houblin de Maucourt's partner in crime. This was the only book besides the Bible that the master of Courbaril Plantation had consented to leaf through in his entire life. But this Teuton, Victor Schœlcher did not stop there. He had persisted in undermining the foundations of Martinique by saddling a new war horse: the abolition of Indian immigration.

'He was a monomaniac with one aim: get everything abolished, while it was clear that the only thing that deserved to be abolished from this Earth, was his abominable self, dammit!' Fumed de Maucourt, when he entertained his colleagues over afternoon punch.

**Promise of Happiness**

Depending on the story teller, the man they called 'The Ancestor' was the son of the first convoy, from *The Aurélie*—or else, the second one. His name was Mourougayan and he was yet to be saddled with the ridiculous Christian name of Victor. He proved to be such a good worker that the father of M. Frédéric de Maucourt, master at that time of the Courbaril Plantation feeling death draw near, decided to perform an act of charity. He offered him a wife, an Indian woman from Karikal.

The White plantation owner had a distant cousin who served as a Justice of the Peace in Karikal, a French trading post in India and with whom he exchanged occasional letters. This 'generous' gesture had an ulterior motive. Mourougayan's term of indenture was drawing to a close; as he had committed no transgression nor contracted any debts, there was no legal way to hold him back in Martinique. M. de Maucourt Senior would have been well and truly obliged to sign his letter of repatriation on the said day, thus losing one of the rare

Indian indentured labourers who had given him complete satisfaction.

Doubtless, this stemmed from the fact that Mourougayan belonged to the *Shanan* caste, responsible for brewing the alcohol drawn from the sap of the coconut tree, the *kalou* which the Coolies preferred to rum at the beginning of their settlement in the colony. He devoted all his free time to this activity, which won him the goodwill of his peers, regardless of caste. To the planter's great astonishment, apparently these people drank a great deal, much more than they did in India, according to what his cousin from Karikal had said. Perhaps it was to forget their exile or to tolerate the persecution by the Negroes. But what was no less miraculous was that Mourougayan himself never swallowed a drop of alchohol. He did not have to be picked up, dead drunk near the plantation shop. Every morning, he was always in great shape and did not object to any of the jobs that the foreman Sosthène assigned to him. An ideal worker he was!

However, the negotiation between the Béké and the indentured labourer did not go well. Mourougayan did not seem enthused by the prospect of a wife, even though he had not known a woman for ages.

Even Negresses of easy virtue refused Indians. If he had held on, suffering stoically, he could still have waited for the remaining four months of indenture to pass. Once back in his native country, armed with his savings he could have looked at leisure for a beautiful and young wife. The master had been particularly crass:

'Hey Victor! When did you last screw a woman? Four-and-a-half years, I presume. Listen, I'm going to give you a gift, old fellow. I'm awaiting a woman from Karikal next week; that is if the boat is not delayed. A woman for you!'

Mourougayan loathed the Creole term that the Whites and Negroes used to designate the act of love: *Coquer*? Screw? Every time he heard it, he saw a cock mounting a hen and pecking the back of her neck, while his rump convulsed two or three times. This kind of brutality was the exact opposite of the prolonged patience which making love in the Indian way takes; at least in the way he remembered it, no matter how evanescent his memories. The bodies slowly drawing close, clothes removed and bodies bared at leisure, the prolonged embrace lasting hours, skin against skin, the light rubbing of the limbs, first the arms, then the legs, finally the cheeks, the progressive penetration of the genitals till ecstasy...all this could seem like eternity. The Negroes and the Whites would never know this. In fact, except for the colour of their skin, nothing differentiated them from each other and the Indians clubbed them together as 'Creole'. *Coquer* could mean to cut, to derail, to crush, to eat, to deflower, to shoot, that is 'to kill' the woman. In any case humiliate her. Instead of lavishing her with grateful thanks in the Indian way.

'I am going to think about it', replied Mourougayan who took this opportunity to reiterate an old demand.

Why were the Indians kept away from the mills and the distilleries? Why couldn't they participate in the manufacture of sugar and rum? Why were these better-paid and more prestigious jobs reserved for the Negroes and the Mulattoes? Why were the Indians and the Chinese confined to field work, to the exhausting work of cutting sugarcane? Why? Why?

Houblin de Maucourt smiled. He had heard these questions ten times, even a hundred times, and every time he gave the same reply:

'You need to know the machines. It is dangerous work. One mistake, one second of distraction and the machines grab a hand or a leg. I don't want to get into trouble with the gentlemen from Immigration Control. And then, you, Indians, you are foreigners, you are not French as far as I know!'

'Boss, there are amongst us boilermakers, carpenters, ironsmiths too. Their caste is called *Panchalatar*. Rangon is one of them, Sacarabany too...'

'Shh—Don't argue! You want this woman or not?'

Mourougayan had mixed feelings, was torn between the temptation of giving in to the call of the senses and his will to hold on till the end of his indenture. For the rest of his life, he must have bitterly regretted choosing the first option and signing on for five more years in exchange for the promise of this creature about whom he knew nothing. She could have been fearfully ugly or lame or scarred by smallpox or worse still, suffering from consumption. Mourougayan's new wife only cohabited with him for two months. She took away the small bonus that M. de Maucourt Senior had given Mourougayan as a reward for staying back in Martinique. She became the concubine of a fat dark Negro in the town of Rivière-Salée. The punishment of the Gods was severe. His penance had been a hundred and four years long, a lifetime without a wife. The Coolie community respectfully called this son of the first convoy, The Ancestor.

The day after, the ire of the master of Courbaril Plantation rose to its zenith. That was the red-letter day when, for the first time, he slapped his mistress Firmine and mistreated his wife. He had received a letter signed by the Governor himself informing the planters of the north that they could no longer hire Indian immigrants. The General Council of Martinique had so decided or was about to decide; the matter was not clearly spelt out in the aforesaid letter. Back to a less dreadful mood, de Maucourt summoned a council of war: his overseer, Laurent de Sainte-Foix—a White man of modest means with a weakness for alcohol; his steward, Marcel Polygone, a taciturn *Câpre* as well as his foreman, the Chabin Sosthène, in whom he had complete confidence; and the latter's assistant, Hermann—the famous *danmyé* fighter. The master received them in the steward's office, a stylish building whose awnings remained closed most of the time as M. Polygone did not take the heat well. Inside, a fan with large blades turned in a chaotic manner as if it were about to come unhinged from the ceiling. On the dusty shelves were piled up ledgers and bills of nearly three decades of business. The more ancient archives had been carried away by a tardy cyclone, one of those that arrived in the beginning of October, just when one expected to be relieved of the menace.

'Gentlemen,' began Houblin de Maucourt in a tired voice,

'It is going from bad to worse! Not only has this fucking beetroot reduced our sugar to nought, but lo and behold, it finally turns out that we are going to be short of hands. *Eh oui!*'

If the planter fully appreciated everything that came from Metropolitan France, particularly the cheeses, he held in great disdain the two things that endangered the prosperity of the colony: sugar from beetroot and wine. At the receptions he organised, he had banished Bordeaux, Bourgogne and even Champagne and bragged about not ever having wet his lips in what he called *jus dẹ raisin-France*, 'badly fermented grape juice from France'.

'Not that I'm unpatriotic, mind you,' he would say, 'Although, since a sinister and infamous 21 January 1793, I have asked myself if we would not have done better being born English or German. But you must confess, dear friends, wine withstands the transatlantic voyage poorly.' Houblin had developed a wholly outrageous theory according to which the consumption of wine could only be appreciated in a temperate climate which was favourable to the growth of vines, besides transportation by ship which required the crossing of several parallels (or meridians, the word he used depended on his inspiration of the moment) during the transportation if the precious beverage 'turned sour'. 'Dear friends, far be it from me to deny that wine is one of the most subtle inventions of the European spirit. The Gods of Olympus themselves were crazy about it, but please, you must acknowledge that in our tropical island, only a few hundred yards away from the Equator, there is something incongruous about drinking it in excess. Let us leave it to the priests who, on Sundays, incidentally only wet their lips with it, ha-ha-ha!'

'Sosthène, how many cutters can we count on this year?' He asked the foreman after a heavy silence had followed his first sentence.

'Hardly...well...I would say about forty, Boss...'

'Less than last year? Impossible!'

'We had nine repatriations to India in December, Sir,' said the manager, 'And that's not counting the four deaths. As you know, these Coolies are quite fragile and...'

'I don't want to hear it!' Houblin de Maucourt screamed, literally screamed. 'Fragile, you say, de Sainte-Foix? Allow me to laugh! In India, the English are in the process of transforming the country completely with the help of millions of Coolies. They are constructing railways everywhere, big roads, imposing buildings, bridges over precipices, and you want me to believe that in this miniscule Martinique, the job of cutting sugarcane is decimating this race?'

A renewed silence settled down in the steward's office, punctuated by the creaking of the blades of the tired fan. De Sainte-Foix, White as he may be, refrained from contradicting the man who had had the goodness to offer him this envied post of the Supervisor at the Courbaril Plantation. De Sainte-Foix's father, a trader at Saint-Pierre, having become bankrupt, had hanged himself to avoid dishonour. The de Sainte-Foix had then dispersed. His older brothers had left for France for good, his younger sister contracted a serendipitous marriage with a Béké from Vauclin and had broken off all ties with him. Considered decadent, his living with a quadroon—who had herself led a dissolute life in her youth but had now become a devout Catholic—was tolerated. Incidentally, it was she who was in charge of catechism for the kids in the countryside. During the rainy season, because of the muddy roads, this flock had refused to trudge up to the presbytery of Macouba.

'And the Negroes,' enquired de Maucourt, 'Are they still with Anthénor and his socialist trade union?'

'I always said that we must dismiss this maniac!' de Sainte-Foix said, perking up.

'Ah yes! And when all those under his thumb take off, *hein*, what will you do? You will take their place in the fields, perhaps? And you too, Polygone? And why not my wife and my daughter as *attacheuses*; they can tie up bundles of cut cane! Enough of this joke! How many hands do we need for a good harvest this year?'

Everyone averted their eyes, pretending to be lost in clever calculations. With two plots lying fallow that needed planting they would need at least eighty people at their disposal to make the next harvest possible. This had already happened in the past, when M. de Maucourt Senior was the master: in 1852 or 1853, the year varied according to memory, an epidemic of bad fevers with unpronounceable names had struck the region, decimating sugarcane cutters, mule-cart-drivers, loadmasters and *attacheuses*. The sugarcane had not been harvested on time and had dried up standing in the fields. The mills had to slow down, and this had almost endangered the very existence of the Courbaril Plantation. It had been saved *in extremis*, thanks to the personal intervention of the Governor of Martinique. He had arranged for a contingent of Indians to be withdrawn from Acajou plantation at Lamentin to work at Courbaril Plantation. And here was his successor today, coldly announcing that Indian immigration was going to be stopped soon! Out there, in France, as usual, the members of Parliment had shown excessive sensitivity about indentured workers. In the wake of Schœlcher, some fault finders presented this as nothing less than a new form of slavery.

'Slavery without chains or whips but slavery nonetheless,' as Anthénor, the Creole trade unionist, would thunder, in the impassioned speeches that he delivered on the first of May.

'May I suggest,' said Marcel Polygone in his affected fashion, 'that we recruit the Chinese? Has not the Governor announced his decision to make two hundred of them available to planters. And that too for free...'

'What! The Chinese? Never again, you hear me!' The master of Courbaril Plantation lost his temper. 'You forget the hassles that Li Feng and the other, what was his name?'

'Chang Sen,' said de Sainte Foix.

'That's right. At this very moment, these two clowns must have been put on trial. I won't be surprised if they are in the Fort-de-France jail or sent to the penal colony of Cagne.'

Houblin de Maucourt, who was one of the first planters to hire Chinese immigrants, was quickly disillusioned. Li and Chang turned out to be dreadful. Not only did they refuse to cut the sugarcane, demanding the easier job of cart drivers, but every evening, they had a bacchanal at the rum shack. Fifteen days after their arrival, they had already cleaned out the wages of a majority of the Negro workers playing Mah-jong. They did not stop causing fights with the Indians, whose women they tried to seduce. Wily, impolite, lazy, quick-tempered when the rum had heated up their heads, these Chinese were a absolute calamity.

'Boss...,' began Sosthène, whose blue eyes clashed with his Negroid features. 'There is perhaps a solution....even two.'

As the half-brother of Houblin de Maucourt, despite his subordinate position of foreman, the master cut him some slack. His temperament might be vindictive but he was a sensible fellow with a practical mind that resolved unexpected problems with simple and obvious ideas that nobody else could have thought of. However this Chabin was a '*chien libre*', free dog, who wandered from bed to bed and who, having no one to keep house for him, drowned in a disorderliness that defied description. His ideas about what was acceptable and what was not did not apply to his own existence.

'Géno's three sons, the farrier, will no longer be of school-going age in a few months,' he continued with his eyes lowered. 'Clotaire and Hermann's children threw their school bags and pencils into the bushes a long time ago.'

'How old is this lot?' asked Maucourt.

'We will have problems with the trade union...' ventured Polygone, the steward.

'And with this little M. Théophile too,' added de Sainte-Foix. 'These school teachers don't understand anything about sugarcane cultivation. They believe that it is with hands covered in chalk that we will feed this country!'

The master of Courbaril Plantation had asked the question as a formality; they knew that none of these children were twelve yet, the age at which they were no longer legally required to attend municipal school. Sosthène was right: if one disregarded this law, then Courbaril Plantation would no longer have any labour problems. Since childhood, Negro pickneys were used to weilding the machete, some to shell coconuts, others to cut the gliricidia branches with which fences were made.

They only had to find machetes both shorter and lighter than the ones used by the adults. In one day of work alone, a good worker could wield a machete up to one thousand seven hundred times. This kind of equipment was easily available abroad, particularly in Asia, but it was not being imported to the Antilles. De Maucourt promised to study his foreman's first proposition. He was all set to take Sire Anthéor, the trade unionist, down a notch or two, and convince the parents of these wretched children that the future of their progeny lay in sugarcane rather than at school.

'And your other idea, what is it?' he asked foreman Sosthène, his voice sounding more reassured now.

The Chabin seemed embarrassed, almost desperately looking to reconsider. But then he caught sight of Polygone and de Saint-Foix smiling mockingly. Both detested him. They were waiting with bated breath for him to make a mistake and he took a perverse pleasure in fixing them at every opportunity.

'Boss....we could hire Indians from Lorrain, even Sainte-Marie. We could attract them to our place.'

'Ha-ha-ha! And how will I go about it, old chap? I'm going to beat the drum in public squares and proclaim that at Courbaril Plantation, in the municipality of Macouba, his Excellency Frédéric Houblin de Maucourt pays higher wages than elsewhere. That's it, *hein*? Do you want all the Békés of Martinique to come down on me like a ton of bricks or what?'

Sosthène smiled, suddenly emboldened.

'I know several Indian women who are hanging around Saint-Pierre without work or accommodation. They have found refuge in the quarter of La Galère where they sell their bodies...we might be able to get them to come here.'

De Maucourt stared in amazement, his eyes round like marbles. He was wondering where his half-brother got such an outrageous idea. Streetwalkers! And that is all he could find to make up for the shortage of hands? And these creatures who were probably sowing crabs, the clap, herpes and syphilis around them? Enough to put the most seasoned of sugarcane cutters out of action considering that entertainment was in short supply in Macouba.

'We could send Mamzelle Nalima to talk to them, Boss...,' said Sosthène, thinking that he was making the most of his edge over the others. 'As soon as they hear that there are Indian women at Courbaril, all the Coolies of the region will rush here. That's what they miss the most...'

'Never!' exploded the Béké. 'Never! Do you hear me? Nalima is not of the same race as those people, gentlemen. Perhaps you have not yet realised, but she has nothing to do with these dark brown Tamil women, who pierce their nose and wear anklets. Nothing at all. She comes from the North of India and that is why she has the light brown complexion like the chickoo. She is a Bengali princess.'

The four men looked at their boss with a mixture of astonishment and admiration. His knowledge surpassed theirs because the old chap had travelled abroad and used to hang around his cousin, the owner of Gradis Plantation, who was reputed to be one of the most intellectual men in Martinique. All these stories of Tamil women, of *Kalikatta* or of the princess of Bengal meant nothing to them. They only saw in the Indian workers cohorts of taciturn creatures who disembarked in the country, year after year. Only their diabolical religion used to intrigue them, but they always avoided going near their ceremonies, including when a certain Z'Oiseau, former Hindu high priest and the only one of his race to occupy the position of foreman on a plantation, and at Gradis to boot, devoted himself to that monkey business.

'Forget I said anything, Boss,' Sosthène faltered.

'*Heu*...come to think of it,' said de Maucourt, 'Maybe you're right. These damned general councillors and this Governor who is under their thumb push us to the brink. In any case, we will have no choice but to find a way to recruit hands for the next harvest. *Ah là là*, what a life.'

He re-read the Governor's missive, crumpled it conscientiously before sending it flying into a dustbin that was overflowing with bills. Without greeting the four men, he withdrew, his face suffused with surliness.

# 6

## Sugarcane, Age-Old Pain, O Tenderness

*In the plantation shop, you find 'Laughing Cow' cheese, slices of dried cod, unfiltered* Mélia *cigarettes, lamp oil, batteries and matchboxes. The shop lady notes everything in a tiny book, especially the impulsive buys (a bottle of vermouth, a watch on a golden bracelet) and at the end of the week, your wage, all pittance of it, cries out in pain. On the verandah of the rum shack, the dominos, cleverly arranged, lie in wait to be fondled before a mean flick dashes them on to the wobbly table. The double-six is obviously the most important! The radio plays Creole mazurkas, biguines, merengues or less frequently* bel-air*; no one twitches with pleasure nor do they beat time. Sometimes the radio speaks in the fancy French from France and you lend an ear for a moment, before shrugging your shoulders.*

*Food doesn't need crockery: you can make do with pots and pans, any container will do: salted pig snout and red peas mixed with* farine-France, *wheat flour, taste better this way. To eat this with your fingers is to experience the secret tenderness of this dish. Because the moment you throw together parsley-spring onion-thyme-allspice, you experience a savoury treat that we like to call 'a pleasure for the palate'. Only men can cook this way.*

*Each day has the same rhythm. It is not a good idea to wait for the excitement of the rain bird, which forecasts the imminent fury of* Compère Général Soleil, *His Highness the Sun. You attack the day before it attacks you. Rows of solemn men let fly a volley of strikes with the machete, cutting stalks of cane to small pieces. Each cutter is followed by his favourite* amarreuse, *the woman who gathers the cut cane and ties it up in bundles; the queen of his heart or the mistress of his senses, as the case may be. The mill groans much later in the morning, waiting for the first batches of cane, but in its entrails, the boilermakers, the cooking stove minders, the fitters, the chief distiller and all the doctors and mechanics bustle about the machines, more particularly those which have not recovered from yesterday's load. They have to repair them, then and there, seal off some, manufacture other parts, service them and oil them again.*

*Sugarcane never lets the Negro out of sight. It becomes one with the aches and pains of his old age. Sugarcane never lets the Indian go. It creeps into his deepest dreams, invades the territory of nostalgia. Then sometimes, overcome by uncontrollable rage, the Negro lights fires which rise in blue flames to the firmament. The White men—their eyes shards of terror—run in all directions, ringing the alarm bell, picking up their guns, letting slip the ferocious dogs they had imported from Cuba in old times, pushing their wives and daughters into a cart to flee before bracing themselves against the last standing walls of their residences.*

*At Basse-Pointe, Patrice de Fabrique, a White man, was beheaded. He was not even a bad guy and the old Negresses cried their hearts out over him. There were Indians among the perpetrators of this unbelievable crime. What a shock! Such a docile, helpful race, their women always ready to spread their legs to receive the seed of the masters. Unthinkable, no? They had run away for days and days into the dense woods of Morne Balai and Hauteurs Courbaril. Their lips were sealed and they wrung their hands in resignation. Till that accursed evening when they were trapped and dragged back to the city, tied up in ropes like cattle from Porto-Rico. They must have been betrayed. A resounding trial was held and: Hector Velaidomestry, Fulbert Allamelou, Jean-Yves Mondésir, Patrice Latchoumia, Raphaël Bonaventure were condemned to death. For once, Indians and Negroes were treated equally. Some vague rumours floated around about this. In the huts of Basse-Pointe and Macouba, were extolled the oratorical exploits of the Mulatto lawyers who succeeded miraculously in getting the case reopened in the city of Bordeaux. The accused were exonerated and they came back as heroes. But no plantation would hire them. Sugarcane is vengeful,* oui! *Sugarcane never forgets the thieves, the arsonists, those who have shed blood and have surrendered to its embrace believing it to be a safe sanctuary. Sugarcane has always been on the White man's side. But when the Negro and the Indian forget this fact, well their buttocks will soon be exposed to the whip, fuck!*

# 7

## Crossing the Sea of Fire

*Deluge of lightning and lustral water falling from skies dark as ink. Wisps of wild sea foam flying over the reptilian hide of a churning sea. Thunder beats time as we implore Shiva and Parvati, our arms raised high, futile, and our eyes wide open staring into the void through which we move forward. Void? Or chimera and darkness tangled up? Will there be a helping hand, a divine hand, to guide our steps?*

Anandam Vellayoudon was one of the first to suffer from a lack of space. Those male immigrants who could not be pushed into the ship's hold were squeezed between decks. As soon as the hour when the lights went off drew near, each one rushed to take up his place, demarcating it with elbow jabs, swearing at the neighbour who had overshot his tiny territory. Reticence compelled some to keep their arms tucked into their bodies as they stretched out so as to touch no other body. This uncomfortable position led to pins and needles in the legs, stiffness of the back and numbness, none of which was conducive to restful sleep—something the passengers of *The White Adder* needed badly.

For the first two days after their departure from Pondicherry, the sea had been slick and smooth. As they continued southwards it grew turbulent, raged with a veritable fury. Adhiyaman felt his heart jump every time a wave hit the ship's prow. He observed from afar his young wife Devi's face, consumed with worry. She was one of the rare persons not to suffer from sea sickness and was constantly coming to the aid of women and children in difficulty. She helped them lean over the rails to vomit or swaddled them in thick woollen blankets that the crew had distributed freely. It was extraordinary that she devoted herself to these tasks without ever letting go of Vinesh, a baby whose mother had been struck by insanity on the fifth day of the voyage. Devi looked after Vinesh with such tender loving care that anyone would bet she was an experienced mother. Incidentally, she wore a yellow sari for seven days after marriage as per custom. When her father Anandam began to complain of rheumatism and was not able to get up for his morning ablutions, Devi, defying opposition from the English sailors, massaged him down with an ointment she had concocted. She avoided talking to her husband but the glances she cast his way spoke volumes about her feelings.

'Don't forget to put some lime juice in your water!' she whispered, while stepping over him to reach the corner where her father lay.

The doctor on board had to explain at length to each passenger that it was indispensable to drink lemon water in order to avoid a terrible malady that he called scurvy. At present, the recalcitrant and the carefree passengers who had not heeded his advice were lying on the raised tables, which served as hospital beds on board for want of space. Adhiyaman hated lemon-flavoured water and found the weekly ration granted to each adult insufficient: five kilos of rice, one-and-a-half kilos of Colombo powder, three hundred and thirty-six grams of salted fish, one hundred and fifty grams of pork or mutton, a few broad beans, and some portions of pumpkin. The sea air had kindled his appetite. Curiously, he had never been one to enjoy a feast even in the good days when his father was one of the richest businessmen of Madurai. In reality, the young man had only just now pulled himself together since he witnessed the horrible spectacle of his parents being dismembered by jackals. Initially he could not swallow a thing.

Although terrible poverty reigned in the provinces that he had crossed before reaching Pondicherry, he had always found a charitable soul who offered him a banana or a piece of corn pancake. Out of politeness he accepted and even pretended to eat but, once his well-wisher had turned his back, he threw the food away after two or three mouthfuls. On the evening of his marriage, the eve of the great departure, he had taken advantage of the poor lighting in the hut to hide his lack of interest in the victuals that his father-in-law had put aside for the event. Once aboard *The White Adder*, though, he started to feel hungry, so hungry that he finished his share of food before his companions and partook of his father-in-law's meals too. Only the lemon juice mixed in water bothered him. Unlike his son-in-law, Anandam lived with little and remained in a state of semi-prostration.

In the beginning, the weather was sunny, the sea calm. To keep boredom away, passengers gathered together region-wise and singing competitions were held. On full moon nights when the crew allowed the men to remain on the bridge longer than the rules and regulations mandated, the musicians made enchanting music. Each one's heart beat faster, confident that this country America, where the ship was taking them, was only a few cable lengths from the Coromandel Coast. Several times, some had thought they saw it in the distance and had let out a shout of joy. But every time it was only the silhouette of some ship or some reef lost in the middle of the ocean. Days went by and a dull anxiety began to seep into the minds of the most optimistic among them. Anandam Vellayoudon's wife, mother-in-law to Adhiyaman, was one such person. She had seen a map showing the sugar island just off the eastern coast of India but was suddenly struck by doubt. She now remembered that the little drawing supposed to represent America was not in the same ink as the one used to draw the neighbouring country, India. La Martinique, capital of America, as proclaimed by the *mestri*, had shone in bright red which caught the eye, eclipsing the dull black colour used for the rest.

'It must have been added by hand!' she exclaimed, stupefied by her discovery. 'By hand, I'm convinced of it.'

Anandam made a resigned gesture towards the sky, as if to call Shiva to witness his distress. But he did not pronounce a word or a prayer and closed his eyes, as if deciding to continue the journey with his eyes shut. The surgeon on board paid him several visits which revealed nothing special except immense fatigue, which on the whole was understandable at his age. Soon the gaze of the sailors hardened. They issued staccato orders, and as they realised that the emigrants were restive, they started moving about with their weapons—formidable looking guns with bayonets attached—and no longer sought to strike up a conversation with the few who spoke some words of broken English. At the slightest sign of panic, at the least scramble, a frequent occurrence when provisions were distributed, they assembled on the poop deck and held three hundred emigrants at gunpoint. Even though they were only about forty, they displayed such determination that nobody could hold their gaze nor object to the cruellest of their decisions.

Like the one to chain a poor wretch of an untouchable at the end of the foredeck, abandoning him to the battering of the waves and the scorching blaze of the sun. What mistake had he commited to merit such punishment? Adhiyaman was present at the beginning of the quarrel which had brought the Shudra into conflict with two Vaishyas from Tanjore. Twice a day, the emigrants queued up, one behind the other and passed wooden bowls of rice to each other that a cook ladled out from a small steaming tub. According to this system, the last one in the queue was served first. The Vaishyas, relatively higher castes, who could not bear the idea of serving the Shudras and even less the untouchables, always stood at the far end of the line. Adhiyaman was one of these happy few while his wife and his in-laws stood in the middle. Adhiyaman saw an untouchable wipe his nose with the reverse side of his *kaīli* before holding out the rice bowl to the next person in the queue. As usual this was passed on to three other people till it reached the young native from Madurai. In turn, he offered the bowl to one of the two Vaishyas without even turning around completely when the man exploded in anger:

'The pariah has spat into it! Dregs of the earth, meanest of mortals, you have dropped your excrement into my meal!'

The offended Vaishya raged up to the untouchable, caught him by the neck and rained blows on him, the other Vaishya helping. The unexpectedness of the attack and its violence stunned the other emigrants. Adhiyaman was tempted to provide assistance to the poor man who was wracked by a bout of shrill coughing. Evidently, he suffered from chest pain because he was so exhausted that he was not even protecting his face from the kicks that his aggressors were raining upon him. The English sailors took forever to intervene, believing that it was some ritual quarrel which erupted between emigrants from different regions. In general, these clashes subsided as fast as they began and so they never looked into the motives thereof. Captain Alwyn observed the scene through the spy glass impassively, then he ordered that the warring parties be isolated and denied the next meal. This time the matter was far more serious. The untouchable who was chained, began to choke and utter incoherent sentences, revealing by his accent that he was a native of the northern province of Dharmapuri. He was struggling to breathe, as if drowning. Finally he died and his death rattle made the Indians and the Europeans shudder. The sailors seized the two Vaishyas who they handcuffed, ignoring their sharp protests.

'No touch me! No touch!' bellowed the first perpetrator in pidgin.

'This pariah spat on our meal!' said the other outraged, turning towards the surgeon who was the only European to speak Tamil.

Captain Alwyn set them free and decided to modify the composition of the groups of emigrants. Henceforth, it would no longer be the men to one side, women and children to the other, and well away from them, the Muslims, but caste-wise clusters: the untouchables, seated alone at the deep end of the cargo hold, the Shudras on the foredeck and the Vaishyas as well as the zealots of Allah at the back of the ship. He ordered the surgeon to negotiate this new distribution with those whom the passengers seemed to accept as figures of authority and took care of the dead body of the untouchable. He asked that the dead man be completely undressed, that a makeshift shroud be made with his *kaïli*. As this garment was too small, the victim's legs stuck out. The corpse looked like a a bale of cotton, almost ludicrous. What was the captain going to do with the dead body? Nobody wanted to believe that it would be thrown into the sea, which had been swelling for some days now. The ship was plunging into enormous hollows while huge waves shattered themselves against its hull, causing such pitching and tossing that it was very difficult to move about. Deep within its hold, Adhiyaman regretted having accepted the proposal of the former workers from his father's spinning mill to emigrate. The tender blue silken skein of the sea which had fascinated him when he first reached Pondicherry now looked like the skin of a crocodile. The constant heaving and rolling turned his stomach and wreaked havoc on his gut. The sea was now a monster, a dragon, on whose back the ship was spinning desperately in all directions with nothing to hold on to. And this America was playing hard to get! The land of bountiful sugarcane was not even a mirage on the horizon. At least that would have kept up the hopes of the emigrants!

Quartermaster Henderson, who served as pastor for the Whites, came up to the enshrouded body of the untouchable, opened a Bible and started reading a passage in a monotonous voice. The distribution of meals continued as if nothing happened, everyone appearing deeply dejected. Devi carried a bowl of rice and a tumbler of lemon water to her father who was lying on the floor. He was trying to get up using his elbows. Anandam Vellayoudon had aged by several years in hardly seventeen days of voyage. His hair had suddenly turned white and he had large dark circles under his eyes. He smiled at his daughter whose hands he took to caress.

'We are still far away?' he asked her.

'I don't know. It seems that in less than a week, we will arrive at our destination. Take it easy, Appa!'

'You know, I believe it is Adhiyaman who will take care of you all, your mother and you. I will not have the strength to wait...On top of that, why did you take in that baby? There are women on board who are mothers and are capable of taking care of it better than you, no?

'Vinesh is my baby, Appa!' retorted Devi digging her heels in.

Adhiyaman, who had drawn close to them, wondered if his wife had eaten. She was always the last to help herself. She never queued up with the other passengers, instead always helped the sick and the children and insisted the cook serve them on priority, something that not everyone appreciated. She lavished so much attention on her protégées that the Captain was deeply touched and vindicated her. Devi took selflessness so far as to leave the food allotted to her at the feet of that strange man that the English called Radjiv and treated with deference. Radjiv isolated himself in a corner of the afterdeck and did not move from there except to relieve himself. Aloof, but not scornful, he thanked the young woman in a low voice but did not touch the bowl of rice that she insisted on bringing him twice a day. A little monkey with a fawn coloured coat stood guard next to him. Anandam Vellayoudon was convinced Radjiv was a Brahmin from north India.

'According to the laws of Manu,' he explained to Devi and Adhiyaman, 'an untouchable, a domesticated pig, a rooster, a dog, a menstruating woman, a eunuch must not observe Brahmins while they eat.'*

Others maintained that he was an Indo-Portuguese of mixed blood or perhaps even an Indo-Arab because the only time he opened his mouth was the moment when the sailors threw the dead body of the untouchable overboard. Then they thought they heard the language that the merchants coming from Arabic-speaking countries spoke.

---

**Manusmriti*, edited and translated by A.J. Prabhu, Pune, Vidarbh Marathwada Book Company, 2003, Book III, verse 239.

Before the Englishman could grab the Tamil country, entire caravans of Arabs had started coming there, in dry weather, to sell Persian carpets, finely carved teapots from Arabia or wool from Kashmir. However, nobody understood the meaning of the imprecation uttered by Radjiv, and all interest in him waned again. For suddenly the sea began to rage. The skies turned ink-black and whirling winds began to knock the ship around. The English sailors rushed to the tops of the masts to fold the sails, while ordering everyone to go down to the hold. Devi and Adhiyaman lifted Anandam up who was clenching his teeth, suffering a thousand deaths. In the great scramble, the emigrants reached the designated refuge area and guessed that in case of a shipwreck, they would not be safe there. Darkness engulfed the place except the rare narrow bands of light which pierced through the hatches. They had to find whatever place they could, squeezed in amongst the barrels of salted meat, casks of sweet water and cordages. Women ended up being thrown to the ground, children were being crushed underfoot. Their cries of pain were louder than the clamour of the waves lashing the ship. Implorations to Shiva and Mariamman flew thick and fast from everywhere, while passengers called out to their near and dear ones to locate them. The storm raged for an entire night and half of the next day.

By an extraordinary accident, Devi and her husband Adhiyaman found themselves side by side. At first the newly married couple noticed nothing. Unknown bodies pressed against them, punched them, and pushed them against the ship cargo. Some people even slumped on them either because they lost consciousness or out of despair when Adhiyaman felt the softness of a hand on his nape. He quivered. That hand, he would have recognised it from a thousand others. From it emanated a nurturing warmth which, little by little, helped him regain his composure. It was of course Devi's hand. He patted her on the face in the dark and discerned from the movement of her lips that she was smiling at him. He came closer, drawing her against him. Placing his chin against her hair, he inhaled that special smell. No more doubts! It was very much the young girl he had married the eve of his departure, without even knowing her well. Devi! While he had not wanted to touch her during their wedding night, he felt a disturbing pressure at the level of his lower abdomen although his legs were barely unfolded, and realised that he was erect. He was all the more surprised because any desire for the female body had vanished on that fateful afternoon, when he had seen a pack of jackals feast on his parents' flesh. How he had run for weeks his eyes fixed on the horizon! He had passed through the provinces of Dindigul and Karur, known for the beauty of their women but he noticed nothing. He could only think of fleeing, fleeing further and further away! At Namakkal, he had accepted bed and board in a family where all the men had emigrated. He had allowed himself a brief and chaste break; but had he only expressed the desire for a woman, there would have certainly been one ready to warm his bed. Was not the semen of the Vaishya always welcome among the lower castes? After all that wandering, when he finally reached the city of Pondicherry, if Andandam Vellayoudon had not more or less twisted his arm, without doubt, he would not have paid attention to the dazzling Devi.

And yet, in the middle of an imminent catastrophe—while the captain was shouting distraught orders as the elements were battering the ship reinforcing the young man's fears—the desire to embrace his wife, to nibble her flesh, to caress her lips, to enter her, prevailed upon him. Incomprehensible. Devi was the one who took the first step. With a clumsy but fevered hand, even a little shaky, she rummaged under his *kaïli* and grabbed his penis which was already quivering. She then began to squeeze it with such gentle force that he screamed aloud but it was lost in the brouhaha of the cargo hold. Tears, groans, prayers, insults mixed with the creaking of the barrels and the casks that had come loose. Someone tried in vain to light a little lamp, without doubt a *Toulken* who was frenetically chanting the name of Allah. It was so dark that you could not even make out the shadows of those who were still moving about trying to find a better place for themselves or looking for a child. Getting rid of her sari, the young woman placed herself upon Adhiyaman, offering him her back, and impaled herself on his turgid shaft. The pain she felt quickly turned into pure pleasure when he gripped Devi's supple thighs and they let their bodies rise and fall with the increasingly powerful rolling of the ship. A sinister crack was heard on the afterdeck. Without doubt, a mast had given way to the repeated assaults by the wind. Around the couple, tears became sobs and hiccups turned to vomit. Soon a foetid odour invaded the cargo hold, a mix of urine, regurgitated meals, sweat and farts. They had become wild animals, distraught fauna facing an imminent cataclysm. Unflappable, Devi continued her movement up and down sometimes changing it into a gentle rotation, lush and delightful to the young man. Even in the days when he had patronized the brothels of Madurai, he had never met a woman of such expertise in the science of love. Their embrace lasted the entire time that the cyclone endured and they ended up falling asleep in that position, welded together like a statue of some barbaric deity.

When they opened their eyes, the ship was no longer moving and most of the other passengers had climbed up to the deck except some sick people including Devi's father. The latter was holding baby Vinesh in his arms. Anandam's skin was sallow. Next to him, seated on her haunches, his wife watched over him, fanning the baby's face with the help of a piece of cloth. Devi stood up and put on her sari again hurriedly.

'He knew that he would not complete this journey...,' her mother said simply.

She had not removed the infant from her husband's arms to mislead the English sailors. She guessed that he would suffer the same fate as the untouchable who had been kicked to death by the two Vaishyas.

'We are not very far from America,' she added. 'The maps don't lie. We will ensure that Anandam gets a funeral pyre worthy of him, once we are ashore. He was a very good husband...'

Devi was in tears and Adhyaman was deeply moved. They noticed that the sailors and emigrants had gathered together on the portside. The emigrants jumped with joy, thanking Kannavédi and Shiva. Out there, at a distance, appeared the contours of a mountainous land surrounded by a blue lagoon. As the ship drew nearer, they discovered magnificent forests, green fields, white dwellings and the golden thread-like outline of roads. The map told the truth! America was not so far away from the Coromandel Coast. However the sailor's gestures expressed denial and the quartermaster struggled hard to temper the enthusiasm of the Indians in pidgin:

'Not America! No! Mauritius!'

Adhiyaman felt the deck give way under his feet. He had never heard about this place. Besides, the ship did not enter into the harbour of the pretty city which stood out as they went past the mountain. The captain ordered that the anchor be dropped and closed himself up in his cabin.

The sailors only responded in dribs and drabs to the pressing questions of the passengers. They were repeating the same old refrain: This is Mauritius! Not America! Towards the middle of the day, a ship of modest size, displaying a British flag, came alongside *The White Adder*. Two officers climbed on board and delivered, after endless greetings, a parchment to Captain Alwyn. Food and water would be replenished before continuing the journey but it would not be possible to berth there: an epidemic of typhoid fever had been raging for several weeks now on this island owned by the British. Almost a thousand people had died. A murmur of disappointment welcomed this announcement. Anandam Vellayoudon's wife approached the doctor, joined her two hands in *anjali mudra* and told him in a beseeching tone:

'My husband is dead. I don't wish to continue without him. Grant us a favour. Please let us disembark here.'

The two officers, the captain and surgeon negotiated for long minutes. The English officers seemed unenthusiastic at the idea of contravening the order of the Governor of Mauritius but ended up giving in. The face of Anandam's widow briefly lit up. She clasped her daughter Devi in her arms, without a single parting word and muttered a prayer to Hanuman, her favourite deity. Then, taking Adhiyaman aside, she said to him:

'You had made a promise to Anandam to watch over Devi, no? Alas, that moment has arrived sooner than we imagined. Much sooner...In America I want you to remember us and most importantly...most importantly, Adhiyaman, never speak to your children about India as a country of misfortune!'

She kissed the young man on the forehead and with a hesitant step began to descend the gangway ladder along which the sailors were sliding her husband's body that they had wrapped up in the same way as the untouchable's body from Dharmapuri. The boat with the officers from Mauritius had not reached the coast when Captain Alwyn gave orders to weigh anchor. As the sea was perfectly calm, the emigrants felt hopeful again. Musicians began to entertain them once more and some started to dance, dragging children into the circle of dancers. The captain had rum from the Antilles distributed freely. It was the first time that most of them drank it. This foretaste of the country of their dreams made their heads spin. Many of them fell down drunk in no time at all as the others laughed and applauded loudly. Adhiyaman did not dare risk wetting his lips with the colourless liquid that his young wife, intrepid of soul, described to him as a delectable drink. Slightly tipsy, she began to hum a risqué refrain that he had often heard from the mouths of his father's servants, in those bygone days that were never to return, when the Dorassamy family was one of the most prosperous of Madurai. It was about a woman who, tired of waiting for her lover to declare his feelings for her, had disguised herself as a demon and blocked his path, one evening when he was returning home. Petrified, the man gave in, that is allowed himself to be stripped, titillated and caressed till he yielded to passion. Devi made eyes at her husband which reminded him of their night together, two days ago when, in the bottom of the cargo hold, hemmed in by other emigrants, jostled about, they had found the strength to make love like the young man had never done before, even though the storm seemed to be about to break the ship.

**Ash Wednesday**

A thousand small mirrors decorated his red devil's costume and black threads hung from his horned mask. He was terrifying. Brandishing a wooden broadsword in one hand and a large whip in the other, he pranced around in the *Grand'Case* courtyard to the great joy of the master's children while the master flung coins at him. Seated in rocking chairs, under their verandah, M. de Maucourt and his wife followed the evolutions of the character with a smile. They applauded when a swarm of little devils, with their tails as simious as their mentor's came hurtling down the front steps screaming meaningless words, especially the mysterious 'Aboubou-Dia!' which made Vinesh quake. His mother had forbidden him, just as all Indian mothers did, from going anywhere near this barbaric festival which started at the beginning of the year. Every Sunday, the Negroes and Mulattoes got carried away by a kind of madness which finally exploded at the end of the month of February. Although the Carnival took place in the alleys of the town of Macouba, it attracted a lot of people from the country, including Hauteurs Courbaril. The foreman Sosthène was the Papa Diable of the quarter, the one who wore the biggest bull head painted bright red. He took pleasure in cracking his whip when he was nearing a house and bellowing:

'*Djab-la ka mandé an timanmay!*' (The Devil wants a small child!)

Even though he avoided the Indian quarter, *peur-cacarelle,* a fear that made them soil their pants, gripped the children here. In fact, the *Négrillons,* Negro pickneys, elsewhere screamed too, petrified. Their parents enjoyed this and sometimes joined the revellers in the Carnival parade wearing only torn trousers or a faded skirt as a disguise. They roared the songs at the top of their voices. The smutty lyrics of their composition jeered at Marcel Polygone who, according to them, groped young girls who had the misfortune of finding themselves in his path but gave lessons in good manners to everybody else. They derided Man Ninise, the plantation shop owner who bought necklaces and gold bracelets from the Syrian peddler Abderramane on the sly and then complained about the high taxes she paid. Then it was the turn of de Sainte-Foix, the overseer! Then Hermann, the valiant *danmyé* fighter! Even the master, the owner of Courbaril Plantation, was not spared because of his unfathomable affection for the Coolie woman, Nalima, but only subtle allusions were made.

'Actually, I like the Carnival time,' said Devi to herself. 'At least the Negroes leave us alone!'

In reality, the Negroes forbade the Indians from participating in the Carnival. Indians were not even allowed to watch. Those who broke this rule, by hiding their smooth hair under a bakoua hat for example, were sprayed with *farine-France,* wheat flour, and then booed by the delirious crowd.

'*Kannaval sé bagay Neg!*' (The Carnival is our business!) The Negroes proclaimed, very proud of those days of total freedom when the power of the Whites magically disappeared.

In general, Adhiyaman and Devi made the most of these dangerous Carnival days to get together. Courbaril Plantation was deserted and they took walks to the river and even bathed there all day long with their younger son, Ganadin. But, their elder son, the turbulent Vinesh, always found a way to give them the slip. Nobody knew when he had slipped under the skin of a Negro pickney: he had learnt Creole very quickly, attended the *joutes de combat-danmyé* on Saturday afternoons after wages, and most surprisingly had become the best friend of Patte Crochue, a little *nègre-griffe,* a dark brown Mulatto, who limped, as his nickname cruelly suggested. Incidentally, it was this little rascal who helped Vinesh escape his parents' watchful eyes on Carnival Monday and resurface only on Ash Wednesday. During the burlesque marriage parade on Sunday along the colonial road with men disguised as brides in white and women fitted out as men with top hats, walking sticks and moustaches drawn in charcoal, Vinesh would start twisting and turning, dancing to the beating drums, turning a deaf ear to his mother's rebukes and his father's threats.

While the Indians of Courbaril Plantation locked

themselves up in their houses, Vinesh slipped into the parade next to Patte Crochue, and participated in the Carnival parade with just a calabash on his head as disguise. Where did he sleep during these three days of madness? Neither Adhiyaman nor Devi ever found out. What did he eat? How did he manage as the only Indian in the swarm of rollicking Negroes? This remained a mystery for the Dorassamy family. In reality, Vinesh feared no one but the Papa Diable and his refrain:

'*Abi! Abi! Mi Djab-la déwò!*' (Brrr! Brrr! The Devil is out!)

Although he knew like everyone else that behind the fearful mask it was Sosthène, the foreman who had a soft corner for his mother, Vinesh shivered and felt his legs turn to jelly. In his eyes, Papa Diable was the reincarnation of Kuvera, the chief of the demons, who devoured men. The Ancestor, who was initiating him into the precepts of Hinduism, had often spoken to him about it: Papa Diable was a filthy evil creature who made kids his prey and threatened to devour them alive. Vinesh's fear kept growing from Sunday and Carnival Monday—when the Devil hardly ventured beyond the main square of Macouba—to Carnival Tuesday when he gave free reign to his omnipotence, surrounded by swarms of little devils, dressed in red. But the most terrifying day was without doubt Ash Wednesday, the last day of the Carnival, when all the participants dressed in black and white as a sign of mourning because the puppet representing the King would be burnt at nightfall in the town square. Papa Diable did not change this quirky disguise during the four days of festivities. His howls made your blood chill and he used to jump on children wandering alone. Vinesh was convinced that he dragged his victims to Naraka, the twenty-one hells where demonic creatures were having fun. He could never erase from his mind that scorching afternoon, when in the middle of a sugarcane field, he found himself face to face with Papa Diable. His yell still ringing out in his ears.

'*Djab-la ka mandé an timanmay!*' (The Devil wants a child!)

Days went by, one after the other, identical, unending. One scoured the sea but no land appeared, except fearful reefs which seemed to guard the doors to invisible palaces. Time and again, a grey hump of a whale would set off shouts of joy amongst the children. Radjiv, the Brahmin who was compelled by the captain to come to the poop deck when the storm was about to hit the ship off the coast of Mauritius, had gone back to his bizarre stance, always with his monkey who enjoyed pilfering other passengers' belongings. The holy man stood immobile again, indifferent to both the conversations and the songs sung by Indians. He ignored the crew who taunted him when the captain was busy in his cabin. Radjiv was held in high esteem by the officers on board. Indeed, his complexion, the colour of old ivory and his slightly hooked nose distinguished him from his Indian compatriots. Sometimes sudden rain drenched his muslin turban and he had to take it off to dry it. Then he folded it again and again, no less than seventy times according to Adhiyaman.

One evening, Adhiyaman, very worried, decided to approach Radjiv. The sea was so calm that the passengers had fallen asleep earlier than usual. The sailors on watch were playing cards on the foredeck. He stopped short when he realised that the Brahmin was snoring, his little pet animal curled into a ball at his feet. Leaning against the railing but upright, his tunic flapping in the wind, he looked like a mast because of his imposing build. The young man could not help laughing softly but quickly controlled himself. Without opening his eyes, Radjiv said in Tamil that had a strong foreign accent:

'*Agattin azhagu mugattile*' (Inner beauty can be seen on the face).

Stretching his skinny body without spreading out his arms or legs, the man seemed to be thanking the God of salutary sleep, the divine Shiva, the one who gives strength to tired bodies.

'Nobody should know that I spoke to you,' he continued. 'Especially not the Whites!'

'Yes...yes, master...'

'Did you leave of your own free will?'

'Yes, yes, master...'

'*Hon*! Are you quite sure? Have you not actually followed a woman you love?'

'That is true, master...'

His gaze suddenly turned harsh. He seemed to read into Adhiyaman, something that troubled the young man so much that he regretted the fact that he had interrupted Radjiv's meditation. Who was this man? Where did his audacity come from?

'The Universe is eternal, without beginning or end,' said the holy man. 'The world in which we live is composed of two substances. One is animate, the *jiva*, the sensitive energy which is the essence of men, of animals, of plants, of wind and of fire; the other is *ajiva*, inanimate, inert, which is found in space, matter and time, in everything that is without a soul. You follow me?'

'Yes, I hear your words...'

'As the very wise Mahavira taught, the purpose of human life is to liberate ourselves from *karma* and to do this, we need several lives of discipline and penitence. In fact, *karma* holds back the *jiva* and causes the transmigration of souls. He who succeeds in purging himself of his passions, of his desires through meditation and the recitation of mantras, in vanquishing his ego, begging forgiveness for his evil actions, concentrating on his soul, avoiding impure acts, will be ready for complete renunciation. Go now. I did not speak to you. You did not come to me. A last piece of advice: never spoil your inner beauty. Go!'

Adhiyaman had to obey although he wanted to prolong this moment of absolute serenity, to listen to the teachings of this great master again and again. What was this holy man doing on this ship? What crime had this man of high caste committed to be condemned to emigrate to the Americas? This journey of no return, was it not reserved for the people of no means, Shudras and untouchables, chased by famine and epidemics? More rarely, intermediary castes like Vaishyas, like himself, also emigrated. Noblemen and Brahmins, disgraceful allies of the English occupant, did they not continue to lead a carefree life? This bunch of questions left unanswered bothered the young man who was tempted to discuss them with Devi. However he preferred to let her mourn in peace. Since the death of her father, the gaze of his young wife was clouded and she was withdrawn, only taking care of Vinesh, the baby she had adopted when his mother lost her mind. Incidentally, Vinesh's mother had disembarked at Mauritius at the same time as Devi's mother. The young woman sorely missed her mother, a reliable and loving presence. 'I am now an orphan,' she said to herself sometimes. 'I only have you and this young boy that the Gods have entrusted me with. I hope it is a sign from above.'

The maps had well and truly lied! As the days passed, Adhiyaman grew more and more convinced about this. Those who claimed that you had to cross two oceans were right as opposed to those who promised that America was a short distance from the Coromandel Coast. Meanwhile, the weather grew cold and the crew distributed woollen blankets. They taught the emigrants to rub their arms and faces with rum to warm themselves. Adhiyaman liked the smell more than the taste of it. It made him dream. When would they reach this country where they would be paid to lay out the sugar in the sun? Each one was beginning to worry aloud. They asked the English sailors who simply shrugged their shoulders and muttered some rubbish in their language. They had better things to do. Card games and binge drinking had stopped and Captain Alwyn had the sails and rigging adjusted and the holds inspected regularly. The sea was beginning to look dangerous again. A new storm was brewing. The huge waves that rose high against an overhanging dark sky did not augur well. Without doubt, this storm was going to be more terrible than the earlier one.

'A mountain! There, look!'

All the emigrants rushed together to starboard, all the eyes riveted in that direction. The man who had spotted it was already jumping for joy, kissing his near and dear ones, crying into his hands, thanking Goddess Parvati for her infinite goodness. The mist hampered a clear view of the strange mountain whose summit was completely flat, a table in stone which was so disproportionate that it covered the entire horizon.

'Africa country! Not America yet!' shouted a sailor in pidgin.

The surgeon explained that the ship was about to round the Cape of Good Hope, at the southernmost tip of the African continent. The meeting of the Indian and Atlantic Oceans was tumultuous and was going to be a veritable ordeal. One man asked:

'Is America then on the other side of the world? In the kingdom of shadows...?'

He did not have time to complete his sentence: a four-metre high wave crashed on the afterdeck, knocking down emigrants and sailors. About ten others followed immediately which tossed the ship in all directions, raising it to the grey menacing sky traversed by lightning and then dashing it into the bottomless pit of the sea. Adhiyaman noticed, between the gusts of wind and cold rain, the lacy silhouette of a pile of reefs which were approaching inexorably. The lookout screamed but his words were lost in the racket of the unleashed elements. The temperature must have plummeted by several degrees. Everybody's teeth were chattering now. The women tried to protect their children with the help of two woollen blankets but they screamed and cried relentlessly, their skin wrinkled from the sudden chill. The emigrants rushed into the hold but the quartermaster had closed the hatches. The surgeon declared in Tamil that there was a leak and water had rushed in, reaching eye level. In truth, the ship was becalmed and slowly going down. Half of the foredeck was almost level with the waves and Captain Alwyn was no longer ordering his crew who wandered about the ship idly, some getting drunk on gin and singing bawdy songs. A groan escaped from the group of low castes, a concert of plaints mixed with intermittent chaotic prayers. They invoked the four-armed God, Shiva Nataraja, the cosmic dancer who keeps time as the world is created and destroyed. At that time he only seemed to be waving his upper left hand, the one that holds *samhara*, the flame of destruction. They called out to Kali, the dark one, whose frenetic dance endangered the equilibrium of the world; to Parvati, most benevolent of all, who lives on the peak of Mount Kailasa with Shiva her husband; and to Matsya, the first *avatara* of Vishnu, who saved the world from the deluge and retrieved the four Vedas from the bottom of the ocean. But nothing happened. On the contrary, the storm raged twice as furiously, two of the three masts of the ship creaked ominously and finally fell. It was impossible to distinguish the sky from the sea and the mountain shaped like a table atop the Cape of Good-Hope had become almost invisible.

'If we don't make it to the end of this journey,' whispered Devi into Adhiyaman's ear, 'I want you to know that I will watch over you in another life. I have committed no offence against the Gods, I am sure I will get a good reincarnation.'

As she protected the baby clutched in her arms, the winds fought over in her hair and her luscious breasts were outlined by her wet clothes. Adhiyaman did not know what to say. Like most Indians, he had become listless after having invoked the Goddess Mariamman, the protector of the poor Tamil people. The English sailors were screaming Christian prayers on their knees, to no avail either. They were constantly making the sign of the cross, confessing their sins, begging the Virgin Mary for forgiveness. The surgeon came back from his cabin with a Bible covered in leather and asked for a *puttagam*, the holy book of the Hindus. Several hands held out their copies. He chose the most voluminous one among them and staggered to the centre of the ship and left the two works there, next to each other. The storm seemed to calm down. For a few minutes, it looked like the Gods of India and Europe combined their efforts to successfully stall the storm. The sailors were already giving thanks, yelling halleluiahs, making the stunning silence which had descended upon the ship resonate. The two Vaishyas who had killed the untouchable began to chant a passage from the *Ramayana*. This was a soothing balm on the aching hearts of the emigrants. If they had survived the first cyclone, it was unlikely that the Gods would make them undergo a similar ordeal again. Yet the curse of the kaala paani, which hangs heavily on the head of every Hindu who leaves the holy land of India, had not been dispelled. Other obstacles would show up on their path but they could not be worse than what they had just confronted.

'Watch out! Wa-a-a-tch-out!' yelled a sailor, interrupting the Vaishya, pointing to the port side where a wave more monstrous than all the earlier ones, was rushing at dizzying speed straight towards the ship even though the rest of the sea appeared to have calmed down and the skies looked serene. That thing, or monster, had wound around itself, dragging along chunks of the sea and foam, making a dreadful sucking sound as it continued on its course. Implacable. Inexorable. Adhiyaman raised his hands to pray to Brahma but gave up almost immediately. Sailors and emigrants were once again holed up in nooks and corners of the afterdeck, pell-mell, mute with terror. There was no doubt that this devilish wave would split the ship in two before grinding it between its teeth. They were all heading for certain death. Even Radjiv had lost his upper caste arrogance and stared incredulously at the monstrous creature. The wave was still rushing, in the middle of a smooth sea as if moved by an unknown force, a force of incomprehensible resentment. It was about twenty meters from the ship's hull when suddenly a *Toulken* got up, removed his immaculate turban, raised his right hand before addressing a desperate prayer to Nagourmira, a Muslim saint who had protected the fisher folk in the coastal region of the Tamil country for centuries. His fellow Muslims imitated him, kneeling down towards the east and repeating the name of Allah so fervently that the Hindus and Christians were petrified. The wave died hardly two meters from the foredeck. It could be seen lurching, deflating, and trying hard to gather strength before finally settling into a gigantic splash of foam. An unending silence followed. Nobody dared to move. The raucous breathing of those who were suffering from chest pain could barely be heard. The sailors began to shed tears as if they were overgrown children. Stupefied, the Hindus watched the group of Muslims, feeling apprehensive and grateful. How could their invisible God—this God who did not tolerate any image, any divine, human or animal representation, this God who was a pure assembly of syllables—Allah, have more magnanimity than all the deities of India put together, the White God included?

Captain Alwyn, who could not believe his eyes either, was the first to react. He had the *Toulken* who had asked for Nagourmira's help come up to the poop deck and embraced him. The man showed neither happiness nor displeasure. As if in a trance, he continued to recite what seemed like prayers through pursed lips.

'Captain, we are going to round the Cape of Good Hope at last!' said the quartermaster with relief.

'From today, the meals of Hindus and Mohammedans are not to be mixed up. Buffalo meat and pork are to be kept separate! We have had enough quarrels on this ship. We will reach the Atlantic Ocean soon and I want the rest of the journey to be peaceful.'

'Aye Aye, Sir!'

'Serve rum to the Indians and green tea to the Mohammedans,' ordered the Captain.

The Tamil emigrants were still in a daze. Adhiyaman would have liked his father, who was hostile to the zealots of Allah because of their frenzied proselytisation, witness this miracle. There was no doubt. This was a spectacular manifestation of a divine presence, a manifestation that rekindled the flame of faith in Adhiyaman's heart. As an adolescent in Madurai he had nurtured this flame with difficulty but when he had stumbled upon his parents being devoured by jackals it had almost been put out. Now the Mohammedan religion revived the light of faith.

'From now onwards we will pray to Nagourmira too...,' he murmured to his wife Devi, who nodded.

'Yes, because we don't know what awaits us there, in America,' she said. 'This land that was described as so close to the Coromandel seems to be a mirage. Maybe it does not exist at all. Maybe the English are taking us to their country in Europe where we will work as their servants.'

# 8

## King Bagiratha

*Our memory slowly dissolves in the fury of the sugarcane fields; in the din of the tip-carts which hurtle down the hillsides, loaded to the brim; in an implacable alignment of godforsaken days. Our language crumbles little by little; our words struggle to drill through the rigorous light of the early mornings. We have lost the meaning of ablutions. We have become dirty, even hideous. Our skin is covered with scabies, yaws, pox, our hands are covered with incurable pressure sores, our toes sprout blisters and rum burns our palates, whipping our minds into sudden madness.*

We called the last survivor of the first convoy The Ancestor both out of respect and out of mute terror. He had no teeth and his hair fell to his knees in long blackish strings when he squatted, always in a simple dhoti, in front of his hut. From his posture, we guessed that he wanted to continue with the story that he insisted on spinning in a strange and beautiful language, a mixture of solemn Tamil and crushed Creole, day after day. The words seemed to form in his bulging stomach which contrasted sharply with his slender limbs. They rumbled there, made his body quiver as they rose up to his throat at a dizzying speed while his Adam's apple bobbed. He never looked us in the eye. As a matter of fact, his pupils were so transparent that the last light of the sun drowned in them, giving him the appearance of a fallen god. He chanted more than he spoke, and for this he needed to feel our heads under the palm of his hand. We subjected ourselves to this insistent caress turn by turn, terrified. The Ancestor knew the names of all the kids of the plantation, even the ones born after he lost his eyesight. As he remained immobile for long hours, his legs folded under his buttocks and his hands joined together, under the shade of the tamarind tree which bore the most delicious fruit in Hauteurs Courbaril, we watched the movement of his eyelids while hiding under the hedge of Guinea grass. In the middle of the day, while a ferocious heat weighed down upon the world, The Ancestor finally seemed to fall into a strange slumber. At that time we walked up to the tree with furtive steps but invariably he called out to the boy whom he smelt or so we thought. Then this boy had to do as he was told. He had to sit against The Ancestor's torso who put his hand on the boy's head and began a litany that froze our blood. One day, as luck would have it, he called my name.

'*Vinesh, vini'w isiya, yich-mwen!*' (Vinesh, come here my son!) You are the son of Adhiyaman, right?

He grabbed my shoulder without waiting for my answer, carefully ran his fingers over my body and gave a grunt of intense satisfaction.

'The White man, he gives you food?' he asked.

'Yes, father.'

'You have rice?'

'Yes, my father.'

A smile lit up his face which had become thoughtful.

'Out there...at home, I mean, I remember the zebus which used to go from window to window looking for a fistful of rice. We named each one. Men and animals, we lived happily till the English landed...well! Go fetch me water! You must always wash your hands before talking about the great deeds of those who preceded us on this earth. Never forget it!'

I ran to the spring hidden under a grove of wild guava trees that was used by the workers who lived there. It was well known for its medicinal value. Did it not come from the entrails of the volcano, which explained why it was tepid? In any case it slaked your thirst more promptly than the water from the river, which was more frequently used. I filled water in a calabash that I carried on my head like the *Négrillons*, the little Negro pickneys, but, being less agile than them, I got wet along the way. I arrived drenched in front of the The Ancestor's hut to realise that he had vanished into thin air! I looked all around in vain. I hesitated to enter. Imagining that he must have gone to relieve himself, I sat on my haunches by the little fire where sweet aromatic plants burned. On the ground, he had drawn complicated characters which I guessed to be Tamil words. Some of my older companions, who had been caught by The Ancestor and compelled to learn some letters, had fun replicating them wherever they could. On tree trunks with the help of a pen knife, on their arms with pieces of charcoal, sometimes on their clothes when they pinched some laundry blue from their mothers. This is how they demonstrated that they were entering the world of adults and we, the younger ones, we bowed down in front of what seemed like inaccessible knowledge to us.

Was The Ancestor going to teach it to me that day? I did not have time to think. The branch of a tamarind tree landed on my shoulders, lacerating my flesh. The pain was so acute that I could not let out the slightest cry. I got up quickly and had to protect my face with both hands. The blows rained heavily on my entire body at present. The Ancestor was frightening. His mouth had deformed into an angry rictus and he heaped insults both in Tamil and in Creole on me.

'I asked you for water to cleanse my hands, little moron!' He shouted, toppling the calabash of water with his foot. 'Go find a *yèlimen tenga*!'

And as I did not understand what he wanted, he pointed to a coconut tree. In spite of the burning sensation on my skin, I managed to climb the tree and pluck a cluster of green coconuts. Without bothering about me anymore, The Ancestor armed himself with a machete and began to lop off the heads of the coconuts with surprising dexterity considering he was so frail and blind too. He grabbed each coconut with his left hand and in a sharp gesture cut off the part which attached it to the cluster. Then he rubbed his cheeks and forehead with coconut water before washing his hands carefully.

'You must know that there is only one kind of water that is pure, just one! It is this one...It has not been soiled with all these bad things that lie around the earth. It is the favourite drink of the gods. Here, look at this coconut here! You see, it is dry while it was still hanging from the tree. Well, it means the Moon has drunk it. The Moon only likes untouched water...' He told me in a voice that was suddenly calm and drew me into his arms once more. I felt his sticky hair against my cheeks and soon his litanies carried me across to the other side of this world. I found myself right on top of such a high mountain that the clouds formed whitish sheets which floated a thousand feet below. I no longer needed to breathe. My heart stopped beating and a great beatitude enchanted my mind.

A voice—The Ancestor's—whispered to me:

'Now you are King Bagiratha...Repeat!'

'I am king...Bha...Bagiratha...'

'You have climbed the slopes of the holy mountain for thirty years, alone, among ferocious beasts, without drinking or eating any food. You have resisted attacks by demons who spin in the air, their wings whistling, their laughter thundering. You set out in the pink of youth when you had just inherited the throne. Here you are now at a moment when age matters no more. You are King Bagiratha, he who set out to implore Brahma, leaving behind his people in a state of desolation because of the Great Drought.'

The earth had emptied itself of its waters. Men wandered about, haggard, tormented by unquenchable thirst. Everywhere, they scrutinised the four cardinal points looking for the oceans but these had disappeared for millennia. In their flight, the oceans had carried away rivers, tributaries, lakes, lotus ponds. It was believed that a sage, in order to vanquish the evil spirits that were disturbing his meditation, had swallowed all this water where they lived. But in doing so he had deprived the earth of its blood; he had taken away from humanity the most essential earthly possession!

'Vinesh, don't let go, you are King Bagiratha, the one who has gone to implore Brahma...,' screamed The Ancestor while shaking me unceremoniously.

I kept waking up time and again with a start and could make out between the strings of his hair, the gang of little Indians who, at a respectable distance, devoted themselves to their favourite game: throwing stones against the low branches of the *manguier bassignac,* mango tree, whose fruits had a flavour of turpentine. Each day of Lent, we stuffed ourselves with this fruit to stave off the hunger gnawing at us. They had forgotten me, the scoundrels! Sometimes a tip cart, loaded with sugarcane, passed along with a deafening *gling-in-ding.* The Negro who was driving it threw us either a prying look or a scornful gaze. Then he attacked the old man, jeering:

'*Kouli, ou pa pèsonn! Ou tou pòtré an zékal piébwa lafoud dérayé. Ou pa té fouti tjenbé madigwàn-ou a pasé dé mwa!*' (Coolie, you're a nobody, an old stump burnt by thunder! You couldn't keep your wife for more than two months!)

The Ancestor did not retaliate. He ignored their insults, the spittle that they directed at us, their eyes red with hate, their menacing gestures. This race was more robust than ours in spite of the miseries that the Whites had put them through; and yet they allowed themselves the indulgences of disbelief and faithlessness.

Some pretended to worship Christian gods and dressed up on Sundays in their best finery to go to the church in town but never stopped swearing, quarrelling, drinking rum, chatting up any woman at hand. We nicknamed them the impure ones because the Negroes did not have gods. In their huts there were neither altars nor holy images. This fact left us flabbergasted. Our mothers pointed this out repeatedly in order to warn us against them. We were convinced that they were demons with their strange hair like pepper corns and flared noses.

'You are King Bagiratha,' resumed The Ancestor, clasping my forehead between his hands so tight that it hurt. 'On top of the highest mountain of the Universe, you implore Brahma but He does not appear. Either he does not grasp your words, or he does not wish to hear your pleas. Your prayers roll about in your heart, as vain as the stones torn off the mountain side by an avalanche. But you do not lose heart! You decide to meditate even though at the court, the high priests hardly had the time to teach you this art. Till now, it is true, you preferred hunting tigers to visiting temples and your beauty was such that every night five young princesses shared your bed. In the morning, they ran out, delighted, into the palace courtyard and the servants thronged to congratulate them. From these fleeting romances were born twelve sons and a daughter, just one daughter who had eyes the colour of emerald...Hey Vinesh, keep your mind clear! This is not a dream.'

When I came to my senses, in my field of vision was a pair of boots being struck nervously by a cane. The Béké! The master of Courbaril Plantation, M. Frédéric Houblin de Maucourt himself! This voice belonging to a White man petrified me. I could not understand a word of what he was shouting but I suddenly felt like I was pulled out from the earth. He had grabbed me by the shoulder and shoved me backwards. The Ancestor did not move an inch. Over there, under the tamarind tree, Sosthène, the foreman, had rounded up my little friends and was whipping them with a riding crop made of mangrove ropes. These lashes hurt so much that you could hardly howl in pain.

'Your name, what is it?' asked the master.

I had become a piece of stone.

'You don't have a name, *hein*? Well, I am going to give you a fucking name, my friend! I don't like to see the children of Coolies roaming around everywhere doing nothing. Learn something from my *Négrillons*, they are all in the fields from morning, while you, *hon*!'

'His name is Vinesh, I believe,' said Sosthène, servile, snivelling. 'It is his father who is bothering us with his letter of repatriation...*oui*.'

The Béké burst out laughing.

'Repatriation! You actually think that I am going to waste my money on your trips back home? India, it's over, done and dusted, get that into your heads. Ha-ha-ha! Vinesh, what's that, *hein*? Henceforth you will be called Vincent. I'm baptising you Vincent. Come, make the sign of the cross so that I see that you have understood...not like that, you little moron! From left to right, with your fingers. And on the shoulder socket, not on the chest. Tell me, Sosthène, de Sainte-Foix's woman, his *bougresse* does she not teach catechism to these little savages? As for you, old man, I'm quite annoyed. What do I do with your smelly carcass? You are not even good enough to be thrown into the mass grave, you and your religion of the devil.'

The foreman hauled us like cattle to Plot Cachiman, the most dreaded part of the plantation, where the grass invaded the stalks of sugarcane so densely that lanceheads found their safest refuge there. They were feared by the Negroes as these reptiles didn't ever attack us because our fathers celebrate Sesha the serpent with a thousand heads, protector of Vishnu, at the end of the harvest. The *Négrillons*, who wore themselves out in the fields from *devant-jour*, before daybreak, were too overwhelmed by the heat and by the red ants, to be able to tease us as they did whenever our paths crossed. Plot Cachiman rose in a gentle slope on the sides of Mount Pelée, sneaking in and out between its faults before almost disappearing into the raggedy clouds that covered the summit. The cane-cutters, Negroes and Indians side by side were right on top, almost impossible to make out, followed halfway down the slope by groups of Negresses in charge of tying up the pieces of cut cane into bundles with dried sugarcane leaves. Carts drawn by fearless mules used a mud path which meandered through the cane. Some men lifted up the bundles of sugarcane, letting out a cry which bursts out from the depths of their being. It was the first time that I discovered this scene from up close. My mother always managed to keep my brother and I from field work. Each time that foreman Sosthène passed by the front window of our hut, she invented a pretext and he pretended to believe it.

'Vinesh is a little feverish today, Sir...as for Ganadin, I have sent him to town to run errands for me, *oui*.'

The foreman was not a kind man. On the contrary, this Chabin was dreaded by all, not only because his late father was the same as the father of the master of Courbaril Plantation, but also because he exploded into devastating rages, sometimes for trifles: if you forgot to take a bundle of daily sugarcane leaves to one of P'tite Mamzelle's horses, if an exhausted worker left his machete behind, if you did not greet the foreman himself deferentially enough. But Sosthène had a soft corner for my mother, Devi, a feeling that he expressed in a strange manner. He did not look her in the face nor did he engage in sweet talk like most of the men at the plantation. He settled for tossing at no one in particular, whenever she was in the vicinity:

'*Fanm kouli enmen chaben, chaben enmen fanm kouli, hon!*' (Indian women like Chabins and Chabin men like Indian women, *hon*!)

When he landed in front of each hut, early in the morning, to recruit small gangs of *Négrillons* and Indian pickneys, he treated Devi a little distantly but accepted, unquestioningly the most implausible excuses that she proffered coldly. My mother made light of the penchant the foreman had for her though she was secretly flattered by it. However, she kept it to herself to avoid triggering my father's wrath. Her attitude had protected us so far. Just when The Ancestor had decided to make me into King Bagiratha—the one who had climbed to the pinnacle of the Himalayas in order to implore Brahma to discharge the Primordial Waters once more into the earth—I found myself rummaging through the cut sugarcane leaves for pieces of sugarcane left behind by the *amarreuses* and trying to clumsily tie the pieces of sugarcane into bundles. Beside me, the *Négrillons* displayed a discouraging dexterity and Ti Milo, the son of the farrier began to jeer at me as if I was his punching bag.

'Hey Coolie, burnt matchstick, don't you know that a bundle must have ten pieces. If the foreman catches you, he will give you a walloping, *oui*!'

Out there, a long way off, I could make out the precise gestures of men who were cutting the stalks of cane in three pieces which they threw promptly on the ground. The *amarreuses* who followed them, rushed to gather these pieces while singing Negro songs full of cheer.

On the narrow side of a small wooded hill, a fellow with a head like a dry coconut was beating such a lively rhythm on a drum that even the Indian cane-cutters tried to match their body movements. I was first struck by fear because it was the first time that I was listening to Negro music from such close quarters. Usually, when they went in for what they called the *bamboula* or a *bel-air,* we Indians withdrew into our huts and our mothers closed the windows and doors.

Time and again, a worker broke into a sad monotonous song so heartrending that the day seemed to stand still. One hardly heard the puffing and the panting of the most exhausted of workers or the hissing of the machete as it struck the stalks. The mules stopped pawing the ground. That day, I must have tied together hardly ten bundles of sugarcane but the foreman came to congratulate me, something that seemed to annoy the other little gangs. Taking me aside, when the afternoon was blending into the evening, he made me an offering of a very fat stalk of cane, yellow with orange stripes and said to me, quickly turning on his heels:

'This is a gift for your mother! The *canne-malavoi* is not good for the mill but in the mouth, it is sweet as honey.'

My brother and I got back to our quarter without saying a single word. Our hands were scratched, our skin suffered from a nasty itch caused by the sugarcane leaves and our lower backs felt broken. My mother was waiting for us at the doorstep. She was beautiful and was not unaware of it. The most beautiful Indian woman in all of the north of Martinique, they said, and doubtlessly one of the most courageous since she looked after us all alone when my father Adhiyaman left for the city looking for a better job. Since then, we had had no news. I had never seen my mother cry or complain. Her pain was deep within, at an unfathomable depth, because some nights when the storm rumbled, she went out, stood in the rain, immobile, getting drenched for hours. I had caught her with her hands joined at the chest, murmuring I don't know what prayers. She stood there unflinching as the fat drops of rain fell on her and drummed on the roof of our hut during the rainy season. My grandmother, or at least the old woman whom my mother had taken in and I had ended up thinking of as my own grandmother, who habitually slept lightly, murmured, without speaking to anyone in particular:

'*Aval paattu paadugiraal...*' (She sings a song...)

That particular evening, my mother ordered us to wash ourselves. An oil barrel served as water tank that monstrous toads invaded as soon as the day ended and before we could even plunge the half-calabash into it to draw water. To me she said, holding out a piece of cassava, 'The Ancestor has not finished with you yet, Vinesh. Go, catch up with him!'

I could not disobey. Besides, it would not have been prudent to leave the narrow path which ran along the shacks in our hamlet for all kinds of spirits took advantage of the dark to give vent to their fantasies. Dreadful malevolent Negro spirits they were, with names like *Anté-Christ, Souclian, Zombi, Petite Sapotille, Manman D'leau, Dorlis* or *Père Labat*. Our deities were powerless against them.

Numb with fear, I quickened my pace till I arrived where The Ancestor lived, in the last hut before the forest. He had not moved from his morning posture and smiled seeing my shadow appear in the weak light of the bamboo torch he had driven on the earth.

'There you are, little king!' He welcomed me in a level voice.

'Good evening, Grandfather.'

'Why did the earth find herself one day deprived of water, Vinesh Dorassamy?'

'Holy men who...meditated on the seashore were constantly disturbed by demons who sprang from the depths and...'

'Holy men about to attain infinite knowledge. Repeat!'

One of the holy men swallowed up the ocean and, thereafter, the clouds disappeared and so also the rain. Then ponds, lakes, tributaries and rivers were also dragged into the void. A great thirst filled up the world for an incalculable number of centuries. Humans, tired of chewing on sour fruit, died like flies. It is then that the venerable King Bagiratha undertook to meet the Immense Being. He was received with benevolence and from that day onwards, water began to pour forth down the slopes of the holy mountains.

The Ancestor used to play a double game: obsequious with the Whites and the foreman Sosthène, who insisted on calling him Victor; fraternal with the Indians, especially the newest arrivals, whom he asked for news about the country and who he helped in every possible way. In fact, it was he who saved Radjiv the Brahmin from the ire of the most ardent protestors who owed allegiance to Anthénor and his socialist trade union. They had not appreciated the fact that Radjiv went to Papa Béké and requested him not to be allotted field work. They kept insisting that his story about being kidnapped was a piece of pure and simple fantasy. He had enlisted willingly because the poverty in the entire Tamil country was such that even the high castes had slowly lost their privileges.

'He is the only one amongst you who can read all our languages,' the old man had argued, 'and without his help, we would risk forgetting all the rites that our books describe. Spare him, I beg of you!'

At the ceremonies, the Brahmin, his little monkey perched on his right shoulder, opened a *pustagam*, book, and, in his slightly effeminate voice, read prayers from it. This was a soothing balm for our hearts even though the younger lot, like me, did not understand everything. During funerals, all too frequent in our community, alas, once again it was he who officiated. However he had refused to teach the kids on the grounds that we had rubbed shoulders with *Négrillons*, and so were lost for good. What's more they attended compulsory catechism lessons given by the wife of the overseer de Sainte-Foix every Thursday afternoon.

'It is like carrying water in a basket,' he had said to The Ancestor, curiously using a typically Creole expression. On the evening of that famous day on which I had been enthroned as an avatar of King Bagiratha, at the end of my very first session of gathering sugarcane, The Ancestor welcomed me as someone he had associated with for ages. Almost like the son he did not have for want of a companion of his race in a country where Indian women were cruelly lacking, since the arrival of the first convoy in the middle of the century. No longer aloof, he prepared tea with the help of an old tinplate box of milk balanced on three rocks. Signalling me to sit down on a bench he had made, he continued to stir the drink, adding some mysterious powders time and again. Soon a heady smell arose from the box, a smell that calmed me down and made me forget to some extent the thousand pains that assailed my limbs. I had a stabbing pain in my lower back, my legs seemed to weigh a ton, and the palms of my hand were strewn with grazes due to the sharp-edged leaves of sugarcane.

'Do you know the difference between us and the others? The Creoles...the Whites and the Negroes, I mean to say.'

'No, Appa...'

'*Hon*! these people live in a permanent frenzy, they are always agitated, in a hurry, worried, angry, enthusiastic. They go from joy to sorrow and back in a blink of an eye. I don't know if they were like this already in their country of origin. Perhaps, it is the fault of that country, I'm almost sure of it.'

He caught hold of the makeshift teapot and blew on the drink with all his might and held it out to me, smiling,

'It is an antidote, ha-ha-ha! Well, I mean that it is the opposite of rum; We Indians, we drink too much rum. Much more than the Whites and the Negroes, and this explains why we are so fragile in the face of sickness. Come, taste this, Vinesh!'

The Ancestor was right! We had adopted sugarcane alcohol. Our mothers rubbed us down with rum and camphor when we had flu or were struck by scabies. They added a few drops to the meals so as to spice up the flavour. Our *poussari* drank excessively during the libations at the end of the ceremonies: indeed before these, there was a long period of abstinence and fasting. As for our fathers, uncles, cousins, they over-indulged as soon as they left the fields at four p.m.; To see a drunk Coolie, staggering on the road, or lying in a ditch, a half-finished bottle in hand, was frighteningly normal. The *Négrillons* had a field day hounding these drunks with rocks or playing nasty tricks on them like taking off their pants, making fun of their penises which they found ridiculously small. The Negresses, not to be outdone, heaped sarcastic remarks upon them, not hesitating to outdo them in vulgarity and even obscenity.

'The day a Coolie mounts me,' Firmine the official mistress of M. Houblin de Maucourt usually bellowed, 'well, on that day, pigs will fly and the dogs will bark with their tails.'

The Ancestor's tea possessed magical virtues. I instantly left the sweltering hut of Courbaril Plantation for the shores of the Kaveri, the river my father had told me about. Once again, I could see the enchanted ageless trees, in whose shade the villagers gathered when twilight fell, to hear the epic of the *Ramayana* from the mouths of storytellers.

# 9

## The Jain's Request

*We had not yet set foot here and sugarcane was already working on building this country, chasing away venerable West Indian locusts, macaw flowers of deep red hue, soft tree ferns and savannahs of* zeb-a-pik. *Sugarcane ventured right up to the coast, lying low as the cyclones blew, only to rear up straight away, haughty, ephemeral stalks in the soft December light. And all around just the sound of chains and the fury of whips, just blood, tears, immense joy, pride in work well done, muffled desperation, demonstrative rage. We did not know those times. The Negroes give it a name, always pronounced with their lips clenched: slavery. They aver, their voices heavy with bitterness, that it had come back because we agreed to take their place.*

All along the perilous crossing of the Sea of Fire, even when the storm raged and Nagourmira, the eminent sage of the Mohammedan faith, miraculously saved us, *he* stayed away, refusing food and medication, drinking only rain water. His name was Radjiv and his skin was so pallid that had it not been for his raven-black, long hair and his aquiline nose, he could have passed off as an Englishman. Incidentally, the sailors did not pester him to go down to the bottom of the cargo hold once the morning ablutions were done. Sometimes in the middle of the night, we would hear him hum prayers in a beautiful and solemn language that we did not understand. Sanskrit, a privilege of the men of great lineage. He was the only one not to howl in desperation when the ship started filling with water and the gloomy veiled sky was striated with countless streaks of lightning. Even captain, Sir Alwyn, had gone down on his knees to implore his god. Our Hindu and Christian prayers had blended into a cacophony with our ardent invocations to the Virgin Mary and to Parvati, the blessed consort of Shiva. We had gathered on the foredeck and all differences between our transporters and ourselves had disappeared. The British arrogance had vanished. We were no more than mere mortals awaiting the most horrible end ever. We were going to plummet into the depths of the ocean, into the eternal kingdom of the demons. Radjiv continued to meditate, solitary and frightening at the same time, and some of us believed we saw an incarnation of Brahma the Almighty in him. When we resolved to ask for Nagourmira's succour and the waves subsided slowly, he remained unmoved. When we gave thanks to Allah's messenger during the remainder of the voyage, he simply looked on contemptuously. Radjiv kept silent even though *The White Adder* had reached the Sea of Darkness, which did not deserve its name because it was gentle. Once the Cape of Good Hope was rounded, the British sailors had gone back to their rowdy selves. They had begun to get drunk again, to beat each other up and even tried groping the group of about thirty women on the ship.

'The Atlantic, we know!' They crowed. 'This sea is less treacherous than the Indian Ocean.'

The arrival at the Americas was greeted with a salvo of cheers. Radjiv straightened up and stretched out. His two-and-a-half months of continuous meditation had made him thin. He looked on, unenthusiastically, at these islands of minced land which filed past. Not a soul could be seen. Only the smoke that spiralled out of these mountain tops assured us that they were not inhabited by evil creatures. We were looking forward to setting foot on terra firma. We had been lured from Pondicherry to a new life full of promise. In America, there was no question of dying of hunger and ending up in the jackal's belly like the thousands of our brothers and sisters who had stayed back in our native land!

Here everything grew in abundance, the fruits were so enormous that one could not eat one in a mouthful. We were already dreaming of soursops, cocoplums, guineps, sea-grapes, and all those delicacies the British bragged about. Furthermore, we were assured that the salaries were ten times higher than in India. At the end of our five-year contract, we would return doubtlessly to our homeland as nawabs. Radjiv, manifestly, did not share our dreams. When the ship had finally docked, we saw him pull a tiny broom out of the cloth tied around his lower back, and, with extreme caution before taking a step, he swept the wood boards of the foredeck, seriously damaged by sea salt. We understood then that he was not a Brahmin but a Jain, a holy man who respects the smallest living creature and who is afraid to crush a simple ant or swallow a midge. We used to see them sometimes wandering in our villages, in the great season of religious migrations, a veil of gauze on their mouth, a duster in hand, never stopping to ask for bed and board. Where we only took a morning to cross a mountain pass, the Jains needed three days as they progressed so slowly.

'He is mad!' exclaimed a British sailor, doubling up with laughter. The respect that the crew had shown him, crumbled in one shot at this strange behaviour and we ourselves, already forgetful of our customs, began to deride him. Once ashore, we were cooped us up in a filthy warehouse while waiting for the port doctors to examine us, or so the Captain said. Nevertheless, the meal that they served was delicious. It consisted of mutton with a strange tuber that the *Kapli*, these creatures, black like us but with peculiar corkscrew hair, called yam. Radjiv refused to touch it, always standing apart. The next day, or the day after, because we had lost the notion of time, we were woken up brutally. Two White men, dressed differently from the British and who expressed themselves in a language less harsh, ordered us to line up in the courtyard adjacent to the warehouse. They mangled our names beyond recognition and split us into four groups. My wife Devi, little Vinesh and I were taken into a cart with the Jain. The Negro who drove it did not say a word to us during the journey which lasted an entire day and half a night. Time and again, the White man turned back and asked us:

'Water? Would you like to drink, *hein*?'

And as we did not understand his language as yet, he held out a calabash ensuring our fingers did not touch his. We crossed several villages peopled with Blacks who cursed us using unintelligible words. However, the natural landscape soothed us. We saw mango trees, tamarind trees, flame of the forest, hibiscus again, our noses were assailed with familiar smells and the sky, though more cloudy, was a sparkling indigo blue. When the cart climbed the hill slope we could hear angry waves crash against the invisible coast. We came out onto a straight pathway, lined with ghostly coconut trees, which led us to a huge two-storied house. We were made to await daybreak in an enclosure for bulls and some of us made the most of it, cleansing our bodies with their beneficial dung. The presence of cows reassured us somewhat even though they were fairly different from the ones we were used to. We were lodged in huts with poles from which hung the remnants of chains. Were these former prisons? Places where recalcitrant cattle were tied? We were extremely perplexed. The Jain was overcome with a nasty rage when a man of yellowish complexion, who looked neither Negro nor White and who seemed to order everyone around, enjoined us to move into these huts in pairs, as per our convenience. The holy man demanded a hut for himself alone and rolled his ferocious eyes. This did not look like it impressed the man who we would shortly learn to call 'Foreman Sosthène'. He showed the Jain a sort of lean-to, which you had to bend low to enter, made of rotten planks. The Jain did not hesitate for a split second. He locked himself up inside right away and we heard him start chanting prayers in his language.

We had hardly slept for an hour when we heard a horse galloping in the distance, just as the sun's first rays peeped out. The rider, dressed in khaki and a wide-brimmed hat was as handsome as a god. He rode striking his mount on the haunches with a stick and by his side ran a Negro, a

*Kapli* who struggled to keep pace. In his wake came another man on a very old horse. When they came up to us, we discovered that the man riding the old horse was none other than the strange individual who welcomed us in the night: he had corkscrew hair like Negroes but yellow in colour like Whites. Furthermore, his skin was white and he had sparkling blue eyes which, as we were to realise later, prevented us from looking him in the eye. It was Sosthène, the *mestri*, the foreman of Courbaril Plantation. One of the Indians who had preceded us here, who had come with the very first convoy, acted as interpreter:

'I introduce you to M. Frédéric Houblin de Maucourt. He is the master here. The harvest began two months ago but your help is most welcome. From tomorrow morning, I will come to pick you up. Go and get a bit of rest today!'

The White man did not open his mouth and set off again in a jog trot, his Negro valet following. The foreman turned towards the Indian interpreter who had avoided mixing with us, only translating the questions that were asked or the orders that were given and asked him to take care of us. The foreman referred to him as Victor but he seemed to take no offense. We would soon call this compatriot, The Ancestor.

However the foreman did not worry about the fate of the woman who was writhing in pain although my mother had begged him to fetch a doctor. On the ship, we had as a matter of fact, a surgeon at our disposal who had looked after us so very well, with so much patience that we had ended up conceding that not all Whites were villainous creatures. My wife looked after the ill woman till late at night. A bad drool crept up to the corners of her lips and her gaze became glazed. Her name was Shakti, like the mother goddess. Her wide hips indicated that she must have given birth several times but she had apparently made this trip alone. In spite of the turmeric water that Devi applied on her temples and the salts she made her smell, the woman was sinking. Her death rattle woke up the entire quarter. The very angry Negroes arrived on the double, brandishing bamboo torches.

*'Sa ki fet? Ki sa ka fet?'* (What's happening here?) They bellowed, pushing us aside unceremoniously. Their bulging muscles intimidated us and we kept staring surreptitiously at their strange hair which looked like sheep wool. Two Indians wanted to protest against their taking Shakti away and a mêlée followed. Insults flew thick and fast on both sides. Suddenly my mother who was holding the head of the sick woman on her knees, removed a vial from her bosom and made her drink it. In a blink, Shakti regained consciousness. Her greenish complexion turned to reddish brown, looking more natural. The Negroes opened their thick lips in astonishment and awe. They were convinced that it was some sort of witchcraft. The others cleared out without further ado. I murmured to her:

'Don't waste the water from the Ganges! We will need it...'

The interpreter led us to our filthy huts, in which there was only one room and light came through a skylight.

He informed us that before the Indians came, the *Kaplis* were lodged here, these Blacks who had been pulled out of their country, Africa, to cut sugarcane in Martinique. The Ancestor described the times of slavery as a terrible era of whips, spit and blood. From what he said, this period must have been over hardly more than five years when he, a son of the very first convoy, disembarked from *The Aurélie*, on the island of Martinique in the year 1853.

'Now you understand why they make us come from so far away...,' he added. 'The Negroes refuse to work in the fields except under duress. And then, the memory of their country had faded over the centuries. They ended up considering Martinique as their native country. But all the land belongs to the Whites.'

The next morning, the *Kaplis*, next to whom we all looked like ghosts, observed us with a surly air, while sharpening their machetes on a grindstone. The grating noise did not seem to bother them in any way. To us, the novices, foreman Sosthène distributed brand new tools, bakoua hats as well as calabashes full of rum. Only then did we realise that the recruiters from Pondicherry had well and truly conned us: our work had nothing to do with putting sugarcane out to dry in the sun. We had to bend over in the fields under a merciless sun and that too for salaries very much inferior to those we were promised.

'Appearances don't matter!' he said when we were nervous. 'What matters is endurance, and Coolies have enough and more of it.'

It was a fact that towards midday, some Negroes left the fields, in spite of the reprimands of the foreman who was constantly moving around on his mule of respectable age. The butt of his revolver was conspicuously sticking out of the back pocket of his pants to intimidate us. In the late afternoon, we found the Negroes in Man Ninise's shop, slumped on the benches. On Saturday, our payday, after settling their dues, they hastened to squander their money on bottles of rum or on a game of dice or dominoes. This invariably led to squabbles which ended with the flash of knives.

We Indians kept away from these excesses because we knew that we had to start saving from the first day of our arrival. Penny pinching for our five years of indenture, even if it meant depriving ourselves, leading a meagre existence in the hope of returning to India with substantial savings. And so we went to the fields in the morning without rebelling, all except the Jain who avoided rubbing shoulders with us, only feeding on fruits that he washed at length in the river adjoining Courbaril Plantation. His strange behaviour had first left foreman Sosthène indifferent, but finally annoyed him when the holy man knocked over a calabash full of water which a child was carrying. If we had our own quota of rum and could use it as we pleased, fresh water was another matter. This was indispensable for the completion of work as painful as cutting sugarcane. For this, we depended on a gang of turbulent *Négrillons,* little Negro and Indian pickneys, who went to and fro between the place where we worked and a spring situated two kilometres away.

*'Sa ka rivé'w?'* (What's happening to you?) foreman Sosthène yelled, shaking the Jain by the arm.

The latter wiped himself quickly, with the help of the undone end of his turban and retorted in broken Creole:

'Nobody has the right to touch me. Neither you nor these infidel Hindus. Incidentally, I have not come here of my free will. I wish to see the boss to explain myself.'

'Ha-ha-ha! You think of yourself as a superior being from what I can see, shitty Coolie!' said the foreman ironically. 'Well then, M. de Maucourt will be delighted to hear what you have to say to him. Delighted! Only, after that don't come back to plead with me on your knees to hire you again. Understood?'

**The Kidnapping**

The arrival of a White man whose goodness exceeded that of the most saintly of the Hindu saints had caused a stir in the entire region. However, he was not proselytising like his peers who were always quick to entreat those whom they called pagans to kiss their cross or swear on their holy book—their one and only holy book—the Bible. This man was the captain of a most impressive three-masted ship. Moved by the frightening poverty that had struck the country, for weeks he had been organising feasts on board, feasts to which the most verminous populace of beggars, paralytics, one-legged, women of ill-virtue and abandoned children, were all invited. Rice was distributed freely, flavoured with rare spices whose taste lingered in the mouth. *Kalou*, palm wine, flowed freely. The very first sip could intoxicate the uninitiated. In the morning, women guests who lived in the suburbs were dropped home in rickshaws. Their children were given candies wrapped in transparent coloured paper. Radjiv, who had been moving around Arcot since the end of the monsoon, delivering teachings to whoever was interested, sleeping on the floor of dilapidated temples, felt a deep curiosity for this Englishman so different from others.

He came from a family of practising Jains who had been largely spared by the invader, while the Hindus had fallen into abject poverty. They could no longer afford to feed the holy men as decreed by the Vedic laws since time immemorial. Of course they were still respectful but their hands were desperately empty. Their fields withered, burnt by the sun, they were compelled to protect their seeds against armies of rats. These rodents scampered through roads and villages in broad daylight, no longer afraid of humans. Nobody had enough strength to chase them away and day after day, they seemed more and more audacious, even fighting jackals, their hereditary enemies, over the smallest dead body. Because of the English, the Indians had been vilified, their gods crushed underfoot, their land violated, their rivers soiled by the waste from coal-powered factories. They manufactured rails, corrugated iron sheets, mechanical ploughs and even guns. Refusing to demean himself, Radjiv did not go near the rare dwellings where the smell of food came from. He even turned his head away when he was humbly invited by a sign of the hand to come in. Sometimes his hunger for a young woman's body led him to a liberally offered bed of pleasure. How many children did he leave behind? He would never know.

He watched for several days the merry-go-round of the White benefactor. Nothing ever changed. Always the same honey-sweet invitations, the same libations aboard the ship which never emptied. Nobody could fathom the real intentions of this Englishman who spoke Tamil almost like a native. When he noticed Radjiv, he held forth with great competence on the Upanishads. When Radjiv heard him recite these sublime verses, he knew that he was in the company of a fine connoisseur of antique texts and a friend of India:

*Om, asatomaa sat gamaya*
*tamasomaa jyotir gamaya*
*mrityormaa amritam gamaya.*

(Take me from unreality to reality
Take me from obscurity to light
Take me from death to immortality.)

On the ninth day after the feast, wherein care had been taken to avoid all meat, he agreed to share the captain's table. His eloquent host kept conferring upon him titles that he did not deserve yet, because he undertook to follow the Path only two years ago. His father, a pious man, who saw the end of his earthly sojourn draw near, had inspired him to take this step.

The meal was the most fabulous one he had ever tasted. Even better than the royal feast served by the Maharaja of Chidambaram for the Dattatraya Jayanti which celebrates the union of Brahma, Vishnu and Shiva. Hundreds of people of all castes had piled on to the steerage of the ship where sailors served them many kinds of Indian and European spirits to accompany the most refined dishes while music boxes played the best tunes in the background. Towards midnight, the captain climbed on the forecastle and clapping his hands to draw his guests' attention, announced an incredible piece of news:

'And now my very dear friends, I would be deeply honoured if you accept to go down to the cargo hold of this ship where I have had the nectar of this dream continent called the Americas stocked, just for you. Thirty barrels of rum are awaiting you! Follow me if you please.'

Radjiv, who was already drunk, joined the crowd of revellers who included the Shudras and the raggedy untouchables. Everyone rushed down to the cargo hold. What followed the Jain could not remember. In fact nobody could! The next day, towards the middle of the morning judging by the glaring sun which burnt their eyes, they were hauled up to the steerage all tied to one another with ropes by the British sailors who had suddenly become aggressive. The captain and his assistants, armed with cudgels, were watching the scene, laughing. When Radjiv fully came back to his senses, he realised that the ship must be in the open sea because no land was visible on the horizon. Not one mountain top nor even the banks of a river in the distance caught his eye. Nothing but the still spread of the sea, a sheet of fire of an unbearable blue hue.

'Listen carefully, Coolies!' yelled the Captain in Tamil. 'If you stay quiet, everything will go well for you. I'm taking you to a country, Martinique, where a better life is awaiting you, a thousand times better than the one you have known so far. A life where you will only have to lay out the sugar under the sun, and for this you will be paid richly. In Martinique, there is no distinction between pure and impure; Brahmins, Shudras or untouchables, it is one and the same! Everyone is equal.'

Radjiv understood that their host, the benefactor who organised the endless feasts when his ship was docked at Pondicherry, had in fact drugged them. As a matter of fact he felt his head throb and this headache had nothing to do with simple alcohols made of coconut water, rice or sugarcane. Visions of grotesque creatures, grimacing masks blurred his eyes and he did not feel the weight of his body anymore. He recognised the captain's voice clearly. It had become menacing now, heavy with disdain and derision. He threatened those who would try to rebel with the worst of punishments. All insurgents would simply be thrown overboard. Radjiv fell asleep. He must have slept for several days. A bone-chilling cold woke him up. A great unrest reigned on the ship. The White sailors pointed to a mountainous land, surrounded by a stormy sea, the colour of clear metal and shouted:

'The Cape of Good Hope!'

They made the sign of the cross, broke into a jig, exchanged small bottles of gin, and congratulated each other like people who had narrowly escaped the claws of hell. About ten Indians, that Radjiv recognised as hailing from Coimbatore, on the fringes of the Tamil country, by their accent, took advantage of this moment to surround the sailors. Though tied up at the wrists and ankles, they managed to jostle their captors when the crack of a gun stopped them suddenly. The cries of the men and the crashing of the waves against the hull of the ship died down magically. Radjiv noticed the captain at the poop deck, calmly blowing on the muzzle of his smoking hand gun, jeering. On the deck, an unlucky man lay in a pool of blood, a gaping hole in his forehead. The prisoners were overcome with despondency. They let themselves be beaten up and collapsed, groaning. Radjiv, who was fortunately far from the ringleaders, was spared. The captain then ordered that two of them be unfettered.

To serve as a warning they were thrown into the sea, under the horrified gaze of their companions.

*

As if indifferent to the sarcastic remarks of the foreman Sosthène, the Jain took the road to the *Grand'Case*, Big House; not the one that meandered through the thickets that the cane-cutters and the mule-drivers took daily but the straight alley lined with coconut trees and hundred-year-old royal palms, the majestic pathway which led to the master, M. Frédéric Houblin de Maucourt's villa. Everyone watched, torn between stupefaction and fear. Only Madame's tilbury, driven by a liveried Negro in a top hat, could go that way. Radjiv heard the Indian workers' supplications. They pleaded with him to come back, to be reasonable, predicted the worst punishments for him and for themselves. The Negroes jeered and guffawed, calling him a 'Coolie with a head ravaged by rum'. The hubbub followed him closely and then faded away as he reached the front steps of the *Grand'Case*. He felt dirty, impure, he would later declare to Adhiyaman, the only human being to whom he condescended to speak. A prayer filled his mind, a harsh belligerent prayer, which infused him with a renewed courage although his fingers were shaking slightly.

'Well, Coolie, you don't want to work today?' said a voice from the first floor of the vast dwelling.

It was the master's voice , the owner of Courbaril Plantation. A surprisingly calm voice, tinged with gentle irony: 'You are ill?'

'No, Sir...I must speak to you.'

'Speak to me? But I have nothing to say to you, man! You have not come here to make conversation. Here we cut sugarcane. It is written in black and white on your indenture contract.'

'I have not signed any contract, Sir...'

Radjiv heard him rush down the indoor staircase. He stiffened, ready to confront the White man's anger which he knew to be devastating. Since their arrival, the Indians had twice witnessed a scene which had left them flabbergasted: a Negro, almost naked, that his brothers qualified as *Nègre marron,* Maroon Negro, had been captured with a lasso like a wild animal. This man who did not speak but grunted was tied to a mango tree and flogged by the master till he bled, while his peers applauded. Then Sosthène, the foreman, had put a rope around his neck before dragging him to the fields. There he was forced to cut an entire plot of sugarcane all alone. Although slavery was abolished well over half a century ago, Radjiv learnt that there still were in the woods of Hauteurs Courbaril, on the foothills of Mount Pelée, creatures who wandered about unaware of this extraordinary event. They had fled the plantations of the region at a young age and survived feeding on wild roots and bird eggs. Now that the sugarcane was gaining ground over their refuge, they had to come out into the open, frightened. Their peers had been waiting patiently for this infamy to end, jeered at them heartlessly. Would the master inflict the same fate as these *Nègres marrons* upon him? He was a Jain, a pious and pure man whom everyone in India respected as a living god. He knew scripture. Just being in his presence allowed people of inferior condition to approach perfection.

Inexplicably, M. Houblin de Maucourt had calmed down. He observed Radjiv with curiosity, as if he was seeing him for the first time. Until then, he may not have spotted him in the shapeless mass of Indian workers who piled up in the courtyard of *Grand'Case* each morning waiting for foreman Sosthène to assign them tasks. The master observed this monotonous ritual from his second floor balcony where his bedroom was. He rarely interfered with the decision the Chabin made. He just made sure that his present mistress, either Indian or Negress, was spared the tough work of gathering pieces of cut cane to tie them up in bundles. These women worked right behind the cane-cutters and tied up the bundles of cut cane in lots of ten. Working non-stop, bent double, these women ended up adopting a hunched gait or on the contrary, an excessively stately one, without losing either their freshness or their beauty. They would proudly call themselves '*mâles-femmes*', masculine-women, and choose their male concubines themselves. They would not stop working when pregnant and would often give birth with no help in the middle of the fields. This gesture of defiance left the men dumbfounded. And they would get back to work two hours later, as soon as the baby had been entrusted to an old relative. Even though the Negro race disgusted Radjiv, who found them ugly and vulgar, all he felt was admiration for the *attacheuses*. They were so much more hardy than Indian women and especially less submissive! He still remembered the time when M. de Maucourt noticed Nalima, that girl with a falsely fragile air, who claimed she came from Bengal and whose skin was the colour of honey. Radjiv was sure that she was from a Brahmin family but had not found time to talk to her. As soon as the convoy of tip-carts appeared in the courtyard, and that Nalima's abundant hair adorned with a green bow—began to sparkle above the heads of her companions of misfortune, the master pointed out to her and shouted:

'That young girl, I'll take care of her! Sosthène, make sure you place five cutters at Plot Duragrin. And *arrimeurs*, headers, are needed at Plot Cachiman, I believe.'

M. Houblin de Maucourt sized up Radjiv from head to toe, without saying a word—something that did not augur well. The Jain in the meanwhile pulled out the holy book from one of his tunic pockets (he had quite simply refused to wear a khaki shirt and trousers like all the other Indians), a volume of the *Ang-agams*, the major texts of great Jain literature and announced:

'In my country, I was going to become a monk...I never wished to come here. I was kidnapped. Incidentally, I have written several letters about it to Queen Victoria and to the Governor of Martinique.'

'Be that as it may, I have in my possession a contract of indenture in your name, duly signed by you or so it seems.'

From the Béké's cordial tone, Radjiv understood that he had won the first round.

'It is a fake! I can prove that my signature has been forged. Over there, in my country, my father owned important businesses and held office as administrator in our government, sir.'

Houblin de Maucourt smiled before grabbing the book that the Jain held out to him and began to leaf through it upside down. Radjiv could not contain his spontaeneous laughter.

'Our script is complicated, Sir...but it can be read left to right like yours. Here, let me help you.'

Then in a loud voice, he began to chant the text. It was so powerfully evocative that you did not have to read Ardhamagadhi to fall under its spell. Mme de Maucourt, spellbound, leaned out of a ground floor window. Da Gervaise, the nanny with a loud hollow voice and gruff manners, had to intervene to restore the normal order of things.

'Frédéric, don't listen to this! It is a whole lot of diablerie, *oui*! This *bougre,* fellow, is looking to con you,' she shouted, looking at Radjiv with hatred. For once the Béké ignored her. He led the Jain monk by the arm to the coconut tree alley. Nobody ever knew what the two men discussed. However, from that day onwards, Radjiv was no longer considered as part of the labour force. He came and went as he pleased between Courbaril and the Gradis Plantation that belonged to M. Frédéric's cousin, the famous Garnier de Cassagnac, a collector of rare books. He was happy to accept one of the holy books the monk had brought from India for his library. Finally, we heard that the holy man had won his case: the Governor had convinced the General Council of the legitimacy of his request and the General Council would underwrite the expenses of his repatriation on the first ship leaving for the Orient. All the Indians of Macouba envied him, but they did not even think it to be a favour, since Jains are superior to common mortals. Besides, the man had become an ascetic, standing on one leg, the other folded at the hips. He neither ate nor drank for months although his ribs poked out more and more and his light brown skin turned greenish. Radjiv's eyes burned bright with an inner fire that was both fascinating and worrisome.

Every now and then, he smiled at Adhiyaman or threw an enigmatic phrase his way. That year, the dry season brought in its wake the usual succession of villainous droughts but he did not move an inch. Pious Indians came to lay at his feet calabashes of rice, of boiled pumpkin, tumblers of fresh water but he did not touch a thing. Quite miraculously neither did the turbulent black birds or the stray dogs! A photographer from Fort-de-France came to immortalise this strange posture. His black box mounted on an excessively high tripod with a black sheet which he pulled over his head to get his machine working. A flash of magnesium spurted forth...

All this greatly excited the interests of the inhabitants of Courbaril. But Radjiv remained indifferent. It seems his photo was published not only in Fort-de-France but also in Paris and in different newspapers of Pondicherry and Karikal.

'He won't last till the rainy season!' people predicted. Foreman Sosthène had taken a deep dislike to him, furious that the plantation had been deprived of a pair of precious working hands.

September, reputedly heralding cyclones, looked truly threatening. Torrents of heavy rain beat the earth, cracking it, sweeping away young trees, cattle and sometimes even houses that had not been properly secured. This year, Martinique would have to contend with a devastating cyclone. The old timers guessed this from the restless behaviour of animals. Mules, reputedly impassive, often beaten to make them move, were fidgety for no reason. Goats and sheep did not stray. La Dorée, M. Houblin de Maucourt's revered mount, refused to be saddled. No birds ventured into the sky, except the majestic *mensfenils*, the chicken hawks, flying well above the highest hills. Over there, on the Atlantic, coming from the coasts of Africa, a cyclone was chafing at the bit, ready to devastate the country. Everybody stocked up water, rice, salted cod and medicines. The master of Courbaril summoned The Ancestor and told him solemnly:

'You are the only person who can talk him round, Victor. Go and tell him that I will offer him food and shelter till his repatriation. A ship is expected on 28 September. It would be a shame if he misses it...If he waits for Queen Victoria to answer he will rot away. That shrew died quite a while ago! Go and speak to this Radjiv! I don't want to have his death on my conscience.'

The Ancestor did as he was told. Without much enthusiasm. He negotiated with the Jain or rather wasted his breath for a long time for the monk did not even bat an eyelid. Soon the air seemed to withdraw from the world. Not a single leaf shook in the mango and tamarind trees that surrounded the *Grand'Case*. A frightening silence settled in, compelling everybody to get back home. The municipal siren started wailing in the town of Macouba. It went on a couple more times and then fell silent. One could swear the end of the world was near. Then they waited. For how long, nobody could tell. Night fell earlier than usual in September. It must have been about three o'clock in the afternoon. Adhiyaman and Devi lit lamps around their little domestic altar and implored Goddess Mariamman to protect their family. In each hut, the Indians muttered prayers which sounded like a kind of purring that rose and fell. Through their shutters, they watched the frail statue-like Jain already pushed around by sudden gusts of wind. He was the only creature not yet holed up, both haughty and derisive in the face of danger that got clearer every minute. Vinesh even had the crazy idea of grabbing Radjiv, tossing him over his shoulder to get him home. After all, this man did not weigh more than a bunch of sugarcane. But his father dissuaded him.

'It is Maldévilin's will!' He declared soberly.

The cyclone was as fearful as predicted. It left not a single tree standing, took off the roof of an entire wing of the *Grand'Case* and swept away Indian and Negro quarters. The rivers swelled and transformed into furious torrents of mud. Cattle had either drowned or had been swept away. Women and children, whipped by the rain, abandoned to the prosecution of the elements; their howls mingling with bellowing, barking, cackling or meowing imbued with utter distress. Helpless, stupefied men were watching months and years of work collapse. Not one house or garden resisted such combined fury. In the morning, the master came on his rounds, on foot for once. La Dorée had been given shelter in the kitchens of the *Grand'Case*. Three Indians and two Negroes had succumbed to the onslaught of the cyclone. Their dead bodies, already swollen and covered with fat black flies, lay in the sludge among the animals that had drowned or had been crushed by tree trunks. Several children were missing, surely carried away by the swollen rivers.

'This country is cursed!' shouted The Ancestor. Coming from a person who spoke so little, it sounded indisputable.

Overcoming their pain, forgetting all racial barriers, the men went about putting up again all that had fallen. The women surrounded the dead and were determinedly ridding them of the coat of mud and leaves that covered the bodies. In order to distribute planks, nails and other kinds of tools, M. de Maucourt got the stockroom opened which had miraculously resisted the raging winds. Nobody had managed to utter a single coherent sentence yet. From time to time, some seemed to be losing their minds and started cursing the sky that had suddenly become peaceful. Some were running helter-skelter, others, almost tearing their hair out. Some were calling out in vain the name of a missing child. Then they slumped, *blip*! Curling up, their face buried in their hands and sobbing. Their insanity was respected. The gods, be they Christian, Shiva, Nagourmira or the African spirits invoked deep into the night had been unfair and even vile with humans. How many Catholic masses, Hindu ceremonies, Negro invocations had been addressed to them since the early warning signs of the approaching cyclone. All in vain. A sacrilegious thought crossed Vinesh's mind: Was Théophile not right after all when he maintained that all religions were a lot of nonsense?

This idea was further confirmed when Radjiv the Jain was found frozen in his hieratic posture, exactly where he chose to stay. Beheaded outright by a corrugated iron sheet that the fury of the winds had ripped off from a roof. His little monkey, terrified, was walking around his head, whining and beating it with its tail. A Negro decided to capture the monkey to sell it in town where the well-off Mulattoes were crazy about this kind of pet. No Indian could summon up the strength to object.

# 10

## Crossing the Sea of Darkness

*First convoy, first terrors. The sweet name of the first ship:* The Aurélie. *The dark shadow of the sin of crossing the kaala paani, hovering over our heads, reminding us that this was the most reprehensible of all sins: to abandon the holy land, India. To set off in search of adventures that will inevitably end in sorrows, anguish, unknown maladies, endless conflicts with people of barbaric tongues and of diabolical beliefs. To leave for the other world, the one where all hope for* moksha, *liberation, is vain.*

Her eyes riveted on the dividing line between the two oceans, Devi felt a flush of joy fill her frail bosom. She gripped Adhiyaman's hand, her nails digging into his palm. He smiled. He too thought that the final hour had come when the storm began tossing the ship like a drifting coconut. For the first time in his life, he had implored Brahma for protection. Indeed, the Supreme Being was too far away from human beings to be addressed directly. He was less familiar with Ganesh or Hanuman with his monkey head, or even Kali, the terrible one, the slayer of evil. Incidentally, he had never learnt a prayer to Brahma but he let his fearful heart speak spontaneously. Around him rose a chorus of pleas to all the gods of India, mixed with the supplications of the British sailors who, having shed their arrogance, were invoking Jesus Christ or God the Father. That is why when the ship crossed the raging waves of the Cape of Good Hope to go from the Indian Ocean into the

Atlantic Ocean, he felt that something profound had changed in his destiny and it astounded him. The *sadhu*, an expert in the Holy Scriptures, whom he had consulted before his departure, had read in the stars that he and his family would be protected during the voyage: he, his beautiful wife Devi whom destiny had bequeathed him, his adopted son Vinesh and this baby which was getting visibly bigger in his wife's womb. In his heart of hearts he had already named the baby after his paternal grandfather Ganadin, forgetful of the Tamil proverb that says:

*'Erumai vangum mun nei vilai pesade, pillai perum mun peyar vaikkade'* (Don't talk of the cost of butter before buying the buffalo, nor name your child before he is born.)

He worried about this child during the storm, fearing that Devi, who was constantly vomiting, would deliver prematurely. He knew that it would have been impossible to keep the little dead body on board. Sir Alwyn, the captain, would have had it thrown overboard and there it would have been devoured by evil spirits.

His entreaty to Brahma was earnestly simple:

'O Brahma, Supreme Being, creator of the sky and the earth, master of infinity, protect my son Ganadin's life!'

However neither Brahma, nor Kali, nor Ganesh, nor Jesus Christ, nor the Virgin Mary had succeeded in appeasing the fury of the elements. Adhiyaman, who was still shattered, did not join in the joyous celebrations of the Indian emigrants and the British sailors which greeted the indigo-blue waters of the Atlantic. Devi, too, seemed fascinated seeing the blue-grey waters of the Indian Ocean recede. She muttered a thanksgiving to Nagourmira who had rescued them from the jaws of death. A Muslim saint! An envoy of Allah! How was it possible? Till then, Adhiyaman had deeply distrusted this religion. He remembered the Arab merchants who, long before the British had settled down on the Tamil soil, buying, selling, trading swords, guns, gold, rare spices and sometimes marrying a girl from the country where they decided to settle. Little by little, they started building mosques, humble structures devoid of all decoration, austere, unlike Hindu temples. These Muslims took advantage of their business travels to preach and attracted to their faith a good number of untouchables who were tired of being the dregs of humanity. Then all of a sudden, these new converts changed their names to Mohammed, Khaled or Fatima, women wrapped themselves in white *gonduras* and strutted about haughtily! The antiquated division of castes did not exist anymore for them! Brahmins, Vaishyas, Shudras or untouchables were one and the same. That was not all. They now consumed beef which they swore they had purified using a bunch of Mohammedan tricks. Even a part of the market was reserved just for this kind of meat. When the British took control of India, conversions increased because the invader showed greater consideration for the sons of Allah than for the sons of Brahma. Apparently Christianity was a cousin of their religion. Adhiyaman had resisted the temptation of converting to Islam. In order to escape his fate after the jackals had devoured his parents, he only had to pronounce the ritual phrase known to all, '*La ilaha illallah Mohammad-ur-rasool Allah*' (There is only one God and Mohammed is his Prophet). After all, he was born in that lush and fertile land of Tamil Nadu, this soil which had given birth to much more ancient deities than the Christian god or Allah! If he had reached the highest echelons of society, it was Brahma's will. Brahma had assigned him an intermediate position between the noble Brahmins and the ignoble untouchables, already a proof of his immense goodness.

A few days later, *The White Adder* made a stopover at the island of Sainte-Hélène where they stocked up on celery and watercress which, when consumed daily, kept scurvy away. Two men affected by the disease were unloaded but alas too late: one of them died just before his scrawny body was hauled up to one of the stretchers from the steerage where the sick were kept to get some sun. The other did not get back on board though it took four long days to refill the tanks with fresh water. After the storm in the Sea of Fire, water stored in metal barrels had taken on a foul acidic taste, making children vomit. The *mestri* who was in charge of Adhiyaman's section, Tamby as he was called, became more conciliatory. Till then he had scrupulously noted the names of those who did not wash properly or did half-heartedly—as their dream of seeing America was receding, their number was increasing. And he cracked his whip too when people jumped the queue at meal times. In the morning, like all the *mestris*, he went to the poop deck where the captain and his quartermaster got together to plan the day and punish the wrongdoers. Tamby kept a watchful eye on women by day and by night, but especially at night, because some of them would go to meet their lovers and this led to scuffles between emigrants. He was implacable towards little Vinesh's aunt who had lost her mind after the stop-over at Mauritius. She wandered from section to section, her mouth full of inanities and incoherent words. During the crossing of the Sea of Fire, the European crew and the *mestris* were too busy to rein her in. Had she not sung and danced on the foredeck during the two storms, indifferent to the fury of the elements? But once the Sea of Darkness was reached, the attitude of the petty officer changed completely. Now Tamby forbade the mad woman from leaving her section even to go kiss her little nephew whom Devi had adopted. As they were on the other side of the ship she had to cross over amidst booing passengers, unable to put up with this messenger of madness. Some thought her insanity was contagious and chased her away. Only Devi treated her like a human being in her own right. She would patiently feed her handfuls of cooked rice and thus commanded admiration, because the mad woman ate so greedily, that she was constantly belching and spraying Devi with spit and half-chewed rice. Devi did not complain and never stopped speaking gently in her ear while rocking Vinesh with her free arm and keeping an eye on the *mestri* who was not happy about all this. Tamby had wanted to have the mad woman chained down in the hold after she had bitten two passengers who had tried to help her with her morning ablutions. However, Devi had pleaded her case with the surgeon on board, who convinced the captain so that the mad woman kept on wandering on the ship as she pleased till the day when she began to howl at regular intervals, one word, just one:

*Irattavati!* (Smallpox!)

Little Vinesh's aunt had just called the curse of Mariamman upon the convoy! How could the unscrupulous recruiters at Pondicherry have allowed the mad woman to embark? It was obvious from her eccentric behaviour that she was going to cause problems around her. This mad woman who was called 'Nameless' obviously spread smallpox around her.

The face and the arms of the two women she bit suddenly got covered with purplish blue pustules. A perfidious fever nailed them to their mats. From their lips sprang forth a filthy mess of saliva, phlegm and blood. Smallpox! For the Indians, there was no doubt this was smallpox although the surgeon on board insisted that it was a simple cutaneous eruption caused by bad hygiene. Ever since *The White Adder* had reached the calmer waters of the Sea of Darkness, the surgeon had relentlessly fought for more bath water for the emigrants. He kept up an unremitting battle with the crew. Every morning, a concert of curses rang out on the steerage as the captain looked on indifferently. The sailors struggled to ration the bath water while the surgeon insisted on two buckets for each emigrant. In the end, the crew understood his refrain:

'Give them two buckets! Two buckets!'

But the surgeon rarely got his way. 'The Atlantic is calm in January,' bellowed petty officer Henderson, 'the cyclones here are in September, contrary to the southern hemisphere. Don't forget the currents! You are not a sailor, old boy. Anything can get us to veer off-course. Can't you see that the winds are light? We could easily lose ten, even fifteen days. What will we do when water runs short, *hein*? Give them sea water to drink or what? I have already completed four crossings and, every time, we were behind schedule. Each one can get one bucket, just one! After Sir Alwyn, I call the shots here.'

The Indians refrained from getting involved in this daily quarrel although most of them felt dirty. The salty air had parched their skins. As they headed westwards, the rain showers became few and far between. But whenever the skies opened, the emigrants rushed to the foredeck, jostling each other unceremoniously, indifferent to the shouts of the *mestri*, and stood under the rain, soaking in the fresh water until they were wet to the bone. Adhiyaman blissfully welcomed these brief moments of freedom and forgot his sorrow. In these moments his mother's face eviscerated by the jackals, her fixed gaze, stopped haunting his thoughts. He thanked Shiva and his beneficial locks that had regenerated rivers and tributaries after centuries and centuries of terrible drought. He, the Supreme Being, had created the Ganges, the spring of humanity, from where came this water that fell from the sky.

It washed away all the impurities he had accumulated since his flight from Madurai. But, at that instant he thought that he had now become an untouchable, like his fellow travellers. Even Radjiv, this man of high caste who stood immobile at the prow of the ship, only dressed in his orange turban, naked since the second storm, whom nobody approached anymore, had he not lost his dignity?

When the husbands of the two women were infected too, the surgeon had to acknowledge that smallpox had declared war on *The White Adder*! And we were in the high seas, far from any inhabited land where *The White Adder* could have made a stop-over to allow the dying to disembark. The maps were inflexible: we were, at the very least, three weeks away from both the Antilles to the north and Brazil to the south. Probably more, because if the petty officer were to be believed for several days the ship had been fighting a current which made it creak on all sides. The *mestris* now refused to have the passengers in their sections stand in queue for the morning ablution or the distribution of meals. Healthy passengers spontaneously stood off from those infected, abandoning parents or children to their fate, indifferent to their cries of pain. They prayed aloud in a cacophony of tongues. Tamil, Telugu, Malayalam jostled each other in futile invocations to Shiva, Kannavédi, Maldévilin and even Nagourmira. This time the Muslim saint was as helpless as the others. And the mad woman kept on wailing day and night:

'Smallpox! Smallpox!'

The sea became perfectly calm, so calm that one felt as if *The White Adder* was at a standstill. The weather was splendid. A gentle light spread over the foredeck where the captain finally decided to assemble those who were not infected. All the Whites had sought refuge on the poop deck, letting the intermittently blowing winds steer the ship. The surgeon alone was brave enough to go down to the hold. He came back with a mixture of lime and sea water. This doubtful medication found takers among those who could still stand on their feet; they smeared themselves frenetically with it. These ghostly creatures were twitching, lacerating their flesh with their nails, crying, shouting and calling out to the deities for help. In vain. Adhiyaman understood that this was the third manifestation of the curse of kaala paani. The transgressors were always punished. Even if the emigrants had escaped the two storms in the Sea of Fire, they would not come through this smallpox outbreak. Such was the Sea of Darkness, its radiance and beauty were misleading. The punishment of the Gods had struck us.

Devi, who clung to Vinesh, Devi the courageous, Devi the helpful, the ever obliging mother of the convoy as some emigrants called her, finally admitted defeat. She no longer combed her long silky hair. She no longer exchanged knowing looks with her husband. She prayed no more. When it came to smallpox, that hideous disease, what could one do but wait? When it had taken it's share of lives, it would go as it came, out of the blue, without warning. Out there, in Madurai, the untouchables were always the first to be afflicted. Endless languishing in the midst of rubbish and rats, in shacks where the dirt floors were flooded in the monsoon, hungry stomachs hardly filled with a bowl of rice. They had taught themselves to come to terms with suffering. With death too. Devi though was sure of a good reincarnation because of her good deeds. But in the present circumstances, she found herself reduced to the same level of degradation as those who ignored divine precepts or blasphemed. She too was in the grip of the terrible kaala paani.

The sick, who were still fit, began to throw the swollen dead bodies of their companions overboard; a shoal of sharks following the ship devoured them immediately. A pestilential smell rose from the aft deck where the victims of smallpox had been cooped up. Some, losing all control of themselves tried to get to the steerage but the captain had given orders to shoot them down. Several gunshots tore the still air of the month of January. The two Vaishyas, who had kicked the untouchable from Dharmapuri to death, were amongst the casualties. As if the Gods had chosen to punish them before anyone else. They broke out in purulent pimples which ended up covering even their eyes. They started ripping off their skin, groaning like wounded animals, unceremoniously pushing away other patients to grab the medication prepared by the surgeon. Their white shadows swayed in the light. When they held up their hands, they looked poised for flight. The one who had accused the untouchable of blowing his nose into his bowl of rice was calling out to the *mestri*. But he could only manage bits of sentences devoid of meaning for his mouth was ravaged by smallpox. For three days, he kept up his concert of imprecations and, on the fourth at dawn, in exasperation, he dragged the other Vaishya beyond the invisible line that separated the world of the healthy from that of the dying. Bullets crashed into their chests with a strange dull sound and their blood, which had turned black, coagulated rapidly on the floor in an enormous cesspool that attracted swarms of flies coming out of nowhere.

Adhiyaman was the first to remember that Mariamman was the goddess of smallpox. His father, Ambu, the most pious of men, had erected a statuette of her in the temple in his orchard. Mariamman, majestically draped in a white sari had been installed on a square stone. In each of her four arms, she carried a ritual object. Although she was a secondary deity in whose honour only a simple oil lamp was lit, the old man Ambu began to worship her from that moment when his spinning mill started declining. He would put a garland of flowers around her neck every morning and, kneeling at length in front of her, he would recite the most common of her thousand names in an exalted voice: Shitala, Abirami, Umaiavale, Penpirenday, Ellamma, Maarimutthe. He enjoined his son to repeat these sacred names after him.

When he was sixteen, his father had taught Adhiyaman about the extraordinary circumstances of the birth of Mariamman at Maléalom, in the seventh sacred mountain. A very wise man who was revered as a guru, Penjaren, constantly begged the gods to grant him a child. His days and nights were dedicated to prayer. He ate nothing, hardly breathed. Sitting in the lotus position, after a few years, he attained the ultimate stage of asceticism, the one beyond which men move the masters of the sky. The Gods manifested themselves in a thick smoke that rose from a *vèpèlè,* neem, a shrub with tiny mauve flowers used to decorate the entrance to the temples before ceremonies. The guru drew near and discovered a resplendent young girl whose long tresses reached to her ankles. Overwhelmed with joy, he decided to adopt her even though strange pustules were scattered over her cheeks. From that day on, Penjaren wandered across the Tamil country to sing her glory. At that time, a terrifying disease struck the country, an unknown disease which started with the eruption of buboes on the skin. Raging fevers dried the blood in the veins of the afflicted. Tens of thousands were dying. No sacrifice to Parvati or Hanuman could stop this scourge. Madouraiviren and Kannavédi remained mute too. People then turned to Mariamman, understanding that she had come to earth to announce the revenge of the gods who felt neglected.

Huge pujas were organised in her honour. Everywhere, her statue was bathed, polished and crowned with garlands of hibiscus and bougainvillea. Camphor and incense sticks were burnt at her feet. She was offered jewellery in gold and silver, precious stones and shimmering textiles. Coconuts, whose water is pure, were broken for her. Vegetarian dishes were laid out. She was offered prayers, and mantras were recited. They pleaded with her for help. The worship of Mariamman became more important than the worship of Parvati. Soon her hideous face, covered with buboes, was given a gentle fullness; it was now perfectly smooth. The horrible evil receded from every district and village. Funeral pyres stopped glowing red on the banks of rivers and tributaries. She had vanquished smallpox, and was now the very symbol of it!

But so far away from the motherland, in the middle of the Atlantic Ocean, the frightening Sea of Darkness, aboard *The White Adder* where the captain and his crew were unable to face adversity, how could Mariamman be invoked? How would it be possible to make ritual offerings to her? Would she accept brackish bowls of rice, the daily meal of the intrepid travellers who had left India in the mad hope of a better life? Would she even hear their incantations full of despair? Every day a new case broke out. Children, although isolated in a box room adjoining Captain Alwyn's cabin as soon as the first alert was sounded, were infected too. First they ran a fever followed by an unbearable itch and finally the terrible eruptions appeared. Even though Adhiyaman was not religious by nature, he was convinced that Mariamman was asking for a sacrifice. He wanted to open up about this to the Brahmin, who stood alone at the prow of the ship, perfectly indifferent to the disease that ravaged his fellow beings. However the Brahmin's pet monkey prevented Adhiyaman from doing so. The animal was about, grunting, baring his teeth and extending his claws, as if ready to pounce on the young man. Adhiyaman could have put the tiny creature out of the way with a simple shove but he suddenly saw again, with his mind's eye, the jackal which had attacked him, bitten his arm when he had come back from collecting rice from the rat holes and discovered the bodies of his parents lying in their blood, disembowelled. He remembered the baying of the jackals, the wails of the children bearing an eerie resemblance. Shuddering, he gave up the idea. Through the intervention of the surgeon on board who spoke Tamil, he asked the petty officer Henderson for permission to sacrifice the couple of peacocks that were kept in the cargo hold. The Britisher, knitting his brows, declined point blank.

'Gift from her Majesty, the Queen of England to the Governor of Martinique!' he said in a dull voice.

He also refused to let Adhiyaman use pumpkins, coconuts, oranges and lemons from the ship's stock, arguing once more that the currents could make *The White Adder* veer from its course, thus postponing their arrival in America.

'We have smallpox already. I don't want famine as well! You know I have had to ration rice and water.' But his voice had lost its authority. He trembled at the very thought of falling victim to this disease against which the ship surgeon's treatment of lime mixed with sea water was powerless. 'All your Hindu monkey tricks will serve no purpose. Nothing at all!'

As the captain did not leave his cabin anymore, the petty officer Henderson was at the helm and out of distress he took more and more contradictory decisions. Now he issued an order to the *mestris* to move those afflicted with smallpox down to the bow-holds. Then he decided to isolate them on the aft deck with a barrier of barrels once and for all. As soon as the moaning of the dying became unbearable, he had buckets of sea water poured on the steerage as a kind of exorcism though the ludicrousness of the exercise soon struck him. He then asked the passengers to strip and stand in the sun in the hope that its rays would kill the germs. *The White Adder* was henceforth navigating downstream. Devi, coming out of her state of prostration, said to her husband: 'It is time to use what my father gave you...'

Adhiyaman had almost forgotten about the little bag containing soil from India. So much turmoil since they left Pondicherry! So many affronts! First the woman's fit of insanity, whose baby—Vinesh—Devi had adopted just two days after leaving the Coromandel Coast. Then the passing away of Anandam, his father-in-law, a week and half later, as much out of despondency as exhaustion. After that, his mother-in-law had disembarked at Mauritius. On top of that, there were the frightening storms, especially the second one that Nagourmira, the Muslim saint, saved them from. Then there was the massacre of the untouchable from Dharmapuri by the two arrogant Vaishyas. In this accumulation of horrors, what endured—though almost like a dream—was only the memory of his night of love with Devi while the storm threatened to dismantle the ship. Adhiyaman searched in his small bundle of things for the last gift from his father-in-law. What a surprise to discover that it did not contain just soil! Between his febrile fingers which were trying to untie it, he felt something crackle. It was probably straw, or crumbled newspaper. He could not believe his eyes when he discovered a small branch of a mango tree, a tiny twig, crowned with three leaves which had become dry and brittle. The mango tree, the sacrificial tree, the holy tree of Kali and Mahabil! When burnt, it exudes a subtle fragrance that almost intoxicates the deities. The smoke that emanates from it is very light too.

This time, Adhiyaman disregarded the petty officer Henderson and turned into a *poussari,* the mediator between men and the immortals. After praying to Goddess Mariamman at length, imploring her to put an end to the epidemic, he set down the mango tree branch in the middle of the steerage and lit it with a little bit of tinder. The fire began to crackle, progressively purifying its surroundings, transmitting its energy to all. For once, the healthy and the sick gathered together, hands joined in prayer, and invited Mariamman to consume their humble offering. Someone drew near and rekindled the fire with *ghee,* sacred butter. Mariamman waited for the mango tree branch to be reduced to ashes to manifest herself. Then each one felt her purifying hands come upon them. All the dirt accumulated during the two months of travel was wiped out little by little. The skin of the smallpox afflicted suddenly peeled off, shaking off the ignoble pustules which the wind carried away. The fever, which made them twist and turn like puppets in a market fair, subsided. Their eyes sparkled again, their hearts beat furiously with joy. Adhiyaman thanked Mariamman in a voice so loud that it drowned out the noise of the waves. Assembled on the poop deck, the European sailors, dumbstruck, observed this new miracle. They lowered the guns that they had brandished when most of the emigrants had drawn near the fire. They thought it was a mutiny. When the petty officer Henderson realised how ridiculous the crew looked, he hoisted the sails of the foremast and asked each crew member to get back to their post. *The White Adder* seemed to awaken from the lethargy that had choked her since the epidemic broke out. She seemed to be shaking herself and even rearing in front of the waves. She was now racing ahead, sure of her course.

'Mariamman will always be with us,' whispered Adhiyaman to his young wife, who was still astonished at the audacity of her man. 'Even when we are out there, in America, I'm sure she will watch over us...'

# 11

## The Itinerant Strike

*The Negroes are reluctant to mention the times when they lived in chains, when the whip lacerated their backs; the very word 'slavery' itself they cannot utter. But their executioner is still there, comfortably settled on the flat and fertile plains and on the hill slopes, he has now reached the outskirts of towns.*

*For his hairy cohorts still toss their green manes haughtily in the wind.*

*It is called sweet reed; its soft name hides a nameless terror.*

Their grandmother, Amma, a self-effacing woman, would say—in her voice full of fear—that these processions were coming from far away, sneaking up when God's back was turned. If one climbed up to the top of Morne Balai, one could make out strange luminous caterpillars which constantly followed the remotest tracks, almost at the forest edge. Time and again, the sound of the drums reached the hamlet, carried by the fickle winds of the Atlantic. It did not augur well. Amma would not stop moaning in subdued tones, which amplified the already muffled sounds of Tamil.

*'Kaalai suttrina paambu, kadiyaamal vidadu'* (If the snake curls around your leg, it means it will bite you).

One morning, the Indian workers found themselves alone in the plantation courtyard when the foreman called out the names. Not a single Negro or Mulatto showed up that day and, for once, the climb uphill to the sugarcane plot was silent.

Vinesh felt a sudden chill in the cleft of his back which had nothing to do with the early morning temperature. He grasped his machete like a robot and fell into step with his companions, wondering what could have happened. No Christian festival had been announced, nor was any important personality from Fort-de-France expected. He remembered the time when the Governor, the head of Martinique, came in person and the Béké had granted everyone an unpaid holiday. Fortunately, the Governor's office had thought of distributing demijohns of rum and boxes of dried cod.

*'Se Neg-la, yo ka fè lagrev,'* (The Negroes, they are on strike) Sandji, the dump-truck driver who officiated in the Indian ceremonies as the drum beater, whispered to him.

Strike! Each time Vinesh heard the word, it sounded even more terrible! It echoed drily, like a bang. The young man got down to work, indifferent to the sting of the sugarcane leaves on his cheeks. The foreman, Sosthène, perched on his horse, harassed them more than usual and every one of them could tell that an irrepressible anger was boiling inside him. They just started harvesting three weeks ago and a good half of the cutters had decided to put down their work tools. This delay would never be made up, especially if the rains were early, as they often were. Vinesh tried hard to the step up the pace and began to feel his arms turn numb; this was good, it would allow him to go on till the hottest hours of the day. Around him, the cane fell relentlessly, sectioned into three equal segments, but there were no *amarreuses* to tie them up in bundles of ten for the dump-trucks to cart off to the mill.

Only Negresses, *mâles-femmes,* masculine women, could do this work for they were strong enough; their Indian sisters' constitution was too weak. Besides there were so few Indian women! Every time a ship coming from India was announced, the rumour in Macouba was that the new contingent of indentured labour coming from Karikal, Yanaon, Calcutta or Pondicherry, would include a fair number of women, but these hopes were quickly dashed. One woman to thirty or forty men, this was the invariable ratio. Unfortunately, if one of these women was of exceptional beauty, the master of the plantation or his overseer hurried to keep them under their thumb by hiring them as cooks or washerwomen for the *Grand' Case*, the Big House. From that moment on, they were out of reach for both the Indians and the Negroes. Once she had settled in and accepted her lot as a White man's *femme-dehors,* mistress, she could benefit from all kinds of favours, especially if she bore the White man's child. Such was the fate of Nalima, that unreal creature who disembarked from Karikal, in February on a day when the sun seemed to stop its course and the usually chirpy birds fell into silence. Vinesh and the rest of his friends had immediately identified her as coming from Calcutta, unlike the overwhelming majority of Indians who came from Malabar, and had taken a dislike to her. He had seen in her the manifestation of Parvati, Shiva's spouse and had convinced himself that she was here to save her race from the hell of the plantation. The very next day after her moving in she disappeared. Well and truly disappeared! Some thought she was a hallucination. All sorts of fantastic tales were spun about her: at times she was a princess from Bengal who had come to enquire from the White man about the fate of Sacred India's sons. At other times she was a witch who was getting ready to unearth the bodies of Indians buried in the dishonourable part of the Christian cemetery. She would then carry their remains to the bottom of the oceans to feed the demons. None of this could stand up to the banal and brutal evidence: Nalima had become the favourite mistress of Béké de Maucourt and, on Sundays, she went to mass in a tilbury, dressed like a fancy European lady. The Béké had built her a little house behind the Big House in great haste, very close to a magnificent garden of allamandas, Chinese roses, yellow hibiscus and bird of paradise flowers. The Indians came to look down upon the young woman and pretended not to notice her when by chance their paths crossed. As for the Negroes, they sniggered to no one in particular:

'Coolie woman has not honour! The White man only has to shower her with money and she will open her legs wide for him.'

In fact, jealousy was gnawing at them because many Negresses allowed themselves to be straddled by the master and paraded Mulatto babies in their arms. It was true that none of them had been put on a pedestal as high as Nalima's. Shaken, Vinesh in turn fell in love with this woman who was despised by everyone. He did not lose hope of a tête-à-tête with her one day and was certain that he would convince her to flee with him to America. Because now he knew that his parents had been tricked into believing that they would be sent to this promised land where their only task would be to spread sugar out in the sun. Neither the Antilles nor Martinique were really America, according to Théophile, a *Blanc-France*, the young White man from France, who worked as a teacher in the primary school of Macouba. Curious about everything, Théophile had got friendly with Vinesh, and asked him to teach him some sentences in Tamil.

*'Annou! Zot ka moli, tonnan di brez! Lajounen-an pòkò fini, non!'* (Get on with it, don't dawdle! The day isn't over!) bellowed the foreman, pulling Vinesh out of this daydream. Only then did he realise that three men had been appointed for gathering the cut cane and tying it up neatly in bundles, the *amarrage*, a task they performed so awkwardly that it was comical.

'A bundle is made of ten pieces of sugarcane, silly fool,' raged the foreman, untying dubious-looking bundles.

He took out his folding rule from his rear pocket to measure the length of the segments. If one of them happened to be less than a metre long, the name of the perpetrator was immediately written down in the foreman's notebook. On the following Saturday, the errant cutter was paid less; if he were lucky, he would be let off with a thrashing. Vinesh had never been treated like this. He was considered a serious worker, a role model, an example to follow, and so he was pilloried by the recalcitrant Negroes. The supreme insult, '*Flatteur de Blanc*' (White ass-licker), flew thick and fast as he walked past and though it was unfair, it shamed him terribly. Had not his father, Adhiyaman, come to this country to work, get rich and go back to India once his five-year contract was over? How could he be hanging around doing nothing like the Negroes? They had lost their country, which they called Guinea, forever and were incapable of even describing its shape. Did they not loathe that obscure place they come from and call each other names like 'damn savage Negro from Guinea'?

At the end of the day, only one-third of Plot Jeannette had been harvested and an unbelievable quantity of segments lay strewn on the ground for want of *amarreuses* and gangs of Negro pickneys. These sugarcane segments would no longer be good for the mill if they were not removed quickly because nothing dries faster than sugarcane. The bark would start taking on a brownish hue before shrivelling up and getting so dry that even bulls and mules refused to eat it. Foreman Sosthène gathered the workers under a mango tree where calabashes of fresh water awaited them. After allowing them to rest briefly, he delivered a virulent speech, rapping out each of his words lest those who could not quite understand Creole, stopped paying attention. 'To go on strike is a Negro matter! The Béké is very upset and ready to crack down on them. He asked the Basse-Pointe Police Station to bring this gang of agitators back to their senses.'

'You, Indians, stay out of all this! It is not for you. You are good workers, you take good care of your families and don't waste your time drinking rum or playing dice. Stay united! Don't let yourself be charmed by the honey-sweet words of Sire Anthénor who is no more than a troublemaker, a socialist! Negroes never liked Indians and if now they pretend to care about your lot, it is only to con you and to sabotage the harvest. Negroes are a cursed race. It is written in the Bible!'

However, as night fell, the luminous glowworms continued to roam the surrounding woods. Workers who had come on foot, sometimes from thirty or forty kilometres away—even from Le Robert and from La Trinité—armed with torches and drums, went from plantation to plantation to urge workers to go on strike. Sleeping under the stars, eating little, fruits gathered on the edge of the road or the remains of a meal that they were offered, they moved inexorably towards Courbaril Plantation.

Meanwhile fear gripped the Indians. These itinerant strikers had the ill reputation of burning everything, thrashing those who refused to join them, assaulting women, stealing jewels and silverware. They had been denounced from the pulpit on Sunday morning by the priests, presented as unpatriotic, denigrators of the national blue-white-red flag by the mayors of the towns they walked through, but they went on, inexorably stopping the harvest. After they visited a plantation, field hands hardly ever resumed work, either because the strikers took away with them most of the plantation workers, or they threatened to cut off the cowards' balls on their way back.

**The Apostles**

My mother had waited in vain for the plantation shop to receive some rice flour, an unknown ingredient in Martinique. Incidentally, Man Ninise had guffawed when I came to ask for it:

'Rice flour? What is this now? Only the Coolies get such ideas. Go and tell your mother that here there are only two types of flour, *farine-France*, wheat flour, and manioc flour. Nothing else! You have to teach these people just about everything.'

Tired of fighting, my mother had to make do with manioc flour which seemed to her softer and purer than wheat flour, perhaps because it was made locally.

She poured a bucket of water on our dirt-floored courtyard. Then she squatted and took a fistful of grain, letting it pour slowly between her fingers as she drew clever patterns. Her confident hand made a series of triangles and circles, dots and strips with a dexterity which left my younger brother Ganadin and I speechless. The figures spread out for almost a metre. She performed this task, whose significance we ignored, with a smile of profound beatitude, as if deeply moved. Lost in this trance, she did not hear our neighbour Kumari warn her:

'*Devi, tansion kò'w, mafi, mi labé-a ka vini!*' (Devi, watch out, my dear, the priest is coming!)

My mother mixed small heaps of manioc flour, some

with blue powder, some with curcuma powder, some with a piece of lipstick bought from the Syrian peddler Abderramane, and others with crushed charcoal. With supreme skill, she undertook to colour the auspicious patterns, which looked magnificent under the June sun.

Seeing us stupefied while we observed her fresco, she jovially quipped:

'Messieurs Vinesh and Ganadin, I hope you will remember how I did this, *hein*...? Ah, I know; *kolam* is not a man thing, but we are in another country, we live another life...these patterns pay homage to our mother Goddess Lakshmi. They are a protection for our home and a sign of welcome for visitors, too. And I am sure...'

She could not finish. The white shadow of Father Xavier, who had come from behind stealthily, covered the fresco. The man was sturdy, almost a giant, and his voice terrorised us on Sundays at the nine o'clock mass when, from his pulpit, he denounced the turpitude of Negroes and the witchcraft of Indians. According to him, the former were but a gang of fornicating-lying-cheating-good-for-nothing braggarts who had to be brought back to the right path, the one shown by 'Our Lord Jesus Christ'. As for the sons of India, he rebuked us for clinging to what he called 'a bunch of pagan practices' and worked on turning us away from them by force. Nobody had forgotten the raid he organised three years ago with the Belgian Redemptorists, a raid during which a number of our holy books and our statues were destroyed. Since that awful day, most Indians from Hauteurs Courbaril headed to the Catholic Church resignedly, while continuing to pray to their own Gods in secret. Little India, a quarter on Gradis plantation whose owner, M. Granier de Cassagnac, was an agnostic, became our refuge. He was not hostile towards us and had even appointed a person of our race to the envied post of foreman. Come what may, Z'Oiseau, as we had nicknamed him, continued to keep alive the tenuous flame of faith which was our last link to Mariamman and Maldévilin.

'What are you doing there?' barked Father Xavier, pointing

to the *kolam* with his square chin which gave him a more military than an ecclesiastic air.

'I am dr...I am drawing the Apostles, Father', said my mother.

'The Apostles...ha-ha-ha! You take me for a fool, don't you? This, this is their face, no doubt...and that their robe, *hon*? It is strange, but I don't recognise any of them.'

The priest squatted next to my mother, and began to examine the patterns with a perplexed eye. Ganadin and I were holding each other's hands, trembling. We wished our father was there but he left for the fields at dawn. Our hamlet was almost deserted and most of the women were too busy with their household work to be interested in us. My mother, who had recovered from her surprise, repeated that she had sought to represent the twelve apostles in the Christian religion. The sincerity of her tone astonished me. In any case she unnerved Father Xavier, who abruptly got up, began to count the intertwining figures with the tip of his fat black boots:

'One, two, three...six, seven...eight...'

After each number, he stopped for a few seconds and tried to decipher the pattern which corresponded to it. His bushy eyebrows, strewn with white hair, knitted together in a way that did not augur well. That man feared none, neither Negro obeahmen, the *quimboiseurs*, nor Indian priests, nor even the master of Courbaril Plantation, M. Houblin de Maucourt. Loud-mouthed, he went about everywhere proclaiming:

'*I* take care of souls! May those who only have an earthly mission do their job and let me do mine.'

Then he continued to count, implacable, an eye on the fresco, the other on my mother who did not move an inch.

'Nine...ten...eleven...twelve! Unbelievable! There are twelve patterns, Devi. I am delighted, dear parishioner. De-lighted! But let me give you a piece of advice, in future, avoid these geometric patterns, these curves, these gaudy colours, all this is a bit pagan, almost voodoo. The Apostles were men like us, quite simply they had a thousand times more affection for Jesus Christ than their peers. Therefore, I know it can be difficult for you, I am scarcely a draughtsman myself, but try at least to give them a human appearance, the next time.'

The Abbot caressed Ganadin's hair, held out a firm hand to me and turned on his heel. His immaculate cassock gave him the appearance of a big bird about to take off. He knocked at our nextdoor neighbour's, Kumari, and went right in without waiting for an answer. My mother straightened up and began to laugh. *Tjip!* Sucking her teeth, like the Negresses, which denoted irritation, derision and 'fuck you' at the same time.

'Vinesh, go get me a pail of water from the barrel, please!' She ordered, holding out the pail. For the rest of the morning, my mother drew her *kolam* in front of our house. In my heart of hearts, I began to count each of the new patterns to finally reach the number...twenty-seven.

As the strike headed towards Courbaril Plantation, Houblin de Maucourt became more and more nervous. One morning, very early, he came on horseback to our quarter, looking gloomy. Two obsequious fellows gathered around La Dorée who seemed very thirsty, as if she had covered several kilometres. They offered her a bucket of fresh water scented with *neem*, a plant our ancestors had introduced into the country and that the Whites preferred to call Indian lilac. Usually, it was used to cleanse the insides of our temples during ceremonies in honour of Shiva and Mariamman.

'I am back from Sainte-Marie,' M. de Maucourt said to us in Creole. 'Things are heating up out there! The Negroes have ransacked a distillery and burnt several sugarcane plantations. They pretend to demand a raise but in reality, what they want is to ruin the colony. Nothing else! You, on the other hand, you are honest and serious people. You are my Indians, my children. I ask you not to get mixed up in this bacchanal. When they get here, rush up to Savane Miguel! Foreman Sosthène will accompany you. I have called the police station for help, they will be here in less than two hours.'

Nobody asked a single question. We all stood, eyes riveted to the ground, unable to hold his blue gaze. Intimidated. Submissive. The Béké came to me and took me by the shoulder.

'It is you, Vincent, right?'

'Yes, yes, Boss...'

'You are young, you are sturdy, I have big plans for you. At Habitation Gradis, my cousin is very satisfied with his Indian foreman. In the beginning, everyone laughed at Z'Oiseau, remember! A Coolie to be in charge of a harvest, who had ever seen the like? I am sure you had your doubts too, but now there is proof that the best amongst you can do as well as the Negroes or the Mulattoes, if not better. Isn't it true?'

'Yes, Boss...'

'From today, consider yourself the person in charge of your people, my dear Vincent. When you are up there, at Savane Miguel, speak to them, explain to them that they should not get involved in this fucking Negro strike...If all goes well, in two or three years, foreman Sosthène will retire and you will take over from him.'

The Béké did not give me time to answer. He got back on his horse, greeted us and trotted back to the Big House. The Ancestor came to congratulate me.

Well stricken in years, he now rarely left his home. Was he not the son of the first convoy? It went back to such a long time ago that most of his companions were dead or had been repatriated to India. He shook my hand affectionately, proud of the promotion just granted to me. My mother, Devi, who had not yet found comfort since my father's departure to *L'En-ville,* the city, cheered up for a brief moment. One by one, young and old came to pledge loyalty, which embarrassed me mightily. I had never learned to command and I reckoned that among them there were men more experienced than myself.

Why had the Béké chosen me? Was it by accident or had it been a well thought out decision? I could not say. I had always kept a careful distance from the world of the *Blancs-pays,* the Whites from France for whom I had neither hatred nor affection. Deep down, the Creole world was similar to ours with its own castes and taboos. Right on top, the Békés—Brahmins; in the middle the Mulatto—Vaishyas, and at the bottom the Negro—Shudras and still further down, we others, the Indians cast as the pariahs. Or so said Théophile, the metropolitan school teacher, and I found it accurate, except that, contrary to India, here no deity had decided this. The Supreme Being in this country was sugarcane. It had created the island from scratch, had shaped it according to its own sweet will, and yet no one worshipped it. No temple had been built to celebrate its glory and if Whites were to benefit most from its generosity, one never saw any of them even come close to it. Wielding a machete under the scorching sun, wearing yourself out cutting sugarcane for half the year, transporting it to the mill in tip-carts or on the back of mules to transform it into sugar and rum: all this was the destiny of Negroes and Indians. Sometimes Chinese, Chabins or Mulattoes. Never Whites. Never.

Two days after M. de Maucourt had appointed me for the job which did not have a name (even if now everyone saddled me with the title of 'Boss'), the itinerant strikers were coming up to Courbaril Plantation. It was announced by the roaring beat of *bel-air* drums at the hottest hour of the day, when most of us had decided to allow ourselves a *pause-tête,* a short break. Without any warning, they occupied fields, savannahs, bull enclosures and the black shack alley as well as our Indian hamlet. Simultaneously, they also surrounded the Big House, the master's sumptuous dwelling. Our women got scared and whipped the children back into their stifling houses and locked themselves up. Some women began to pray, invoking the help of Maldévilin or Nagourmira. We men did not move an inch. We were taken completely unawares.

We expected the strikers four or five days later; and meanwhile I meant to plan our escape to Savane Miquel, up there, in the woods. Anthénor, the trade unionist, led the strike, surrounded by more than a hundred cane-cutters, mule-cart-drivers, *amarreuses* and mill workers. Some were brandishing machetes, others pitchforks or cudgels, yet others simple bamboo pikes, weapons which looked derisory but were extremely dangerous in such hands. And they sang war chants in a Creole so unusually solemn, that we, Indians from

Courbaril Plantation, were rooted to the spot. I felt like a lame duck, my throat dry. Gathering the little courage I had left, I walked up to the strikers, some of whom had eyes reddened by tafia.

*'Sé wou ki majò pasé pèsonn!'* (You are the bravest!) Anthénor threw at me with biting irony.

'Bloody traitors! Coolie bastards! White men's dogs!' the crowd began to scream.

'We will crush you, you'll see!' added a raging woman.

Behind me, I knew my people were petrified. They did not have the strength to breathe, much less to run away. And where would they run? The whole of Courbaril was under Negro control. The Maucourt family was barricaded in their castle even though the master had six-shot rifles at his disposal, which he fired in August at the opening of the hunting season.

'Are you with us or against us?' shouted Anthénor. 'Vinesh, don't tell me you've become the White man's pimp. Your father, Adhiyaman, was a good man. He never flattered anyone.'

'What do you want from us?' I managed to get out, ever more at a loss.

'Don't act like a fuckwit!' raged a man with no teeth. 'Until White men increase our wages, not a single stalk of sugarcane will be cut, and you, Coolies, watch out for your arses if you think you can support their villainy.'

With a gesture, Anthénor calmed the crowd that was ready to fight. He stood on his toes to scan the crowd and shouted:

'Moutoussamy, where are you? Come forward, comrade!'

There was an Indian amongst them! I was both flabbergasted and a little reassured. There were surely about thirty Moutoussamys in the region, I did not know them all, and doubtlessly in the municipalities of Sainte-Marie or Le Lorrain, from where the strikers had come, there were just as many. I was far from expecting a legendary being to appear in front of me on this scorching afternoon.

But there he was: Moutoussamy of the ninth convoy in person! I had heard about him from my very early childhood. The Ancestor, Foreman Sosthène, Z'Oiseau, the priest who had dedicated his life to Maldévilin, my own father had all spoken about this rebel's life in such glowing terms that I had come to look upon him as a hero from our ancient epics. He was equal to Narasimha, the Lion-Man, the fourth avatar of Vishnu, who vanquished the demon Hiranyakashipu who had been granted invulnerable powers by Brahma himself. Moutoussamy was equal to Rama, an avatar of Vishnu, who was exiled by his jealous stepmother to the forest. There his wife, Sita, was kidnapped by Ravana, king of Lanka, and Rama defeated him in battle.

Moutoussamy was there in front of me, in the flesh, a human among humans, Indian among Negroes, the itinerant striker, exhausted from having walked, without a break, the forty-odd kilometres between La Trinité and Macouba, full of unwavering determination. His story could be summed up in a couple of words: the Sepoy Mutiny. An expression ceaselessly repeated by those who mentioned him and it took me quite a while to decipher it. The story was so captivating that it could pass for a legend from the *Ramayana*. Rejecting a marriage arranged by his father, Moutoussamy fled the Tamil country for Dali, stopping along the way at various work sites that the British invader had opened, to get a job. After working as road-mender, navvy laying tracks, rice sack carrier, carpenter and even cook, he had ended up enlisting in the prestigious Fifth Sepoy Regiment. This elite corps was the native jewel of Her Gracious Majesty's army and he was sent wherever rebellions broke out. He put all of them down successfully.

The uniform was beautiful, all red and bordered with black velvet. He won his first stripes when his company put an end to the atrocities committed by the dacoits, these gangs of thieves who terrorised the Lucknow area. They did not hesitate to plunder English convoys, putting the guards to the sword, be they Indian or European. The booty was then transferred to an inaccessible mountainous region, which Moutoussamy's regiment besieged for close to three months before dislodging the *dacoits* from there. But if the people were grateful to the sepoys for maintaining law and order, they rebelled more and more against the intrusion of the British into their daily life and against their contempt for local customs. The compulsory vaccination campaigns against smallpox provoked riots around Banaras and Allahabad because people feared that it would challenge the will of the Gods. The annihilation of the power of Maharajas and Muslim princes ended up outraging the people: Hindus, Jains, Muslims and Zoroastrians, Brahmins, Kshatriyas, Vaishyas and untouchables, men, women and children, and even the elderly stopped toeing the line. The British invader was assaulting the holy land, reducing its inhabitants to the state of pariahs. If nothing were done to stand in the way, Brahma himself would lose interest in their fate. Nevertheless, what sparked things off was an incomprehensible provocation by the chiefs of the Army of India who distributed rifles with cartridges coated with beef and pork fat to the sepoy battalions. They tried to compel the Indian soldiers to tear these cartridges with their teeth, provoking the revolt of the Meerut garrison quickly followed by the Kanpur and Lucknow garrisons. The people joined the rebels, massacring all Whites including the soldiers, administrators, missionaries and doctors. Portraits of Queen Victoria were torn or burnt, the Union Jack reduced to shreds. Victory seemed close at hand when the invaders called upon the bloodthirsty Sikh warriors and Gurkhas. These men did not fear death and fought to the last. The sepoys had to beat a retreat and withdraw into Delhi where they were surrounded. At the end of a four-month siege, the city fell and Moutoussamy was made prisoner, escaping miraculously while the local population was exterminated. Amnesty was declared after the surrender of the last rebels. These rebels were given a choice. They could either rot in jail till the end of their days or leave to work on the sugarcane plantations in America. Moutoussamy chose the second option. Against his will.

Thus Moutoussamy walked to the front of the procession. Wearing a large bakoua hat and a shirt in khaki, he might have looked like a perfect Creole had it not been for his pony tail fluttering in the wind. Some said he was almost as old as

The Ancestor but in spite of his advanced age, his stature was as imposing as his light brown eyes, an uncommon feature among Indians. Unlike his Negro companions who were all reasonably excited, there was great calm in him. He carried no weapon. He came up to each of us, without saying a word, stared at us with a paternal air. This reassured me. Suddenly he grabbed my wrist and said to me in Tamil:

'You are the boss if I'm not wrong!'

'*Va...vanakkam...Neengal nalama?*' (Greetings...How are you?) I stammered stupidly.

'You are supporting the White man, young chap!' he asserted. There was no sharpness in his voice, it was as if he were stating the obvious. Turning towards the strikers, he enjoined them to wait patiently under the shade of the mango trees which bordered the colonial road. They obeyed immediately. We were shocked. Moutoussamy, the Coolie, had the upper hand over these Negro Creoles who saw us as a race of traitors? These Negroes who said we had sold ourselves to the Whites, who referred to us as White Man's rags?

*'Vini'w!'* (Come here!) he said to me.

We walked to the manioc mill from which smoke had been rising for several days. The pleasant smell emanating from it seemed to soften Moutoussamy even more. This was despite the fact that Indians didn't care as much for cassava as Negroes did; we found its taste bland. For us it would never replace the taste of rice. Although rice did not grow in Martinique, we found it in plenty at Man Ninise's shop, and when it was in short supply we preferred to buy bread made with French wheat flour instead of manioc pancakes. Leaning against the mill, Moutoussamy crossed his arms and, looking me in the eye, told me:

'Indians and Negroes, Negroes and Indians, same thing! Is our skin not the same black colour? The White man has always tried to divide us but, now, we must hold our heads high. Just because we have signed a contract, we don't have to obey him to the letter, dammit!'

His last sentence, pronounced in a tone of contained rage,

rattled me. He was using the same language as the socialist trade unionist Anthénor, the only one among the strikers to be champing at the bit. This was dangerous language, seditious even. Very few sugarcane workers dared to use it for fear of receiving a letter from foreman Sosthène.

Negro-pimps were not uncommon on Courbaril Plantation. The most abominable among them was none other than the keeper of the Spanish fighter cocks that belonged to M. de Maucourt, *Bec-en-or*, Gold Beak, so named because his teeth were yellowed by strong Macouba tobacco. Used to make raw cigars that were called *boutes* in Creole, as aggressive as *brûle-gueule*, short-stemmed cigars, they gave out a thick and foul smelling smoke. These cigars were thus the prerogative of braggarts and those who, like *Bec-en-or*, enjoyed a privileged position. We, Indians, settled for simple cigarettes: Mélia. Although *Bec-en-or* kept tabs on his people on a priority basis, and was always prompt to protest against the way they were treated, he did not forget us either. On that matter, he would hammer his philosophy in all possible manners and when it was least expected.

'The Negro rejects the sugarcane because he is a good for nothing, the Indian because he becomes mad!'

Anthénor was the only one not to fear the Negro-pimp because he was a war veteran, having fought in the Dardanelles and that was very prestigious. Although he was an enemy of the Christian faith, on Sundays he put on a suit and tie like his peers and strutted around the town church forecourt, his chest covered in medals. As a result, neither Békés nor the European police dared go after such a valiant defender of the motherland, although deep down, they were hoping that one day, the proud trade unionist would be found stabbed in the back. That he should obey Moutoussamy's order to wait patiently stupefied us. Much later on, I heard Anthénor declare that compared to the sepoy mutiny, the battle of the Dardanelles was mongoose piss. According to him, although Moutoussamy had received no medals, he was head and shoulders above Anthénor in bravery.

'The only thing I ask you,' said Moutoussamy, observing that I was not reacting, 'is to lay down your machetes, fuck! We don't need you to join us or to pick a fight with the Whites. Stop work right now and you'll be okay, that's all.'

I was distraught, it was a terrible decision for the brand-new chief that I was. I knew the consequences: my family would be thrown out of Courbaril plantation and we would run the risk of not finding a job in the North, where M. de Maucourt had the ear of the big planters. I thought of my mother, Devi, who had gone through so much trouble getting her life back on track after my father's departure to Fort-de-France; of Ganadin, my younger brother, whose meagre education would not save him from labouring in the fields. And of me: my dream of taking over from Sosthène as foreman in a few years as M. de Maucourt promised? That would go up in smoke too. Once more, we would become 'Coolies without a master', be homeless, surviving on the fringes of plantations or in the most squalid quarter of Macouba, built against a gigantic cliff lashed by the Atlantic during the rainy season.

'Vinesh Dorassamy, I spoke to you, yes, you!'

Moutoussamy was yelling now. Out there, near Colonial Road, some Negro strikers had begun to curse Indians. Anthénor, regaining his *sang-froid* as a trade unionist, had to calm them down. I looked for the wrinkled face of The Ancestor, a pathetic life-saving buoy. I saw that my mother was crying, softly, motionless under the merciless sun as the morning ended. What gloomy premonitions were tormenting her? Would our Gods betray us once again? Had we not deployed all the fervour that we were capable of to celebrate Mariamman and Maldévilin, Nagourmira and Kali? I became aware at that moment that we were alone, abandoned on this island separated from India, the country of our ancestors, by two oceans, on an island, Martinique, where a solitary unjust God reigned: sugarcane.

'*Nou...nou la épi zot...*' (We...we are with you...) I managed to stammer, taken aback by such audacity.

Shouts of joy erupted from the group of strikers who

began to sway to the sound of an imaginary drum. Negroes and Indians mingled as brothers immediately, the Negroes more demonstrative than sincere, the Indians torn between incredulity and relief. My mother came up to me and put her head against my chest. Her temples were throbbing. We did not have time to congratulate each other: a troop of policemen on horseback came hurtling upon us, clubs and guns in their hands. What followed cannot be told: the crashing of breaking bones, frightened cries of fear of women and children, hand-to-hand fights, bayonets against machetes, all peppered with abuses in French, Creole and Tamil. The loud report of shots fired. The bucking of horses, panic stricken by the rain of rocks which was falling on them. Calls for help. The groans of despair. And then silence. Excessively disproportionate silence in the stifling midday air. Time had stopped dead. Moutoussamy lying lifeless, disembowelled, his eyes strangely laughing. Anthénor riddled with bullets, one of which decorated his chest almost like a star. Negroes and Indians plunged in the same irrefutable distress. Itinerant strikers were itinerant no more. It was time, high time to find the way back to the cane fields. From the very next day, at the first song of the rain-bird. As if nothing had happened. Foreman Sosthène, still draped in his deep-rooted agressiveness. The Béké Frédéric Houblin de Maucourt, imperial as ever, riding his mount, la Dorée, whom we would have to greet. Only the tales told during the wakes would now celebrate the exploits of two warriors fallen on the battle field: the hero of the Dardanelles wounded in his flesh but who managed to cling to life, and the rebellious sepoy who lost his.

# 12

## Dream on the Banks of the Ganges

*Godless, lawless animals, the jackals roam on the banks of the river where the dying are laid out. During the day, they hide. We are too weak to howl. Our desperation drives us into silence. The times of impurity have come; beggary reigns, spinelessness and cowardice abound. Even the* Mahabharata *has stopped pouring out its verses; its grandeur now means nothing to us.*

Every night, I dream of a great band of light flowing from the tresses of Shiva the Benevolent, marking the end of centuries of intercession. For King Bagiratha had finally won his case. Ganga, the daughter of the Great Himalaya, had first refused the terrestrial sojourn her father had offered her and the great distress of humanity continued unabated with lamentations and cries of agony filling the air. Shiva, whose words are sweeter than honey and more refined than cardamom, found a way to convince her to pour forth on our heads. The God contained the fury of her waves within his excessively long tresses before letting them hurtle down the enchanting slopes of the Holy Mountain and spread out on the plains, covering thousands of kilometres. On her path, she regenerated millet and paddy fields, banana plantations; she healed the wounds of lepers, restored eyesight to the blind, and consoled the victims of misfortune and mourning, like a mother who had been long deprived of her progeny would. O Ganges, beautiful and sacred lifeblood!

My mother, Devi, bathed me in it the day I was born. She remained in water, which reached her waist for three entire days. On the eve of our departure for the Americas, she insisted on diving in it one last time, her hands clutching my little body against her breasts. In reality, it was the Kaveri River, an avatar of the Ganges in her mind. She begged to be forgiven for leaving India and disobeying the tutelary deities' orders! She had to. Since in our region the British had dispossessed the farmers of their land and had settled there to grow cotton and cotton only, a terrible hunger had begun to gnaw at us. We survived on boiled leaves and tender roots. Birds began to die and finally, the weakest of us collapsed from exhaustion, lying face down, eyes eaten by the ochre dust of the roads. Then hordes of emboldened jackals came out of the woods to devour our bodies, even those in which a remainder of life continued to flicker. A race of demons—the British with their red hair and chalk-colour skin—had seized our country and dictated a rule inappropriate for our customs. They looked down upon us, jeered at our temples and declared our statues hideous. We had to leave!

I never knew whether I was born a few weeks before we left India or on the ship, in the high seas, on the Sea of Fire or the Sea of Darkness. My parents remembered the name of the ship, *The White Adder*. Or perhaps I was born on Courbaril Plantation, some time after my parents, Adhiyaman and Devi were sent there. Opinions differ on the subject. At the time when my father was still invested in the world, he said that I was a son of this new land, this Martinique for which I felt a muffled and enduring mistrust. He never spoke of the lost land and paradoxically tried to make me love this new country by inciting me to partake in the games of the *Négrillons*, Negro pickneys, whose quarrelsome and often belligerent nature intimidated me. As for Tamil, he kept it for whispered conversations with my mother when we, kids, had gone to bed and they believed we were asleep. To my brother Ganadin and to me, he only spoke a chaotic Creole which he had managed to glean from the mouths of foremen. On the contrary, my mother swore on her life that I was born out there, not far from the Great River, that it was this blood that flowed in my veins as in the veins of true Indians. A pious woman, she maintained a tiny altar in a corner of our house, honouring Goddess Mariamman. A lamp burned night and day in front of an etching which represented the Goddess. We had to ensure this quivering wick continued to burn even in her absence. If by some mischance, the wind were to put out the lamp, we would lose divine protection forever. Nobody asked for my opinion, but I believed that I was born in the middle of the Atlantic Ocean and its unexpected storms. This idea came to me when the school teacher, Théophile, marvelled at what he observed as my rolling gait. Everyone noticed my style of walking, something they took for arrogance. Envious Negroes were wont to throw this in my face:

'Look at that Coolie! Who does he think he is? As if the earth were not good enough for him, *oui*!'

They were mistaken about me. How could they ever guess that since my early childhood I had lived a double life? During the day, I was the son of this country, the generous soil of Martinique, a hundred times more generous than the Madurai soil, out there in India, where my family was born. I spoke Creole and a little French, especially since Nalima, the gorgeous woman from Calcutta had granted me secret rendez-vous every time her lover M. de Maucourt had business in the city. I experienced none of the difficulties which paralysed my parents who had never been able to get used to these strange languages. I was the son of the last convoy and felt no shame about it. The son of the fifty-fifth convoy, as Théophile, the young school teacher from France, says. I took an instant liking to him the day I saw him stand up to our master and to foreman Sosthène. These two were always looking for more hands to work on the plantation and did not hesitate to lure young Indians from school with sums of money that the children thought were stupendous.

My younger brother, Ganadin, who was getting ready for his fourth year of primary school, had responded to the sirens' song without our knowledge, and this for a good half of the harvest. That very year, the First World War broke out in Europe. Negroes enlisted by the dozen to defend what they called their motherland, thus deserting plantations to the great displeasure of Békés. They said they wanted to pay their blood tax, a tax that would forever sanctify their affiliation to the French nation. We, Indians, were kept away from this patriotic unrest. Parades, with tricolour flags proudly raised and triumphant marching bands, were not for us. We remained foreigners. Did our contract of indenture not provide for our repatriation to India at the end of five years of good and faithful service? M. de Maucourt had got into a memorable fury when at least half his Negro workers had favourably responded to the call for conscription. A military camp had been set up between the municipalities of Macouba, Basse-Pointe and Ajoupa-Bouillon in order to sign up volunteers from the far north. Poor fellows who usually wallowed in insignificance now paraded in uniform, an army cap perched on their heads. Cane-cutters exhausted by years of hard labour, mule-drivers and labourers in charge of the loads, workers from the sugar mills and distilleries, who considered themselves superior to the humbler *gratteurs de terre*, earth scrapers, as they called those who worked in the fields. Under the direction of three European non-commissioned officers, this entire troop learnt how to the march, to assemble-disassemble-reassemble guns, to shoot, to read ordinance survey maps. Including those who could not read nor deliver a proper French sentence.

'Because of these stupid Teutons,' the master of Courbaril Plantation raved, 'Negroes in Martinique, Negroes have managed to get promoted. *Hon*!'

'You are not French,' he harangued us. 'This war does not concern you. India has not declared war against anyone, as far as I know. You have come here to work, not to laze around.'

So, that was how labour became scarce and M. de Maucourt decided to recruit Indian children. At age twelve, we were thrown into the sugarcane field, machetes in hand. At age ten, we joined the little gangs to gather segments of cane. At age eight, we were brave enough to go back and forth from the plantation to the spring, with enormous calabashes on our heads. Then we went from one plot of cane to the next to quench the thirst of cutters. Young Indian women, although very skinny, made good *attacheuses*. Foreman Sosthène, who knew all the plantation workers (over a hundred), did not assign kids who he had pulled out of school in the same fields as their parents. Adults were quite surprised to see their neighbours' children working so hard along with them on the plantation but Hindu reticence forbade them from asking questions. Each imagined that their parents gave their consent! It was Théophile who, worried about my brother Ganadin's repeated absences, planted this idea in our head. Ganadin, the puny fellow, played the foreman's game so well that we could never have guessed that when he put on his plastic sandals, arranged his notebooks in his school bag and hitched it on to his back, in reality he was heading for Savane Miguel, a bullock enclosure in the hills. There, Indian kids were warmly welcomed. Sosthène and Marcel Polygone, the steward distributed an appetising snack washed down with a tumbler of pure rum. Then these kids were assigned to a sugarcane plot where, in gangs of three or four, they spent the entire day. Little Indians received no salary but they had unlimited credit at Man Ninise's shop. They were let off one hour before the adults and headed straight for the plantation shop where they stuffed themselves with sweets, potato cakes, slabs of chocolate and guzzled bright pink or green sodas that drew them like flies. Then with the connivance of the plantation shop owner, they gathered around the metal keg filled with rain water and washed themselves clean with Marseille soap. At four pm, they returned to their parent's home with their school bags on their backs. This merry-go-round lasted forever. Long enough in any case for Théophile to blow his top. There were three school teachers in the town of Macouba but Théophile was the only one who really bothered with country kids. His colleagues were a Negro always wearing a business suit, sporting a monocle and using a walking stick with a silver handle, and an unreliable Mulatto who spent half his time making students repeat by rote the names of the different cities and villages of France. Both considered themselves superior beings because they came from the city. The Negro, Nestor Pommier, quoted Alfred de Vigny or Albert Samain at wedding banquets, baptisms and even funerals, which made him very highly regarded among *la négraille,* Negroes. The Mulatto was nicknamed *Alexis-grands-mouvements,* Alexis-the-jumping-jack, a lasting nickname, which caused his real name to be forgotten. The two men mildly appreciated Théophile's efforts to convince plantation hands to send their children to school.

'We must first form a black elite,' said Pommier, losing his temper. 'Later, we'll see.'

'Black and Mulatto!' *Alexis-grands-mouvements* corrected him with a guffaw.

'The Mulattoes have already obtained more than their due. Look at the General Council of Martinique, all councillors have been Mulattoes since the end of the nineteenth century.'

'Pommier, you are jealous, man! Ha-ha-ha!'

The two men agreed on one point: little Indians, not being French, had no right to reap the benefits of the republican school. This attitude revolted Théophile, the European school teacher, who was younger than them by ten years and not attuned to the racial subtleties of the little insular world. That is why he ended up going to Courbaril Plantation and thereby discovering the truth after he had conducted a survey. He felt great affection for my father Adhiyaman, who was not very communicative but had told Théophile the story of his flight from Madurai, the Indian province where he was born. Théophile was the first to speak to me about the terrible story of the jackals who had devoured my father's parents during the famine that ravaged India, a good number of years earlier. Neither my father, nor Devi, my mother, had wished to confirm his claims.

'This little White man has too much imagination!' my mother snorted when I was bothering her a little too much about that. 'We did not come here willingly. I already told you this ever so many times, Vinesh, we were kidnapped!'

In fact, she was only weaving the same legend that most Indians repeated over and over again. Even if I did not speak Tamil to perfection, even if I stumbled upon some words too difficult to pronounce, I understood everything. All Coolie families, without exception insisted on this. Be it my mother's family, the Vellayoudons or the Velaidomestrys or the Singaravelous or even the Saithsoothanes who were very fair skinned and Muslim, a fact that they kept secret, but which I guessed from the way they stayed scrupulously away from Hindu ceremonies in honour of Mariamman or Kali. Nevertheless, they all refused to admit that they had signed a contract of indenture as per rules and regulations. As a consequence, on the ominous day when my father asked to be repatriated to India and the Béké refused citing the considerable debts that we had accumulated at the plantation shop, I did not understand my father's anger. He began to brandish his indenture contract and to scream:

'I signed for five years, damn it all! It's written there. I never wanted to end my life in America.'

Alas! Nobody was moved.

As a rational boy, I saw a contradiction between the idea of us as victims of kidnapping and the fact that our parents had this precious document. Wrapped in dried banana leaves which are more resistant to termites and humidity than regular paper or newspaper, this indenture contract was hidden most often under their straw mattress. When Théophile revealed to my parents that my younger brother Ganadin had deserted school for a good two months, their reactions were very dissimilar. At the sudden gleam that lit up my father's usually dull gaze, I understood that he was deeply satisfied. He had always dreaded that the White man's school would make us forget Tamil and give up our Hindu religion. Till then, he had only expressed his feelings in veiled terms and, now, I discovered in him another man. I was imbued with pride. The sad and scrawny person whom I was a little ashamed of had just transformed into a warrior in front of my eyes. Yes, there was no other word to describe his bristling up when the school teacher argued that school was the only path to salvation for little Indians. My father, Adhiyaman Dorassamy, was a warrior! I regretted that I had not realised it earlier. I had looked down on him in my heart.

'Those who don't go back to India,' he said in a voice so sententious that it left Théophile gaping, '*eh ben*, they will buy bullocks, they will buy land and you will see, in no time, they will stand up to White men. I can assure you!'

My mother exploded. Never had her beautiful face been deformed by such irritation. She was busy preparing lunch, peeling our daily breadfruit, putting the quarters to soak in half a calabash of water in which some slices of dried cod, cloves, allspice leaves and a little bit of Colombo paste were floating.

We did not think for a minute that she was paying the slightest attention to what the two men were saying. My mother, Devi, was always so reserved. So tender too. So courageous in adversity. Always ready to help her neighbours without them asking for it. In all these years I had never seen her get angry. Never! I was astonished to hear her express herself in flowing Creole and full of analogies like the Negressses whom she hung out with only on Mondays, when they went to the river to do the washing.

'*Genyen tè, élivé bef, ou di? Men, Adhiyaman, ou ka révé tou doubout! Ou konpwann sé Bétjé-a key kité Kouli maché anlè pié-yo? Ou pa ka wè nou sé dènié ras apré kapolad ba sé moun-tala?*' (Buy land, rear bullocks you say? But Adhiyaman, you are daydreaming! Do you imagine that White men will let Coolies walk all over them? Don't you see that they consider us like the worst of races, even worse than the monstrous toad?)

She added: 'When the school was built in Macouba, it was too late for Vinesh. But Ganadin can still be saved. He does not look his age, fortunately! I want him to become a doctor or a lawyer. There is no future for our children on the plantation. None. If they remain here, they will go on cutting cane forever. Besides they will be the only ones, because look at little Negroes, almost all of them go to school. Their parents fight for them to escape from the land, while you want to chain yours to the canefields. At least if we were allowed to work at the mill or the distilleries, they could have become fitters, welders, coppersmiths and mechanics. For this, you have to be able to read-write-count and the Saturday wage is better. To cut cane you only need strong arms and immense resignation.'

My father seemed stunned by this diatribe. Only Negresses dared to stand up to their men. Indian women were a model of discretion and obedience. Then the warrior changed into a violent husband. He slapped Devi and barked:

'*Ou mèyè ka koké épi koumandè-a, hen? Sé pou sa Sostèn pa té ka blijé Vinesh ek Ganaden travay adan sé tibann-lan? Atjèman, man ka sézi!*' (No doubt you fuck the foreman, *hein*? That is why this bastard Sosthène does not force Vinesh and Ganadin to work in the little gangs. Now I understand!)

Théophile intervened. Had he been a *natif-natal*, a local Creole, my parents would have murdered each other in front of the entire neighbourhood who had gathered there because of their noisy altercation. But the school teacher was White, not a *Blanc-pays*, a descendant of the White plantation owners from France. He had come from this great faraway country, France itself, which we imagined as rich and beautiful. Martinique was only a tiny colony of this country, lost in a remote place of the Americas.

When I had to pick up Ganadin from school, the days when the rainy season unleashed torrential rains, turning the paths into rivers of slush, I could not keep myself from stretching my neck through the class window to admire the French map which adorned the walls covered with mould. Théophile had taught me to decipher the names of provinces each of which was coloured in pink, or sky blue, or green or blood red, the entire thing topped with small black drawings representing vineyards, smoking factories, railways, cities with tall buildings: *l'Aquitaine, Le Bassin Parisien, La Bretagne, La Lorraine*. As many strange and attractive words which echoed in my head like magical doors to a life that I could not imagine. Nevertheless, I knew it was better than mine here. Incomparably better. However, on the way back, I cursed France just the same. Wasn't this country the cause of our misfortune? Had it not shamelessly snatched us, Indians, from our native land to throw us onto this island, the antechamber of hell? If you only looked at it hard enough, you realised that it was just a gigantic sugarcane field whether you went down south or crossed it from east to west. Here, in the North, in Macouba, my family was settled, on that Courbaril Plantation which belonged to that heartless Béké, Houblin de Maucourt. The plantation covered three-fourths of the quarter which went by the same name and sugarcane ruled supreme, leaving only bits of barren land to build huts and grow vegetable gardens.

The metropolitan school teacher was persuasive. The warrior lowered his guard, apologised to Devi and clasped her to his chest in a rare gesture of indiscretion. When our neighbours learnt about foreman Sosthène's villainy, they were indignant and promised that, as of the following day, their progeny would find their way back to school, come what might. And if Papa Béké dared object to this, they would not hesitate to call the socialists who incidentally had just won local elections in the neighbouring town of Basse-Pointe. Till then, Indians had kept away from strikes, they had neither rebelled against their derisory wages nor protested too violently against the stalling tactics aimed at preventing them from being repatriated to India but now, enough was enough! To have school-age children work in canefields was against the law, even though M. de Maucourt ceaselessly boasted of being the sole master after God, master of his plantation workers. If he persisted, they would appeal to Immigration Control.

'They seem to be getting ready to replace the governor but that will change nothing, ladies and gentlemen! The power of these brass hats stops at the outskirts of my properties. Never forget Courbaril Plantation had belonged to my family for six generations. My ancestor arrived from Anjou in 1694!' Our boss laughed mockingly. Nothing could be done. The Immigration Control officers were the only ones who could give us justice.

Thus, during the day I was living here, in this country, La Martinique, on this plantation where I cut sugarcane without any hope of escaping my fate even if for some time now, the name of Henri Sidambarom had been mentioned quite a bit. He was a Tamil from Guadeloupe, who had been struggling for the Indians to get French nationality. However at night, as soon as sleep overtook me, which happened the moment I hit my bed—rags laid out on a cask of dried cod—I travelled in a dream to the India of my parents. It mattered little whether I was born a few weeks before they embarked on a ship for the Antilles or at Courbaril Plantation itself. This uncertainty, cleverly maintained by my parents, only needled me during the day. As soon as darkness began to fall on our hamlet, I became Indian again, little by little. I no longer saw rows and rows of canefields, the manioc flour mill, the stables, the corrugated iron roof of Man Ninise's shop, the monumental volumes of the *Grand'Case*, the Big House, with its straight avenue lined with ageless royal palms. This filled me with a sense of immeasurable well-being. I felt soothed, ready for meditation. It was certainly not a feeling of happiness—a state forbidden to us! I felt progressively freed from the heaviness of my surroundings. Even though none of us spoke about it, I was certain that all Indians, even the sons of the first convoy, who arrived aeons ago and got ultimately used to Courbaril Plantation, experienced the same elation as me. I guessed it from the hint of a smile which adorned my mother's face when she was getting ready for her nocturnal ablutions behind our house. I felt it when my father lit his terracotta pipe and enjoyed tobacco imported from a country called Madagascar. And when velvety silence engulfed our Indian quarter despite the shouts of joy or swear words of Negroes striking their dominoes on the greasy tables of the rum shack. Despite the irritating chirping of *cabris-des-bois*, local crickets, and croaking of frogs in the thickets or stray dogs barking at the moon, India seeped imperceptibly, inexorably into Courbaril Plantation. Neither Whites nor Negroes had any inkling of this. These frenetic Creoles were enjoying themselves in another dimension, on another time scale.

As a matter of fact, only a handful of us were capable of setting out in a dream on the return journey to the Madras Presidency, as some wistfully called it. Z'Oiseau, my initiator, a foreman at the adjoining Gradis plantation, the only one of our race to hold such an important job, an eminent *vatialou* who could convoke the gods and regularly practiced *kotumpavi*—a ceremony performed during severe droughts to beseech the rain gods—preferred to call it *Pays Z'Indiens*, 'country of the Indians'. His parents were from the ninth convoy but people insisted on calling it the tenth convoy. This was perhaps to honour the tragic memory of the ship named *Souvenance* which left from Pondicherry after the fateful date of 15th March, and never reached her destination. Z'Oiseau had never set foot on Indian soil and yet he described it in great detail to the recently arrived emigrants. He simply said:

'Every night I return to *Pays Z'Indiens*.'

Out of respect, no one expressed any doubts.

One afternoon, as I was going back home after catching some crayfish, I left my little companions near a canefield to answer the call of nature. Immediately my friends taunted me:

'*Vinesh, pa kaka an bagay Bétjé-a!*' (Vinesh, don't shit on the Whiteman's belongings!)

At Courbaril Plantation, everything was the 'White man's belongings'. Crops, fruit trees, cattle, dirt roads—not the paved roads though, which belonged to the town—springs, rivers belonged to the Whites. Even obscure valleys filled with an inextricable mesh of guava trees, rose apple, custard-apple trees and *zeb-a-pik* where long-beasts with big fangs are hidden; all these were the White man's property.

Negroes, superstitious at heart, called snakes 'long-beasts' because they were convinced that if you uttered the word, a serpent could suddenly appear. They wondered why they did not scare us. The fact is that, out there in Madras, we had learned the art of charming these reptiles, some of which were far more dangerous than the lancehead which haunts sugarcane plots. Negroes accused us of being as deceitful or treacherous as reptiles. 'Coolies or long-beasts, that's one and same thing,' they taught their children. They did not appreciate that we didn't share their hatred of sugarcane and treated us like new slaves.

Just when I was about to lower my shorts to squat, a mocking voice made me jump!

'*Hé,* little *Z'Indien,* what are you doing? Don't you respect your parent's work or what? Tomorrow, when they come to cut cane, do you want them to tread on your stinking shit or what?'

Shamefaced, I wanted to steal away but the man held my arm. His grip was soft but firm. Surprised that my father had not taught me to relieve myself the Indian way, he pulled out a banana leaf, spread it on the soil, and turning his back, asked me to empty the contents of my bowels, an expression that seemed very funny to me. I let two plops of shit drop and hurried to put my clothes back on when once again, he stopped me. Breaking a large yautia leaf sprinkled with water droplets, he flung it at me:

'We, *Z'Indiens,* we are clean people. Wipe yourself with this! By the way, where do you come from? I've never seen your face in Gradis?'

'I...I'm from Courbaril...'

'Aaah! From my boss's cousin's place? Do you know what becomes of Nalima? You know, that beautiful *Z'Indienne* that he keeps at his place?'

I shook my head. I knew that we had become the laughing stock of the Indians and non-Indians of Macouba. For once, they had a superb Coolie woman and the Béké had grabbed her. If the planters had all the women who worked for them at their disposal, they allowed them to cohabit with whom they liked as long as these women rushed back to the White master whenever he snapped his fingers. It was even an honour for a number of Negresses, Mulatto, Chabin and even Indian women, otherwise so reserved, to bear a child for the White man and their companions were rarely offended by this. These men did not think they were cuckolded when their partners slept with the White man, no matter of honour here. Besides, many favours were heaped upon the chosen one of the moment. She was spared hard work in the fields, her companion could take as much time off as he wished without a cent being cut from his wages. And to crown it all, when a baby was born, the Béké would become godfather to his own child. On each New Year's Day, this child would receive clothes and toys; later he would be spared joining gangs of Negro pickneys. He would go to school wearing real shoes and have brand new books. When he grew older, he could receive his share of the inheritance. Not much though! A few acres of land close to the woods, a loan to buy a lorry or a *taxi-pays*, a local bus to convey passengers to and from Fort-de-France, corrugated iron and bricks to build his house or a few letters of recommendation to *Béké d'En-Ville*, a Béké in the city, a wholesale trader or a shipowner who would hire him straightaway.

Nalima's case, the princess of Bengal, was another matter. M. Frédéric Houblin de Maucourt had practically made her his second wife, openly and publicly. His wife Eugénie and his longstanding mistress Firmine were well aware of it. The little house he got built for her, next to the botanical garden where he grew rare plants and trees, made tongues wag; but no one dared criticise this in public. People grumbled in kitchens, spat into the dishes which the master wanted to be delivered daily to his new favourite. Washerwomen would lose or spoil Nalima's linen purposely. In addition to these envious Negresses, Indian women themselves were outraged by this unusual union and gossiped in hushed tones. Honestly speaking, the transformation of this young girl into a zealous Christian scandalized them.

Luckily Z'Oiseau lost interest in Nalima's fate and asked me about my family. He seemed to respect my father, Adhiyaman, with whom he had a chance to speak during a Hindu marriage celebrated last year. The Dorassamys were a high-profile family in Madurai, he said pensively, they used to own a spinning mill, they were rich, but along came the British and they ruined them. He held forth for a while, telling me facts that neither my father nor my mother had thought useful to reveal to me thus far. I got yet another confirmation that my paternal grandparents died of hunger and were devoured by *chiens marrons,* wild dogs, in front of their son, under Adhiyaman's eyes.

'We call them wild dogs,' said Z'Oiseau, 'but they are not really dogs. They are insatiable creatures, jackal is their real name.' I tried to imagine them and felt the hairs on my arm stand on end. I saw a monstrous animal with the body of a dog, the head of chicken-hawk, the legs of a toad and the skin of a snake.

'Your father is a brave man,' he continued, taking my hand. 'He crossed the entire Tamil country on foot to reach the city of Pondicherry. Come! I have something to show you, Vinesh.'

We walked down a track that burrowed into the heart of the plantation. It was bordered with tall sugarcane which proudly displayed their flowers, the myriad miniscule white stars that withstood both rain and wind. We reached a circular savannah in the middle of which was a wooden shack. Two tall bamboo poles stood on either side, at the end of which fluttered small flags bearing drawings and inscriptions that I could not make out. Suddenly I felt a change come about Z'Oiseau. He was more sure-footed, his right hand rested firmly on my shoulder. His voice became tremulous too. It was less hoarse, less Creole, deeper. He came up to a stone stake painted a gaudy yellow, standing at the entrance to what I understood to be a Hindu temple.

'It is a *minédien,* the guardian of this place. Greet him!' he said, joining the palms of his hands.

Z'Oiseau began a complicated prayer in Tamil which he asked me to repeat after him. I was stumbling over the words, losing myself in the complex arrangement of sentences, terrified for fear of offending our Gods. But little by little, I too, left my physical body and grew lighter. I felt like I was floating a few centimetres off the ground and the sunlight did not make me blink. An infinite sense of well-being settled in and around me. I was one with the world. One with Z'Oiseau. One with this temple, no matter how derelict. The foreman of Gradis plantation pointed out the different statues to me, addressing some words of appeasement to each. Here was Mariamman, the mother goddess, at the centre of the altar, surrounded by lamps that shone in the semi darkness; there Maldévilin on his horse, brandishing his vengeful sword; further up Kannavédi with his elephant head and Katavarayen. They were all painted yellow except for Maldévilin; he was white.

'They are angry with us...' murmured Z'Oiseau, 'therefore, we must constantly appease them. If not...'

Stopping in front of an exquisite female statuette, he turned and stared at me for a long moment before declaring:

'Henceforth you are under the protection of Kalimaï. Venerate her whenever you can! She is hardly demanding. Two lamps, a ripe banana, some poppies and a little incense, it is all she asks for.'

Coming out of the temple, I was dazzled by the brightness of the sky. I abruptly fell back into a world familiar to me, the world of the plantation. And once again, in the distance, I could hear the mule-drivers shout in anger at their unmanageable mounts. I adored the obstinate and stubborn nature of mules. They looked a little like beasts but as soon as they were left to themselves, they mischievously set off to steal the sugarcane leaves which the workers had prepared as fodder for their bullocks. I felt relieved of a great burden. Z'Oiseau smiled, enigmatically. But he did not intimidate me now and I walked by his side as if he were my own father.

'Why are the gods angry with us?' I asked, gathering my courage.

'Too long a story. Some other time! Well...If you really want to know...we *Z'Indiens*, we can't leave our country to live in another. Here, in Martinique, we are not really at home. Besides, that is what Negroes say repeatedly. They don't like us because when the Whites removed their chains—the Negroes had been slaves for quite some time—they could not understand why we came from so far away to work in their stead. They hated us for it! Now, our parents could not speak their language and Negroes could not understand ours. Therefore our parents could not explain to them that they had not come to this country to do their job but to lay out sugar in the sun. You are smiling...? Well yes, it is with this rubbish that in Pondicherry or in Karikal, they encouraged us to emigrate, to feel such an irrepressible desire to reach this paradise, named America. And sugar, our parents had seen nothing of sugar because we have always been forbidden access to the mills. Mechanical work was for Negroes, cutting cane stalks for Indians! We can't be coppersmiths, or so they say. Neither fitters nor boilers—highly skilled workers—nor any of that. We are just good enough for cutting cane as if we were new slaves and our gods are not happy. Little by little, we are forgetting them. We are abandoning our temples...'

# 13

## Asking Maldévilin for Grace

*On your yellow horse, similar to Dessingou Raja's mount, Barassadi, which sometimes descends from the sky, you gallop, your sword drawn, your eyes simmering with vengeful blood. Nobody can stop your flight as you strike at Evil, as you rip Misfortune to shreds, as you make demons retreat, as you establish the reign of Brahma on this earth eroded by impurities. O Maldévilin, dream warrior!*

For the second time my father's request for repatriation was rejected. He had buried himself in silence which had become so unbearable that when he came back from the fields, my mother encouraged us, my brother Ganadin and I, to go play outside. And she went about performing her evening ablutions with the rain water we used to collect in an old rusty barrel. Ensuring that there were no Negroes around, she called out to the women who were our closest neighbours in a voice filled with a sudden gaiety, and they began to take off their clothes, to soap each other, to play, flinging handfuls of water into each other's eyes, laughing like little girls. These moments of pure happiness, although too brief, enchanted me. I loved my mother's calm face, the care she took to perfume her long, jet-black hair with sandalwood oil. Had she forgotten that I had grown up? That I was no longer the little rowdy boy, one of the few to stand up to the Negro pickneys? The sight of women's firm breasts and large hips excited me and I had trouble hiding it. I pretended to be interested in Ganadin's favourite game. It consisted in digging a small hole, preferably below a tree, and tossing three kernels of the cashew fruit into it while standing a good distance away. If you managed to throw them in the hole, you won! I was too old now to take pleasure in something so simple. Ogling Kumari, although a middle-aged woman, I dreamt of improbable embraces, of endless kisses on the entire stretch of her slender legs, which, at the height of the pelvis, curved to form a magnificent lap. With her clothes on, this *amarreuse* did not catch the eye. Undressed, she overshadowed her younger companions, including Devi, my mother. This was a true mystery to me. I began to spy on her, at the same time becoming jealous of her husband, a famous *vatialou*, one of these interpreters who translated the words of the priests possessed by the Gods into Creole. She had a boy my age upon whom I lavished kindness with the sole aim of getting to know the Mouttoupoullé family better. When I received my Saturday wages, I bought him cakes and sodas at Man Ninise's shop. I protected him from attacks by Negro rascals who were always ready to have a fight, and most often over mere trifles. He informed me that his mother did not go to the river on Monday mornings like all the other washerwomen of Courbaril Plantation. She preferred to wait until early afternoon, when the water was warmer according to her and so the laundry was easier to scour. When some insinuated that it was a pretext, she got annoyed:

'I don't like to mix up with Negresses! They jabber too much, *oui*!'

My mother always took on a knowing air when someone made an allusion to this curious habit that Kumari had of leaving for the river just when all the other women of the plantation came back from there. Sometimes, she shook her head with a half indifferent, half critical air but never made a comment. So I was determined to discover for myself what drew our neighbour to this faraway place where it was dangerous to venture alone. Snakes had bitten some washerwomen there. Sometimes, a brigand might try to assault the women who dragged their feet. Two or three Indian women were raped by Negroes. Always by Negroes. In some families, thus was explained the birth of *échappés-Coulis* babies, babies born of Indian and Negro parentage. For the Creoles, these children had escaped the curse weighing down on our race. Kumari, had never complained about anybody or anything, and that reassured her husband. 'The fool!' jeered Patte Crochue, my best friend, 'she goes there to get screwed by Foreman Sosthène. And nobody, starting with her poor husband, is clueless.'

Other tongues, swollen with nastiness, claimed that our neighbour's lover was de Sainte-Foix himself, the overseer, because he was so indulgent with her. He who was so arrogant and so harsh with Indians, rarely checked the bundles of cane that she had tied and gave her leave of absence whenever she wanted. Unlike his fellow White Creoles, he seemed to appreciate the Negroes more than us, calling us the sly race. Did he not repeat endlessly that if the *Kapli* were good for nothings and drinkers, at least they were frank? With them one knew what to expect, while with us, you always had to be wary. But I could quickly come to my own conclusions: at the time when Kumari reached the river, Sosthène, the foreman, was making sure the mules were back in their enclosure and had been rubbed down. As for M. de Sainte Foix, he was taking a nap in the stylish official accommodation provided by the master of Courbaril Plantation. In fact at two o'clock in the afternoon, on Mondays, all the men in our hamlet came back from the fields if it was harvest time. In the rainy season, the Negroes tramped across the countryside, a fighter rooster under one arm, to reach the cockfight arena of Hauteurs Bourbon or Hackaert. They left the rum shack free for Indians, who were only too happy to make the most of this godsend. Could Kumari's lover be a stranger to our region? An unknown person, perhaps even a field worker? One of those Mulatto tax inspectors that independent distillers dreaded, for example... or a Syrian peddler? Abderramane was the most skilful of all of those peddlers who sold: reproductions of *Le Semeur*—a work by a famous painter named Millet, black leather Bibles, ointments to treat rheumatisms, necklaces supposedly in gold from Cayenne, black panties meant to protect young girls in full bloom from the machinations of incubuses. People said he was so clever that he could have sold his mother at a small discount. My suspicions were confirmed when I noticed that he only came to Courbaril on Mondays, and very early at that, before the women went with their rags to the river. At eight am, he had already sold off the all the merchandise he had brought in a bundle and would say with a laugh:

'My brrrothers, my day is done, I must go back to town, rightaway.'

In reality, as soon as he was out of sight of the inhabitants of our hamlet, the Syrian turned towards the river. As he was rather tubby, he trod heavily on the track that the washerwomen's feet had opened up over time. I could hear him panting, I could see him stop, look around with worry then set off again. As soon as the regular swishing of the water could be heard, Abderramane removed his shoes, tied the laces together and put them around his neck. As he walked, he rid himself of his trousers, almost stumbling, removed his white silk shirt, until he was only in trunks. Kumari was waiting for him, sitting on a rock, smiling. Without any further talk, they threw themselves into each other's arms and rolled onto the bank. The Indian woman was moaning as the Syrian rammed into her repeatedly. She bit her fingers to stifle her screams, struggling like someone about to drown, writhing constantly. And he screwed her with a vigour that nobody could have suspected he had in him, this man known to be constantly complaining of exhaustion.

'Being on the rrroad, always, is not fair, no!' was his favourite sentence, the one which made Negresses feel sorry for him and buy expensive trinkets they did not need.

When he straightened up, at the end of an hour of intense fornication, his chest stupefied me. It was unbelievably hairy. His shoulders and back were no different. I was overcome with sudden nausea. I had never seen something like this in Indian men, even less in Negroes, and if White men had hair in the same spots, it was a fine fuzz, not this repulsive blackish bush. It did not seem to have the same effect on Kumari who snuggled up to her lover, without a word, till the sun began to go down at around four o'clock in the afternoon. There was something grotesque in this mismatched couple and yet there was such tenderness in their bodies bound together that nature herself seemed to be their accomplice. In the river, the water glittered in a thousand places, tinged with the deep green of the tall trees whose branches overhung it in places. An extraordinary if ephemeral peace set in, broken by the furtive beating of the hummingbird's wings. When the sky turned red upstream, the Syrian detached himself from Kumari, spread his clothes on the sand, knelt down to pray to his god, bending forward several times till his forehead touched the ground, repeating the name of Allah. Then they got dressed and went their separate ways, not saying good bye, the man suddenly in a hurry, the woman hitching her basket of dirty laundry on her head and climbing up the river to the pond where the water was still tepid. I decided to follow her, still intrigued by her behaviour. Kumari looked for the best place to stop, and her skirt up at mid-thigh, she set about scrubbing, soaping, wringing out, beating, rinsing and spreading her husband's khaki shirts and trousers on the grass. My foot must have snapped a dead twig because she turned in my direction and scrutinized the wild cherry thicket where I had hidden myself.

'*Ki moun ki la?*' (Who is there?) she asked in Creole, and when there was no response she repeated her question in Tamil. I was rooted to the spot, or rather stretched out on my stomach, trying not to breathe. The woman came ahead, two round stones in hand, with a menacing look and shouted again:

'Hey you, pimp! You've been watching me for a while, I know. Come out or I'm going to break your head...Sosthène, is it you? You bastard! Those Negresses are not enough for you, are they? Do you have to chase after Indian women now? Sos-thè-ne!'

Discovering me, Kumari had a strange reaction: instead of heaping reproach on me or even giving me a slap, she burst out laughing. Laughter with a touch of relief. Curiosity too. When she realised that I was Adhiyaman and Devi Dorassamy's eldest son, she became worried.

'I will not lie if I tell you that I have much affection for your father but I feel he is not doing well. Not well at all. I was told that he has not spoken for months now, is it true?'

'Yes, Madam.'

'*Hon*! I admired him when he arrived in Courbaril, you know. Pity I was the daughter of the twenty-third convoy. Too early then! Otherwise I would have made him my husband and you, young man, you would have been my son. Ha-ha-ha! And you would not have been ogling my breasts and my buttocks, bloody little scoundrel that you are!'

Her mirth won me over. I was also relieved at the idea that she did not get huffy about what I now saw was a crime. I knew she wouldn't tell my parents. Just thinking of the whipping my mother would have given me, made me faint. Kumari dragged me to the river, dived in completely dressed and chuckling like a *capistrelle*, a ten-year old carefree young girl, she took my hands and placed them alternately on her breasts, her stomach, her lap, her thighs, rubbing them gently on her firm flesh.

'Touch! Don't be scared, boy! It is time you know what a woman is,' she said and burst out laughing again.

I had been absorbed in this voluptuous petting for such a long time that the night was about to fall on our heads. At the end of the month of August, twilight is already surprisingly brief.

'I know what can cure your father,' she added before gathering her laundry. 'Only Maldévilin can save him!'

### Son of the Levant

When Uncle Abdulhamid came back from Argentina—dressed in a linen suit, a panama hat with a black ribbon on his head, he was at the steering wheel of a brand new Chevrolet and began to throw money around—everyone in the village of

Djebel Barisha ended up admitting that Mansour, Chafik, Farouk and Ali, who had had travelled to the other side of the Atlantic before him, had not told tall tales. All of them had boasted about having made their fortune in America, this one in Sao Paulo, that one in Caracas, yet another in Havana or in Panama. These exotic names made people dream but nobody truly believed that these good-for-nothings had ever really set foot there. It was believed that they had rather reached the lowly back streets of Beirut where all kinds of swindlers, opium and cannabis dealers, ship robbers and assassins traditionally found refuge.

Uncle Abdulhamid had only daughters and so the seventeen-year-old Abderramane quickly became his uncle's favourite. Abdulhamid offered Abderramane's parents to take the young man with him to the land of plenty, namely America. This meant guaranteed happiness. In those days, the English and the French preyed upon Syria, claiming they had come to free the country from the Ottoman yoke. However, nothing had changed: the same lasting poverty gripped the lives of Djebel Barisha farmers. Adberramane's parents immediately gave their consent, only too happy at the idea that in ten or even fifteen years, their son would come back as rich as his uncle. They were already dreaming of a pleasant old age, a sweet revenge on a life of unrewarding labour and endless suffering.

'I set a condition to my offer,' announced Abdulhamid. 'Just one: that my nephew Abderramane marry his cousin Houria.'

Abderramane did not have any say in the matter. He had never exchanged more than greetings with this beanpole with sad eyes; some people even claimed that she would never marry. Their wedding was a princely affair, Uncle Abdulhamid spared no expense. On the other hand, their wedding night was abominable, the young girl refusing to be touched and accepting at dawn a brief embrace which would prove, thanks to the bed sheets stained with blood, that she had just lost her virginity. At the time of departure for the port of

Lattaquié where a French ship was supposed to take them first to Palerme, then to Marseille, Abderramane did not shed a tear.

As a believer, he was certain that Allah would protect his parents during his absence. He was going to be away only for a short period. At Djebel Barisha, he had a reputation as a sensible and hard worker. Out there, on the other side of the Atlantic, he was sure he would succeed as well as his uncle, if not better, and would come back for his wife. For were not his uncle and he carrying a cargo of Oriental rugs and delicate textiles which, according to Abdulhamid, the people of America were crazy about? Alas, the voyage turned into a tragedy; off the coast of Malta dysentery caused the death of seven passengers among whom was his venerable uncle. Abderramane thought for a moment about getting off at La Valette to take the next ship home but he picked up courage, swallowed his pain and promised to honour his departed uncle. At the stopover at Marseille, he did not even go ashore and during the rest of the crossing, hardly left the cabin he was sharing with other Levantine emigrants. Violent tempests regularly nailed him to the bunk and it was only on the eve of their arrival that he discovered that the captain had decided to reroute the ship towards the north because of major damage. Argentina could wait, hello Martinique!

He had never heard of the name of this island before, and in spite of his disappointment, it sounded full of panache; it rattled like the blades of two swords. He knew nobody there and wandered for half a day on the wharves of the dry dock. Then, gathering courage, he hitched his bundle of carpets over his shoulder and went into Fort-de-France, such a strange name for a place in the Americas. He had not yet reached Démosthène Bridge when two old Negresses in gleaming finery, their neck and arms loaded with jewels visibly in solid gold, accosted him with these words:

'*Pauv' ti doudou-chéri,* (Dear little darling) you just landed, *hein*? You are completely pale like a freshly-plucked *cristophine*. What do you have to sell, my friend?'

And without waiting, they helped him unload his merchandise and upon discovering so many marvels from the Orient, they burst into shouts of amazement and delight. Such a din drew a good number of women from the quarter as well as men from seedy bars. Abderramane, stunned, saw the whole of his silk wraps, embroidered Persian style rugs, shimmering fabrics which the Negresses did not stop caressing, and even his baggy pants were sold out in a blink. He had arrived almost without a cent and now he found himself holding a thick wad of notes and an unbelievable amount of coins. Better still, after each buy the women covered him with wet kisses saying:

'Aaah! Thank you, thank you, *p'tit chéri*, you will make me the princess of Démosthène Bridge, yeah!'

So, Abderramane decided to strike Argentina from his plans. He had discovered the country of his dreams, the one where money came to him without the slightest effort. An old man offered to lead him to what he called the 'Syrian Road', an expression in which Abderramane only recognised the first word. They crossed the city, quite hot at this hour but still lively. On their way, people said with a genuine cheerfulness: 'Good morning, Syria! Welcome, man!'

The reception from his compatriots was far more reserved. In fact, most of them were Lebanese and Maronite Christians. They put him up for a week. In return, he helped them in various shops. One morning, his host, Boutros, told him:

'Go to the North, friend! Out there you can make money more easily. There are already enough of us here.'

Abderramane hesitated. He did not know yet that Martinique was no bigger than the palm of his hand. But he had been taught to obey his elders and he came to terms with it. He reached Le Lorrain, then Basse-Pointe and ended up establishing his general headquarters at Macouba where he quickly became a famous peddler who scoured the countryside!

*

Adhiyaman was finally convinced to implore the intercession of Maldévilin, the brave fighter who routed the gangs of thieves who were pillaging Madurai in the ancient times. Would this powerful God make M. de Maucourt see reason? Would Maldévilin compel the Béké to sign the document confirming that Adhiyaman had completed not one but two cycles of the five year contract, during which he served the colony faithfully to the best of his ability, as stipulated? Adhiyaman agreed to the ritual but demanded that The Ancestor, who, for many years, had been teaching the Indian children the rudiments of Hindu religion, officiate as *poussari,* head priest. Devi, Kumari as well as three other reputedly pious, women took turns talking to the old man in order to obtain his consent. It was a huge enterprise, almost hopeless. Every time they went to meet him, before any of them had the time to express her wish, the Ancestor began to quiz them relentlessly. The moment he caught them out, he sent them right back. He asked Devi:

'The King and the queen of Kaçi, wanting a child, knelt down on a needle on the seashore and begged the Almighty to come to their aid. Touched by the couple's sincerity, God asked his younger son Maldévilin to be born in their home...'

'Maldévilin had...two wives,' she hurriedly continued, 'and he was not happy to be separated from them. His wish to see them reborn among humans was granted. The first wife was named Bomi and the second one Vèllèanman.'

The pious old man nodded in satisfaction. He had hardly exchanged a few words with Adhiyaman's wife. Too many years separated The Ancestor, the son of the first convoy, from Devi, the daughter of the fifty-fifth and last convoy. Yet he knew her to be devoted to the Indian deities. Although he had become almost completely blind, he was not unaware of the fact that the foreman, Sosthène, hung around her and appreciated that she resisted him year after year, unlike these depraved Indian women who abjured their race by living as concubines with Negroes or by accepting Christian baptism. But he also knew that memory was one of the most fragile attributes of earthly beings. On this accursed island, so far from mother India, among the sugarcane fields which occupied even the smallest piece of arable land, clogging the horizon, memory could disintegrate and be lost forever. So much sweat, suffering and madness, so many sudden deaths were fatal! Unless you struggled against forgetfulness, your teeth clenched, all humiliation swallowed, unless you keep repeating the legends of the Gods, often alone with yourself, clutching at words from this language like buoys, a language more lively at night, in the midst of dreams, than in broad daylight.

'The Queen of Kashi became pregnant immediately,' continued Devi, 'and her husband invited an astrologer to predict the future. Alas, the astrologer revealed that while the Queen would bear a boy he would have to be killed at birth because he would be endowed with a strength too great for the kingdom. Furious, the King threw the astrologer in jail and asked for a second astrologer. But he confirmed the ominous prediction. The King called upon executioners to kill the child, asking them to bring him back their sabres covered with the baby's blood although the Queen begged him and shrieked in pain. But on the way, the...'

'But on the way the executioners noticed that the child's beauty kept growing. Moved, they refused to kill the child and placed it on a golden tray, dressed in a tunic embroidered with gold threads, under the shade of a big tree,' intervened The Ancestor, suddenly happy.

'The Almighty took pity on the child. Honey dropped into his mouth from a beehive on a branch of the tree above him and so he was fed. Naga-Pembou, the celestial five-headed serpent, shielded him from sun and rain. The child survived and an untouchable woman found him by chance. She took him in and breastfed him. Madouraiviren, such was the name of this child, brought great riches to his guardian and her spouse.'

'Madouraiviren became a famous hunter. Nothing escaped his sword: neither deer nor tiger, nor lion, nor elephant. One day, he desired the daughter of a king, what was her name?' asked The Ancestor abruptly.

'Ka...Kanikandra...'

'No!'

'Magdègèsi...'

'No!'

Twisting the folds of her sari, Devi grew more and more nervous. Her memory was failing. She closed her eyes and tried to clear her mind of its thoughts. She erased the familiar sounds of the plantation. In the silence, she felt she could hear her heart beat. The Tamil country and its paddy fields, her beloved land, scented with mangoes and tamarind, penetrated her and she was filled with an immense happiness. Adhiyaman had to be cured of his melancholy so that they go back there! But only The Ancestor could intercede with the gods on his behalf because he was the last one who knew the exact protocol to be followed to conduct these ceremonies. His tongue did not slip as he chanted the prayers. Alas, the name of the young girl that Madouraiviren desired did not come to Devi's mind and she burst into tears before returning home, staggering as if she had drunk too much *tafia*.

The Ancestor reminded Kumari, the unfaithful woman, the Syrian peddler's lover, of Arimala's story, the girl of royal blood who fell in love with a handsome untouchable man, a valiant warrior named Kattaravayan. Defying the *Laws of Manu,* the lovers ran away into a faraway village where they lived happily ever after.

'But the Brahmins demanded that he be sentenced to capital punishment,' said the old man staring into Kumari's eyes.

'The King then asked Kattaravayan's father to go and get him,' continued Kumari, undeterred. 'One fine day, he discovered where his son was hiding. He was living with a large number of wives of all castes. His father begged him to go to the palace, otherwise his entire family would be executed. Kattaravayan sought audience with the king and convinced him that love could very well exist between persons of different castes.'

'But the Brahmins asserted that an untouchable cannot behave as he likes and forced the king to order Kattaravayan's public execution.'

'Which was done.'

The Ancestor crossed his hands under his wrinkled chin and waited. An aeon passed as Kumari looked desperately for the remainder of this fabulous story that she had heard a hundred times in her childhood at Karikal. Her face was bathed in sweat. Her hands began to tremble.

'Who decided on Kattaravayan's fate?' asked the old man, enunciating each syllable. 'And why?'

Kumari's haughty and sensual gaze suddenly clouded. Dropping Tamil, she piteously called out in Creole:

'*Man...man pa sav ankò, Appa...*' (I...I don't know anymore, grandfather...)

'Get out of here! You are a wretched sinner, the shame of our race. In point of fact, Kattaravayan was punished by Shiva, the All-Powerful, because he had dared to engage in love games with several divine virgins in Kaïlayame, the residence of the gods. Get out!'

The three other women who had come to implore The Ancestor were no more successful than Devi or Kumari. The Ancestor was inflexible. He would not officiate for Adhiyaman!

'What is the point of fooling yourselves?' he shouted, losing his temper. 'You have all deserted our religion in favour of Christian monkey tricks. You proudly wear a cross around your neck and your children take catechism lessons from Mme de Sainte-Foix. Now, you are no more than Creoles just like the godless and lawless Whites and Negroes who populate this country.'

A month passed at Courbaril where the resounding failure of the five women spread a sort of sadness and torpor on the Indian quarter. The attempt to find a treatment turned out to be worse than the disease: Adhiyaman had come out of his silence and was now raging in a totally unknown language. The school teacher, Théophile, suggested that Devi institutionalise him but M. de Maucourt opposed it. Adhiyaman had debts to the plantation and till he paid up, there was no question of his leaving the place. Immigration laws in the French colonies were crystal clear on the matter. Vinesh understood that he was the only one capable of resolving the problem. He spoke for four continuous days with the Ancestor and succeeded where the women had failed. When he was asked about the arguments he had used to achieve such surprising success, he just said, humble and serious at the same time:

'I don't need a complicated plea. I submitted that my father is already on the path of piety and he would not even need to fast in anticipation of the ceremony. He doesn't drink alcohol any more. He hardly eats. He no longer touches my mother. He no longer associates with people; he has no more reason to quarrel with anyone, curse or covet the smallest material possession. My father is not mad! He simply needs Maldévilin to give him courage again to wait until they agree to repatriate us.'

The Ancestor gave Vinesh the responsibility of preparing the *katti*, the ritual machete which would decapitate the roosters and the sheep to be sacrificed in honour of Maldévilin. Vinesh first sharpened it on a millstone purified with coconut water. Then he sharpened the machete on a slate stone bathed in olive oil before covering it with a red cloth. Next he subjected himself to such a severe fast that he fainted twice. Devi became confident about the future and did not stop singing at night when heavy rain fell. She stood there getting drenched to the bone, indifferent to the threat of flu or pleurisy. Adhiyaman's wife thanked her neighbour Kumari every day for the good idea she had of appealing to The Ancestor, the only *poussari* still capable of moving the implacable Maldévilin. For seven days, the eldest son of the adulterous Kumari took up the job of preparing *ghee*, the ritual butter. It would be poured on to the burning mango tree wood to implore Agni, the god of fire, to grant the wishes of his followers. Devi would get up before daybreak to observe Kumari's son seated under a small *ajoupa*,* his face full of concentration as he churned fresh cow's milk in a bucket till it curdled. He tied a rope to a pole,

*In the Caribbean: a wooden-framed hut or shelter with a thatched roof and (sometimes) open sides.

which he then coiled around the churn, and without touching it, the bucket containing the precious liquid jammed between his knees, he activated his strange device with both hands. In fact, the entire Indian community of Courbaril decided, without any preliminary consultation, to contribute whatever they could for the successful conduct of the ceremony. Too poor to offer Devi money, men and women followed each other to her house, very discreetly saying to her quite simply:

'*Mi sa man pòté ba'w, chè...*' (This is what I bring you, dear lady).

A litre of fortified wine, white cotton cloth, red cotton cloth, a new saucepan, ground turmeric, bananas, rice, sugar, a jar of honey, kippers, a ball of string, a box of local cigars, pieces of camphor, eggs, neem leaves, green lemons, in short everything that was indispensable to the ritual piled up at the back of Devi's house, who on the given day, only had to gather a cluster of green coconuts. The ceremony was all set to a propitious start. Only the offerings to Maldévilin had to be bought but the young woman hesitated to spend the small nest egg that Adhiyaman had amassed in view of their return to India. He had hidden it in two purses under a floor-board. Although indifferent to the sounds of the world, immobile on his bed, his eyes riveted to the ceiling, the man would no doubt notice if his most precious belonging was touched.

Devi knew that his reaction, combined with coming insanity, could be devastating! In the city of Ajouba-Bouillon, an Indian had thus beheaded his entire family when he noticed that his hard earned savings of five years had been squandered by one of his sons on cock fights. What could she do then? Who would be kind enough to offer the Dorassamy family, the animals whose blood sacrifice Maldévilin demanded? Who?

Two days before the ceremony, Devi had still not solved the problem. Vinesh's request for an advance on his wages had been refused several times by the steward, Marcel Polygone. Mother and son were desperate when, on the eve of the ceremony, Anthénor showed up at the front window of their house with two Creole roosters under his arms. He was also pulling at three sheep which were bleating heartrendingly as if they knew the fate awaiting them.

'*Pa di ayen! Sé nou menm ki la.*' (Don't say anything! We are all in this together.)

Then he handed Devi an envelope before turning on his heels. It contained several notes which would be useful to offer The Ancestor as honorarium. Ganadin helped in deciphering the inscription on it: 'from Théophile'. On the morning of the ceremony, Devi and her two sons washed their house thoroughly. They got Adhiyaman to his feet, washed him with water mixed with curcuma and neem leaves, dressed him in a brand new white garment, a gift from the Syrian peddler, Abderramane. Vinesh lit pieces of camphor in the three pans that he had laid out in the room. Some unknown peace seemed to engulf the world. Foreday morning, usual noises seemed muted. It was time to go and meet The Ancestor whose hut adjoined the woods. Outside, they were surprised to discover that most of their neighbours were already waiting, all dressed in white, all praying in hushed tones, hands clasped. They joined the Dorassamy family on the path which meandered through the thickets, with Devi leading the procession, followed by Vinesh and Ganadin. After them came Kumari and her eldest son and other faces who were less familiar but very fervent. The ambient air warmed up with a sudden flood of sun. Dew glistened on the large leaves of yautia which The Ancestor had planted around his house. The place was silent. Too silent. In front of the house, a fire burnt between three rocks but the tinplate box which was perched on it was empty and sizzling unpleasantly. It was even partly knocked over. Devi stopped, her face clouded with dark foreboding:

'He is gone...' she said as if to herself. 'Gone, *oui*...'

'Gone where?' Vinesh asked, incredulous.

'He got back to India...Appa rode Barassadi, the celestial horse and returned to his homeland.'

Those accompanying them were torn between stupefied sorrow and joy. As soon as Devi opened the door, a frightening smell forced each one to take two steps back and cover their noses quickly. The son of the first convoy's dead body had decomposed quickly because of extreme dry season heat. Overcoming their disgust, the women went about cleansing and clothing the dead body. Kumari seemed distraught. Had not she convinced Vinesh that only a ceremony in honour of Maldévilin could save his father from the despondency he was sinking deeper and deeper into? On the day when she caught Vinesh spying on her as she was making love with Abderramane, the Syrian peddler? Was it not Vinesh, who had moved heaven and earth to convince his mother who did not want to hear anything about this ceremony?

'Why solicit Maldévilin?' She argued. 'There are more generous Gods than him: Mariamman, Nagourmira, Bomi and even Paklayen.'

But she ended up giving in to her son's scolding! And now, everything had gone up in smoke. The Ancestor alone had the requisite knowledge and more importantly, the faith to invoke Maldévilin, who, many believed, was the alter ego of Saint Michael, the Archangel. He was a deity who could go on a rampage against humans if there was ever the smallest mistake in the organisation of rites. A deity who could kill if his anger was provoked. The only one who could have made Houblin de Maucourt see reason!

# 14

## Goddess Mariamman and the Coromantee Negro

*Her hunger is never satiated; she does not stop demanding alms, more alms and still more alms. Sugarcane, o avatar of the monster Varahi! You have dragged us mercilessly from the cotton fields of Madras, from the paddy fields of Canton and from the forests of Congo, with false promises of happiness. You plunged us into a terrible torpor before crushing us; from now on, we will be the dregs of the earth. But in front of Mariamman, so beautiful and dressed in saffron, our Goddess without a face, you must admit defeat!*

Everyone remembered Théophile Leroux's arrival at Macouba. It was the year which followed the Catastrophe, what the Whites and the *nouveau riche* Mulattos called the Mount Pelée eruption at the turn of the century. Everyone at Hauteurs Courbaril had lost a family member, some a friend, some an acquaintance and the number of those charred to death took you totally aback and grieved you: thirty thousand people. How could such a large population manage to pile up in the cramped lanes of the city of Saint-Pierre? Vinesh had been there only once. Two or three months before the terrible event in March or April 1902. He did not remember it very well. When Béké de Maucourt refused to sign Adhiyaman's letter of repatriation to India citing imaginary debts contracted at the plantation shop (May Kali the dark one, strike Man

Ninise the shop owner, with her sword), Adhiyaman resolved to go to Saint-Pierre to claim his rights. He took his family there, making the most of the brief period of leave between the end of one cane harvest and the point when the cuttings were replanted, between the end of June and the middle of August. He already knew the place, having accompanied the steward, Marcel Polygone and the foreman Sosthène to pick up barrels of salted meat, crates of dried codfish and machetes ordered by the Courbaril Plantation. Adhiyaman thought that it looked like a replica of the port of Pondicherry: noisy wharves, crowded with goods coming from the whole universe where laughing *gabariers,* barge sailors, paced around; import-export shop assistants in detachable collars; *femmes-matadors,* coquettish and overbearing women, who sashayed about ravishingly, wearing dashing Creole dresses; gangs of idle youngsters looking to play a prank; sinister-looking swindlers; Indians adrift. The miserable fate of his compatriots in Saint-Pierre terrified him. Dressed in torn rags, drunk as old skunks, they wandered about the wharfs, trying to get hired on one of the innumerable ships flying so many different flags, which crowded the harbour. Most of them had fled hinterland plantations to end up in the infamous quarter of La Galère, the city's garbage dump at the mouth of the River Roxelane. There—in the middle of gallows-bird Negroes, boorish White men who had recently arrived from Europe, their faces sown with scars that bore witness to their sinister feats, and toothless wily Chinese who ran illegal mahjong parlors—these Indians lived a hopeless existence. Some were but stumps of humanity, their bodies ravaged by smallpox or syphilis. With little or no knowledge of Creole, they could not communicate and had become the whipping boys of *Négrillons,* Negro pickneys, who guffawed at these Indians that staggered down the road. The *Négrillons* enjoyed throwing at them anything they could lay their hands on while shouting:

'Coolie, you smell of piss! Coolie beggar! Coolie dog eaters!'

Other Indians, less flea-ridden but just as unfortunate, awaited their repatriation in a shack of the Le Mouillage quarter, called Coolie Warehouse. These had kept up a semblance of dignity even though they had to do unpaid work for the municipality. In return, at midday they were served the leftovers of the meals from the Bethlehem Home. Most of them worked for the cleansing department of the city as street sweepers or latrine bucket cleaners. When evening approached, mixed groups of women and men came into the city, at least into the rich quarters, hugging the stone walls of the White traders or bourgeois Mulattoes' dwellings, their eyes always lowered because of the immense shame that choked them. They went in groups of six, two at a time, carrying a tank made of zinc in which the others quickly emptied the chamber pots from Aubagne. Once the tank was full to the brim, clenching their jaws in order to be able to bear the stink, they lifted it together and rushed to the banks of the Roxelane to empty it. This operation had to be repeated four or five times in the course of an evening depending on the number of chamber pots that had been set out by the inhabitants, some of whom had not put the pots out for several days at a stretch, out of negligence. These reeked like rotting carcasses and the foul smell permeated the Indian cleaners' clothes; even sea water could not completely dissipate it. This gave a chance to the Creoles to invent a new term of abuse:

'Shit smelling Coolie, dog!'

Suppressed anger choked Adhiyaman, especially as neither the steward, Polygone, nor the foreman Sosthène, busy with their business, seemed unaffected at this awful sight which was repeated everyday of their week in Saint-Pierre. Upon his return, thinking the boys were asleep, he told Devi:

'It is a very beautiful city. There is even a theatre where people go all dressed up in a tramway that links the two ends of the city, but it is hell for the people of our race. Hell!'

However, he had decided to take his family there to try and clandestinely embark on some British ship, in charge of repatriating the many indentured labourers from the French islands and the British colonies. They sailed up the river Demerara in British Guyana, then berthed at Trinidad—the southernmost island of the entire archipelago—making short stops at Saint Vincent, Grenada and Saint Lucia before stopping at Saint-Pierre in Martinique. Adhiyaman had thought of contacting an interpreter on board to bribe him with the savings which he had put away over seven years and eight months of hard work at Courbaril Plantation. The operation was perilous, because if unfortunately, he were caught, he would be sent to jail and his wife and children would be dispersed across plantations on the Caribbean coast—plantations where the land was barren and unproductive, and work was back-breaking.

To allay her suspicions, he did not tell Devi about his plans and carried no material possessions, except for some notes which he hid in his underpants. He claimed that it was a simple pleasure trip, something that thrilled her because she hardly left the plantation and avoided the town of Macouba, where men tried to seduce her with a coarseness that never ceased to surprise her. Like that day, when a black giant with a dazzling set of teeth, doubtlessly already drunk even though it was only nine a.m., grabbed her arm in the middle of the road and shouted, holding his testicles:

'Coolie woman, don't you want to taste this? I have one that is longer and larger than four Malabars put together. Ha-ha-ha! They say your pussy hair is razor-sharp, I'd love to see that.'

The passers-by just laughed as Devi ran away, terrified.

Since then she went to Macouba only under duress, preferring to entrust her shopping to her boys. But Saint-Pierre? That would be different! The name of the city itself made her dream. Those lucky enough to have been there brought back vibrant stories that made her long to see it for herself.

And so Devi, usually so wise, accepted her husband's offer eagerly. She was surprised at his insistence on leaving their house untidy and wide open as if they planned to come back the same evening. She knew that on foot, it took a day-and-a-half through the woods to reach the other end of the country, unless you were lucky enough to get a ride on a sugarcane cart; and honestly speaking, that was easier if one were alone. Adhiyaman insisted that their door latch remain conspicuously unlocked. As an obedient wife, Devi made no comment and, early on a chilly July morning, they took the path that led to the neighbouring town of Ajoupa-Bouillon, each of them only carrying a shoulder bag containing grilled sweet potatoes and pieces of cassava. The two boys, Vinesh and Ganadin, were delighted; the elder to be spared post-harvest chores, and the younger a day at school. His school teacher, Théophile, a young *Blanc-France*, a White man from France, although extremely friendly with little Indians, tolerated neither unruliness nor laziness, even less unauthorised absences though the school year was almost over. This time, Ganadin, had not played truant. His father could apologise when the time came.

'Into the thicket, quick!' Adhiyaman shouted each time they noticed someone. Hidden among *zeb-a-pik*, jackass-bitters, and wild guava trees, the Dorassamy family would wait for the person to move away before going on with their trek. More and more intrigued, Devi watched her husband out of the corner of her eye, waiting for him to reveal the reason behind these strange manœuvres. But the man kept his mouth shut. The thousands of creases lining his forehead told her he was worried. Time and again he ordered them to hurry, especially when they crossed exposed places: grassland or fords, for instance.

'We must reach Le Morne-Rouge before nightfall,' he said in Tamil, giving himself away. 'We will sleep at my friend Aladèn's place. He is a Muslim but he makes no distinction...'

Adhiyaman gave them a break on the banks of River La Falaise, doubtless because it was embedded between two rocky mounds and it was impossible to spot the slightest activity from the Colonial Road. He stripped bare, to the shock of his two boys who had never seen their father naked before. He asked them to undress. He himself undressed a flabbergasted Devi, and dragged all four of them, holding their hands, into the ice-cold water, which came from Mount Pelée. Then he began to pray to Mariamman with a fervor that was so contagious that his wife did as he did, inciting Vinesh and Ganadin to follow suit. Alas! The two boys did not know these prayers well; they had always sounded beautiful though the words were obscure. They stumbled over unfamiliar phrases and ended up muttering just about anything. This enraged Adhiyaman who, once his ablutions were over, pinched their ears, shouting:

'It can be expected from Ganadin, but from you, Vinesh, no; what were you doing when we sent you to The Ancestor's, *hein*? Didn't he make you repeat these prayers?'

The young boy lowered his head, embarrassed. He was scared to confess that the story of the adventures of Rama or King Bagiratha had always interested him more than the boring recitations that the son of the first convoy inflicted upon him.

'Well! I have never been a devotee myself. Am I right, Devi?' said Adhiyaman, suddenly reassured. 'But I was born in India, my father had a temple in his orchard, out there in Madurai, and I regularly went to Sri Meenakshi temple. O my sons, if you could see that marvel! Next to it, Christian churches look like hovels. You, on the other hand, were born here, in this accursed country. Only our religion can save you. It's the only thing we have preserved, alas, one and only and besides...'

'I was born in Pondicherry, Appa!' murmured Vinesh, surprised at his own audacity.

'Who put that idea into your head? Is it you, Devi? Why do you tell such moronic stories to the boy? No, man, you were born on Courbaril Plantation, two months after we moved in.'

'Adhiyaman, you are a man full of goodness, I have no complaints about you!' Devi exclaimed. 'Every day I thank Parvati and Shiva for having led my parents to choose a husband like you for me! But I must tell Vinesh the truth. He is my elder son! Vinesh, you were born neither in India nor in Martinique but on the ship that brought us here. Yes, right in the middle of the Sea of Fire, just before weathering a terrible storm and Nagourmira, the holy man revered by the Muslims, came to our aid. That is the truth!'

'Okay, okay! What does it matter where Vinesh was born? He must still learn to speak Tamil and honour our gods. Ganadin too, actually.'

Adhiyaman ordered each one to get dressed even though they were not completely dry. Just as they were about ready to get going again, shouts rang out from the woods. A hoarse and chaotic voice yelled impenetrable sentences, whose echo shattered against the cliffs. A Negro's voice, but an unusual one. A voice which was not Creole, crying out despair, anger, hate, and bewilderment. A man, with a torn canvas cloth wrapped around his body, suddenly appeared. He was as stunned to see them as they were to see him. Adhiyaman immediately understood that this Negro was not a local. They stared at each other in silence, the latter whirling his club on which he had sculpted vulgar designs.

'*Mwen, moun Kongo! Mwen, lakay-mwen, viré! Viré!*' (I Coromantee Man! I home go back! Go back!) the Negro started screaming in bad Creole. His eyes were as round as his head. This would have made him look funny, had it not been for the frightening rictus that adorned his lips. He was drooling but all things considered, he seemed more desperate than threatening. He had probably lost his mind because he did not stop pointing upstream, where the river lost itself among intertwining tree ferns, repeating 'Coromantee! Country-Congo!'

Adhiyaman took a few steps towards him, very calmly, and told him he understood, that both of them were indentured labourers who had been cheated about the munificence of this island and its sugar supposedly easy to manufacture.

'You Africa! Me India! We both, same-same!' He added, adopting the Negro's distorted Creole.

'*Kréyol, nasion mové!*' (Creole, bad country!) The African shouted, his eyes bulging.

Adhiyaman drew closer and placed a hand on his shoulder. Devi and the boys had, as a precaution, crossed River La

Falaise and were observing the two men from the other bank. She regretted not having carried a machette with her, a useful weapon for travelers in this country where the backcountry was infested with both lancehead snakes and '*Nègre-bourse-ou-la-vie*,' 'Negro—your-money-or-your-life,' as they said in Creole. Truth be told, the African looked nothing like a highwayman. Instead, he looked like someone who had been lost for several days and was desperately hungry. He was eyeing Adhiyaman's rucksack from which a piece of cassava stuck out, as he repeated his refrain: 'Country-Congo! Country-Congo!'

Adhiyaman offered him some, remaining calm. The poor fellow devoured it, simultaneously quieting down. Then he drank greedily from the bottle of rum that the Indian offered him.

'*An péyi ta mwen, lé viré! N'Kanza, li, viré!*' (In my country, want to return! N'Kanza, he, return!), he struck his chest and spoke in a voice that was suddenly more human. He squatted, pulling Adhiyaman down to do likewise and began to pour out his story, in bits and pieces.

*

Unlike most indentured labourers who had come from Congo, N'Kanza had signed no contract. He had not even heard of Martinique before. It was on landing in this country that he had seen a sugarcane field for the first time. He was kidnapped! He should never have left his village in the heart of the forest. He should never have forsaken his family, the people of Luo, because they had always been generous with him. Orphaned early, he was taken in by one of his maternal uncles who treated him like his own son and when he became a young man, built him a house, taught him to operate a canoe and fish on the river. The prettiest girls of the village offered themselves to N'Kanza and, when the time came, he would only have had to choose three or four of them as wives. It is just that people from the coast had begun scouring the bush, distributing extraordinary objects which they said came from well-wishers with white skin, creatures that nobody in the village had ever seen. Nothing to do with our albinos, the inhabitants of the coast assured them, because, in truth, the latter's skin is pink while the Europeans' is really white!

'*Yo toulitan répété Ewop! Ewopéyen!*' (Them always repeat Europe! Europeans!) said N'Kanza.

These magic words finally infatuated him. Each time they came, these men from the coast had brought along mirrors, knives, saucepans, rifles and glassware to gratify the village chief and his family, arousing envy and covetousness among the poorest of the Luos. The chief's wives strutted about with gold necklaces and scarves, disdaining ordinary women. Their children went hunting with rifles and brought back more game, and in a shorter time than those who used bows and assegais. N'Kanza could not bear it. He was short-tempered and regretted it bitterly today. One day, he struck up a conversation with a man from the coast who spoke to him of a country beyond the seas—America which overflowed with all kinds of riches. If you just bent down and looked into a river, you could see gold. Even houses were built of this precious metal! It was a vast orchard where fruits were so abundant that the inhabitants did not even bother to pick them all. There were no wild animals infesting the forests as in the Luos country. No lions, no hyenas, no crocodiles, no hippopotamuses, no scorpions.

'There the Gods reside,' added the man from the coast, 'and in their immense goodness, they have agreed to let humans have a small place but not just anyone! Only to those who deserve it, those who have always led an exemplary life, those who do not balk at work.'

N'Kanza decided to follow him without saying a word to his maternal uncle. All the way downstream, the man from the coast managed to convince other men to follow him, young and healthy men. N'Kanza got to know a multitude of peoples whom he had not even suspected existed: the Mongo, Zande, Chokwe, and Lunda. Some were simply keen to see the River Without End which was said to be blue and whose water was salty. Others were outcasts, thieves or criminals, ostracized by their tribe, and who had nothing to lose. Or they were war prisoners, freed on the condition that they left for America. Their guide tried in vain to recruit women with trinkets or vials of perfume. Only one Zande woman, a creature of haughty bearing, with disproportionate legs and a warrior's gait joined them because she was a widow and inconsolable. They all had great difficulty understanding each other and had to communicate with gestures. The man from the coast alone knew the main languages of the river and in the evening, around the fire, he enjoyed the misunderstandings arising among his protégés, some identical words in two languages could have opposite meanings. N'Kanza felt light hearted. After having walked for ten days, he forgot about his family. A new life, full of surprises, awaited him and he welcomed each new dawn with an enthusiasm which surprised him. If he had not quite taken the decision to brave the River Without End or to move to the country of the Gods, this America that the man from the coast boasted about endlessly, he was sure that he would not go back to the forest soon.

'Your mind is made up, my son?' The guide would ask him, again and again.

'I'll see when I'm there, Uncle,' he would reply in a placid tone that seemed to annoy the guide.

'High time you let me know. The tickets for America are expensive, very expensive,' he groused.

Arriving in the city of Matombo was an enchantment for N'Kanza. He had never seen houses this high, roads this large and clean. The horse-drawn vehicles in which the White men moved about left him spellbound but their owners did not bode well to him. In fact, their skin was in no way the colour of the clouds as the guide had declared, nor pink like those of albinos but sometimes rather reddish, other times brown like grilled corn. They smiled little, were very agitated, and sweated a lot in spite of their straw hats. The guide led the gang to the port on the banks of the River Without End but the river itself was a disappointing sight.

Its water was dirty, muddy, crowded with gigantic boats on which sailors were busy. They were loading all kinds of goods: rare wood, elephant tusks, coffee, animal skins, and live animals in cages. They were settled in a shack where a considerable number of candidates were already waiting. From time to time, a medicine-man, a European, came to examine them and provided medicines. Every morning, about twenty lucky chosen ones left the place with a joyful din that would wrench N'Kanza out of his stupor. Each night as the sun set, the watchmen compelled them to lie down on their pallets. N'Kanza was used to sleeping on a simple mat on the floor and could not sleep on these pallets whose planks were full of cockroaches and ants.

Their guide, now dressed European style, was distinctly less friendly and repeatedly asked: 'Have you made up your mind?'

N'Kanza wanted to get some information on this fabulous destination about which he now harboured a few doubts. An old beggar with whom he was chatting in the afternoon told him that beyond the ocean, there was nothing but the Kingdom of Ghosts. The men with their reddish skin, who came from Europe, were their servants. Their mission was to bring Coromantee Negroes as fodder for the Ghosts.

'None of our people have ever come back from there', the beggar said. Driven by an increasing curiosity, the young man learnt to speak this strange language, which was a mixture of Congo tongues and Portuguese. Everyone used this language to communicate along the coast. At the darkest hour of the night, he gave his friends the slip, hopped over the high fences around the group of shacks and got lost in the city's seedy quarters. Taverns and licensed brothels formed an endless line where there were no social barriers: no more Blacks or Whites, men from the coast or the hinterland, brass hats or recruiters with their baleful eyes, honest washerwomen or cooks or easy virtue Mulattoes, but just one and only human fauna, addicted to the pleasures of palm wine, card games and paid fornication. A universe that quite simply fascinated N'Kanza.

*

'*Kon sa, mwen, kò-mwen, pèdi!*' (So that way, me, my body, lost myself!), he told Adhiyaman, who was captivated by his story and had not noticed that on the other bank of La Falaise River, his wife and two sons were beginning to get impatient. Devi was afraid that by tarrying too long, they would not reach the town of Morne Rouge before night.

'Adhiyaman!' She called out unsuccessfully. 'Leave that mad Negro to his madness! Let's get out of here, *oui.*'

N'Kanza had got into the habit of playing dice with European sailors, losing, one by one, the gifts given to him by the man from the coast: a finely crafted music box, a fob watch, a little oval mirror in a silver frame, two glass necklaces, a comb made of tortoiseshell. Although saddened, he gathered the information he was seeking, putting together bits and pieces of conversation. Out there in America, they grew a plant named sugarcane, a sort of reed which had to be cut into pieces before it was crushed in mills. The products, sugar and rum, had great value and yielded huge profits when they were sold in Europe. For this the White men needed hands to work because America was almost empty of inhabitants. They also offered the Congolese contracts of indentureship, contracts at the end of which they were guaranteed free passage back to their native country. On returning, they would be rich until the end of their lives.

Adhiyaman could not stop himself from smiling.

'*Wou, mwen motjé?*' (You laugh me?) The Coromantee Negro got suddenly angry and stood up.

'No, but this story is not unknown to me...' he retorted, his face darkening.

*

The man from the coast kept asking the same question for the months which N'Kanza spent in the shack. He was getting more and more impatient and threatened the young man that he would send him back to his village. However, one evening, he organised a banquet, brought a lot of food and drink, gifts and prostitutes. He smiled, moved from group to group with a kind word for each, including N'Kanza. Afterwards, the young man's memory was just a big black hole. He felt sick, he could no longer stand and his eyes only saw myriads of white dots on a stretch of dark blue. The ship was underway, all sails unfurled. She was pitching as the waves were crashing against her hull. Around N'Kanza, several dozen men were painfully waking up from their orgy. They were all dazed, even petrified. They were all piled up on the afterdeck. Swear words and lamentations flew fast and furious in languages unknown to the young man.

'Like this, me landed in this country Martinique,' he said to Adhiyaman who was now tangled in the threads of this story. 'Moved to plantation Morne Capot, in the Lorrain, White men very nasty, Negroes from here very nasty. Creoles them bad nation!'

Then, sinking back into his original frenzied state, he started to bellow again, shouting meaningless words, writhing and twisting. The white of his eyes turned purple. Pushing the Indian back violently, he crossed the river with swaying strides, rushed to Devi and started tearing her clothes. Vinesh was dealt a knock on his temple with the man's club and collapsed while Ganadin, distraught, ran for his life. N'Kanza began kneading Devi's breasts, his features full of intense satisfaction. Toppling her to the ground, he dug his head between her thighs and tried to lap her up. Adhiyaman, gathering his wits, broke a branch of the guava tree, crossed the river in turn, and hit him on the back with all his energy, shouting:

'Let her go or I'm going to kill you. Stop!'

The Coromantee Negro's skin was criss-crossed with marks of recent whippings, probably, which burst and let thick blood flow. It ran onto Devi's face and into her silky hair. She had not moved. She had not struggled. She stared fixedly at her aggressor, in dignified silence. Adhiyaman was wearing himself out hitting N'Kanza, on the head now, without the Coromantee Negro showing the slightest sign of pain. On the other hand, he grabbed his engorged penis with both hands and, spreading out the thighs of the Indian woman a little wider, got ready to impale her. Devi put up no resistance. She just said:

'Mariamman, please protect me! O Mariamman, mother of our race!'

N'Kanza froze. His penis went limp. His arms started trembling suddenly. Adhiyaman kept on raining blows upon him without realising that the African had just died. Devi pulled herself out, not even out of breath, went to wash herself in the river whose water was now freezing because of the approaching night.

'He...he is dead!' stammered Adhiyaman.

'No, he is not. Mariamman has simply put him to sleep.'

'I'm telling you he is dead, Devi. Look, he is not breathing anymore....'

The Coromantee Negro, a statue of grotesque flesh, was on his knees, immobile, his arms dangling, his eyelids shut. Vinesh had a bump on his right temple. He and Ganadin went up to their mother who was putting her torn clothes calmly back on. Adhiyaman threw the bloody guava branch into the river, which swept it away immediately. He had lost the haughtiness of a family head. Not knowing what to do, he sat on a rock in the middle of leaping waves, as if he was waiting for the dark night to arrive.

'Don't worry, Adhiyaman!' Devi went on. 'You did not kill him. It is Mariamman who cut short his life.'

N'Kanza began to roar suddenly. His chest inflated and a powerful breath came out of his nostrils. Distraught, he spun around and around before rushing towards the woods screaming once more: '*Péyi Kongo, lé viré, mwen!*' (Country-Congo, want to go back, me!)

A few minutes elapsed before Adhiyaman reacted. Without saying a word, he started back on his journey, Ganadin astride his back. It was difficult to see the path in the dark. They tripped over stumps, slipped on steep or muddy stretches. Thorny thickets scratched their arms but nobody complained. They were impatient to flee this place, this river with diaphanous waters where Adhiyaman had had the bad idea of stopping. The moon finally stopped playing hide and seek between the clouds, and enveloped the earth with tender brightness. Devi sang, her voice drowning the sounds of toads and crickets. The lyrics were a vibrant thanksgiving to Goddess Mariamman who had saved her from being most horribly tainted. They reached Morne-Rouge around two a.m. and found Aladèn, the fair-skinned Indian, looking very anxious. He thought that they got lost in the forest or that the Negroes-purse-or-your life stopped them on the way. He was getting ready to go and meet them, two bamboo torches in either hand.

'Vinesh had a fall,' announced Devi. 'We had to stop on the banks of the river, La Falaise. Would you have something for his bump?'

'This is what happens to unruly boys!' said the relieved Muslim, pretending to scold Vinesh.

He served them a delicious meal and, leading Devi and her children into a room where mats were laid out on empty casks of dried cod, wished them good night. Adhiyaman would share his room. In actual fact, the two men sat on the minuscule verandah of the dwelling where they chatted till daybreak. Vinesh's sleep was lulled by the drone of their voices even though they were doing their best to keep their voices low. From time to time, he heard his father say the word 'repatriation'. In the morning, the young man noticed that his father addressed his mother with uncommon deference. He even seemed to have left the direction of operations to her because he did not object to her asking a bullock cart driver to give them a lift. The man, an *échappé-Couli*, half Indian, half Negro then, was going to Pécoul Plantation which overlooked Saint-Pierre. He showed them that, from there, they only had to go down the slope which would take less than half an hour. He was right.

The city was a revelation for Vinesh and Ganadin. A faint excitement pushed them to walk faster even though their legs felt as heavy as lead. At the foot of the Trois-Ponts quarter where they saw the magnificent trees of a botanical garden, they boarded a tramway that dropped them off at Mouillage. Vinesh stared with wide-eyed wonder at the hustle and the bustle of the roads, the shining clothes worn by the women and their white parasols which spun around like butterflies, the incessant coming and going of hand carts pulled by Negroes of Herculean build and White gentlemen comfortably seated in tilburies wearing white pith helmets. And these vast dwellings completely built out of stone, tightly packed against each other. On the balconies sat languid Mulatto women gently plying hand fans in rich colours! (Saint-Pierre was baking hot.) Obviously, the breeze was a rare commodity and passers-by bent over sculpted fountains to moisten their faces. In front of the Coolie warehouse, a multitude of scruffy, sullen Indian men sat on a floor of scorching cobblestones, waiting for a schooner to Fort-de-France, emaciated dogs lounging around them. They did not respond to Adhiyaman's greetings but devoured Devi with their eyes. A sherbet vendor was shouting herself hoarse in front of a building whose entrance was sealed shut.

'Come, boys! I will buy you some,' said Devi, joyfully.

Adhiyaman got into the Warehouse alone. He stayed there for two hours. Devi allowed Vinesh and Ganadin to go and play in the black sand of the shore, forbidding them to go close to the sea where rowdy boys were swimming. She tried to identify the boats which flew the British flag, the only one she actually knew besides the French flag. Her heart tightened with a strange foreboding. For quite a while now, she had known that her husband meant to disregard M. Houblin de Maucourt's decision and get back to India! This was what he had wanted ever since he disembarked on this island. See Pondicherry again, get back to Madurai where he planned to rebuild his parents' home where jackals had shamefully devoured them, in short, to start all over again. Devi had stopped believing in it all, even though she did think about her mother who had disembarked at Mauritius and from whom she had never heard anything again. She had got accustomed to life on the plantation, to humiliations, to the hard work in the fields, to foreman Sosthène's repeated, though discreet, advances. Sometimes, she even caught herself thinking in Creole, and no longer in Tamil, and grew tense at the idea that she was changing. Imperceptibly she was beginning to be like these Indian women who were born in Martinique and for whom Madras, Madurai, Pondicherry, Karikal, Yanaon were mere words, albeit glittering, but insubstantial. They were women who had a small altar at home and attended Hindu ceremonies but did not hesitate to wear a cross and never missed Sunday Mass. No difference between them and the Creoles.

'No ship for six months', Adhiyaman whispered to her when he came out of the Warehouse. 'Six months...'

His face was a mask of desperation; it had suddenly grown old. Refusing to tarry any further in Saint-Pierre, in spite of protests from the two boys, he started back, forgetting that they had hardly eaten in the day. Devi raised no objection. Did he not often quote this precept from the ninth book of the Manusmriti?

*A sterile woman must be replaced in the eight year; the one whose children are all dead in the tenth year; the one who gives birth only to girls in the eleventh year; the one who speaks sourly on the spot.**

When the night came upon them, they slept under a mango tree that protected them from the rain which began to fall heavily although the rainy season was still far away. Adhiyaman did not want to stop over at his friend Aladèn's place and kept hurrying, turning back time and again to encourage his family. They walked the whole day. As they were getting close to Courbaril Plantation, a little before sunrise, they met Théophile, the metropolitan school teacher.

---

*A barren wife may be superseded in the eight year; one whose children have died in the tenth year; one who bears only daughters in the eleventh; but one who says unpleasant things (may be superseded) immediately. Verse 81, chapter IX, *The Laws of Manu*, translated by Wendy Doniger with Brian K. Smith, London, Penguin Classics, 1991, p. 207.

'Ganadin has not come to school for a while! I have come to see if he is not bedridden. With this nasty diarrhoea which is common these days, half my class is absent,' he said.

'We had work in Saint-Pierre,' replied Devi. 'My boys are well, don't worry.'

'I offered to teach your elder son to read, Madam. Even if he is above schooling age, it could always be useful.'

'Useful for what?' Adhiyaman interrupted. 'To cut cane, one doesn't need education. Strong arms and solid legs are enough!'

These were his last words before he locked himself up in silence for several years.

The school teacher ruffled Vinesh's locks in a friendly manner. Their jet-black colour never stopped fascinating him.

'If you want to get out of the plantation, you Indians, there is only one way: education. Look at the Blacks! They have understood it for a long time now,' he said in a level voice as he moved away.

# 15

## The School Teacher from France

*Fate wrenches some out of their native lands; these poor unfortunates find themselves turning round and round in the dugout canoe of life without knowing if the wind wants to laugh or cry. Mute with terror, they cling to bits of languages, impervious masks of deities who demand more and more sacrifices. Of these it is said that despair impels them forward. Quite unlike he who, always solitary and reckless, decides to confront exile.*

Now, once slavery was abolished, it was decided that Negroes would be taught the art of reading and writing, something they had been deprived of for two-and-a-half centuries. M. Schœlcher, an Alsatian whom the Great White Men had vowed to bring to his knees, won his case: schools would be opened everywhere at the cost of the colonies and all children would attend it till the age of twelve. But Macouba, being one of the remotest of all towns in Martinique, saw nothing coming its way. Everywhere, the Brothers of Christian Instruction and other less famous congregations worked at putting up schools. Sometimes a shanty was enough, with some benches and a blackboard. The alphabet became the new 'Open sesame', the key that unlocked the prison door that was the Plantation so that Negroes could now flee far from it. Multiplication tables, conjugation charts, maps of France, the fables of La Fontaine, the names of Henri IV and Louis XIV were venerated like icons. Or at least as much as catechism books. The Houblin de Maucourt, the main planters of Macouba, congratulated themselves in secret that for once, the remoteness of their place was an advantage. Because their alter egos from Lamentin, Le François, Rivière-Salée and Le Lorrain were complaining about the shortage of gangs of *Négrillons* who were thrown into the fields from the age of ten. No such thing occurred at Courbaril Plantation. Thus Aymard Houblin de Maucourt, before Félicien Houblin de Maucourt who passed the baton to his son, Frédéric Houblin de Maucourt, just around the turn of the century, which began with the eruption of Mount Pelée. But times changed and the teaching imparted by the priests was replaced by secular republican schools, both free and compulsory. In the pantheon of demons hated by *Grands Blancs*, the rich White planters, Jules Ferry found a place of honour next to Robespierre, Danton, Voltaire, Lamartine and of course the abolitionist, Victor Schœlcher.

'I heard that the arseholes of the General Council are having a school built in town,' said M. Frédéric to his workers. 'All of this is just waste! Money thrown down the drain, *oui*! When your children finish school, they won't even know how to handle a machete. It's land and not books that has made Martinique rich. No reason to change that, boy!'

His fears were unfounded. The two school teachers—a Negro and a Mulatto, both in their late thirties—who landed at Macouba one morning, hurried to pay their respects to him. They only intended to educate the children whose parents lived in town. Children from the countryside would be left in peace! If these children wanted to come, they would not object to it either—they actually did not have the right to do so—but they would do nothing to incite them to come to school.

'Our aim is to create an elite,' said the Negro, Nestor Pommier, pompously. He was a character who wore a ruffled collar and was quite full of himself. 'No point divulging knowledge left, right and centre to just about anyone. Especially to those for whom it will be perfectly useless!'

'I am paid to teach those who are eager to learn, not to

play policeman,' added the Mulatto, who had been nicknamed *Alexis-grands-movements,* Alexis-the-jumping-jack, because of the permanent state of restlessness of his body. 'Whether my class has forty pupils or only ten, it's all the same to me!'

These words reassured Houblin de Maucourt who could sleep soundly till Théophile Leroux, a very young school teacher from France, with his pretentious airs and his revolutionary ideas, arrived at Macouba, three long years later. A native of Orléans, he refused all the posts which were offered to him when he graduated from the *École normale.** When he learnt that they were recruiting for the colonies, he did not hesitate for a second because old Europe weighed him down. There, he felt like a prisoner, incapable of giving the best of himself. Although he was no rebel or adventurer like Rimbaud—the poet he admired above all—he wanted to see the world, meet other peoples, hear and speak other languages, get interested in other gods, taste other flesh. When he saw an advertisement for volunteers for the islands of Martinique and Guadeloupe, he sent in his application, asking for Martinique because its name had no religious connotation. The young man was a militant atheist who had devoured all the books dealing with the French Revolution, who considered Saint-Just as the sharpest mind that humanity had ever produced since Spartacus, venerated the Supreme Being and strived to use the names of the months in the French Republican calendar,** which made him look like a sweet eccentric to his colleagues.

Thus on a rainy day of Vendémiaire,† he embarked from the docks of Bordeaux with only a small suitcase of summer clothes and a huge trunk of books in which he had piled up, in

*Teacher's training college.

**The French Republican Calendar was created and implemented during the French Revolution, and used by the French government for about 12 years from late 1793 to 1805. The revolutionary system was designed in part to remove all religious and royalist influences from the calendar, and was part of a larger attempt at decimalisation in France.

†First month of the French republican calendar from 21 or 22 or 23 September to 21 or 22 or 23 October.

addition to his favourite books—Montaigne's essays, *Jocelyn* by Lamartine, *Zadig* by Voltaire and *La Bête humaine* by Zola—a series of grammar books and French dictionaries which he knew he would not find easily in the colonies. His sense of being on a mission helped him overcome the sudden nostalgia that assailed him at the moment when the ship weighed anchor: to help the natives of Martinique, recently emancipated from several centuries of slavery, to reintegrate them into humankind. To tell the truth, he had never spent enough time with Blacks to know their way of thinking. He knew intuitively that those he had seen in the taverns of Bordeaux—and they were many, to his great astonishment—had rubbed shoulders with Europeans for too long to be considered representative of their race. During the first two days of the voyage, he kept away from the other travelers, most of whom were European traders and white Creole families returning home after holidays in Metropolitan France. Their behaviour was a revelation! If he had spent time with Italians, Spaniards and a few Germans during his student days, all of whom were political refugees who saw in France a haven of democracy, he had never been close to Creoles. Despite their princely American airs, their vulgarity struck him immediately. These men smoked imposing cigars whose foul smoke hung all over the dining room, and were unaffected by the discomfort so caused; or they exchanged coarse jokes in their peculiar drawl, slapping their thighs. That is when Théophile heard the Creole language for the first time and it induced both irritation and frustration because, although he recognised some words, he could not understand even the shortest sentence. The planters's wives remained aloof, spending most of their time in their cabins where their meals were brought to them, only coming out at the end of the afternoon for fresh air, always in a group, quite unobtrusive, even diffident, their heads hidden under large straw hats. As for their children, they were escorted by dozens of black nannies dressed in their most beautiful Creole outfits and extravagant gold necklaces. The other passengers exchanged amused smiles at this most curious gathering, as when some Creole, trying to impress one of his peers, called them to witness.

Then on the seventh day of a smooth crossing, Théophile was addressed by one of them, who announced his name as François-Marie Dupin de la Valmenière. The man could not have imagined that his extended surname, instead of impressing Théophile, reminded him that if the guillotine had cut many heads amongst the colonial nobility in Guadeloupe, Guiana and Santo Domingo, it had spared Martinique. In fact, right after the first abolition of slavery, in 1794, the White Creoles got the island transferred under British jurisdiction even though France and England were sworn enemies at that time. The school teacher had scoured rare books of history which dealt with this country where he asked to be posted. He was deeply dissatisfied that these books only spoke about the actions of governors, lieutenant generals and the *Grands Blancs*, rich white plantation owners. The original inhabitants, the Caribs and the Blacks who had been imported as slaves from Africa, were only summarily alluded to.

'Well, you are off to see the world, young man? *Hon*!'

'In the past, Martinique was a magnificent island, a small Garden of Eden,' said de la Valmenière. 'When I say the "in the past", I mean well over half a century ago, before this maniac of a Victor Schœlcher began making our lives a misery. Because of him, Negroes don't want to work any more and Mulattoes are arrogant as ever. I don't mean to pry, but, why are you coming to our island?'

'I am coming to teach.'

'Ah good! At the Séminaire-Collège, I presume. It is the best school in all of Martinique and the oldest. Nothing like the republican dumps where sixty or more pickneys are packed! My elder son is in the rhetorics class. He has a passion for literature, yes. But from next year onwards, I will get him down to work. He must grapple with the gruelling job of a rum distiller. Books are all very well but they don't feed the man. In any case, not on our island...'

When two other Békés, full of disdain for Théophile,

arrived, Dupin de la Valmière's attention was diverted and he followed them into a little salon on the upper deck where the Creoles played poker or bridge after lunch until early evening. This was the time when the chaplain convened the passengers to a common prayer. Théophile, who did not participate, noticed a young man with a rather dark complexion, leaning against the rail, reading. His elegant clothing had caught Théophile's eye while boarding, but their paths had not crossed since. But then the ship was transporting nearly two hundred passengers and, in any case, he was not travelling second class like Théophile and certainly not third, a sinister place down in the hold, where the noise of engines was so unpleasant that one could hardly imagine that a normal person could get sleep there. The hold was reserved for the White Creoles' menials and for two or three adventurers. On the tenth day of the voyage—Théophile conscientiously ticked off the days on an almanac, so great was his hurry to arrive at the destination—the school teacher had followed a young Black nanny who had not stopped making eyes at him. Barely speaking French, Yvelise, as she called herself, dragged him by the hand, laughing loudly, with that extraordinary Negro laugh that he would learn to like. They went down four stairs at a time, leading to the third-class section. She quite simply threw him onto the heap of mattresses where the planter's servants were crammed at night.

'Make me a Mulatto child!' she said to him, laughing even more. 'I want him to have a fair complexion, a *peau sauvée,* beautiful smooth hair and thin lips. Ha-ha-ha! Go on, take off your clothes, *mon bougre,* dear fellow!'

What followed was sheer delight. Théophile felt enveloped, engulfed by this black firm flesh, so astonishingly sensual, softer to touch than the skin of White women, whom he had known so far. He had hesitated to caress her frizzy hair and, when he had ended up overcoming his apprehension, to his great astonishment, he realised that it was hardly coarse; it was even fragile, like mousse. Yvelise had masterly guided their lovemaking, riding him at leisure, driving her mischievous tongue into his ear, nibbling his shoulder. Théophile had exploded with a pleasure he had never known before; it left him exhausted for about an hour. When he woke up, the young girl had disappeared. Two fat older nannies were dusting the mattresses and sweeping the cabin making lewd comments on his being naked.

'*Hé,* Little White Man!' shouted one of them. 'Mamzelle Yvelise has sucked you dry. Ha-ha-ha! Be careful with your body, she is a she-devil, *oui*!'

'In Martinique,' added the other, 'you'll meet she-devils every day. Negresses like Yvelise but also *Câpresses*, Chabin women, Mulattresses. Watch out!'

'And the Coolie women too! Those are the most dangerous. Not only do they tie your mind up with diableries but their pussy fur is sharp like razor blades!'

And the two women guffawed as they gently chased Théophile out with a broom. The following days, he tried in vain to renew contact with the creature who had given him the most extraordinary pleasure which he had ever felt in his twenty-three years of life but Yvelise pretended she did not know him. She turned her gaze away when she felt he was observing her and took care never to move about except in the middle of a group of nannies who chattered, joked or quarreled while looking after their White wards. If their paths crossed, she put on a mask of both surliness and arrogance, and hurried past so that Théophile could not strike up a conversation with her. Such an attitude disconcerted the school teacher. Was this the famous Creole temperament which he heard so much about at the end of his training at the *École normale*? Former colonials had been invited to speak to the future envoys of the republican school to different countries where they wished to go, which was by definition secular, free and compulsory. The man who spoke about the Antilles lived in Martinique for nearly twenty years where he held the post of Administrator of the Navy. He had not drawn a very exciting picture of these two French islands otherwise reputed to be enchanting:

'Out there, you have to worry about mosquitoes, gentlemen!

They are everywhere and bloody fat, not these small ridiculous insects that one finds on the shores of our ponds in Europe. In the tropics these bitches suck your blood and if you are not careful, at the end of the week, your arms and legs will be covered with pustules which, in this hellish climate, get infected very quickly. You must regularly rub yourself with camphor oil. Ah! I know it stinks, but there is no better protection. Then avoid walking alone through fields and steer clear the woods: they are infested with venomous serpents. These Negro bush doctors claim they can cure snakebites by sucking the wound, but that is all fucking rubbish! I did see with my very own eyes, the reptile's fangs deep into the victims' thighs or calves; they were writhing in pain and died three or four hours later. Watch out gentlemen! Got that? Well...You must also be wary of centipedes as fat as your middle finger; violet spiders which over there the Negroes call "*matoutou-falaise*", tarantulas. They are the size of my fist and they'll leave you with very high fever for fifteen days. So much about disgusting dangerous bugs! The Antilles is not quite Africa! No lions, tigers, hyenas or crocodiles. But the greatest danger that awaits you gentlemen is the Creole temperament. Don't you imagine that the Whites on these islands are any different from their Negroes! They have all wallowed in the same cooking pot for centuries now; they speak the same Creole; they eat the same food and the planters, they still blithely exercise the *droit du seigneur* as in mediaeval times. That is the origin of the mixed-blood multitude comprised of people of all colours whom you will meet there. Among these, Mulattoes are the most dangerous and Chabins are the most villainous. Finally, you will learn to know them once you get there...the Creole temperament, as I was telling you, is something which is unpredictable. The same person can smile at you, fawn upon you in the morning and stab you in the back with a machete in the afternoon. And this without the slightest reason! Without a valid reason, I mean. Because, to the Creoles's eyes, both White and Black, what is no more than some inconsequential joke for us can be a serious insult. These people don't reason like us, my young gentlemen! Don't look so glum; it's still a very pleasant place. I survived, why shouldn't you?'

Théophile, who had dismissed the words of the colonial as blabbering of a half alcoholic, just got proof that he was telling the truth. He felt mortified and lost interest in Yvelise who now took a mean pleasure in enticing him. She began to make eyes at him again and, when she bumped into him, she said in a lewd tone: 'Well, Little White Man, don't you miss my honey box? The journey will still last another ten days because of a stubborn wind refusing to blow. If you want we can make love right away, man. Standing up if you like, that does not bother me! Ha-ha-ha!'

**Surprise Visit**

Frédéric Houblin de Maucourt had not quieted down since he woke up that morning in his mistress, Firmine's bed. The splendid Mulattress was still asleep next to him. He could hear the waves of the Atlantic crash against the cliffs of Macouba in a regular and monotonous rhythm. Except a few higglers from the countryside who were jabbering, each one more than the other, and a couple of drunks waiting for the seedy joints to open, no human movement was perceptible. Decent people, Mulattoes and Negroes, so proud of no longer working in the fields, all the bakers, traders, mechanics, butchers or school teachers, slept in. De Maucourt realised that it was Sunday. Normally, he never spent his Saturday night away from his home. He made it a duty to drive his legitimate wife and his daughter to the seven a.m. Mass, which was not attended by many coloured people who preferred the 9 o'clock High Mass. He saw red when he heard Simon, one of the most faithful mule-drivers of Courbaril Plantation, call out to him from outside when it was still dark:

'*Papa, papa! Fok ou doubout vitman-présé, ni an kontwolè ki pou rivé jòdi-a.*' (Papa, Papa! You must wake up, an Inspector is coming today.)

Houblin de Maucourt had to get dressed in no time, not

even sparing a minute to wash his face or kiss Firmine who was still snoring away. He rushed back to the plantation where the overseer, de Sainte-Foix, the steward, Marcel Polygone, and the foreman, Sosthène, awaited him with contrite faces. They were the three pillars of Courbaril upon whom the master counted when he took off for a few months to holiday in France. They all had in mind the severe sanctions which were taken against L'Habitation La Crique, at La Trinité, L'Habitation Fonds d'Or at Marigot, because two over-zealous inspectors had supposedly discovered that the Indian emigrants not only rotted in the most abject poverty—those were the very terms of the report which they submitted to the administration—but were mistreated too. This was followed by an entire list of abuses ranging from unjustified wage cuts, to thrashings and sexual exploitation of Coolie women. The incriminated Békés denied these accusations to no avail. They had to face a coalition of socialist trade unions entrenched in their plantations, of penpushers running the Administration at Fort-de-France, of Metropolitans and General Councillors largely belonging to the Mulatto class.

'The Inspector mustn't talk with Anthénor!' de Maucourt shouted, getting off the horse. 'Does anyone know where he is?'

'*Hon*! Probably attending a meeting, boss,' Polygone replied. 'The fellow doesn't show up except a couple of days a week. The rest of his salary is paid by his trade union!'

'In any case, send in people to clean up the area around the Indians' houses! Sosthène, go and see the Dorassamy family and tell them I will sign their repatriation ticket; they must not badmouth us. If they do, they are in for a hiding!'

The immigration controller arrived at Hauteurs Courbaril at ten a.m. Two policemen from Basse-Pointe, *Blancs-France*, Whites from France just like him, were with him. He was dressed in a drill suit, and didn't look easy-going. He refused the punch that M. de Maucourt offered him pointblank and asked to consult the ledgers which he read attentively, stopping to say to no one in particular:

'Four Indians dead this year? That's not bad! Not bad at all...Let's have a look, Sylvain Mouttoupoullé, gangrene, Ernest Virappoulé, typhoid fever, Héloïse Mangamalle, died in childbirth, Léon Tangamen, fall...what kind of a fall?'

'A tip-cart...fell on him...' stammered de Sainte-Foix while Houblin de Maucourt looked away.

'Really? Then why did you write "fall"? You should have written "accident", dear Sir. And then tell me, how is it that the hospital in Le Lorrain admitted so many sick Indians these last months? I'm coming from there you see, and the doctors speak of poor food, exhaustion and even ill treatment.'

The foreman, Sosthène, took the plunge to protect his half-brother and boss.

'Indians don't have a very strong constitution, you must know that...besides they drink a lot and fight each other...'

'Each other? Don't make me laugh! The Negroes are always trying to pick a fight with them, *oui*!' The Inspector got angry. 'I want to see where your emigrants are accommodated, please.'

When the little group came up to the Indian hamlet, M. de Maucourt was most surprised. The place had been transformed. The path that led there had been weeded, the potholes filled. Kumari's house, the first one, was covered with corrugated iron, newly arrived material in the colony which blazed in the sun. Dorassamy's door had been changed and the common pond, where spring water came down from the mountains, scoured. In less than two hours, his men achieved the impossible, sprucing up the place. When the Inspector asked the inhabitants, they pretended to not understand his Creole and replied hurriedly 'Yes' to all his questions.

Yes, they were treated well. Yes, they received their pay regularly, every Saturday afternoon!

Yes, their children went to school! Yes! They were well taken care of when they were ill! Yes, their women were respected! Yes! Yes! Yes! Perplexed, the controller wanted to go inside some houses and found nothing to complain about. He tried to exchange some words in Tamil with Adhiyaman Dorassamy who, for once, wore an affable face, and assured him that all was well in the best of worlds. M. Houblin de Maucourt was thrilled but tried to keep an impassive face. He said nothing, letting his assistants take the trouble of giving the controller all supplementary necessary information: number of working days since the beginning of the harvest four months ago, quantity of sugarcane delivered to the distilleries and to the sugar mill in Basse-Pointe, list of the sicknesses which struck the workers, number of marriages, deaths, and repatriations to India. Everything was covered. Ultimately, the intruder faced facts: he would not uncover the slightest transgression of the strict rules and regulations which protected Indian emigrants. Nothing to sink his teeth into, poor chap! He ended up accepting a snack at the *Grand'Case*, the Big House, not before casting a prying glance over the area. It was then, that his gaze fell miraculously upon a most astounding human creature. A man, almost naked, except for a cloth wrapped around his hips like Christ, his hands joined at the chest, his eyes half closed, standing on one leg like an egret, the other leg bent at his waist. Around him, a little monkey was moving freely, with a mocking air, nibbling on tamarinds fallen from a nearby tree.

'He is a yogi,' said M. de Maucourt who had found his tongue again. 'A holy man, from what I understand. He is much respected by his compatriots.'

'What is he doing in Martinique? Why have you not informed our services?' Retorted the Immigration Inspector, happy to have found something to criticise. 'I find him quite emaciated. Don't you give him food?'

'Radjiv doesn't want to eat anything, Sir,' said the steward, Marcel Polygone. 'We leave platters of food for him every day but to no avail, he doesn't touch a thing.'

Disappointed at this, the Inspector patted his forehead in a tired gesture. He was dripping with sweat; the bad sweat of an insufficiently acclimatised European. He must have been there for a few months only. He was about to throw in the towel when, for the first time since he settled at Hauteurs Courbaril, Radjiv, the supposedly holy man, the Jain who had written several letters to Queen Victoria to protest against his kidnapping and his deportation to Martinique, had come down upon the Inspector and had begun, in spite of his frail condition, to rain blows on him. Then he grabbed him by the neck, which almost finished the poor fellow. Neither Houblin de Maucourt nor his assistants reacted. The European—a man taken unawares is a beaten man, as they say in Creole—only owed his life to Adhiyaman and Vinesh's intervention. His drill suit was now grey because of the dust from the dirt courtyard. His cheeks had been grazed by the gravel. The man trembled in amazement and rage. He followed de Maucourt to the *Grand'Case* where Da Gervaise, the old Black nanny, made him look more presentable and worthy of his eminent position. He drank many a glass of rum before getting back on his horse with comical clumsiness, as the planter continued to explain to him that the Jain held the French administration responsible for his deportation to La Martinique.

'Have a safe trip, *Monsieur le contrôleur*!' The master of Habitation Courbaril said to him, rather ironically while patting the Inspector's horse. 'And come back when you like! The pleasure will be entirely ours. Ha-ha-ha!'

*

The young Mulatto, who seemed to have sea legs, introduced himself to Théophile without a fuss. He was coming back from Berlin where he had studied music and philosophy, so he said. His name was Pierre-Marie Danglemont and he too was going to Martinique to teach. He was proud of his native city, Saint-Pierre, which he described as much more beautiful and industrious than a number of similar cities of provincial France. In comparison, he affirmed that Tours, Besançon, Carpentras or Dijon were god-forsaken places.

'You'll see our theatre, it is an exact replica, though smaller in size, of Bordeaux's and we have a tramway, a stock exchange building. Besides the entire city, except the seedy quarters, of course, are electrified.'

He would teach at the most prestigious school of the island: the Lycée Saint Louis de Gonzague. But as he pronounced this imposing name, the Mulatto's face clouded over, noted Théophile. He ended up confessing that this establishment only welcomed offspring of traders and planters of the white race, except a handful of Mulattoes from rich families.

'I chose the republican school,' said Théophile, 'and I am not assigned to Saint-Pierre, nor even Fort-de-France, but a small village, Macouba. Know it?'

Pierre-Marie Danglemont burst out laughing, the same shattering laughter like most White planters playing poker, the same as Yvelise's and the black nannies', those women whose profession was called 'da' in Creole, as the young man learnt, a strange word which reminded him of its Russian homonym, 'Yes'. Théophile had made the acquaintance of a dowager from Moscow at the theatre. She used to take up residence in Paris in the winters and kept saying 'da' to him. Stranger still, a mystery of sheer chance, the nannies, when their mistresses addressed them invariably responded 'Oui m'dame', never a word more!

'My dear friend, you are truly a hero,' said Pierre-Marie, suddenly thoughtful. 'I don't know Macouba but I can easily imagine it. It must look like an immense sugarcane field with a wretched market town in the middle, having no more than a couple of streets. In the countryside, there will be the plantations of White Creoles and their sumptuous villas surrounded by the huts of Negroes and Indians. Nothing very exciting!'

Once again he was speaking highly of his dear Saint-Pierre where three daily newspapers were published: *Les Antilles,* and *Le Bien Public,* the White Creole class' media; and *Les Colonies,* run by their Mulatto rivals. Opera companies from Europe and North America came regularly to perform. Groups of poets competed in inventiveness and were as good as Hugo, Lamartine or Baudelaire.

'Well, I'm exaggerating somewhat here, he conceded. 'In reality, our men of letters are imitators, perfect imitators but still imitators! You will meet them when you come to Saint-Pierre. I do recommend the Carnival period, Romantic Creoles, Naturalist Creoles, Parnassian Creoles and more recently even Symbolist Creoles, according to what I was told. Ha-ha-ha!'

Théophile was fascinated by the complex and contradictory personality of Pierre-Marie Danglemont. He remembered the odious work which the colonialist had highly recommended when he spoke with the school teachers assigned to the Antilles at the end of their training at the *École normale* in Orléans: *Essai sur l'inégalité des races humaines* (An Essay on the Inequality of the Human Races), by a certain Count Gobineau. 'Everything is in there!' he declared. To understand Negroes and other coloured human races, there was no better guide according to him. Théophile had been horrified by this reading. Gobineau proposed a quasi-zoological classification of the human races using so-called cranial measurements. According to his hierarchy of races, the Aryan race was allegedly superior—Negroes being, of course, at the bottom of the ladder. This point of view was in complete contradiction with Théophile's egalitarian convictions which were based on his in-depth reading of Danton and Robespierre. However he had noted that Gobineau was less critical of persons of mixed-race, born of Whites and Blacks, Mulattoes to be precise, in whom he condescended to recognise some, albeit modest, qualities. Did Danglemont have some? In any case he seemed very lonely on board this ship overloaded with Europeans at odds with society and descendants of pro-slavery planters, with their stupid, groveling servants. If one could accuse Danglemont of being slightly conceited, one had to admit that he weighed each of his words and cherished a certain number of ideals which were, when closely examined, not very far from Théophile's. Simply put, although he was an islander, the young Mulatto was a city slicker through and through. He was incapable of settling down in the peace and quiet of the country without getting bored. The two ended up becoming friends and spending the rest of the voyage together.

Each morning, Pierre-Marie welcomed Théophile with a

resounding: 'Good morning, Educator of the People!' The latter retorted in the same mocking tone:

'Good morning, Educator of the Elite!' Their acquaintance did not go unnoticed. Two days before arrival, which was confirmed by the frequent appearance of sea birds, François-Marie Dupin de La Valmenière took the republican school teacher aside and warned him about mixing with Mulattoes. According to him, this bastard race was worse than Negroes because they deployed artifice and hypocrisy with consummate skill, in order to lull the Whites whom they hated the most. In Martinique, their main goal was to oust the Whites from all the important political positions, with the help of Metropolitan democrats or socialists who were quite unaware of colonial customs.

'Mulattoes use the *Blancs-France*, white man from France, to destroy the White Creole,' he said, getting angry all of a sudden. 'And Victor Schœlcher, this *saboteur* of the French Empire gave them a damn good helping hand! Let me give you some advice, dear Sir, if you really want to mix with coloured people, well then choose the Negroes. At least they can be good and frank provided you can keep them in their place, while the Mulattoes are hopeless and deceitful rogues.'

The semi-circular harbour of Saint-Pierre, the proud mountain shaped like a cone which overlooked it, enchanted Théophile. The din and bustle of the docks, crowded with barrels of salted meat, sacks of rice and lentils, cartons of dried cod and barrels of rum, captivated him. The heady aromas that emanated from the outskirts of the Mouillage Market, a subtle mix of cloves, allspice, vanilla, cocoa and other spices and the scent of fruits that he did not know yet, turned his head, to the great amusement of Pierre-Marie Danglemont. Carts took turns to transport the White Creoles and their servants amid a crowd of porters, one more obsequious than the other. Yvelise, the young chambermaid who had initiated Théophile into Negro sensuality, told him merrily as she passed:

'Eh, Little White Man, thank you for the baby, *oui*!'

'No sooner ashore, and you are a father already!'

Danglemont teased him, shaking his hand. 'If one day you feel like escaping the boredom of Macouba, know that you can always find me at *La Taverne de la Flibuste* from 8 p.m. my dear friend. This dive is at the end of the city, over there, not far from the river Roxelane. Well, good luck!'

They hugged for a long time. A Negro dressed in dark clothes, who was holding two horses by the halter, came up to Théophile and asked him:

'You are M. Leroux?'

'That is me!'

'The Macouba Town Hall sent me. My name is Gustave. Can you ride a horse?'

'A little...In fact, very little...'

'No fears! This one is as gentle as a lamb. Don't startle him, that's all. We must leave at once if we don't want the night to come suddenly upon us.'

They rode together in silence through grassy plains and hills, the Negro at the front, turning round, time and again, to encourage the school teacher. It was barely five o'clock when the sun started going down. They had reached a tiny village, perched on a slope with a strange name, Ajoupa-Bouillon, which reminded Théophile of the valiant knight Godefroi de Bouillon. People made welcoming gestures, some calling out in a jovial tone:

'Good morning, White man, have you just landed or what? Your skin is the colour of cassava.'

Some children tried to follow their horses running fast behind and begged for a few coins or sweets. The Negro chased them away with his riding crop and stepped up the pace without warning. Théophile had difficulty keeping up. His back, his hips, and his legs were burning. The pain made him clench his teeth. At the end of an exhausting Atlantic crossing, he should have given himself a day or two of rest at Saint-Pierre. Manifestly he had overestimated his strength.

'The most difficult part is over,' his guide reassured him. 'Once we arrive at Basse-Pointe, it is all flat or a downward slope. Chin up!'

The man seemed worried. As evening fell, he cast furtive glances around him as if he feared an attack by highwaymen. The road was deserted at present; in such darkness, it was like a belt of stones whose light grey guided the almost sleepy steps of the horses.

'We may come across...a coffin,' said the Negro in a tremulous voice. 'If that ever happens just dismount immediately, *Monsieur,* and hold your mount by his halter. I know what to do...'

Théophile held back a smile. He had read pages and pages on superstitions in the Antilles and on this famous *quimbois,* obeah, a mix of Negro witchcraft and White magic, which even men as reasonable and cultured as Pierre Danglemont feared. The latter had, in fact, refused to deny the existence of zombies, just saying that he knew nothing about it, in a manner which could be interpreted in so many ways. In fact, he too was scared, but in front of a European, he preferred not to show it, thought Théophile. Finally, at Basse-Pointe, the road became broader and became straight, bordered on both sides by rows and rows of canefields. The evening wind was threading its way through the cane with a murmur that sounded like a long drawn moan. This made the guide shudder. Instead of galloping away, he got into a slow trot, his eyes watchful and asked Théophile to stay close to him. Suddenly he shouted:

'There! Look there, dammit!'

The metropolitan school teacher could only distinguish a formless brownish mass which could have been anything. A bullock sleeping across the road. A bundle of linen fallen from a cart. Or a simple mound of mud because the wet grass suggested that there had been a heavy downpour a few hours earlier. Honestly speaking, it was quite clearly a coffin! The school teacher thought it was a joke. Danglemont had warned him that Negroes were pranksters at heart. They loved to play nasty tricks on Europeans who were fresh off the boat.

According to the philosopher musician, it amused the Negroes to no end to see the White man's face change colour, turn from white to red. But in this case, Théophile was neither the victim of a *macaquerie*, monkey trick—a Creole expression he had picked up from Yvelise—nor a hallucination. It was indeed a coffin. Massive. Oblong. Brilliant as if it had just been polished, with golden handles which shone in the dark. The two men got off the horse at the same time and the Negro started walking ahead slowly, his eyes focussed on the object. He was no longer shuddering and a cold determination could be read on his drawn features. When he was ten steps away from the coffin, he held out his horse's halter to Théophile and told him:

'*Monsieur*, if anything happens to me, jump on your horse and get out of here!'

He stepped even closer, very carefully, taking umpteen precautions. About a metre from the coffin, he suddenly turned his back, squatted before doing a back jump and straddled this mysterious object. There was a mournful hissing sound, then the thing taking the shape of a spiral of fire flew over the sugarcane fields which flattened out as if a gust of wind was blowing. The horses reared. The guide came back to him. He did not utter a word. He reassured his agitated mount, whispering softly in his ear and mounted. The rest of the journey took less than twenty minutes. From the noise of the sea below the cliffs, Théophile knew that he had reached the town of Macouba which had only one main road lit by a single street light. A disparate group of houses in wood or stone, their windows and doors firmly shut, lined this road. It was only 8 p.m. though. The house assigned to the school teacher was in an annexe of the town hall where a huge tricolour flag fluttered in the sea breeze. All night he was gently lulled by the backwash and did not really fall asleep before the early hours. A lady, who introduced herself proudly as a town worker brought him a tray of fruits and a bowl of *café* flavoured with cinnamon. She hummed while dusting his bed without bothering about him and seeing he was intimidated, she said to him:

'White man, go have a wash! *Mussieu le maire,* the Mayor is waiting for you, *oui*!'

Théophile was surprised when, an hour later, he went into the office of the First Town Councillor of Macouba; there, he found three White planters entirely dressed in khaki fanning themselves with their pith helmets. The mayor, an elderly Mulatto who sat sunk in an armchair that seemed too deep for him, observed him with an inquisitive look from behind his spectacles. He welcomed him and invited him to be seated. The planters examined the young man from head to foot as if they were dealing with a strange animal.

'That's our little M. Leroux, I presume?' One of them asked the Mayor. 'He seems rather young to me...How old are you, dear Sir?'

'Hardly twenty, I bet,' said another one without letting Théophile answer. 'I told you, de Maucourt, the Republic recruits them from the cradle. That way, they have more malleable brains and they can disseminate their venom in all innocence.'

'Gentlemen, gentlemen, I urge you to...,' the Mayor tried to intervene in an ill-assured voice. 'Our duty is welcome a valiant son of our homeland, who chose deliberately to sacrifice his youth for the sole purpose of the spiritual elevation of colonial populations who have long been deprived of the benefits of education. I believe...'

'*Ga sa, éleksion bout, Edmon ! Arété basinen nou épi lo pawol initil ou a! Sé dépi yo rivé Matinik, fok nou fè yo konpwann ki manniè bagay-la ka woulé isiya,*' (Listen, the elections are over, Edmond! Stop your bullshit! As soon as they come to Martinique, they must be made to understand how things work here) said the man who was called de Maucourt.

He turned to Théophile: 'To tell you the truth, dear Sir, your age matters little. The main point is that you have to accept that school is not absolutely indispensable for Negro boys. It is even a luxury! For your information, you have to know that our dear island of Martinique lives off sugarcane and we need hands to harvest it. I have no objections to Negroes learning to read and write, but frankly, I can't see how this will contribute to the prosperity of the colony. All the more so as Mulattoes... you do know what Mulattoes are?'

'Yes...yes, I know,' stammered Théophile.

'Well, then these people already sufficiently leech off the resources of the country without the Negroes joining the ranks. But Mr Mayor is right, let us begin with the introductions. My name is Frédéric Houblin de Maucourt. I own Courbaril Plantation, located in the Hauteurs Courbaril quarter. One hundred and twelve hectares of sugarcane, about sixty workers, Negro and Indian.'

'De Lavigne de Saint-Jorre, at your service! As for me, I own Eyma Plantation, at Basse-Pointe,' said the second one.

'De Marcillac!' added the third, greeting him with a nod. 'Poterie Plantation and Distillery Saint-Hilaire. I make one of the best rums in Martinique.'

'We are, so to speak, and to use a very erudite word dear to our venerable Mayor, the quintessence of the town council of Macouba. Ha-ha-ha!' said de Maucourt.

The municipal councillor then informed Théophile that two Martiniquan colleagues already taught in the primary school and he would provide precious assistance because their classes were already overcrowded.

'Our women give birth to quite a few children,' he added with a tired look. 'Eight, ten, twelve sometimes! It is true that whooping cough and dysentery take a good half of them before they reach adolescence.'

He was anxious to find out if the young man was vaccinated against yellow fever, 'more common in the south than here in the north,' he hurriedly added. He then offered him, as a welcome gift, a stick sculpted in the shape of a sugarcane.

'A gift from these gentlemen,' said the Mayor, pointing with his chin to the White Creoles.

'Don't forget, young man,' said de Maucourt, getting up to take his leave, instantly followed by his peers. 'Don't ever forget that here sugarcane will always take precedence over books!'

# 16

## Repatriation

*There comes a time when suffering ends, there comes a time, a day, a week, a month, a year during which—it is written in the contract, fuck!—You are filled with limitless joy. The air suddenly seems lighter, the mud of the dirt tracks across the sugarcane fields feels less burdensome. You admire the flight of the broad-winged hawks, the mad audacity with which they fly so close to the sun, and you feel like them, free of all ties. No woman's caress could turn us away from the glory of that day.*

Vinesh came up to the rock which emerged between the thin, long wader bird-like roots of the oldest mango tree of the Plantation. There, for years he had prayed to Kannavédi, the elephant-headed god, unknown to the Negroes and the Whites, who would never have been able to discern the fine yellow stripes that he had drawn on it. It was the favourite meeting place of cane-cutters and mule-drivers at the end of the harvest. Dice were rolled there, invoking the magical number eleven, *tafia* was slept off, the latest news exchanged, chances with new women estimated. It was also right there that the men shamelessly emptied their bladders. Over-ripe fruits were strewn everywhere, rotting, but nobody bothered. As a result the place had a partly-nauseating, partly-intoxicating smell. Vinesh had followed The Ancestor's advice: 'Choose your patron God and consecrate an altar for him. Anywhere. What is important is the love you dedicate to him.'

From Kannavédi, the young man had asked for two boons: the first one was not to die in this accursed country, this godless and lawless island of Martinique, which had no ancestral religion, which was dedicated to profit and debauchery, this island of sudden and unreasonable violence; the other was to obtain a seat on the last ship repatriating his compatriots back to India which would drop anchor this year, 1912, in the bay of Saint-Pierre. The first boon had been granted: Vinesh had escaped many dangers, the worst among them, melancholy. This disease which no *poussari* or White doctor or *quimboiseur*, obeahman, could cure seemed to particularly afflict the Indian race. It manifested itself in strange behaviours like remaining silent for entire weeks or not even moaning when some treacherous illness fell upon you. At the beginning, the Béké had been stupefied. He went about telling one and all that Indians were the silent type. Nothing to do with the Negroes for whom turbulence and cheerfulness were apparently second nature. For the Negroes, the Indians were a sneaky gang, unreliable people, always ready to break strikes and kowtow to foremen and overseers.

'Look at Singara!' they declared. 'This fellow has been living with us for almost fifteen years now and, we swear by the Lord that we have only heard him speak twice.'

Singara was a secretive creature who lived in a somewhat secluded hut damaged every year by the September cyclones, a hut which he had given up repairing. He did not even participate in Indian ceremonies and no joy ever lit up his face when *Pongal* came in January, at the time when work in the fields began. For four days and nights the Indians behaved as if they had taken leave of their senses. They washed their houses several times a day to chase away the miasma of the previous year, scrubbed their battered kitchen utensils, darned their clothes, decked up their roofs with crowns of red and yellow hibiscus and danced with a frenzy which stupefied the Negroes. They danced alone, focused, faces imbued with a supreme happiness, and from time to time ran to a large pot of water or a pond or a river to dunk their heads. They then raised their heads briskly shaking them as if they were hand fans; their drenched hair resembled a peacock's nuptial parade. 'To celebrate *Pongal*' was indispensable for those who wanted to escape the pitfalls of the year that was beginning and certain Negroes, reading in it some Indian magic, got involved in this madness too. Only Singara ignored this ritual. As he ignored talking with anyone. As he ignored eating. As thin as the shadow of a string, he carried out all the tasks that the foreman entrusted him with, never begged for the least favor. He did not even grant himself two pennyworth of rest. In the evening, he was never seen hanging out in the rum shack, at least not on the only bench reserved for Indians in the dimmer section of the establishment. He did not have a credit account with Man Ninise, the owner, who had been the mistress of M. de Maucourt's father in her youth. How every single day he managed to raise his emaciated body from the pallet on which he slept was a mystery. Vinesh had tried to talk to him, keen on discovering his secret.

'M. Singara, I heard that you are a very wise man...', he had begun.

The man had stared through Vinesh as if he were transparent. And so Vinesh sought to understand his story. Every Indian in this country was a story. So many twists and turns since the departure from sacred India! So many humiliations silently suffered! Nobody had told Vinesh Singara's full story but thanks to the bits and pieces, which he had gleaned here and there, he managed to put together an almost complete picture of his destiny. First, he discovered that the fellow was not born in India or, more precisely, that he came into this world in the middle of the ocean. Which one? The Sea of Fire or the Sea of Darkness? Opinions diverged. In any case, he was the son of the malevolent spirits that have populated the deep seas since eternity. These creatures must have attacked the ship which transported the emigrants and, in the dead of night, they had forced themselves on his mother. She gave birth in just three months without anybody's help because the vainglorious British sailors felt an irrepressible fear when faced with such impossible events. Were the women not cooped up in a shelter on the foredeck when the men were sent down to the hold as soon as the stars started twinkling? All this while armed sailors and mean *mestris* kept a careful watch. Usually, the few children who were born aboard were fair-skinned because some British recruiters felt the need to satisfy their instincts in the trading posts where candidates for emigration were crammed for months on end. Now, Singara was as black as a blackbird! Indians and Whites decreed that his mother had fallen prey to an invisible malevolent creature. Upon disembarking in Martinique, his story got around the plantations and the Negroes only called him by the nickname, 'Son of the Devil Incarnate'.

Out of compassion for him, an old Indian woman told Vinesh another facet of the tragedy: Singara had not managed to protect the two holy books which his mother had brought from the Madras Presidency. She was related to a man from one of the first convoys who was working as a mule-cart-driver on Séguineau Plantation, in the Lorrain quarter. She was supposed to hand the famous *puttagam*, holy book, over to him so that he could fortify his faith and, more importantly, propagate it. He was one of the rare Indians of Martinique who could read Tamil and people came from all over the island to consult him. The prayers to be recited when a close relative was dying, the exact ingredients to be used to prepare offerings to Goddess Mariamman or quite simply to write letters of complaint to plantation masters, mayors and to His Excellency M. le Gouverneur himself, if you were bold enough. Obviously nobody understood anything of this Dravidian script which some qualified as scribble. But with the passage of time, the learned man's memory began to falter. He therefore required the help of works describing the precise rituals. His distant niece, Singara's mother, was entrusted with the task of taking these *puttagam* to Martinique because it was easier for a woman to hide them in her sari. Having travelled with the seventh convoy, she arrived in Martinique at a time when the fury of iconoclastic priests was raging. These white bearded men, wearing heavy wooden crucifixes around their necks, dressed in hurriedly ironed cassocks and wearing sandals, were no longer happy to officiate in their churches. They roamed the countryside along with a congregation of fanatics, Belgian Redemptorists, in order to spread what they called the Good Word, hunting down the slightest signs of Hindu presence. As soon as they spotted a mast on which a little triangular flag in honour of Nagourmira fluttered, they convinced the *Békés* to have it razed at once. The smallest altar, the most dilapidated shack used as temple was mercilessly consigned to the flames. And on Thursday afternoons, Indian children were taken almost forcibly to the presbytery to study Catechism.

'And yet, Singara's mother had honourably accomplished the task,' continued the old woman. 'On the boat, nobody suspected for a minute that she was hugging the two holy books to her stomach. Nobody! Even in the thick of the storms on the Sea of Fire, she remained stoic. On the Sea of Darkness, when the English captain had water rationed on board, the young woman chose not to bathe for weeks and weeks in order to protect the *puttagam* from prying eyes. But her heart gave way as the Antilles drew near, then the onerous task of accomplishing the rest of the mission lay with Singara, her little boy. He was placed in a bourgeois family with no children and they raised him till the age of ten. His foster parents put the holy books away in a canvas bag containing his few personal belongings and the child was unaware of the value of what he was carrying on his back. He was tossed from plantation to plantation because his frail constitution made him useless to the Békés. Indians died so quickly and sometimes because of a simple flu! Or even a small cut on the foot which would begin to fester and turn gangrenous. Sometimes diarrhoea, which would keep neither Negroes nor Whites in bed, would finish the Indians off. Then there were those who let themselves perish, refusing one day to eat for no reason whatsoever. Vinesh, my boy, you did not know those times, the first years of our settlement in this gruesome country. You were too young to realise that almost every week, we mourned the death of one of our people. And no question of burning the dead bodies! For Christians, these were barbaric customs. They preferred the slow rotting in these boxes with gilded ornaments, which they called coffins. What an awful word "coffin" *hon*!'

Ultimately, Singara ended up at Fonds d'Or Plantation, in the north of the country, where he was appointed to cart calabashes of water to quench the thirst of workers. Honestly, this was no painful job and the boy regained his strength, toughened up, began to learn Creole and play with Negro pickneys in spite of the taunts they always heaped on him. He became a puny mischievous boy with dark brown eyes which enchanted women. The holy books which he did not know what to do with, unaware of the whereabouts of his great-uncle, remained in a corner of his house, in broad daylight, till the day when an overseer decided to organize a round of inspections. Thefts were increasing on the plantation. One evening, when his family and he had gone to a banquet in a neighbouring quarter, the Fonds d'Or *Béké* was robbed. Silver candlesticks, creole jewels in gold from Cayenne, wads of bank notes, fine linen sheets, bottles of Bordeaux wine, paintings, everything had been carried away after the swindlers had poisoned his dogs. His flunkeys, who had their evening off, were busy having a bash and had heard nothing. In the morning, Negroes and Indians were gathered together and interrogated by the police. All in vain. Mad with anger, the Béké gave his foreman his marching orders and replaced him with two Mulattoes from Vauclin in the South, whose hair was yellow like the *mangue-zéphirine,* the local mango. Tolerance was not one of their virtues. The pace of cane-cutting was stepped up, the punishments for those who lagged behind were increased and frequent inspections of their houses were organized in the hope of getting a lead. It was thus that one of the new overseers fell upon the two books, which he immediately brought back to the Béké who got rid of them.

'It is believed that he burnt them,' said the old woman

in a whisper, 'but I know that he kept them for himself. The Whites have a passion for objects. It is amazing! They collect anything: clocks, stamps, engravings, precious stones, terracotta vases. Believe me, Vinesh, I was a chambermaid all my life. I lived in close contact with them for more than thirty years. Sometimes these people attach greater importance to their trinkets than to their children! The fact remains that the day the *puttagams* were seized, scourges pelted down on the unfortunate Singara. Nameless hardships began to obstruct his path. To punish him for having kept what the Whites qualified as works of sorcery, he was thrown into the fields. He who had never held a machete found himself plunged in the sugarcane hell overnight. His palms were getting ripped, his frail body was bending and aging, his hair began to fall. Singara became quite simply hideous. Uglier than a cardinal sin, *oui*! When the master of Fonds d'Or realised that he was good for nothing, he exchanged him with his buddy for a pair of mules. *Eh oui!* I'm not joking. For two exhausted mules who had to be whipped to carry the bundles of sugarcane.'

Little by little, Singara sank into depression. He forgot that his time of indenture was over and did not ask for his repatriation to India. His brothers in misery begged him to see reason.

'You cannot die in this country! You have already devoted the most beautiful years of your life to it. It is time you go and purify your tired body in the waters of the Ganges.' But Singara kept his lips sealed. He did not so much as bat an eyelid. They finally forgot about him and left him to his madness.

Vinesh thought of him the day when he walked to the hundred-year-old mango tree shading the rock that he had dedicated to Ganesh. Indeed, for some time now, he had felt a muted foreboding rise in him, like a buzzing in his ears, which made him distracted, insensitive to the sounds of the world, indifferent to the gentle words of his mother, to the secrets of his young brother who was assiduously courting a *capistrelle*, a young girl, from the town of Macouba. And to the ceaseless taunts of the Negroes too. Was this the first signs of the melancholy that had struck Singara? This was not the time to give in to despondency because in four months, his indenture contract was coming to an end. Incidentally he had notched a rock, marking months and years, this unending time, this awful time, which did not stop gnawing at the mind of the most seasoned of Indians. Vinesh joined his hands and said a prayer to his guardian deity, his eyes half shut. A sudden coolness bathed his temples in spite of the ferocious heat. He felt himself being transported far from Courbaril Plantation. He floated in the air, like King Bagiratha, who for centuries had climbed the slopes of the Himalayas alone in order to implore Brahma to bring back the monsoons. A cry interrupted his meditation. The cry of a woman distraught and in love at the same time. Vinesh took three steps back and looked for his machete, he had dumped it on the ground but could not find it. He cast a glance all around the grassland where the flames-of-the-forest displayed their crimson petals as if competing insolently with the sun. Nobody around. Not a living soul. However, he would have recognized this voice among a thousand others. How was it possible? It was Nalima, the most seductive Indian woman who ever disembarked in Martinique. She hardly ever left the surroundings of the *Grand'Case*, the Big House, so as to be always available for the master. No, he was not dreaming: she was emerging from behind the thickets, dapper in a white organdy dress. Her magnificent bosom was bouncing, caressed by her tousled hair with tawny highlights which came down to her hips. As resplendent as Sita, Rama's wife, the victorious king of Ayodhya, Sita, the one who was celebrated in the songs that accompanied the *nadrons*.

'Talking to yourself?' She quipped, laughing, and her laughter, a luminous cascade, lit up the young man with great happiness. She drew close enough to touch him. He could feel her short breath on his cheek. Her small teeth shone like pure ivory.

'Speak to me Vinesh! I'm not going to eat you up, *non*. Ha-ha-ha!'

'*Man té ka chaché koutla-mwen. Talè-a...man...man té mété'y la ek disparet anni pwan'y...*' (I was looking for my machete. Just now...I...I put it down here and it has disappeared.)

'Here it is!' She said, laughing twice as much.

Vinesh noticed the slenderness of her fingers, the yellow shimmer of her palms. He was fascinated. He could not find words, especially as the young woman's French, full of sharp notes and squeaks, made his Creole so much more miserable. The horror of it was that his bastard language, violent, maimed, lewd had ended up becoming the language of the majority of Indians, inexorably blurring Tamil, the language of their ancestors and their rituals.

'I heard that you asked the *Béké* to fix the date of your repatriation? You want to leave us then? Don't you feel good here? I will never go back to India. Never!' said the young woman. She drew nearer, snuggling up to him although he did not fold his arms around her. Vinesh felt an irrepressible chill envelop him, the hair on his arms standing on end as if this beautiful creature were a serpent.

'Here, I am free,' she continued, 'no mother-in-law to tyrannize me, no jealous good-for-nothing husband, and then I've become Christian! Why keep on praying to gods who could not even protect us when we were in distress, *hein*? Say something! Speak, *mon bougre*, my dear fellow!'

Suddenly it became crystal clear to Vinesh. Could he have misjudged her? This woman who aroused his senses, who was trying to wrest him from the world of Indians and drive him into the world of the Whites, this woman here was a woman of ill virtue out there, in Calcutta! She had the lyrical insolence of those who have no honor to protect anymore and who decide to make a gift of their bodies to all the men whom love has disdained. On the nights when he would not touch her and she had to go out in the rain to cool her ardours, how many times had he heard his mother reproach his father for having associated with such girls in his youth? In Madurai, at the time when he was his father's dearest son, the heir to Ambu Dorassamy, the rich owner of a spinning mill? Her grievances took the form of a long monotonous complaint, almost like a song, in the hoarse Tamil of the low castes. Believing her two sons were asleep, Devi struggled with her husband, rolled on him, covered him with kisses, tried to take off his night rags, but Adhiyaman remained stonily indifferent. Ever since he had lost all hope of going back to Madras, he had wrapped himself in a silence that nobody could shake him out of. In the morning, he went to the fields like a automaton, cut cane relentlessly, finished the work allotted to him before the other workers, went back home early, indifferent to the mocking greetings of Negresses on his way, indifferent to everything, to the wind, to the rain, to the sun, to the storm, to dust.

Adhiyaman had unfortunately shared with his wife details of his youthful escapades. In those days he assiduously patronized houses of pleasure in the seedy quarters of Madurai where he was received like a prince. There, he had developed a taste for these women, experts in erotic sciences, inherited from the ancient times, illustrated in the sculptures of Khajuraho, codified in the *Kama-sutra*. These courtesans knew that the coming together of bodies was only a prelude to the much more exalting ecstasy of meditation, a reflection, albeit pale, of the celestial union of divine couples. He was still haunted by the memory of the hours spent exploring their bodies perfumed with sandalwood, looking for tiny spots of infinite pleasure, without this necessarily culminating in the act of penetration.

'In this country', he murmured, stretched out on his straw mattress, 'I unlearnt the art of love. Neither the Whites nor the Negroes know what it is about. They behave like savage beasts. Hardly have they begun and they are already in a hurry to finish with it!'

Vinesh's father had had a brief liaison with an *attacheuse*, who would not stop provoking him. She was a widow and had sworn that she would evaluate the virile qualities of all the men in Macouba, whatever their colour, before Basile—as Negroes used to call death—carried her away in his arms.

Nicknamed Coucoune Diable, she never settled on any

plantation. Everything depended on her current mood or the man she had set her eyes on. And so she would turn up early in the morning in the courtyard of *Grand'Case*, when men and women were beginning their workday; she arrived from Eyma, Gradis or more distant plantations, and demanded that foreman Sosthène put her behind the cane-cutter she had chosen for herself. The Chabin complied, no doubt out of fear that she would deride him just as she had done with Marcel Polygone, the steward. This *Câpre*, born of a Mulatto and a Negress, who hated being taken for an *échappé-Couli*, a half-breed, born of adultery between a Negro and an Indian, was a pretentious character, always nattily dressed, speaking polished French, and vilifying Creole. He was very proud to be a man who got married in church and in the Town Hall. He never missed any opportunity to admonish unmarried cohabitation, (most present on Courbaril Plantation), and to denounce what he pedantically called fornication. One day he had objected to Coucoune Diable being hired after she had disappeared for two weeks right in the middle of harvest. Who could have suspected that this noble soul would have succumbed to the advances of a she-devil? It was unthinkable and yet there was such a ring of truth in her words that nobody questioned what the merry widow declared when she denounced him, providing a salacious description of his virile member: the tail of a creole pig, a ridiculous corkscrew, that was what this M. Marcel Polygone was hiding in his flannel pants! And what is more, after having done *djouk-djouk* like a rabbit, he would slump, more exhausted than a fellow who had run twenty kilometres on the double.

Adhiyaman was one of the rare men on the Courbaril Plantation to resist this witch, not that he feared like some thought, that she would mock the size of his penis, but because in the past, in another life which he had lived out there in Madurai, he had known nautch girls, women far more skilled in matters of carnal pleasures than this harlot. And if he respected these women, in whom, at the risk of sounding sacrilegious, he saw incarnations of goddesses, he only felt a deep disdain for the Negresses who sold themselves to the highest bidder and the deranged Indian women, at odds with authority, who imitated them. Coucoune Diable, far from being offended by the repeated refusals of Adhiyaman, pursued him assiduously for months, managing to be his *attacheuse* in the fields, remaining hot on his heels as he returned home, pattering provocative words all the while. She even dared to come up close to the Dorassamy house and challenge him with these words:

'Hey Coolie, your wife has sweet candy between her legs or what? You're always stuck there, but I can offer you ten times better. Ha-ha-ha! Mine is a barrel of *sirop-batterie*, wet sugar, *oui*!'

Adhiyaman had ended up being the laughing stock of rum drinkers and domino players who laid siege to Man Ninise's shop as soon as the twilight settled and swarms of bats began to streak the sky. Even his Indian peers, who had taken part in Coucoune Diable's game, only too happy to escape their forced abstinence, found it difficult to understand his attitude. They wrongly imagined that his wife Devi, known for her strong willed nature, kept him on a tight leash. However, getting tired of this racket, she pushed him to satisfy the insatiable curiosity of the widow.

'*Karumbu kattodu irundaal, yerumbu thaane varum*' (Where there is a bundle of sugar cane, there come ants), she told him in an enigmatic tone. It was a bad move because from that ill-fated day—when Adhiyaman let himself be knocked over in the middle of the fields by that witch in the stifling hours of the early afternoon—he stopped touching Devi. Not that he had taken to the savage mounting that Coucoune Diable inflicted upon him—the matter was concluded in ten minutes—but *because* it had made his stomach churn. The stench of the Negress' sweat had suffocated him and he still bore the scratch marks she had inflicted on his forearms. All this allowed Vinesh to understand the surprising goodwill which his father had long shown Nalima when she let herself be snatched up by the master of Courbaril Plantation.

Imagining that White Creoles behaved differently from Negroes in matters of the heart, he used to defend her with so much conviction in front of Indians that Vinesh ended up imitating him. So Vinesh was dumbfounded, when he caught the overseer de Sainte-Foix—a downgraded White but White all the same—riding one of the cooks of the *Grand'Case*, standing against the door behind the steward's office.

Thanks to the secrets he overheard his father share with his mother during the nights when Devi harassed him because Adhiyaman desired her no more, Vinesh had begun to respect women who devoted their life to the practice of the refined art of the mystic-carnal ecstasy. Sacarabany, an Indian prankster who amused his brothers of misery in Tamil and entertained the Negroes in Creole, made the most of the celebrations on the patron saint's day. He had a box of explicit etchings probably from the famous *Kama-sutra* and allowed adults and children to feast their eyes on for five francs and five cents respectively. Vinesh did not deny himself this secret pleasure. If beautiful Nalima could strike equally acrobatic and sensual poses, he could only admire her. He could even consider her as the thirteenth avatara of Vishnu, Mohini, the Enchantress according to the *Bhagavata Purana*, a book which the Ancestor happened to recite. Vinesh could still hear the words of the old man resonate in his head:

'Whoever takes refuge in Me through intense pure and unalloyed devotion, an enemy, a woman prostitute, or a man born in a family of non-believers, can attain perfection of existence.'

Wasn't Nalima all this at the same time? An enemy of her people whom she had betrayed in a White man's bed, a prostitute, an infidel who had turned up her nose at the Hindu faith which she rubbished as vulgar paganism like Father Xavier, her confessor at the Macouba church. What was this aura which surrounded her person and dissipated all hatred for her from the very moment she appeared?

'If you return to India', she said to him again, 'you will be lost. You never lived there from what I know. You have no idea of the squalor our people live in over there. I am older than you. I arrived with the third from last convoy, when I was already fifteen years old. I know what I'm talking about, Vinesh. I beg you, do give up this absurd idea of repatriation! Henceforth our country is this one. Without the work of Indians, the plantations would have collapsed, the Whites would have been ruined and the Negroes condemned to beg for a chunk of bread from dogs. We have reconstructed Martinique. It is ours too, now.'

The young man believed he was hearing Anthénor, the trade unionist who dreamt of uniting Negro and Indian workers against the hegemony of the Whites. But this left him indifferent. Martinique? India? Repatriation? Courbaril Plantation? Poverty? Strike? All these words did not mean anything to him anymore because the presence of this young woman wiped them from his mind. Only she existed and he began, stupidly without doubt, to recite this poem by Auguste Joyau to her. Théophile, the school teacher, *Blanc-France*, White man from France, had taught him to read using this poem. He felt a particular affection for this text, which had pulled him out of ignorance and which he had learnt by heart:

Silhouette
I like to see you walk on the savanah in the evening,
When the crescent wanes in the firmament,
When solitude lingers in the more serene air,
Giving each single word the softness of a promise.
Parading your exquisite grace on the path,
You leave behind a happy trail;
Sometimes a word, soaring in the breeze,
Brings me something of you in the misty evening.
Under the pale rays falling from the night sky,
Your mystery wavers and grows charmingly;
Because the silvery night, knocking down its urn,
Slipped into your hair like a shimmer.

Nalima remained speechless. Vinesh's passionate recitation did not impress her at all (her lover, Houblin de Maucourt, lavished her with honey-sweet words too) but quite simply surprised her. This young man could read and probably write! And what's more, in the language of the Whites. Fierce jealousy seized her. Her eyes turned violet and her charm suddenly vanished into thin air. Moving away from him, Nalima said:

'You are a talented sweet talker, I can hear that. You have everything you need to sway the hearts of women, *hon*! But tell me, when did you last step out of the Plantation?'

She broke a stalk of century plant and began to pick her teeth, she was incredibly vulgar. Vinesh was hypnotised by the gold cross which hung from her neck, the conspicuous symbol of her conversion to Christianity, the religion that his father, in Madurai, used to call *Paravedam*, or Veda of the pariahs.

'Since when?' she started again. 'Since the end of the war, I bet? You don't even know that this business of repatriation is over, *mon bougre*. Over, well and proper! Now, we Indians have become French just like the Creoles. Don't you know that?'

Vinesh was ashamed to admit that he had never left Courbaril hamlet. Except when he went with his father and mother to the city of Saint-Pierre, a little before the volcano erupted, when this Coromantee-Negro attacked them on the banks of the River La Falaise and was finally found hanging from a tree. Sometimes he walked to the town of Macouba where his younger brother Ganadin finally settled down with a *Câpresse*. He hardly ever went to the neighbouring town of Basse-Pointe to take part in some *danmyé* fight, on which occasion Vinesh caused a stir as he was the one and only Indian to practise this Negro dance-fight.

Of Martinique, which was described as no bigger than a rice grain, he knew only these three places. Neither Le Lamentin, which had the most flourishing plantations, nor Fort-de-France, the capital city, where his compatriots, who were no longer attached to any plantation, had started experiencing the worst downfall. Did they not sweep gutters and empty the chamber pots in Fort-de-France? Honestly speaking, Vinesh was no exception, far from it. The Coolie was riveted to his plantation like a nail to its plank. Most often, to venture out amounted to being exposed to the cruelest taunts from the Creoles and running the risk of permanent unemployment. Because could he do anything else but cut sugarcane? Tie it up in bundles? Load the carts? Transport it to distilleries and mills where only Negroes and Mulattoes were hired? If he went off into the blue, it would be like vanishing into thin air, being forgotten by his kin. Such was his father's destiny. Adhiyaman Dorassmay fled Madurai on foot about thirty years earlier and in Pondicherry boarded a ship bound for the Americas. Where was he now? Probably in one of the seedy areas of the city: Au Béraud, that infamously disreputable quarter; and cramped in the Grand Dépôt, a shack crowded with Indians living in permanent fear of the nearby river flooding. Unbelievable stories had reached Courbaril: houses swept away to sea in the middle of the night; drowned children; coffins floating on the waves, yanked from cemeteries by the fury of the waters. Yes, where was Adhiyaman Dorassamy now, the father he revered so deeply?

Nalima had calmed down. Without losing her ironical air, she was addressing him in a less hoarse voice.

'I'm not telling you no lies, my boy. It's been ages now since the colony does not repatriate any of us to Madras. The Whites dangle this carrot to make you work even harder. Do you know that since the Negro soldiers came back from *En-France*, they have been objecting to receiving orders? They proudly declare: "I fought the Battle of the Marne! I shed my blood for the motherland! No White Creole will ever walk over me anymore, fuck!" Did you know this Vinesh?'

The young man, who had preciously preserved his father's repatriation booklet and had over time indulged his dreams of returning to Pondicherry, suddenly became aware that he had been far from what was going on in the world for too long. Courbaril Plantation and its sugarcane was his only horizon. Four months after the eruption which had wiped out Saint-Pierre and its pomp, Mount Pélée erupted again, this time destroying the town of Morne-Rouge where many Indians lived; this had brought him out of his torpor. There was a great hustle and bustle about the departure of the Negroes for the battlefields of Europe. In Man Ninise's rum shack on Saturday evenings, once wages had been paid, he listened attentively to the story of their exploits against the troops of Emperor William II. But he was completely indifferent to the efforts made by a certain Govindin, a native of Karikal, to obtain French citizenship for the Indian emigrants. Likewise, Sidambarom, a lawyer from Guadeloupe, had delivered impassioned speeches which Théophile had made him decipher in a newspaper, left him just as indifferent. Time had stood still for him because he had come with the fifty-fifth and last convoy. Year after year, fresh waves of emigrants used to bring the latest news from India but this had stopped suddenly with the landing of his family.

Some considered the Dorassamys a repository of the memories of the India they had left behind, they were their last refuge. They came from all over the island, from Basse-Pointe, Ajoupa-Bouillon or Le Lorrain, to ask them for advice about some medication or some ritual. If his parents had played along with good grace, Vinesh pretended to be ignorant about these matters. He had even been initiated into the martial art of *danmyé* by the Negroes of Hauteurs Bourdon and, to everyone's amazement, he had become a seasoned fighter. Nobody had guessed that this was a façade and that in his heart of hearts, he had kept alive his desire to go back to Madurai, this province where his father, Adhiyaman, was born. He had even reconstructed this city in his mind, piece by piece with the help of overheard conversations and glorious stories taught by the Ancestor. The *vatialou* Z'Oiseau had initiated him into the finer nuances of the Goddess Mariamman cult. And above all, he was captivated by sketches and photographs of paddy fields, temples in the Tamil country, and dancers bedecked in jewels and swaying hips. Between the end of the afternoon, when work stopped in the fields, and early evening, when they all got together, as a family for the Indians, at the rum shack for the Negroes, he gazed upon these pictures for hours on end. He sat by himself between the tall roots of the silk-cotton tree and let his mind wander or dozed off till his mother, Devi, called him to supper.

'Vinesh, I'm going to tell you a secret. I don't love the Béké, I have never loved this White man. I hate their religion, even if I wear a cross around my neck. All this is just play acting...I have been observing you for years now. I need someone of your calibre. Let's leave this place. I'm not joking. There is no future for us here. Sugarcane will become our tomb. You only have to say one word; just one, and tomorrow morning, you and I can go away to Fort-de-France. I have acquaintances there. We will be welcomed warmly. You will find work at the port, and I can get by with pastry making.'

The young man looked the nautch girl in the eye, stunned. Was it possible that she took pleasure in poking fun at him? He was a plantation Coolie with toenails encrusted with mud; arms scarred and scabbed by sugarcane leaves. He felt a thousand times more comfortable speaking Creole than French. How could he think of being associated with the wealthiest planter of Macouba's muse, M. Frédéric Houblin de Maucourt, the fifth generation owner of Courbaril Plantation?

Furious he said: 'And this White man's child that is growing in your belly, what shall we do with it?'

Nalima's pregnancy was hardly visible, except for her breasts, which were swollen and made her even more desirable. She thought that Vinesh wanted to simply postpone his answer. She exclaimed:

'But what are you talking of? At his age, do you think the White man can still make love to me?

'I may be an idiot but Da Gervaise cannot talk nonsense. She is a matron everyone respects.'

The planter's nanny, who was not exactly Nalima's bosom buddy, had betrayed her. She had guessed before anyone else, perhaps even before the young woman herself, that Nalima was pregnant or '*en situation*', as they say in Creole!

'Keep your White Coolie for yourself!' Vinesh said, grabbing his machete. 'You feel comfortable between the White man's thighs. He has built you a house, you never spent a single day working your fingers to the bone cutting cane and here you are now, bearing him a child. What else do you want, *hein*? Let me struggle in my own misery, fuck!'

He left saying nothing, neither good day nor goodbye. Behind him, he heard beautiful Nalima, the princess of Bengal, burst into tears but he did not turn back.

# 17

# The Son of the Indian Woman and the Negro

*And then there is the time of forbidden love, furtive looks, a brief touch on the back of a hand grabbing a machete or a whip. This unusual accident provokes rage, disdain, jealousy, condescension and all this tinged with incredulity because who knows what will spring forth from such unions? What indomitable new blood will come to disrupt the order of things?*

Anthénor was probably one of the few Negroes in Macouba who made no distinction between the people of his own race and the Indians. Hired when he was very young as a mule-driver on Courbaril Plantation, he had declined the much desired position of foreman when M. Frédéric Houblin de Maucourt's father offered him the job, preferring to commit himself to trade union action. This had cost him all sorts of affronts, including losing his fiancée whom some managed to convince about the diabolical nature of socialists; some people had started calling them by the strange name of 'communists' for some time now. This young woman from town had learnt how to iron clothes and went from house to house offering her services. Balancing a heavy basket on her head with no help from her hands, she gathered Sunday shirts and trousers, formal dresses, lace bed sheets, in short all the precious linen that the Negroes spent fortunes buying from the Syrian peddler so as to give the impression that they were comfortably off. They had set the date of their wedding: it would be on the eve of 14th July, Bastille Day, a French public holiday. Anthénor actually adored France which, according to him, had managed to make the White Creoles see reason, first by abolishing slavery, then by voting laws that protected the rights of workers.

'If I had not been too young in 1870', he loved to declare, 'you can be sure that I would have volunteered to defend the homeland against German persecutors!' During the First World War, he was mobilized and he came back bedecked with medals.

'Either you forget about this trade union business, or it's over between us!' his exasperated fiancée told him.

With a heavy heart, Anthénor chose to keep on defending his brothers in misery who wore themselves out in the sugarcane fields for next to nothing, as they said bitterly. From then on, he became a confirmed bachelor, entirely devoted to 'The Cause', words that he always pronounced emphatically. As soon as the harvest drew near—generally around January—he transformed his home into a permanent meeting room and became Béké de Maucourt's, steward Polygone's, foreman Sosthène's bête noire; the latter was a quick-tempered Chabin who would not allow the slightest form of protest once he had assigned the daily chores. Anthénor had taught *l'Internationale* to the cane-cutters and the mule-drivers of Courbaril Plantation; they soon made it a habit to sing it bel-air style, accompanied by drums roaring through the itinerant strikes. He frequently mentioned a country called the Soviet Union, which he described as a worker's paradise, talked of fabulous characters like Lenin and Stalin whose photographs he had cut out from the magazine *Justice*. The pictures of these two characters—Lenin, emaciated with almost Asiatic eyes, and Stalin, his square face adorned with a fat moustache—were stuck on the partition wall of his house and presided over the endless debates which sometimes lasted until early morning. Anthénor hammered into his friends' heads: 'This land does not belong to the Békés, they stole it from the Caribs. Then our Negro ancestors cultivated it for centuries and today without the Indians it would remain fallow. We must unite, fight for our rights and demand that the State nationalize it.'

The Negroes of Courbaril, Eyma and Gradis Plantations did not understand everything Anthénor said, but they respected him so much that when he missed one or two days of work, they collected money for him after the Saturday wages to compensate for his loss.

For Anthénor often had to go to Fort-de-France, to the trade union headquarters from where he would bring back fresh news, leaflets, newspapers and most of all, an inexhaustible stock of combativeness. Even Hermann, the much dreaded *danmyé* fighter, respected him, which was saying a lot! There was just one contentious issue between Anthénor and his friends: the solicitude he showed the Coolies. First, he forbade anyone to utter this word in his presence, demanding that they be called 'Indians'. Then, he refused to call them traitors and strike breakers even when the majority of them kept carefully away from the protest movements which troubled the plantations for a good half of the year. He had also made friends with Adhiyaman Dorassamy, a fellow who kept clamouring for his repatriation to Madras when it had long been discontinued. Worse, Anthénor, though very rarely, attended Hindu ceremonies conducted by Z'Oiseau, the Indian foreman of Gradis Plantation. All this while claiming to be an atheist who made it a duty never to set foot in the Macouba church, even for burials.

'We can't even say that a Coolie woman turned his head,' they commented, perplexed. 'The gentleman does not associate with such hussies. And, to be honest, he is good looking!'

Always eager to justify his attitude, Anthénor would just frown and say that Negroes and Indians 'were all in the same boat', an expression he must have picked up in Fort-de-France. Then he would suddenly get impassioned, embarking on a vibrant and inexplicable defence of Mariamman zealots. When Abbot Xavier and the Belgian Redemptorists had plundered their houses and burnt what the latter called idols, everybody was surprised to see Anthénor stand up for them. He had sharply criticized the Negroes who were complicit in this pillaging and, as a retaliatory measure, he had organized a bash in the streets of Macouba in order to obstruct the Holy Week procession. It was therefore less surprising when, following Adhiyaman Dorassamy's departure for L'En-Ville, the city, from where he sent no more news, the trade unionist became imperceptibly closer to his wife, beautiful and gentle Devi. It was joked about in Man Ninise's rum shack:

'Good God and his Mother, there's going to be a fight, ladies and gentlemen! Do you realise, two sworn enemies like Sosthène and Anthénor fighting over the same *bougresse*, the same dame, *oui*!'

The Chabin, intimidated by Devi in spite of his position as foreman on Courbaril Plantation, did not dare confess his feelings to her. On the other hand, Anthénor got straight to the point. At the end of five months of loneliness, when everyone, beginning with Devi, had to face the fact that her husband had left her for good and that henceforth she had to manage all by herself with her two boys, the trade unionist came one evening to her house and asked her to 'live' with him. His words were dramatically simple: 'Devi, you are still in your child bearing years. I'm a working Negro, my two hands belong to me. If you wish, we could live together.'

Adhiyaman's wife, who was still having a hard time grieving, was taken aback. Not so much because she felt she was being unfaithful but because he was a man from another race. Of the other race. The one that rubbed shoulders with Indians on a daily basis while ignoring them or heaping taunts on them. These Negroes from Africa seemed to have completely forgotten their country of origin and though they were still poor and most of them illiterate, they were not afraid to stand up to the Whites. They were an intrepid race, jovial, carefree, violent sometimes, so different from Indians, who were deemed to be placid and to accept their fate. Usually, the Negroes considered Coolie women as less than nothing, creatures whom they could throw down on a dirt track and screw hastily, then they would complain that their pussy hair was sharper than Gillette blades. As for Black women, they accused Indian women of practising witchcraft to entice their men—these bitches—eager as they were for their male members, reputed to be long and thick. Of these furtive unions, which Théophile, the metropolitan school teacher, did not hesitate to call rapes, were born mixed-race beings, the échappés-Coulis, who, like the Mulattoes, went about disowning their mothers. Only the 'White Coolies', the offsprings of White masters and Indian women, enjoyed a certain respect in the Creole world which is pitiless in matters of skin. Devi considered all this as she weighed Anthénor's proposition. He was not the type to insist and after revealing his feelings once, he made no further attempts. Fortunately, an itinerant strike began to wreak havoc in the north of the country. From La Trinité and the sugarcane fields of La Caravelle Peninsula it swept up to the doors of Macouba across Sainte-Marie, Marigot, Le Lorrain and Basse-Pointe, as if an immense fever had gripped the plantation workers. Courbaril Plantation had lived through several such strikes but this one was of a new kind. All sorts of insane rumours circulated relayed by hawkers and *taxi-pays,* drivers, from town to town: the itinerant strikers were not only asking for a raise, but they set fire to everything on their way, and armed with weapons they clashed with the police; they beat up half-hearted workers and emasculated traitors. Not very different from what had set the south of Martinique ablaze in 1870, almost sending the island the Haiti way. At that time, some hoped for Toussaint Louverture and Dessalines, the heroes of the revolution which liberated the great Northern island from the yoke of slavery. But all in vain; almost a century had gone by and only the spirits of these leaders encouraged the insurgents.

'This time it will be the right one!' proclaimed Anthénor who went from place to place to spread the good word.

He organized many meetings during which he preached the union of Negroes and Indians against what he described in the pompous language of the trade unionist as the White Creole plutarchy. Devi had a chance to admire Anthénor's determination when the sincerity of the Indians, who had the reputation of having sold themselves, body and soul, to M. Houblin de Maucourt, was questioned. It is true that the closer the itinerant strike came, the more pressure the Béké put on them, alternating between threats of dismissal and inexplicable favours, like doubling the pay of those who came to work the day after Hindu ceremonies. Anthénor came to Devi's house only once during this troubled period. He wanted to speak to Vinesh whom he took aside for a long chat. What exactly transpired between them she never found out, since her son refused to say anything. From his gloomy look, she understood that the future did not bode well. Since their arrival in this country, the Indians, had always found themselves caught between the devil and the deep blue sea—between the Negro and the White man. Whipping boys, scapegoats, expiatory victims, cast-offs, such had been their fate since they had left the parched paddy fields of the Tamil country for the sugarcane fields of Martinique. Devi thought sadly about her husband, Adhiyaman, who was said to be working as a septic tank cleaner in the city. How many ordeals they had faced together! First, they had been cramped for weeks on end in that foul-smelling house at the port of Pondicherry. Then the terrible storm in the Sea of Fire, which almost wrecked the ship and which they survived thanks to Nagourmira! Next the smallpox epidemic which broke out during the bleak crossing of the Sea of Darkness. Through these experiences Devi had understood that the husband imposed on her by her father was a man of exceptional goodness. Once they reached Fort-de-France they had been quarantined in the famous Warehouse in which Indians awaiting repatriation were rotting and finally they had moved to Courbaril Plantation in the distant quarter of Macouba where they discovered the *mestri's* false promise: no, their job did not consist of laying sugar out in the sun.

And after all this, why was Adhiyaman not sending her news of his whereabouts? Was he dead, could she henceforth consider herself a widow? Dreadful though this itinerant strike was, work would have to resume one day or another. Then would she be justified in casting her lot with Anthénor whose inner strength impressed her more than his knotted muscles, built by fifteen years of back-breaking work in the cane fields?

*

**Letter to the Governor**

Victory to Rama

To his Excellency, Monsieur le Governeur of Martinique, tall like the beautiful Mount Himalaya and bestowed with the esteem of the King. A prayer addressed with the deep respect of a thousand salaams by Radjiv, farmer for M. Frédéric Houblin de Maucourt at Macouba:

Queen Victoria, informed about the evils which hit our country for want of regular rains, sent a Gentleman to India, in the month of Karthigai on an independent mission to find out more about it.

I was not a labourer in my country, but a salaried employee of the Government working for my town quarter.

Having learnt about the arrival of the delegate, first to Madras and then to Manjacoupam, I sought an audience with him to present our situation of great misfortune. On the way, a *mestri* from Pondicherry told me that this Gentleman was in Pondicherry; he cheated me, hired me and finally imprisoned me at Pondicherry, in the premises called Magasin. In this Magasin, it was not possible to communicate with the outside world, neither with a letter nor anything at all, and I was put aboard a ship. No justice out there.

Upon my arrival in Fort-de-France, I wanted to speak to the authorities, but it was useless. Nobody understood me, there was no interpreter.

I wrote six letters to Queen Victoria but not one seems to have reached her. And as for the letters I addressed to my family, I have just received an answer in which I am told that my fate being unknown, I'm considered dead in a foreign country. Under the pretext that there are no other loyal subjects of Queen Victoria in my family capable of assuming the office that I held with the attendant rights and duties, the same is being transferred to a stranger, from the month of July. Now it is clear to me that I will die in this country where I presently find myself.

If you will only be kind enough to forward this letter, even though it is written in Tamil, to Queen Victoria, she will certainly do whatever is necessary to retain this aforesaid office in my family, failing which, my family will die of starvation. I will bear all the expenses incurred to send my letter from Martinique to Her Majesty the Queen.

Please find it in the goodness of your heart to listen to your humble servant who solicits your Greatness to dispatch this letter to Europe, who must secure a living for his family who will bless and honour your name.

I salute you with a thousand salaams and with deep respect

Signed Radjiv
At Courbaril Plantation, Macouba
On the 25th of the month of Chittirai
Of the year Calacutty (1918)

*

Kumari was the first to guess Devi's pregnancy. On a Monday, when Devi was coming back from the river with a pile of laundry on her head, completely drenched, the Syrian peddler Abderrramane's mistress caressed her bosom.

'Your breasts have grown bigger, dear Devi', she exclaimed, 'although you have remained as slim as a dragon fly. Ha-ha-ha. M. Anthénor is doing his job properly as I can see. Congratulations!'

The young woman's companions could not believe their eyes. They surrounded her and, turn by turn, shyly feeling her breasts with their engorged areolae, which did indeed seem to be ready to burst out of her bodice. Most of them had not appreciated Devi cohabiting with the person considered as the leader of the revolt which ravaged the region three months earlier and provoked the death of three workers including

Moutoussamy, this Coolie who had commanded the respect of Negroes by his imposing bearing and his unfailing courage. The man who had succeeded The Ancestor as the oldest Indian of the plantation had just shut them up by announcing that there was nothing unhealthy about this union because it was time to kiss the dream of returning to India goodbye. It was, he said, time to admit that Martinique had become their country, even if there was no question of forgetting the ancestral gods. Mariamman, Maldévilin and Nagourmira would go on watching over the Indian race but their benevolence would stop there. Coming from a person who had dedicated his life to keep the flame of the Tamil language and the knowledge of sacred texts burning, while pretending to toe the line of the White man and his henchmen, these iconoclastic words threw the little Indian community of Courbaril Plantation into complete confusion. This helped Devi to get used to the daily presence of Anthénor around her, especially as the fellow was amazingly helpful. Without being asked, he organized a group of helping hands to repair the houses that had been damaged by the cyclones. He built a pen for the few cows which provided the area with fresh milk. He persuaded the more reticent families to send their brood to the school in town, with the complicity of his great friend, the school teacher Théophile. He intervened several times when foreman Sosthène or the overseer Sainte-Foix were about to commit some injustice.

'Anthénor is a Negro,' murmured the Indians 'but he is not nasty.'

No disciplinary action had been taken against him once the itinerant strike had ended, no doubt because he took several weeks to recover from the hail of bullets which he had harvested. As usual, the two camps estimated that each one had paid its dues: the White planters had lost a good part of their harvest, the Negroes had lost three of their people, who were shot. They were quits. At least for that year. Work was resumed as if nothing had happened. The sugar mills and the distilleries, still out of bounds for Indians, began to crush cane 'for the greatest profit of the colony' which delighted

M. de Maucourt. However, the master cancelled the promotion he had promised Vinesh, by which he would replace Sosthène as foreman in a few years.

'Since neither the Indians, nor the Chinese, nor the Congolese are trustworthy,' he said sourly, 'well, I will suggest the General Council to import Madeirans! These people already know the cultivation of sugarcane and, what's more, they are almost White. Swarthy for sure but almost White.'

'I gathered some information from Fort-de-France,' jeered Anthénor. 'People from Madeira are experts in wine, not rum. De Maucourt has become a sourpuss, which is why he is talking rubbish!'

To tell the truth, everyone had grown older by ten years. Some had even caught a 'shot of snow', according to an expression which enchanted Théophile, that is to say that their hair had turned white overnight. Only Anthénor had preserved a sturdiness like that rare rot-resistant guaiac wood. He settled down with his meagre belongings in Devi's house without her formal consent. It had been enough for the two to look at each other because, as the proverb goes, 'when four eyes meet, there are no lies'. The first night, Anthénor slept on the floor in the young woman's room, rolled in a simple canvas cloth cover. When she had stepped over him to rekindle the oil lamps at the feet of a picture of Kali, he had just smiled. As usual, Devi had waited for the dark before performing her ablutions, which took her so long that when she returned the Negro was sleeping soundly. Shortly before dawn, he was awakened by Devi who was muttering and moaning in her sleep. It was a heart-breaking sight. He crawled up to her bed and examined her beautiful face with its pinched nose, so different from those of Negresses. He put a hand on her hair whose roughness surprised him. You could have sworn it was a horse's mane! Smooth hair was not the necessary equivalent to soft hair. This discovery bothered him greatly. Snatches of sentences sprung out of Devi's thin lips in a language that Anthénor gathered to be Tamil. He only recognized the words he had heard from Adhiyaman when they happened to chat at the rum shack quite a few years ago:

'Madurai...Kaveri...*Mestri*...Madras...Pondicherry... Coromandel...' These words were like the beads of a broken rosary, irreversibly scattered. At the first glimmer of day, Devi, turned on her back again, rubbed her eyes and let out a faint cry as she saw a shadow bent over her. She smiled and held out her arms to Anthénor who did not hesitate. Their embrace which was both wild and sweet, reminded her of that night of the storm, in the middle of the Sea of Fire when she had united with Adhiyaman for the first time down in the hold of *The White Adder*. Anthénor's infinite tenderness swept her apprehensions away. After all, not all Negroes were brutes, sozzled with rum, ready to screw women of all races, hurling coarse and smutty abuses at them, when these helpless creatures had the misfortune of crossing their path in a cane field. And this inordinately large male member which they boasted about so much was perhaps only a legend. For Devi there was no significant difference between her former husband and her present lover. The pleasure she felt, although different, was in no way any the more ineffable. Reassured, she poured out all the love she carried in her on Anthénor. Later on when Kumari made her realise that her breasts had swollen, she knew beyond doubt that this child who was now growing in her belly was conceived on that bright morning. This son of India and Africa could only claim to be from one country: La Martinique. But the hardest part lay ahead. Actually, the majority of Indian women had ended up accepting her relationship with Anthénor, some declaring that they even envied her because of the supposed sexual prowess of the Negro; whereas the men, a number of them having no companion of their own race, looked askance at her. They answered her greetings only reticently or turned away when they met. Sandji, a mule-driver who had set his heart on her as soon as Adhiyaman left, almost went mad. He began to drink excessively, to pick a fight with anybody, to swear, even to blaspheme, he was unable to contend with a burly fellow like Anthénor. He yelled:

'*Man pa Kouli! Pa kriyé mwen Kouli ankò! Landjet manman*

*ras-taa, tonnè di Dié!*' (I am no Coolie! Don't call me that! Fuck this race, dammit!)

His pain moved Devi who asked herself if she had betrayed her people. What would her father, Anandam Vellayoudon, think of this union? And her poor mother, if she were not already dead, was probably moping around the island of Mauritius. Devi could not imagine what this island was like though Théophile, the school teacher, had explained to her that it was quite similar to Martinique. Only the joy of her sons, Vinesh and Ganadin, lifted her spirits. They had accepted Anthénor as a new father and obeyed him implicitly. Ganadin had not missed a single day of school since the trade unionist had convinced him that by learning to read and write, he would surely land a job in the mill at Basse-Pointe. Indians could not remain eternally riveted to the land, he had assured them. Some day, they would also become fitters, boilermakers, cooks or mechanics. They would in turn manufacture sugar and rum in the midst of these noisy machines which gave out thick trails of whitish steam and could be made out from a kilometre away.

'And you, Vinesh,' Anthénor used to say half seriously and half jokingly, 'Don't worry, you'll get yours. The Béké will soon realise that you are the only one who can take over from Sosthène. Not just anyone can become a foreman!'

When Devi's belly began to grow, some jealous Negresses wished her the worst misfortunes. Firmine, M. de Maucourt's now repudiated mistress, a superb Mulatress whose only fault was her sterility, never missed a chance to stop by Devi's house when she knew that Anthénor was in the fields and hurl terrifying portents:

'From the shape of your stomach I am ready to bet that you'll give birth to a little ugly monkey, Devi. Unless it's a two-headed monster, *oui*!'

Or,

'Don't you know a pregnant woman mustn't eat pineapple? Continue like that and you'll have a miscarriage!'

Devi bore these affronts stoically. She vaguely knew

that it was the price to pay for the Indian race to be finally accepted by the Creoles. Indians had to become Creoles too. To be a Creole is to be a native child of this magnificent and ferocious land, excessively cramped but infinite in its way of putting together languages, musical styles, cuisines, religions, peoples. Théophile, who had recently developed a passion for archaeology, had showed them his treasures one day when they had invited him to share a meal: terracotta vases decorated with red and black designs, a fragment was always missing, cut stone tools, all sorts of amulets chiselled in a green stone with the most exquisite brilliance, arrowheads.

'This country does not belong to anyone', he declared to a flabbergasted Anthénor, who claimed that Martinique should belong to the Negroes and Indians alone, the Whites never having sweated under the sun, a machete or a hoe in hand. 'Martinique belonged to the people who manufactured these objects, the Caribs!'

Devi's new husband had run his hand over these shards and potsherds, perplexed. Like everyone else, he had vaguely heard about the first inhabitants of Martinique and the day when two Caribs from the neighbouring island of Dominica had drifted along till the Macouba Beach. Their *gomiyé* fishing boat had not been able to resist the treacherous current. He had rushed to see them. He had been disappointed: these fellows looked very Chinese, a little Indian, with a touch of Negro. Nothing very extraordinary. And what was more, they spoke Creole, although with a curious accent! However, according to Théophile, this child that Devi was carrying would be a Carib, a new species of Carib, a creature born of the very humus of the island, who would owe nothing to the ancient worlds from where his progenitors came. 'He will be the one, Devi!'

The school teacher insisted that the Indian-Negro mixed breed, even if denigrated as *échappé-couli,* would be what the Mulatto could never be. This was because the Mulattoes born of White and Negro parents remained attached to their White planter fathers and to the values of Europe. And so it was suggested that the boy—there seemed to be no doubt about the gender of this unborn child—should be named Acayouman after a valiant Carib warrior, one of the last to have combatted the French colonists.

The metropolitan school teacher was not the only one to worry about finding a name. The brand new Ancestor, who had recently taken charge of the community, developed a theory according to which whatever emerged from the entrails of an Indian woman was Indian and should, consequently, receive a Tamil name. Only one name! 'Because in our country, first names don't exist. They have never existed. It was the European traders and their accomplices, the *mestris,* who before embarking at Pondicherry or at Karikal had saddled us with it, and you, like idiots, when the government here finally accepted to grant you French nationality, you have continued in the same way. Devi Dorassamy, Sandji Virapoullé, Antoine Tengamen! What a joke! According to the stars, this child who is going to be born can't be called anything but Caroupanin.'

But times had changed since the arrival of the first convoys; the century had ended with the fifty-fifth and last convoy, and no one received any news from India. With the new century, the number of Coolies born in Martinique exceeded those who were born in the territory of Madras. The Tamil language had given way to Creole and in the religious ceremonies only. Some asserted loud and clear:

'We are in the twentieth century, the century of science and progress, what is the point of looking back? The sugarcane itself is in the throes of death. Look at the Békés. They no longer have their former powers.'

And they were right. If the First World War had been profitable to the colony, rum having served as a warming element and a medicine in the trenches, an unknown and terrible phrase intruded into all conversations: production and distribution quotas. In the year of 1921, the alcohol from sugarcane had restricted entry into the metropolitan market. Beet sugar had already almost killed its insular alter ego, cane sugar. Now wine, cognac and champagne were about to do the same thing to rum. There was no future for the Negroes and the Indians on the plantations. This was more of a concern for Anthénor than finding a name for his son. Besides, deep down, he yearned for a daughter. Year after year, the planted surfaces of Courabaril Plantation shrank and dozens of newly jobless workers were compelled to emigrate to the city. Frédéric Houblin de Maucourt continued to live in style thanks to his annuities and investments, not because he supplied sugarcane to the Macouba distilleries and the Basse-Pointe sugar mill. The harvest, still customarily called '*roulaison*', was carried out as a matter of routine. Sosthène did not need to raise his voice, that incensed Chabin voice which used to make the most conscientious workers tremble. The overseer de Sainte-Foix was less finicky about the deductions he had to make from the Saturday wages. Man Ninise, the shop owner, no longer jumped on those whose credit book began to inflate overly. It is true that nobody objected to going to the fields, nobody complained about the harshness of the work. Anthénor, the seasoned trade unionist, was heartbroken. Henceforth a force, superior to that of the White Creoles, weighed heavily upon the country and everybody knew perfectly well it was beyond reach. We would only hear whispered: the Government.

Thus as she reached her forties, Devi Dorassamy, who arrived in Martinique at the age of fourteen with the last convoy, gave birth to a superb boy whom she called Adhinor. This time she succeeded in imposing it on the bureaucrats of the Macouba town hall who could do nothing about it, for Indians had become French like everybody else. It was thought to be one of those pompous names from Ancient Greece or Rome, like Thémistocle or Rémus, which the most destitute liked, while rich Whites and Mulattoes preferred Jean-Michel or Charles-André. Nobody at Courbaril Plantation, asked Devi about this strange first name, not even her new companion. Therefore she alone knew that this name was made of the beginning of Adhiyaman and the end of Anthénor. Once the matron had left to bury the umbilical cord under a tree in a nearby forest, the new father, lifting his child towards the sun, just said these words:

'This little boy mustn't rot in Coubaril! Devi, in a few months, we'll leave the place, *oui*! The city will be better for Adhinor...'

## 18

# New Times

*Those who left, defying anew the fury of two oceans, forgot those who stayed behind. Those who stayed behind undertook to plod on, not so much in the memory of the ancestral gods, nor in the supreme taste of 'kolbou' but by inscribing it all in Creole Time—O sacred geometry of vermillions, yellows and greens on the Madras cotton—as History builds up, heaping upon the Time of the Caribs that of Europe and of Africa.*

He had lost his memory. The Plantation had ended up wearing him out even though he had persisted in reciting the sacred texts to those among the young Indians who were not afraid of his hideous appearance. The Ancestor, presently aged one hundred and four years, had decided to make me, Vinesh Dorassamy, his disciple, the one who would continue on the Path that leads to the Almighty Being and to the ever sought-after *samadhi*. I was the one who visited him most frequently, who never tired of his long litanies interspersed with even longer meditative silences. He was gifted with patience of the rarest kind, in this country of permanent frenzy. The Ancestor believed he had convinced me that the purpose of human life was to attain, or at least to look for perfection.

*Yadaa yadaa hi dharmasya glanirbhavati bhaarata*
*Abhyutaanaamadharmasya tadaatmaanam srijaamyaham*
*Paritraanaaya saadhunaam vinaashaaya cha dushkritaam*
*Dharma samsthapanaarthaay sambhavaami yuge yuge*

'Whenever and wherever in the Universe, spirituality declines and ungodliness rises, O Descendant of Bharata, I will come down there in Person,' the old man recited to welcome me.

But the years rolled on, time chased time and the Gods of India continued to live hidden in sordid, dilapidated temples on the fringe of the plantations, venerated by people who had lost the rich Tamil language completely. When in a trance, they still managed to break into bits of prayer, the onomatopoeia of ritual, but that was all. There came a time when only The Ancestor and Z'Oiseau were able to talk freely in Tamil without resorting to Creole. The convoys with fresh emigrants from India had ceased, depriving us, the Indian workers, of the revitalizing source of our culture. The umbilical cord that linked us to Madras had been cut forever. We had become prisoners of this land without Gods, of brutal, cynical, depraved, fatalistic Martinique, peopled with Whites who only worshipped money; with Mulattoes for whom the knowledge of books meant everything; and Negroes who were compelled to resort to Br'er Rabbit's wily tricks* to keep their head above water. As for that strange race to which Foreman Sosthène belonged—he was a Chabin, a paradoxical mixture of Whites and Negresses—and he was broken by sickness. They counted only on the rage boiling in them to throw their weight around. In any case, all these Creoles behaved as if after their life on earth there was nothing, even though they pretended to follow the precepts of the Catholic religion which promised paradise to the most deserving.

'Vinesh, I can't find my words anymore,' grumbled The Ancestor when I went looking to persuade him to intercede for my father, Adhiyaman, with God Maldévilin. 'I think I'm going to die soon.'

'*Appa*, your time has not yet come and I...'

'Be quiet! There's no sense upsetting the gods. I only have

---

**Compère Bouki pi Compère Lapin*, Créole folktales from the Carribean featuring a clever Rabbit.

one desire. Just one: That Brahma should appear in front of my eyes just before my tired heart stops beating...'

And the old man kept repeating like a refrain the only prayer that he remembered:

O my Lord, preserver of life,
Your radiance dazzles me and hides your true face
Remove I pray this veil of light
And reveal yourself to your pure devotee!

Suddenly all the words he had taught me with infinite patience seeped into me, Tamil words, repeated a thousand times till the pronunciation reached perfection, words which allowed me to make my great nocturnal voyage to India and converse with those of my family who had not dared to defy the taboo of the kaala paani or who had not been enlisted in the ports of Yanaon, Karikal, Mahé or Pondicherry. Now, I wanted each of these words to accompany The Ancestor during his descent to the Kingdom of the Dead. This was not at all in the mad hope that he might retrieve his memory, but so that he would know that in Martinique, the sons of the last convoy like me would continue to perpetuate the language, the only one which our divinities understood, the language without which we would be lost as in an endless fog. When he was in the throes of death, I repeated in a voice loud enough to drown The Ancestor's death rattle:

'*Veylu,* sun...*nela,* moon...*paalu,* milk...*uppu,* salt...*vazhi,* road...'

His face, a nest of shapeless wrinkles, brightened up and gripping my hands in a supreme and vain effort to raise himself on his elbow, he followed through:

'*Puu,* flower...*aaru,* river...*muku,* nose...'

Time seemed to stop. Or rather self-destruct. The Plantation and its perpetual headlong rush, this insane and frenetic sugarcane harvest did not clutch us in its tentacles. Each of the Tamil words took us away from this narrow godforsaken world. The Ancestor and I were perceiving the Transcendent now! The Creator on his lotus, He who has no beginning, no centre, no end! A thousand suns appearing together in all their splendour could not have come any closer to the radiance of the great soul. In Vishnu, we saw—o incredible sight!—all the Gods and living beings as a single whole.

Later, it would be said that the death throes of the first convoy's last survivor had dragged on for two days and two nights. This is not true. Those who filed past his house, Indians wishing to seek his blessings but already disbelievers at heart, Negroes, pretending to be compassionate but simply eaten up by curiosity, Mulattoes and Chabins murmuring opportunistic condolences, Whites of great or minor extraction were there to reaffirm an age-old superiority. All these people did not even suspect that The Ancestor and I left long ago. That, throughout this span of time, which could only be measured as covering several human lifetimes rather than two derisory days and nights, we were in Him, the Immanent, and in His spheres.

I also heard the members of my community declare in an undertone:

'This young fellow is inconsolable, yes! The Ancestor had become a second father to him ever since Adhiyaman desisted from speaking.'

Their derisory words in Creole and sometimes in French reached me like a faraway murmur, a faint sign from a universe which had no longer the power to affect me. With their Indian moans and laments, their grotesque gesticulations, their Negro and White faces distorted by make-believe sorrow, they looked like a swarm of panic-stricken bees. I was bathing in the celestial light of the One who wore the crescent moon as a crown, the Unchanging, the Lord of the Mountains, the Being with three eyes and five faces, from whose matted locks the Ganga poured forth. Once the visits from the people of Hauteurs Courbaril had ended, The Ancestor came back to earth for the last time. Holding me with his gentle hand, he said to me:

'There is only one master, Shiva, the One who commands the three energies without which there is no knowledge. Do you know them?'

I lowered my head with shame. I had never been very pious, following the example of my father, Adhiyaman. The latter had told to me during one of the rare face-to-face conversations which we had, that his father, Ambu, had a *koïlu* built at the end of the orchard which surrounded his beautiful residence, over there in Madurai. Adhiyaman objected to sweeping every morning the room where a statue of Murugan had the pride of place. He did not like to light the oil lamps placed at the idol's feet. The daily recitation of the mantras of Manu was an ordeal for him. But he was not a non-believer either because he enjoyed going with his parents to the monumental Minakshisundareshwara temple during the Ganesh Chaturthi festival in the month of September. During the preceding weeks, everybody was busy preparing effigies of the elephant-headed God, some made of paper, some others of cloth, some of clay or of metal. My father loved to paint Ganesh on those cardboard sheets which were used in his father's spinning mill for drying saris. He was ecstatic when the faithful, at the end of the festivities, went to the river in order to immerse statues and pictures.

'There are three energies', the Ancestor continued, 'and it is Shiva, with the help of Goddess Shakti, who is their dispenser. First *Jnana*, Knowledge, which allows us, simple human beings, to be different from animals; then *Iccha*, Desire, the force that moves us deep within ourselves, from the tiniest ant up to the elephant, but which, in us in tempered by Comprehension. Do you follow me, Vinesh?'

'Yes, master I'm here...'

'Finally there is *Kriya*, Action, everything that we undertake at any moment of our lives from the simple fact of drinking a little water right up to the wars we wage. He who does not respect the order of the three energies is condemned to get lost, to wander in the darkness of a life without a goal. The White men, reckless beings, often begin with the third, sometimes the second, never with the first. That is why, their knowledge, even if it is impressive, always remains at the level of material reality. It does not attain the sphere of the Spirit, the one which enables us, Hindus, to detach ourselves from it...'

Opening his eyes wide, he tried in vain to rise on his elbows and said to me:

'Take the box over there!'

I could only see a pile of dirty laundry, shirts and khaki pants, patched up several times, testimonies to thirty years of cane-cutting.

Hidden below it, there was a very old trunk, the kind which in the early days was brought from Pondicherry and in which certain families kept their daubings, statuettes, holy books, grains of *mandja,* turmeric, and *vèpèlè,* neem, and the other plants needed for rituals. The Ancestor's did not contain any of these. In the darkness, my questing hands discovered a shapeless mass, which sometimes felt rounded, and at other times elongated. There were strings of jute attached to it.

'Now, Vinesh', he said to me in a voice that had become less short-winded while I was holding replicas of breasts in my hands, 'you will dance for the Goddess!'

I was dumbfounded. Even distraught. Because even if I participated in the ceremonies in honour of the Gods as drum-*tappu* player, I had never taken any pleasure in the *nadron*, these evenings of song and dance which in the past lasted for several nights in a row at the time of the Pongal festival, in the month of January when the cane harvest was about to take off. Or rather, if this orgy of sparkling costumes, grimacing masks, sacred movements of the hands which we used to call *mudra* in our language, captivated my eyes, it was incapable of breathing into my limbs these quiverings which took hold of my mother Devi, my younger brother Ganadin, Kumari, Abderramane the Syrian's lover, Sandji, the mule-driver and most Indians from Courbaril and the neighbouring plantations. Not once had I given way to making the smallest hint of a dance move. I was stiff, riveted to the ground by some invisible force and I had to make do with being seated in the shadows, ignored by all. Dumbstruck. Shamefaced. From time to time they came to me saying:

'Come on Vinesh! Move your body, my boy! If you don't dance for Mariamman, how do you think she will protect you?'

I was cross with myself especially because such paralysis did not hit me when, during Carnival, I haunted the Paillote. This disused warehouse was half way between the town of Macouba and the countryside. There Negroes, Chabins and Mulattoes went wild dancing frenzied creole mazurkas, crazy biguines, boleros or waltzes. I was one of the rare Indians to go there and they did more than tolerate me: the women fought to take me in their arms, went into raptures about the nimbleness of my steps. I was assigned the title of the most accomplished dance partner in the region, to the greatest displeasure of *Alexis-grands-mouvements,* Alexis-the-jumping-jack. This Mulatto school teacher, born in the city of Saint-Pierre which he constantly boasted was the most beautiful of the entire Antilles archipelago, used to impress everyone by performing dances of foreign origin like tango or charleston. His colleague, Pommier, on the other hand, locked himself up at home between Carnival Sunday and Ash Wednesday. He had a rather high opinion of his person and kept harping on his mission to 'train a Negro elite'. Alexis, a libertine at heart, made the most of the Carnival to charm the young girls in full bloom who, under normal circumstances, would have lowered their eyes and hurried away when the poor fellow tried to entice them in the street. They thought of themselves as a species different from the country girls because the palms of their hands had never swollen with blisters for they had never wielded the machete nor tied up too many stacks of sugarcane. In general, these young ladies looked down upon those whom they derided as *Nègres-gros-orteils* 'Negro-fat-toes'. They were so-called because, walking barefoot most of the time, they waddled grotesquely in their shoes, which they only used for Sunday Mass, funerals, baptisms and Carnival dances. A hundred times, they would try over and over again, insensitive to the rejections, even more stubborn than stubbornness itself. They twisted into knots to bow gracefully, but Firmine, M. Houblin de Maucourt's mistress, the queen of the Paillote dismissed them summarily, calling these valiant attempts mere gorilla antics. In her heyday, she would announce right from Carnival Saturday:

*'Kannaval rivé, manmay, man lib ! Sa ki lé pwan mwen, sa ki ni fos pwan mwen,*

*pwan mwen, fout!'* (The Carnival is here and I am free, friends! He who wants to take me, he who has the strength to take me, may he do so, *fout*!)

And in all earnest, she forgot everything to amuse herself during the five nights of dance which constituted the only interval of happiness in the life of Negroes. If a man could seduce her with some original dance moves, she would readily offer him her body, but she was brutal in rejecting dance partners too clumsy for her, even in the middle of a dance. No one took offence nor did they pick fights with her. Her verdict was merciless. Consequently, very few country Negroes dared to come up to her. And what is more, one mistake in the French language usage, a masculine possessive adjective instead of a feminine one was enough to make Firmine drive you round the bend brazenly, and transform you into a carnival puppet. This is what happened to Hermann, the assistant foreman of Courbaril Plantation, the grand master of *danmyé* fight. Years later, kids used to shout out to him from afar, before scurrying off:

'Hey Hermann, dance partner Hermann look! His dress is beautiful *oui*!'

The Béké de Maucourt, by tacit agreement did not hold these excesses against Firmine. He knew that she was used to romping with all and sundry because of the 'heat of the Carnival'. The day after Ash Wednesday, he would get to her house in town, holding his head high, tie up la Dorée in front of it as if nothing had happened during the preceding days, and screw Firmine relentlessly till the evening. Many women, who would have been delighted that a, *Grand Blanc*, Wealthy White honoured them in such a manner, envied Firmine for having such a temperament while feeling sorry that she had a womb so desperately sterile. As long as she was the favourite of the master, I did not dare, even though I was recognised as an outstanding dancer, to beg her for a dance. If she refused Negroes from the fields, what a rebuff would she not have reserved for a Coolie-dog-eater? But then came Nalima and this princess of Bengal ejected the Mulatto woman from her position of first concubine. Firmine's haughty airs received a fatal blow: younger and sexier women began to challenge her title as queen of the Pailotte. People murmured:

'Firmine still has some vestiges of beauty but she is done! Done-done-done!'

I was thinking of all this when, once I had taken the *nadron* costume out of the box, the Ancestor in his death throes ordered me to dance for the Goddess. With consummate clumsiness, I slipped on a silk tunic with gold trimmings and tied a mask on my face. I decked myself out in fake breasts and tied little bells around my ankles. Finally I painted the contour of my lips red.

'Dance for the Goddess, Vinesh! Dance!' I could hear his voice grow weaker and weaker but still pleading, desperately pleading. He who had lived for a century in the company of divinities, who had helped us preserve the prayers which pleased them, here he was at the end of his terrestrial journey, with nobody but me by his side in his last moments! Then I began to make my body move, trying to imitate the accomplished *nadron* dancers' solemn hand gestures and sudden rolling of the eyes. I raised my knees, pivoting alternately to the left and to the right, and trying to keep a perfectly straight chest. The Ancestor, who could only open one eye, a glassy eye already covered with the veil of death, cried out to me:

'This is not our dance step! Vinesh, this is *danmyé*, here. Your dance steps are those of the Negroes, *oui*...'

He was right. The death throes had not completely taken away his lucidity. I was ridiculous. These dance movements, which I thought so diligently performed, were no more than those of the dance combat inherited from Africa. I learnt *danmyé* fighting on Saturday evenings,, without my parents' knowing. After collecting my wages, when the cane-cutters, mule-drivers and loaders gathered behind Man Ninise's shop, I used to join them in the glow of torches when they engaged in fights which sometimes drew blood. The *danmyé* is what gives the Negro his strength! Thanks to it, he had been able to survive through three centuries of slavery and the life full of humiliations which followed. I could dance the *danmyé* and not the subtle dance steps which so delighted our Goddess Shakti! No matter how I resisted the brute force which made my arms and legs move, there was nothing I could do about it. Under my beautiful Indian disguise, a Creole energy expressed itself and even heightened, which stupefied me.

'Vinesh, I pray for you...,' whispered the old man.

Effectively, I managed to recover my balance gradually. The force which filled me vanished and I kept still for a long time. In the dark house, the son of the first convoy, who disembarked from *The Aurélie*, this mythical ship which had victoriously triumphed over the fury of two oceans, was dying. The Ancestor held out his arms to me, his eyes shut now. More and more violent spasms shook his chest. I knelt by the straw mattress and arranged the grey strands of his hair. The palm of his hand was icy with sweat, which made me quake.

'It is...nothing my son...,' he stammered, 'but beware of the night! In the night always fear Ayyanar and his cavalcade of stranglers...'

With these strange words, in one stroke he reached the ancestral land, our beloved mother India and *moksha*, this finitude that our gods reserve for men of unshakeable piety. The death throes lasted an indeterminate length of time. His funeral brought together Indians, Negroes, Chabins, Mulattoes, Chinese, Syrians and Békés, who rushed from all over the North of Martinique, the entire Creole people usually doggedly tearing each other apart. Each being aware that New Times were coming and that new words, stripped of their grime of hate, had to be invented in order to live on.

The Béké Houblin de Maucourt had repudiated Firmine for good. The path was finally clear. I won her over with these lines from a poem by Baudelaire which Théophile, the young teacher from the school in Macouba, had taught me:

*Your feet are as slender as your hands and your hips*
*Are broad; they'd make the fairest white woman jealous**....

(Fort-de-France, August 2001–June 2003)

---

*'To a Malabar Woman', *The Flowers of Evil*, Charles Baudelaire, trans. Geoffrey Wagner, NY, Grove Press, 1974.

# Glossary

***Amarreuse/attacheuse:*** women who work behind the cane-cutter, tying up the cut cane in bundles of ten and knotting it skillfully so that a loader can then put it into a mule-cart and send it off to the mill

***Arrimeur:*** load master

***Bamboula:*** party where food and drink are aplenty, originally an African drum and also the dance performed to this percussion instrument

***Béké:*** White French colonialist plantation owners

***Blanc(he)-pays:*** White (wo)man from France

***Bondamanjak:*** the spiciest chilly in the Antilles, peculiar in shape

***Bondieuseuse:*** the woman who gives cathechism lessons

***Bougre:*** chap, fellow

***Bougresse:*** woman, dame

***Canne malavoi:*** very juicy variety of sugarcane

***Capistrelle:*** young pretty chatty woman

***Câpre-Câpresse:*** born of a Black and a Mulatto

***Case-à-rhum:*** rum shack

***colombo:*** a mixture of spices, also a gravy dish

***Combat damier:*** danmyé fight

***Cristophine:*** a small, pale, ridged pumpkin

***Droit du seigneur:*** customary right of the feudal lord to have sexual relations with his vassals bride on her wedding night

***Échappé-couli:*** a half-breed, born of Negro and Indian parentage

***En ville:*** city

***En-France:*** France

***Farine-France:*** wheat flour

***Femme-dehors:*** mistress

***Femme-matador:*** a coquettish, domineering woman

***Fils-dehors:*** illegitimate child

***Gaule:*** traditional attire worn by women at home in the Antilles

***Grand Blanc:*** Rich White man

***Grand'Case:*** Big House

***Grands-Blancs:*** wealthy Whites

***Hardes-cabane:*** rags wrapped around the arms and legs to protect them from the sharp sugarcane leaves

**Higgler**: Jamaican English word for vegetable vendor

***Kaala paani:*** the proscription of crossing the seas for Hindus

***Kaïli:*** lungi

***Kalou:*** locally brewed alcohol

***Kapli:*** creolized version of Karuppan or Karuppi, the darkskinned one in Tamil

***Katti:*** ritual machete used for animal sacrifices

***Koïlu:*** shrine

***Kolbou:*** from the Tamil word kozhumbu, made of tamarind and spices

***Kotumpavi:*** a ceremony performed during severe droughts to beseech the rain gods

***Mâle-femme:*** masculine-woman

***Mandja:*** turmeric

***Mestri:*** Indian recruitment agent who worked for the British to recruit indentured labour to work in the sugarcane plantations

***Minédien:*** from the Tamil word Munnadiyaan, guardian deity in front of a shrine of a local God or Goddess

***Morne:*** créole word for a flat-topped mountain of variable height, a typical geographical feature of the Antilles, Mauritius and La Réunion.

***Mulâtre:*** born of a White and a Negro

***Nadron:*** musical mythological play

***Nègre griffe:*** born of a Mulatto and a Black

***Nègre marron:*** Negro who escapes from the Plantation

***Negrillons:*** little Negro and Indian people

***Paravedam:*** Veda of the pariahs.

***Pays Z'Indiens:*** India

***Peau sauvée:*** fair skin

***Peur-cacarelle:*** fear that made you soil your pants

***Pickney:*** Jamaican English for child

***Poussari:*** the priests who conducts religious ceremonies

***Poustengon/puttagam:*** book in Tamil and holy book of the Hindus in the Antilles

***Quateron(ne):*** a person who is one-quarter Black by descent, quadroon

***Quimbois:*** obeah

***Tafia:*** inferior rum made from distilled sugarcane juice

***Taxi pays:*** local buses

***Ti-bandes:*** group of child labourers in the plantations

***Toulken:*** muslim

***Vatialou:*** interpreters who translated the words of the priests, possessed by the Gods, into Creole

***Vèpèle:*** neem

***Yellimen tenga:*** creolized version of yelani tenga or tender/green coconuts with sweet water inside

***Z'Indien:*** Indian man

# Translator's Acknowledgements

All translation is a fruitful, generous collaboration.

My grateful thanks to Christine Raguet, for introducing me to Raphaël Confiant and his work, patiently re-reading my translation, answering endless questions, pouring over dictionaries, cross-referencing and researching cultural details about Martinique which she knows so well and loves truly. Without her active participation and support through testing times, this translation would never have seen the light of day.

Jerry Pinto, who gave unstintingly his time, talent, energy and hand-held me through the entire process both as a translator and a writer.

Shoba Venkatesh-Ghosh, who was always there to brainstorm, to think through an idea, untangle a thought.

Appasamy Murugaiyan, who generously shared his knowledge of the Carribean Tamil culture, patiently guided me through Tamil words that had been creolized beyond recognition.

Madhavi Narsalay, who vetted the Sanskrit translations, sourced the verses of the *Manusmriti*, *Upanishads*, and *Bhagavad Geeta*.

Jyothsana Narasimhan, for her scrupulous proof reading, valuable inputs and friendship.

Ravi Singh and Renuka Chatterjee of Speaking Tiger and Christine Cornet of IFI, for their faith in the project.

Caroline Heubert, Minakshi Carien, Anusha D'souza, Christelle Lozère, Marek Ahnee, Sowmya Vencatesan, and Shreya Gupta for their unfailing support and incisive insights.